Copyright Burdizzo Books 2019

Edited by Em Dehaney - Burdizzo Books
All rights reserved. No part of this book may be reproduced in any form or by any means, except by inclusion of brief quotations in a review, without permission in writing from the publisher.

This book is a work of fiction. The characters and situations in this book are imaginary. No resemblance is intended between these characters and any persons, living or dead.

This book is sold subject to the condition that it shall not, by way of trade or otherwise, be lent, resold, hired out or otherwise circulated without the publisher's prior consent in any form or binding or cover other than that in which it is published and without similar condition including this condition being imposed on the subsequent purchaser

Published in Great Britain in 2019 by Matthew Cash/Em Dehaney Burdizzo Books Walsall, UK

G000036861

B DATE
N.R.   Em's Mega Mix
○ YES ○ NO

1. Down By The Water – J. R. Park

2. Maps – David Court

3. Indigo – Matthew Cash

4. Lady Grinning Soul – Laura Mauro

5. JUNE – Kayleigh Marie Edwards

6. Mountain People – C. L. Raven

7. Rain Dogs – Richard Wall

8. Pick Your Path and I'll Pray – Jessica McHugh

9. Hot Knife – C. H. Baum

10. Isobel – Paul M Feeney

A DATE
N.R.   MATT - BOB'S BADASS CHOOOONS! ○ YES ○ NO

1. BONES OF AN IMPRESSIVE ROMANCE – J.G. CLAY

2. SPIRIT IN THE SKY – DUNCAN P BRADSHAW

3. BLACK SABBATH – LEX H. JONES

4. CARAVAN OF LOVE – EM DEHANEY

5. DON'T FEAR THE REAPER – JONATHAN BUTCHER

6. HERE, THERE AND EVERYWHERE – C.M. FRANKLYN

7. A RAINY NIGHT IN SOHO – DARYL DUNCAN

8. FUNNY LITTLE FROG – CHRISTOPHER LAW

9. IT MIGHT AS WELL RAIN UNTIL SEPTEMBER – CATHAN CHALMERS

* NO PAGE NUMBERS = NO SHILPIM

For Cordelia,

The sweetest song of 2019

Love

Matty-Bob & Em

Xxx

Foreword

It was through our shared love of punk, of playing harder, louder and faster than the boys in the bands that we went to see, that we formed Red Aunts. We were punk as fuck, and played dirty, crazy, noisy rock and roll. We weren't following the rules because we didn't know there were any rules.

Playing live was always our favourite thing. It's a high like no other. We were just four best friends, rocking out and kicking ass. When we got a chance to reunite for some live shows in 2018, we thought it would be the start of a new chapter for Red Aunts, but sadly it was not to be. Life is cruel, and our bassist and dear friend Debi Martini was taken from us.

We are still devastated by the loss of Debi, so our message to the readers of this book is this: start that band, write that book, paint that picture, sing that song. Life is short, fill it with the things you love.

Xo

Terri Wahl, Kerry Davis and Lesley Ishino of Red Aunts

Matty-Bob's Foreword

Where do I start? Music, aside from books, has to be the most important thing ever, for me. There has always been music in the background to the history of this Matty-Bob. As some of you wonderfully weird and much-loved devoted Matty-Bobbians will remember, I am the last in a line of five children. Those who have paid attention and read some of my little autobiographical encounters will know I have one older brother and had three older sisters.

My musical background stems from my mum and sisters mostly. Along with her love for horror, I inherited my mother's love for music, and in particular singers with distinctive voices. Country and western crooners singing about murder and love gone wrong.

There was always music being played in our house; my sisters were adults when I was born and they grew up in the sixties where radio and music was everything.

Zina's walls would be covered with Sky and Roxy Music posters, pin-ups of Arnold Schwarzenegger, Dolph Lundgren and epic drawings of Greek warriors battling mythical monsters. She would be forever fitness obsessed, and would blare out sixties and seventies pop that skirted on the boundaries of rock music.

Gela, of who I have often referred to as 'the witch sister' (it's something she's always been proud of) looked like she'd fallen out of an old Black Sabbath poster with her waist length black hair, dark clothes, ridiculous amounts of silver jewellery and a cat obsession. Her musical taste has always been far more evolved than any of the rest of us. She was heavily into the psychedelia scene and how there isn't a secret history of drug usage in her past is beyond me. She also has the amazing talent of Bill Bailey when it comes to musical instruments, something I've always envied.

My brother and I were closer in age, six years apart, and Gela's daughter, my niece, Jenny is five years older than me, so we grew up like brothers and sisters too. We were surrounded by the latest offerings on Top Of The Pops, something that was watched religiously every Thursday night just before the chip van came around. Jenny subscribed to Look-In magazine and Smash Hits , and once the NOW tapes came out they were a routine Christmas present for one of us three.

I can remember the first ever cassette tape I got given. It was Jive Bunny. I wonder what he's up to nowadays; probably in an old people's home unable to have a conversation with anyone without suddenly spontaneously stuttering and lapsing into "c'mon everybody." I played that tape over and over again on my new black and white Walkman. I thought it was brilliant, especially when the battery power ran down and they started singing like a doom metal group (obviously I didn't know what that was then.)

I went through a phase of ploughing through my mum's tapes, all the sixties pop bands and stuff I recognised from my Jive Bunny album. This even escalated to me going to my first gig with my mum and sisters to see Bobby Vee, Tommy Roe and Gerry and the Pacemakers. I met them all afterwards too.

When I started High School a couple of years later I found out that listening to this kind of stuff wasn't cool and if there was one thing this shy fat kid didn't want to do it was give people more fuel to mock me. I began taking note of what my friends were listening to and got into heavy metal. I raided Gela's stash for Alice Cooper, Def Leppard and Black Sabbath whilst secretly, behind closed doors still listening to the sixties stuff and falling hopelessly and deeply in love with Cyndi Lauper and Belinda Carlisle. My tastes expanded at an alarming rate, I could not and would not stick to one genre no matter what I was 'told' to listen to and never once did I pretend to like something I didn't.

I got into heavier music at the same time as the emergence of britpop and female fronted bands such as The Cranberries, Echobelly and The Cardigans. My tastes were always diverse, to say the least.

When I left school I finally had more freedom to be myself and openly like what I liked and I loved everything I have ever loved. I had a major crush on my Australian friend who in turn heavily influenced me in Australian music, told me who Nick Cave was and the rest has just unfurled from there like a huge cacophony from the world's most mental orchestra that will never stop playing.

Me and my partner in grime Em managed to narrow some of our favourite songs down a throw the list at some of our favourite writers to do with as they pleased. Most of these miscreants tend to have a fondness for the murkier side of fiction but we're given no restrictions, just to pop the song on and see where their muse took them.

In no particular order, my songs for this volume got cut down to these beauties, and here in my own half-arsed way I'll try and tell you why I chose them.

Don't fear the reaper - Blue Öyster Cult

I'm going to say one sentence about this song and if you don't get it then you don't get it but I know that seasoned horror fans will, and if they don't then they should. Ready for the sentence? (I'll put it in italics so you know when I'm saying it and you all don't think this is part of the sentence and I'm so crap I don't know what a sentence is)
Stephen King's The Stand TV Series.
There, that's my explanation for why I love this song. I liked it before then but after then I loved it. It's amazing what a glorious piece of cinematography can do for a piece of music and vice versa. Kinda given it away there but what the hey.

Caravan of love - The Housemartins

I was a little kid when I saw the video of this and all I remember was four rough-looking skinheads with crosses shaved into their heads. Whilst I instantly thought that was cool, I automatically had it built in to me that they looked like thugs and would beat you up and that they should not be singing songs about that sort of thing in such harmonic melodies. This obviously made me love it, that and the fact that me and my brother, Andrew, would always sing along in high-pitched voices and stand up out of our chairs whenever Paul Heaton sang 'stand up.' Later on I became a fan of The Beautiful South and when I discovered that the band before them were the four skinheads who did 'the stand up song' I was a-quiver at discovering an older, more raw and enjoyable band The Housemartins.

Funny Little Frog - Belle and Sebastian

There aren't many bands who can pull off album after album after album and still float my boat. Belle and Sebastian and The Divine Comedy are about the only ones who do in my eyes, and ears. I wanted to pick a song from them as they're one of my favourite bands but it really is an impossible task, so I narrowed it down to an album and then I thought I'd just be cruel and pick the toughest sounding title to work from. No, not really, I love this song, the imagery it inspires and everything. Or am I just saying that?

Here, There And Everywhere - The Beatles

One of the best Beatles songs ever in my opinion.

All Across The Sands - The Stone Roses

The Stone Roses just remind me of happy times being high on life, pissed as a fart and spinning around and around and around before collapsing on the floor, sofa, girlfriend, pet. Almost all of their songs make me feel physically lighter, weight watchers should listen to them before weekly weigh-in.

It Might As Well Just Rain Until September - Carole King

When I first heard this song I thought it would sound perfect to be played right at the end of a really brutally gory horror film, or something a little more 'grungy' like one of Rob Zombie's 'good' movies. There's an old nineties, I think, film starring Randy Quaid and...umm...other people (no shit) called 'The Parents' that I can't be arsed to Google, about cannibalistic parents that uses this method of inappropriate music at a nasty ending perfectly. I think they use a famous ballet piece or something but it worked wonderfully and nobody has a clue what I'm on about so I'll shut up.

Rainy Night In Soho - The Pogues

I fucking love The Pogues. Shane MacGowan is a medical wonder. I honestly believe he is a living Mummy, that the amount of alcohol and drugs he has consumed in his life is actually preserving him and will make him immortal. (Disclaimer: if, since writing this foreword, he has died, it's all lies, LIES! HE LIVES ON! LIKE ELVIS) Almost every Pogues song is a lyrical masterpiece where every line should, would, and could inspire a fucking novel, and if you don't believe me go listen to this song and another called 'The Sickbed of Cuchulainn.'

Spirit In The Sky - Doctor and The Medics
The eighties version was a complete horror show, they looked like Spitting Image does a cross between Slade and Kiss but this was one of the soundtrack to my youth. Then

years later I heard the original and was blown away! The original is a slow, hippy, get high in a field, festival type number that's completely different but just as awesome.

Black Sabbath - Black Sabbath

The best Black Sabbath song ever with the most ominous, most horror intro ever with the heavy rainfall and the toll a solitary bell. I used to get tunnel vision and hear this intro whenever I used to see a certain barmaid that worked in my local rock pub The Trough back in the day.

Like I have said, a small amount, not even a millisecond in the grand scheme of my musical love, is captured, in this book via stories inspired by some of my favourite songs. You should read the stories and check them out.

Matty-Bob June 2019

What music means to...

Lesley Ishino – Red Aunts Drummer

I was extremely shy as a child - like, MEGA shy. One of those kids who'd hide behind their mother's legs or behind the furniture when people came around. I would rarely reply when adults who weren't my parents talked to me. I was like this for my first 7 or 8 years. My family was musical and we were always listening to music: my mom played acoustic guitar, my brother, my dad loved to sing. Starting in about 8th grade, I realized a lot of others liked the same music I did and it gave me something to talk about with friends. So, I started opening up a little. As I got into my preteens, I would stay in my room for hours listening to the radio or albums on my stereo, pretending to be the bold, confident singer in every band, prancing around on stage and belting out various emotions. I took piano for several years and tried violin and guitar. When I asked for a drum set, my mom surprisingly said yes. Something clicked when I played drums. I loved playing the drums. And playing drums gave me a greater sense of self - a confidence that kind of melted away a lot of my shyness. When I started playing shows with the Red Aunts, getting on stage was frightening yet exhilarating. The music we played gave me power - gave me strength - because I didn't care that I was terrified. I just wanted to play music. Music forced me out of my shell because I was drawn to feeling it gave me. Even though the stage still makes me nervous, music has transformed me into a performer - a confident person. A person who doesn't have to hide behind the furniture anymore.

at music means to...

Emma Wilson – Blues Singer

Music is like air, constantly surrounding me. It brushes against me, it's an energy, a force.

I breathe it in. I breathe out and I find I can create a note, and another and more, I relax and the notes fall out of me, I tense myself and I can form shapes with the notes. Are these *my* notes? Is this *my* music? I try a word, now I can join together the sound, my thoughts, my body, my soul, my blues.

What a thrill! An endless thrill! A fabulous ride where the dodgems and the roller coasters and sometimes simply little boats on ponds are inside me and with my voice, my instrument I can let them out, I can share the ride with you.

Music is a universal radio and I'm a channel.

So are you, so twist your dial and tune in.

You can find out more about The Emma Wilson Blues band at www.emmawilson.net

ACOUSTIC CASSETTE   N.R.[   ] □IN □OUT
A *BONES OF AN IMPRESSIVE ROMANCE - J.G. CLAY*

Normal Bias 120µsEQ A|60

Inspired by Stone Roses "All Across The Sands"

I used to think that romance was dead, a swelling gas-filled corpse rising to the surface of a polluted dull existence, organs removed and replaced by wilting flowers and tumorous hearts. Relationships birthed in the glow of expectation and hope soured after time, leaving a taste of ash and defeat at the back of the throat and a dull thud of anger at the base of the skull, an ache deadened by alcohol, cocaine and the occasional torturing of an animal; fleeting seconds of satisfaction, wholeness, focus evaporating in the mists of a cold dawn. All I wanted was to capture the thrill felt at the beginning of a partnership. All I was left with was the sour tang of stale booze, aching sinuses and the blood of pets seeping into the pores of my palms.

Until I caught *her* attention.

I straighten up, breath slobbering out from between dry cracked lips, stretching to ease the metronomic throbbing at the base of my spine. Preparing *her* gifts is hard work. Preparing this final token is torture. I feel the exertion more these days. Must be my age. The knife in my aching hand is dull from overuse. It doesn't matter. *There*'s plenty more in the holdall tucked away under a rock ledge nearby. I discard the used blade.

In the distance, a freight train rattles its way to a destination unknown. The noise is unsettling, the laugh of a broken demented clown drifting over the roof of my cliff top residence and echoing out towards the sea. The waves have a rhythm of their own, a roar more threatening and ominous than the train noise. It comforts me.

I know *She'll* be coming soon.

I reach into my tool kit, numb fingertips searching for a new blade. A faint breeze coats me in a fog of blood, meat and agony. My lips, cracked as they are, twitch into a grin.

She'll be pleased, no doubt. Such a perfume is erotic to *her*. And to me. At least it is now. It never used to be. Funny how love can change you; your appetites, your sense of self, your soul. That rush of hormones can turn a hardened lunatic into the gentlest of souls. Conversely, it can turn librarians into raving monsters.

Love has turned me into something else. I can empathise. I've gone from an ordinary, albeit successful life to an existence undreamed of. I've seen things beyond my own childish imaginings, felt sensations far in advance of the ultra-hedonistic, learned secrets safe with all the world yet hidden in plain sight.

All because of *her*. *She's* given me so much. Its only fair to requite this love.

Clasping my new blade, I stand and make my way back, pausing a moment to admire my handiwork. The light of the moon is strong this evening, its white *She*en illuminating the concentric circles of bone, scattered in angles yet forming a perfect circle with sigils. Some of the bone is still slick with blood, clotted with the flesh of previous owners.

But *She* won't mind. *She* enjoys *her* appetizers as much as *She* enjoys me.

A thrill of pleasure makes me shudder, my mind recalling past couplings; the frantic tearing at each ot*her*, the heat of *her* as I enter, the spark of ecstasy in those black marble eyes as I increase the pace.

She'll be coming soon.

We both will.

Laughing at the bad joke, I crouch, flipping the corpse over. *Her* face – a pneumatic supermodel in life, is contorted into a mask of fear, eyes once azure and sparkling now scratched dull from lying face down on sand. *Her* mouth is stretched wide open, bloated tongue standing stiff and upright in a salute towards the moon. The *substance* works its magic again. A little dab on my lips, a kiss and bingo; a hard death for the sacrifice with zero harm to me.

She gave me immunity.

Victims? Ha. The tribute's last moments have to be filled with wretched fear and unendurable agony. Affects the taste of the bone or so I've been told in those magical moments when we hold each ot*her* in the dark, flesh to cool flesh, groin to the heat between *her* thighs. Only the female tributes taste the *substance*. It makes them more compliant. Males have to die violently, traumatically. Again, it's some chemical thing unique to men, a substance released during bouts of anger. I don't mind. The *Sh*eep I picked for slaughter were ones who I wanted to kill anyway. Every machete cut gave me a grim satisfaction.

The*re* is one ot*her* condition *She* attached to this ritual of love. The tributes must be people I know personally and loath exquisitely. Love is powerful but hate rivals the intensity of that emotion. If both can be felt in equal measure, the balanced energies can purify the air, the water, even the atomic level itself.

Fortunately for me, my occupation has brought me into

contact with people who I fall in hate with very quickly. Journalists, political types, celebrities and the inevitable hangers on, all of these and more are inflicted on me, day by day, week by week. I bear it, the practised grin ramping my cheekbones as I inject humour towards my eyes. Laughing in the right places, enduring the clammy, pulsating fat palms thrust towards me, mockingly enjoying the flirting, I seethe within. A kaleidoscope of horrors plays out behind the throbbing bone of my forehead – the whisper of a razor parting flesh, blood pattering to earth, a rich perfume stinging my nostrils as my hand grips and pulls muscle back to reveal crimsons, yellows and green. I'm glad these people can't mind read.

The first time I caught *her* eye was also the first time I flayed someone. The Universe conspires, throwing people toget*her* through the strangest of circumstances. *She* maintains that *She* felt, rat*her* smelled or heard, my intention. I believe *her*. *She* has gifts that leave me awestruck and not just in the bedroom department. *She* knows things, sees things, feels things at a hig*her* level than most, even me. It's not just love talking. It's an established fact.

I remember feeling vague disappointment as the keening cries, so terrifying yet so lyrical, began to ebb as I pulled more muscle away, slashing at stubborn tissue whilst unwrapping. Blood poured downward, greasing the victim's still visible lungs, expanding and contracting. Life fights on, even after wounding. It still amazes me. Enraptured by the emotion, I didn't hear *her* at first. The motion of agonal breathing, seen live and raw under the week light of the moon, hypnotised me.

"You have an artist's eye."

I spun round, knife up and raised, startled but ready to kill again. Our eyes, mine brown with pupils still dilated from the kill, *hers* a solid ebon set in alabaster skin, met. The blade slipped from my now boneless hands as *She* glided towards me. Dressed in a gossamer white dress, *her* form seemed to dance to a terrible dark tune playing at a frequency only heard by *her*. *She* drew closer, a smile promising mischief and more tenderly sculpted onto an elfin face framed by a lush black bob of hair.

We were inches from each other. *She* bent down, *her* crown brushing my groin, making me instantly and painfully erect.

"Please. Don't stop on my account. I hate to interrupt a maestro at work."

Placing the knife in my hand, *She* leant closer. "There's an opportunity to showcase your talent for an appreciative audience. For me. A stimulating proposition, no?"

In that dark stinking blood-filled moment, *She* had me.

The bones have been scattered all across the sands. Random to the untrained eye, I see the pattern, the message, the story. *She* – a shell painted and pretty - enjoys packing people off to Hell. It's *her* call, the siren song that plays deep in *her* DNA. I write, *She* collects. These are the things we're programmed for.

This I do willingly. I'm no hired hand, a mercenary killing for money. I do it out of love and desire, an urge to please my girl.

Out there, beyond the fringes of my limited vison, I hear something.

Her call.

She's coming. Warmth envelopes me as I recognise the tortured howling drawing closer and closer. From a forgotten corner of my mind, regret and sadness well up. I look around at the cove, our playpen, bought on the back of my power with words and I realise something.

I'll never come here again. The forgotten part of me agrees.

We agree. Tonight is final. *There's* no going back. I look back to the scattered remains, my monument to an impressive romance, an idiot grin stretching my face. Bone sinks into sand, encircled by thick ropes of black muscle. Some vanish instantly, pulled under the surface of the blood-soaked sand. A new orchestral arrangement embellishes the ever louder moaning – the grisly crunch of bones being squeezed to bursting, slurping and grunting as the soft prize within is gulped down.

She must be hungry.

Almost unknowingly, I stepped forward towards the water's edge, carefully avoiding the tentacles writhing sluggishly in the throes of post-meal drowsiness. A voice whispers in my ear - *her* normal voice.

Now you see the real me, realise why our romance was so special, so impressive.

I nod, awaiting *her* arrival.

"I kissed the girls. Made them die."

Why I say that, I have no idea. The waves bubble before me, a dark bulk rising from the water. My teeth clatter together, love and terror dumping adrenaline into my system as *She* reveals *her*self; wider, taller, taut flesh sliding beneath tough mottled skin as *She* emerges from sleep or exile. *Her* mouth opens in a yawn, revealing rows and rows of needle-sharp teeth that glint in the moonlight. Beady yellow eyes glance down at me, thick lips twitching into the parody of a smile.

"Aren't you pleased to see me?" The *thing* says breathless, girlish and excited. Stupefied, I nod as knowledge awakens. The woman I slept with, dined with, killed for, learnt from; nothing more than a pretty painted shell after all. A lure, a bait to capture and captivate a willing participant. Something whips from the dark, encircling my torso. I try to gasp as it tightens, squeezing my organs.

I was the hired hand after all. Now, I'm just bone.

As *She* lifts me, the pressure becoming relentless, *She* speaks once more.

"For my part, it was an impressive romance. A human coupling with my kind. How can you not be impressed?"

I try to find some consolation in that as the tooth-filled mouth draws nearer.

The freight train laughs in the distance. I wonder if I'll ever be found, scattered all across the sands.

She bites.

I leave, knowing I'll never come *her*e again, play *her*e again, live *her*e again.

Inspired by Doctor and The Medics "Spirit In The Sky"

History is littered with tales of epic quests and mine is no different, though maybe less epic and more along the lines of, 'why in the name of everything that is honest and decent did you do that for?' Like any good yarn, it's best to begin at the beginning, there will undoubtedly be a middle, and by jingo, you can bet the last plastic monetary disc in your scabbed-over pocket that there will be an end.

In order to preserve some of the mystery, I'm not going to divulge my current location. There would be little point in you reading what happened, if I went and blurted out that I'm living in a leopard-print high heel shoe just outside of Bala, north-Wales.

That's a joke.

Probably.

So, what did happen? Why? How? To whom? Did it create a vortex sufficient to lift an empty caravan into the air? Enough with the questions and allow me to begin!

Honestly.

It started - as all truly great adventures usually do - one evening in my local pub, The Rabbit and Jugular. Like everyone else, I was making sure that I necked my daily intake of alcohol. For me, that was six pints of beer or lager, at least 4.8% ABV, topped off with a single shot of something from the top shelf.

On this particular day, a Tuesday, I opted for a gin and tonic. Since the government introduced the Daily Booze Law, the populace had learned to adapt and make sure they had their daily allowance. I'm not saying it was easy to begin with, but over time everyone from school kids to those in vegetative states learned how to slot the legal requirements in with their everyday lives.

Some chose to have theirs first thing in the morning. Owen from Accounts arrived at his desk thirty minutes before he was due to start, just so he could have his bottle of wine. On the days where he'd missed breakfast, it wasn't unusual for him to be seen drowning his bran flakes with a nice Bordeaux in the winter, or a clean and crisp Sauvignon Blanc in the warmer months. Sure, morning meetings with him could prove... interesting, but he only got lairy a few times and very rarely assaulted anyone with the projector screen.

I tried morning drinking only once, but it didn't agree with me. I got my hangover mid-afternoon and it completely ruined my post-work game of Tiddly-Winks. After a bit of schedule jiggling, I settled on having my quota after work, mainly for one reason... my best friend in the entire world, Portuguese cloud darner, Jesus de la Pogatch. We'd been friends since we were abandoned by our real parents, having fought each other in the gladiatorial pits in the Lucky Boy Orphanage down in Bournemouth. As he charged at me with his spear, I hopped to one side, entangling him within my net, and brought my trident up to strike. Looking down at the poor stricken fool, I felt something I had never experienced before.

Pity.

Up until that point, I had hacked and maimed my way

through every opponent I had faced without any compunction, but staring into those glassy orbs we call eyes - reminiscent of council estate rock pools - I hesitated. This cost me dearly, as he brought his foot up swiftly and incapacitated me with a kick to my testicles.

When I came to in hospital a few days later, who was the first person I saw? You got it. Sister Harriet. For she was the one who brought people out of bollock-trauma related comas. But behind her, looking sheepish, was Jesus.

Ever since that moment, we were as thick as thieves. Wherever he went, I followed, and vice versa. On some days, we'd forget who was supposed to be following whom, and we would be stuck in one place for twenty-four hours, waiting for the other person to go somewhere. Although we had very different jobs, him with his mobile cloud repair gig, and me being a mid-level extractor at the company that made the sticky substance in chewing gum, we made sure that we got a place of our own together.

We both finished work at five, and by ten past, we were in our local, clutching our alco-vouchers in one hand and the first drink of the day in the other. The landlord would force every personalised voucher into the Government-endorsed pelican, who would verify their validity and make the appropriate mark in the ledger. Woe betide anyone who didn't get their daily drink on. You'd get a knock on the door the next morning and WOOSH, you'd be disappeared.

I heard those poor souls were whisked away to become underwater piping for the transportation of official curses and lamentations, but it's probably just a myth.

Back to the story. The day *it* happened was like any other day. I negotiated with my peers as to who should get in the lunchtime enemas, oblivious to what fate had in store for me that evening. As soon as the end-of-day klaxon sounded, I was sliding down the brass exit pole and on my way to meet up with Jesus at The Rabbit.

With my pint ordered and a double sherry for J-Dog (you always come up with nicknames for best friends), we sat down at our usual table, ready for the ten second bursts of subliminal programming from whichever company had sponsored that week. As we received the first course, BUY JUBILEE MINTS, THE BEST MINTS EVER MADE BY HUMAN HANDS, we both supped our drinks.

We chatted away about our respective days, our top score at Fish Raiders, the latest gaming sensation sweeping the nation, and reminisced about days gone by. Before we knew it, I'd just finished my final pint, and J-Bop emptied the dregs of his penultimate sherry. As soon as the barmaid draped the slice of salami on the rim of my glass, I turned around, straight into *him*.

You know in life when you meet some people and you take an instant dislike to them? That was Merv Trutskin, apostrophe poacher, internet philanderer and abuser of Greenwich Mean-Time. He had a face like a swollen prostate and a body that jutted out like a pigeon-chested Autobot. Even his voice - so nasal that it sounded as if he had a perpetual bout of sixth stage Hepatitis K8 - put my back up.

Anyway, I turned around as he walked forward, seemingly oblivious to my existence in that space, but the smirk he had as I toppled backwards onto the vulcanised rubber floor, told me that he knew what he was doing. Trying to arrest my fall, I put out my back hand, which did little except help to catapult my gin and tonic skyward. Before the liquid splashed on my face, the salami slapped over my mouth and tried to suffocate me. Alas, pork products have never forgiven me since I rode that pig round the Orphanage in my teens, dressed as Rapunzel. Me, not the swine. Who knows what punishment they would dole out for that offence.

Desperately, I tried to suck and slurp the errant booze up as best as I could. Wringing out the salami, teasing every last drop of juniper berry effluence into my gob. Sure I got most of it, but as I picked myself up, I could see that the floor was awash with my drink. Well… I was furious. I jumped up and demanded an explanation, and you know what I got in return?

Nothing.

Merv simply picked his nose, excavating a particularly stringy bogey, complete with drooping snot tail, and wiped it on the middle of my forehead. Wrestling the slice of salami from me, he slapped it against his pickings. He winked, turned and walked out of the pub, into the humid night.

As I struggled to come to terms with what had happened, I realised that the entire public house was quiet. Even the jukebox, the incarcerated musical baby ghosts who were halfway through a nifty rendition of Blondie's 'Rapture', came to a halt. Spinning around to the barmaid, she shook her head and served another customer. A hand slapped on my shoulder, a familiar Portuguese lilt in my ears. "Come on, buddy. Let's go home."

Walking back to our one-storey zeppelin, the world rocked from side to side. The moon, bloated like a sad old sow, poured pity on me with extra moonbeams, trying to cheer me up. To no avail. I knew I would be safe from official sanction, I had after all presented my daily chit of vouchers and they had been verified and sent to regional head office, but it didn't feel right.

For two years, I had spent every day having my exact allowance of booze, and now this? I swear, there was a slight spring in my step, where before I would have tottered slightly. Jay-Zeus and I usually spent the walk home talking utter bollocks, singing song lyrics, pushing each other into the sleeping deadly killer bushes of certain death, but that night, we walked in silence.

For all of his altruism, as soon as we got home, J-de-la-P made his excuses and went into his room. Before too long I could hear him taking out his eyeballs and polishing them up to a glossy sheen. I was left in the same spot I'd stopped at when I'd walked in through the front door. Not even the gentle rocking as our zeppelin jostled for space with the other blimps helped soothe me. As I struggled to comprehend what had happened, I heard a cracking sound from within. Like ice dumped into a glass of warm cider. Sobbing gently, I closed my eyes and denied myself the comfort of my bed, choosing to sleep where I stood.

The next morning I awoke with a start. Looking straight at me, without any hint of embarrassment, was a completely naked Jesus. As I wondered where his beard ended and the mat of thick chest hair began, he opened my mouth and placed the smaller of his hands deep inside. Grabbing hold of my uvula, he reeled me in closer. All I could see were those eyes of his, set within a face so smooth it was as if it were carved from soap.

"I have been meditating on the events of the evening all night long. I think I know what needs to be done," he whispered. His voice barely audible over the morning song call of the native fire hydrants.

I was in a fugue state, struggling to come to terms with what had happened, and being awake with only a mild hangover.

He took my silence to mean he could continue, which, in hindsight I thought to be highly presumptive. "I'm going to recommend you." His free index finger pointed up at the ceiling. His words struggled to penetrate my crusty ears, I mumbled my favourite Rutger Hauer soliloquy in sober reply.

"There is someone who I will call upon to help you. In case this should happen again. For I fear that Merv will continue with his baiting of you."

By this point, I could feel the cauldron of life bubbling beneath me, ready to jettison the day's new-born babies skywards from the geyser of conception. Jayzuz sensed this and rested his forehead against mine, ignoring the reformed meat disc that clung resolutely to my skin. "I will beseech them to help you. Trust in me, my friend. If you hear a voice call to you from above, do not be afraid."

Easy for him to say. Everyone knew that the overlords from the Asiatic mountains often called out to people from aboard their *papier-mâché* aircraft, luring hapless folk to their doom down potholes and rents in the Earth's crust.

"Do you trust me?"

I nodded. His words were nought but heresy and madness. I could feel my second stomach clench as they digested his consonants.

Jesus moved to my side, the salami choosing to stick to his head as he did so. Our temples joined together, he still pointed upwards, to the painting we had commissioned of our first battle. "Listen to the words from the sky. They will do you no harm. They mean only to help. They will give you what you so badly crave. But first… "

I gulped. Jesus swung back into my eyeline, lightning flickered across his retinas as he received an incoming email notification. "Yes?" The word tumbled from my lip.

"…you must suffer."

And he was gone. His face and the entire muscular-skeletal structure that supported it, disappeared into a waterfall of black and white static. Thick blocky pixels pelted the floor and exploded into greasy droplets, which in turn hissed and condensed into steam. This rose past my frozen body, hit the ceiling, before seeping out through the bad dream hatch, reserved for night-terrors and lithe cat burglars.

I was alone.

No.

I was terrified *and* alone.

What a heady concoction that is, dear reader. WHAT AN EARTHY MIX INDEED!

Sorry, I always get a bit carried away by that bit. Nothing like a bit of over-reacting to something. Truth be told,

Jesus liked nothing more than to turn into vapour every once in a while. He'd always manifest nearby, sometimes in a bicycle inner tube, or a child's pencil case. Once, he squeezed himself into my shampoo bottle. You should've seen the look on my face when I had a shower a few months later!

Anyway, I shook myself free of my catatonia, wriggled out of my now useless Tuesday skin sheath and set about preparing myself for the daily grind. With a tune ready to be whistled in the wrong key, and a fresh pair of gossamer thin undergarments on, I trotted into work, cautious of the day ahead.

Work was mediocre at best, I could barely milk the sticky-yaks properly as I was lost in thoughts of the previous day. When the klaxon sounded, I decided against the brass pole, and threw myself out of my cubicle window, landing atop the freshly prepared pile of martyrs who had given their life so that others more worthwhile may live.

I tumbled to The Rabbit, performing roly-polys and headstands along the way, trying to forestall my appearance. *He probably won't even be there.* I hoped. But I knew what would happen. As I pushed open the doors, I took a quick glance around, and saw that I had been spared his presence. Determined to complete my quota, I set about my drinking with a gusto unheard of since the last Great Lager War. For fourteen weeks straight, we drank nothing but organic lager, made by the landlord, Ted. People back then not only had their own allocation to drink, but also those who were engaged in the furious battles up and down the continent.

As the Prime Minister of the time, Timothy 'Pork-pie' Cathedral, said; "Ask not what you can drink for yourself, but what you can drink for your country!" Stirring words indeed. The impact was lessened a tad as he was completely inebriated, but you can't knock the sentiment. With the old and infirm out fighting for freedom from the evil Hops-barons, the fit and healthy remained at home, but with a heavy burden. The daily allowance was not lowered, and every man, woman and child had to pick up the slack of those unable to have their daily drink.

There were times when I was having six or seven people's drinks a day, in addition to my own. Needless to say, work was a write-off, but this was for the good of all, to shake off the shackles of ale-tyranny. Sure, it had been a while, but when the occasion called for it, I could drink as quickly as anyone.

Forgoing chitchat, I slammed my alco-vouchers on the bar, demanding that my six pints were poured and prepared immediately. No sooner had the barman put one drink down, I had finished the one previously. We worked in tandem like a well-greased apple bobber. As I raised the sixth and final glass to my lips, I pointed to the shelf beyond. "Uno tequila, por favor."

Wiping the froth from my lips, and letting out a ferocious belch, I pushed the empty pint glasses aside and grabbed hold of the shot glass. Nodding a thanks to the good barkeep, I pulled the sickly liquid towards me. Just as I was about to sling the fiery nectar into my gaping mouth, I felt something sharp connect with the back of my knee. The world spiralled before me, and try as I might, the glass flew over my shoulder, hitting a man square in the crotch. As the wet patch blossomed, I looked up to see Merv, that smirk affixed to his face, even in spite of his meat and two veg shrivelling up as the tequila soaked his nether regions.

I went to ask why, managing nothing but a. "W-" before the fiend turned on his heels and marched out of the pub, not even once patting himself down.

So it continued. The next day, my bourbon and Coke sailed over my head, as he kicked out the other knee. My Campari faring little better the day after as he pulled out my stool, and I threw the glass and its contents into the cigarette-mashing machine in the lobby.

Thinking I could stay one step ahead of him, I concealed myself behind the bar the day after, much to the barmaid's consternation. Yet as the smell of Martini assailed my nose, the glass shattered upon hearing a note in the key of E#, played through an out-of-date harmonica. Who was playing that dread instrument? Well, yeah, it was Merv. Obviously.

I was at rock bottom. I staggered out into the night, tearful and scared. Shunning the contempt radiating off Merv and the rest of the pub who were becoming quite used to the scene that played out night after night.

Dragging myself down Cannonball Boulevard, the moon, a slither of a crescent seductively winking at me, I heard a voice. "Oi. Mate."

Wiping my tears on yesterday's newspapers, I looked around, trying to locate the source of the sound.

"Oi. Knobber. Up here."

Remembering my dear friend's words, I craned my neck upwards and was aghast at what I saw. Floating there, just out of reach, was a bottle of sixteen-year-old Scotch. My taste buds instinctively fired up. Salivating to the point where the entire lowlands of my mouth was flooded out, scores of jaw-people were drowned, their bodies carried into my gullet, borne aloft on my own spit.

A nondescript face - really just a pair of eyes and a mouth - appeared in the bottle. "Yes. Yes! I have come to save you from your predicament."

I felt compelled to kneel, even though my brain told me that I would then be further away from the whisky. I did it anyway. As I sunk to the ground, the bottle floated down the commensurate distance.

Which I thought was jolly nice of it.

Struggling to find words, I called upon it. "Who are you? What do you want with me?"

The smile grew wide, an eye winked. "It's good to have a friend in Jesus, eh?"

Of course! I knew my friend would not forsake me. "That it is, oh noble bottle. Pray tell, what must I do, to sup on your innards?"

The bottle laughed, a hearty one, full of belly-wobbling and merriment, it made me feel safe. "Oh little one, I am not an ordinary bottle, oh no. Only those who are dedicated, firm of loin and soft of heart can take me into their stomach. I wonder... are you such a fellow?"

"Oh yes! I am, I am!" I implored. Any lingering doubt I had, had vanished. Sure, we've all heard the stories about trusting nefarious bottles of alcohol, but this was no rogue can of scrumpy, this was some kind of god!

Probably.

You have to remember that I was going through alcohol withdrawal, I'm pretty sure a figure clad in the skin of my work colleagues, brandishing a blood-soaked halibut and heaving a sack filled with human heads on their back, promising to give me an Amaretto and Coke would've been appealing at that point in time.

The bottle pulled in close, its top corkscrewing off slowly as it descended. The peaty musk oozed from the gap, encasing my head in its wonder. "If you want me. You have to show me you're serious. For only the most dedicated and serious can enjoy my oaky goodness."

"Anything! I'll do anything. Just tell me what I must do!"

I didn't think such a thing could make a facial expression like this, but the bottle leered. Its top screwed back on tight. Nodding across to an abandoned parcel thresher, the bottle drawled. "All you gotta do now..."

In that moment, I knew what it intended for me. "No."

"Ah, come on now, don't you want to drink me all up?"

"There has to be another way. Surely?"

"It'll be over real quick. You won't feel a thing."

I looked across to the thresher, the gleaming steel blades caught what little moonlight seeped from the sickly not-a-planet in the night sky. Sensing my uncertainty, the bottle hovered in front of me, blocking out my view of the solitary light in the sky. "If you do it. You can drink me all up. Every day."

"Really?"

"Oh yes. There won't be anyone who will barge into you. You'll be…"

"Yes?"

The bottle gave his best salesman toothy grin. "…free."

My brain was a befuddled mess, I knew that if I just went to a different pub I would be free of Merv and his wanton ways. But why should I? The other closest pub was The Strangled Babysitter, and that smelt funny. Besides, what had I achieved in this life? Nothing of note. Here was a bottle of booze offering me something tangible.

"Fine. But you promise?"

The bottle nodded, the act sloshed the scotch around inside the glass. "I do. Scout's honour. Forever."

It was easy enough to climb into the thresher, the sharp teeth sliced through my clothes and lacerated my feet and legs. The tricky bit was turning the damn thing on. I managed to lay sideways, the bottom of my torso within the stationary blades, and using my keyring chain, I was finally able to hit the button which kicked the machinery into action.

To be fair to the bottle of scotch, it was right, I didn't feel a thing. It must've chewed me up real good. No messing about whatsoever. So here I am. In heaven, which is basically a giant pub in the clouds. Guess that's how Jesus knew all about it, given his job. All my family and friends are here, which would be nice except I don't have many. So I spend my days sitting on a bar stool, watching repeats of my favourite television shows. I have to say, this place really is the best, probably because there is no-one up here intent on spilling my drinks.

So now, after I've had a few pints of quite frankly the

best beer I've ever had, I gesture to the barman that it's time. Sure enough, he waltzes on over, places a glass in front of me, pulls out a bottle from the top shelf of my choosing, and I can finally drink whatever spirit I want, up here, in the sky.

Inspired by Black Sabbath "Black Sabbath"

The open fire popped and crackled as Boone stared into it, the embers drifting upwards and slightly sideways in the night breeze that the open plains graciously provided. The night air was cold, and his thick grey blanket was held tightly around his shoulders. The much older man who sat across from him had stopped eating his pan of beans and simply stared at the ground in front of Boone. His jaw remained open, and several beans had taken up residence in his scraggy grey beard.

"What's the problem, old timer?" asked Boone, looking up slightly to see beneath the rim of his black Stetson.

"Your shadow," said the old man, pointing towards Boone's feet with a shaking metal spoon.

"What about it?"

"You aint got one."

"How about that?" said Boone. It was hardly the first time anyone had noticed this, after all. "Must be a trick of the light. It's plenty dark out, full moon keeps slipping behind the clouds, and that fire's roaring wild casting light all over in an uneven manner."

"I don't know, sure looks like…"

"What's more likely, old timer? That you're old and seeing shit that ain't there, or that I don't have a shadow?"

"Suppose." The old man shrugged, returning to his pan of beans but hardly daring to take his eyes off Boone.

"I don't mean to harm you none, shadow or no shadow. I just asked to share your fire, to which you obliged me. I been walking plenty, a sit would do me good."

"And I said yes to that because I didn't know you was some devil-worshipping…"

"What'd you just say?" asked Boone, moving his blanket back slightly to reveal the revolver tucked in the holster beneath his left arm.

"Nothing." The old man shook his head, turning his gaze away from Boone's cold eyes.

"That's right. Nothing. Now eat your damn beans."

"I aint the one who's damned," the old man muttered.

"Sure sounds like you got something to say, old timer. Let's have it." Boone sat back on his log and folded his arms.

"That mark, on your hand there." The old man pointed his spoon at Boone's right hand. Just above the joint at the base of his thumb was a deep red scar in the shape of a pentagram. "I know what that means."

"Is that right?" Boone laughed. "Then why don't you educate me, old man."

"Means you belong to him. To Old Scratch. That you sold your soul to him and someday he's gonna come collect."

"Smarter than I gave you credit for, old man. But you ain't right about either of those things. I didn't sell my soul to nobody. And second, you think the Devil got time for shit like that? He's waging the biggest war there is. One that makes that mess Lincoln started look like a whole lot of nothing."

"Well, if not him, then one of his soldiers."

"Alright, you're getting warmer now, I'll give you that."

Boone tugged his sleeve down to cover the mark on his hand. "Speaking of warm, throw some more grass on that fire, there's a chill in the air."

"Weren't before you came and sat down," the old man muttered, throwing some dry grass on the fire nonetheless.

"Brazen old cuss, ain't you?" Boone laughed, taking a sip from the canteen that hung from his side.

"I ain't comfortable around you, stranger. I make no secret of that. But I ain't exactly inexperienced with fear neither. I seen things. Done things. Regret a lot of them. But they give me a form of confidence a man don't get if he seen nothing and done nothing."

"You fight in the war?" asked Boone.

"I did."

"Which side?"

"What's it matter? Lincoln won, and that's the end of it."

"Name's Boone, by the way. Might as well tell me yours since we're swapping stories."

"Carson. Least it used to be. Ain't sure if I got a name no more. Been awhile since anyone used it."

"Everyone needs a name, Carson. Helps you remember who you are, and where you come from."

"Or what you're running from," Carson suggested, taking another mouthful of beans.

"Tell me Carson; did that keen eye of yours piss off everyone so much that you had to go live as a hermit in the middle of nowhere?"

"I left town to find gold. Never did get my hands on any. But I saw what it did to those luckier than me. Saw how it affects people. And that's the way this country is going. Pursuit of wealth and nothing more. Forgetting God and hope and all that brought us here. That made me sick of the sight of people, so I left them behind."

"I can respect that," said Boone, taking another drink and then offering the canteen to Carson. He declined.

"What about you, then? What's behind you wandering out here alone? Ain't no gold in those hills anymore, and the nearest town with work is behind you, not in front."

"Ain't looking for work, Carson."

"What are you looking for, then?"

"Salvation."

"Ain't no churches nearby."

"Church ain't no better than any other building in that regard."

"You don't believe in God?"

"I do. But he ain't what you think. And none of it works how you think. A church is bricks and stone. Jesus is a man on the cross. It's all names and places. Physical things. The stuff of our world. Not theirs. That ain't what gods and devils are about. They predate all of that."

"You sound like a man who's seen something to back that up."

"More than I'd like."

"You want to explain that mark on your hand? Perhaps tell me where it is you hail from?" Carson suggested.

"I think the answer to one might well give you the answer to both. In any case, I come from a town called Pleasance. Heard of that?"

The beans that Carson now swallowed down in one slow gulp seemed to have become heavy lumps of ice in his throat at the mention of that name. The expression this brought to his face gave Boone his answer without any words needing to be said.

"Reckon that's a mighty powerful yes, I'd wager," said Boone. "Why don't you tell me what it is you heard about good old Pleasance, Arizona?"

"It's probably a load of hearsay and horseshit," said Carson, lowering his eyes to the dirt. "Don't want to offend you none."

"I'm long past town pride, old-timer. Spill, tell me what you heard."

"Well... I guess they say that Pleasance was one of the first towns founded in the expansion. There were rivers, good soil, not too many hills, and it was far enough away from the redskins to not be getting attacked or nothing either. Except it all went wrong after a bad drought. Crops died, river went dry, soil couldn't be made to grow nothing no matter how hard it was worked."

"Right enough but it weren't just one season. Spell of bad luck came over those lands. It was like the weather was against it from the outset," Boone corrected him.

"Well, as you say. But yup, that's what I hear. Things got bad. Townsfolk started leaving, or those that could, anyway. Them that stayed behind started praying. Guess that's what folk do when they're desperate. Just start begging and pleading to anyone that might answer. And as I hear it, someone did."

"God? Is that what you heard, Carson? That God himself came down and made the lands fertile, the livestock good and fat, and the river run blue and strong again?"

"Nope." Carson shook his head, locking eyes with Boone as he chewed his beans. "Something else. I heard the Devil, but you already corrected me on that."

"Just me being pedantic, I get like that sometimes." Boone dismissed the remark with a wave of his hand. "You aint too far off with that, old timer. Might not have been Satan himself, but it certainly was something from the same sort of region. Go on with your story."

"All that's left to say is that the townsfolk got what they wanted, and Pleasance became prosperous. But in return, they had to pay. They started a new religion, to worship and give thanks to whatever it was that had settled in with them. I hear they'd light big fires, dance naked around it, toss live lambs and calves into the flames and sing songs to their saviour. The whole thing was like some kind of Old Testament Mount Sinai bullshit. Like an unholy Sabbath. I don't know nothing else, except the whole place burned down when one of their fires got out of control. And now nobody'll even go near the ghost of that place. Not even the redskins."

"You're close, but there's more to it. Unless you just plain don't want to hear. For which I wouldn't actually blame you. It ain't a nice story to get to sleep on."

"I don't sleep much anyway. Already got a head full of nightmares, one more won't hurt." Carson shrugged, placing down his empty pan and leaning forward to listen.

"The Sabbaths weren't the payment. They were just a bit of frivolity to worship the thing that had saved the town. But Pleasance still had a bill that needed paying. Once a year, on the night of All Hallows, the price was paid. That price was one child, every year. The holder of the town's debt would come in through the shadows and claim the life and soul of the child scarred with his mark, and then depart, leaving the town healthy and happy for another year. Went on like that for years, until it was my turn."

"That mark." Carson realised.

"Yep. My daddy done marked me up like a prize pig. It was my folks' turn to pay, just like all the other townspeople had. Many of them had two children, so at least they had one left after paying their way. For a while, at least, until that thing came back around and nobody had a spare child no more. But my parents never had a second child. Not for want of trying, but they always thought a sickness had gotten to my mother and made her barren after I was born. Probably for the best. Fewer children born into that town, the better.

"So my turn came up when I was close to ten years old, but my old man went and had a change of heart. Funny how that happens when it becomes personal, ain't it? Fine to stand by and watch some fiend take away your neighbour's children, but when it's your turn, suddenly you have an attack of moral fibre.

He told me to run, my daddy did. The night before All Hallows. Snuck into my room, helped me out the window, put me on our best horse and told me to run and never look back. I did the first part, but I couldn't help the second. I looked back in time to see my father pouring lantern oil round the doorways of every other house in the town, whilst those inside them slept.

Few hours later I could see the flames reaching up to the sky, even with the distance the horse had managed to take me. Could hear the screams, too. And something else. Like a… a primal roar of anger. It weren't happy. Not one bit. Maybe it knew it was being betrayed, or maybe it could just see its meal ticket going up in smoke. Either way, anger took hold of it that night. And never left."

"What happened to you? Where did you go?" asked Carson, barely blinking as he listened, enthralled with Boone's story.

"Next town over, to start. Place called Pure Water. Somewhat ironically, I might add, given the filthy state of what they were drinking. But it was safe. Weren't no child sacrifice going on, and they even had a church. I'd never seen a church before, but I'd heard about them. The church in Pleasance had been knocked down when I was too young to remember, so the novelty of seeing one wasn't lost on me. I enjoyed being near it, felt safer somehow without really understanding why. Well, I'd barely been in Pure Water a week when the illusion of my safety was made undeniably clear to me.

"I'd been taken in by a loving, Christian family. God-fearing folk, but decent. Not the kind who'd beat you for not knowing Bible verse, in any case. None too sure that they wanted a child to take care of in their advanced years, but one turned up desperate and hungry and no self-described Christian could rightly turn them away. So they didn't. Anyway, that one night, the last one I spent at that nice little homestead, I was laying asleep in the cot they'd made up for me. Something woke me up, but I can't rightly say what it was. As I sat up, I noticed straight away there was a cold draft in my room, but the unnatural kind of cold. Not from the night air, but the kind that feels like air from the mouth of something born from the darkness, breathing right down your neck.

"I looked around, squinting into the darkness, could I could see nothing. I could hear it, though, when I listened real good. It wasn't breathing, not exactly. Not even sure that what I could hear was the sort of thing that needed to breathe. But it was more like the steady movement of air, caused by the presence of something else in that room besides myself. I lit the candle the old couple had given me, and looked around. All I could see was my shadow, stretching out below me. Until it wasn't. What I'm saying is I watched as my shadow actually grew and stretched, pulling away from me and then changing shape into something else that loomed up the wall and ceiling over my head. It was a black shape, hard to define but probably something close to a bat, I'd reckon. Couldn't see no features except two eyes of pure fire. It was whispering something, but I couldn't understand none of it. Not that I was truly listening. Only words I caught were something about payment being due. It stretched out a clawed hand and pointed at me. No question that thing knew I was exactly who it was looking for.

"Even at that age, I weren't no dummy. They kept us mostly in the dark at Pleasance about what went on at the Black Sabbaths, and what they were for, but I knew enough. Least enough to understand the basic concept of what it was that had now followed me here to Pure Water. That same knowledge spurred me to grab the wooden cross from the wall above my head, and clutch it close to my chest, over my heart. Soon as I gone and done that, the thing shrieked like a banshee and withered into the corner of the room, merging with the other shadows until it was gone. I lay awake the rest of that night holding that cross like a mother holds onto her baby. Then I left the next morning. Been moving ever since, never staying anywhere too long."

"Wasn't it dead? That shadow thing?"

"No. I don't think it's something you can kill. And it's never going to stop coming, which is why I can't stop either. I've managed to keep a few days ahead of it, giving myself time to stop and rest a night or two at each place before moving on. Learned a few tricks too. Staying near churches or graveyards keeps it away, hides my scent from it. Crossing water seems to help too. Learned that one from the redskins themselves. The Quechan tribe, to be specific."

"You stayed with Indians?"

"I've stayed with lots, over the years. Been on the run twenty-some years now. A man learns to be a lot less judgemental about the ways and looks of other folks when he's desperate."

"Twenty years? Why is still after you? Surely it would have just found other souls to take by now?" asked Carson.

"Time ain't like it is to you and me, not to something like that. I think it's all relative to the thing counting it down. You and I wouldn't judge a minute as particularly long, but to the horseflies that only live a day? The human race, least in our part of the world, we got what? Sixty, seventy years on this land before it reclaims us. But that thing chasing me, it was here before the first man ever set foot on this planet. And it'll be here long after, I reckon. So what's a couple of decades chasing after its meal to something like that? Probably about the same as the time you or I would spend leaning over to pick up a coin that dropped out of our pocket. It aint going to get tired or bored."

"Is it close now? Will it come?" Carson tensed suddenly and looked all around him, scanning the darkness and focusing on every movement in the underbrush that the night's breeze caused.

"Relax, old timer. I'm a few days ahead of it. Crossed a few streams, left a few drops a blood at a couple of crossroads along the way."

"How do you know to do things like that? Indians again?"

"Yep. I stayed with them a few months, longest I've ever been able to avoid it. The way I see it, they been sharing this land with things like that for longer than we have. They know how to hide from them, how to cast them away."

"But they wouldn't have the sign of the cross, like you used at that homestead," said Carson.

"Aint about the sign of the cross itself, Carson. It's what it represents. Faith. The power of belief in something good and pure and light. You might call it God, the Quechan would call it something else entirely. The Great Spirit, I guess. But it don't matter none what name you put on it, or even if you give it one at all. Fact of the matter is, they believe, or rather they know, about a lot of things the white folk have forgotten or never even knew. And that included knowing exactly what the folks at Pleasance, Arizona had been up to. I always figured that in times past, during a bad hunting season or some such, their own people might have made a similar pact and lived to regret it. Or at least enough of them did to warn future generations against it.

"The Quechan taught me how the shadow thing doesn't like to cross running water, and how a crossroads can confuse it if you leave a little bit of yourself behind there. Don't rightly know if that's similar to leaving a blood trail to confuse a hunting dog or if it's a little more complex than that. All I know is it works, and it's bought me a few days rest here and then when I've needed it. They also taught me that you can transfer the thing's attachment to you to someone else by way of giving them your mark. But it has to be voluntarily, mind. You can't just go drawing the thing on just anyone.

That's not how a bargain works."

Boone took a swig from his cantina, then tipped it upside down to show it was now empty.

"Guess we're onto the reserve for the remainder of the night. That's alright, this stuff's better anyhow." He shrugged, taking two silver hip flasks from his waist. He handed one to Carson who accepted it, evidently feeling its contents might help to ward off the increasingly cold night air.

"Why would anyone agree to take on-board that kind of a curse? To be willingly hunted down by that thing?" asked Carson, unable to let the point rest.

"Well… that's a good point. Truth be told, I ain't never found anyone. I mean the ritual itself is pretty simplistic. You break bread together, share a drink of wine, welcome the person into your home, share your truths under the light of a full moon and then pass the mark over. But, like you said, can't see much chance of anyone agreeing to that. Only reason I can see for such a fact existing is for loved ones to give someone they truly care about a reprise. So perhaps the parents might take it on for their children, for instance."

"Your daddy could have done that for you."

"You're right, he could have. He was so determined to save me in the end, and that little ritual was a way he could have done it. I always supposed that he didn't know that it was an option. Not exactly common knowledge, is it? Only ancient folks like the redskins seem to have that kind of awareness. Everyone else just touches on the fringes of it whenever they start to play around with things they don't truly understand. But that's about it, old timer. That's my story."

"Sure is a dark one, friend. Can't have been easy. Never resting, never slowing down. Never being able to find yourself a girl, or start a family."

"It's getting harder, the older I get. Ain't as fast as I used to be. And about that last part. I did find a girl, actually. Met her once and spent a few nights with her, and then looped back round to see her again, taking the new railroad on one part to stay well ahead of that thing. It ain't dumb but the iron on the railroads seem to be one more thing it ain't fond of. Anyhow on that second visit, it turned out she was carrying a little surprise for me."

"Aw shit, I'm sorry Boone," Carson remarked, taking a long drink from the flask Boone had given him.

"Supposed to be good news, aint it?"

"But that kid's going to grow up never knowing its daddy. Not properly. I mean I guess you could stop by every once in awhile, but…"

"No." Boone stopped him. "I aint going near either of 'em again now I know. Not with this thing on my back. It's my burden, not theirs."

"You seem a good man, if a little curt. I might have misjudged you to start with. If I could help with your burden then I would."

"You're an old gent, Carson." Boone smiled, taking a drink from his own flask. "And you're right, I ain't particularly polite. Probably a combination of the years spent mostly alone, and the desire to keep away them folk that tried to get close. I ain't the easiest to get along with, and you've been more welcoming than I rightly deserve."

"It's a hard world out there, Boone. Getting harder all the time. More folk coming along to take what little there is. The ones who already got more than their share of it don't wanna offer any of it out to those that come next. Man's horror to one another is getting worse every day, and that's not even taking into consideration the kind of horrors that you and I know exist."

"You too, huh? You seen some of the same kind of thing, old man?"

"I aint seen no Devils, I wouldn't claim that. But I seen ghosts aplenty. Walking the roads out here, lost and not sure where they're going. I saw a few on the battlefields too, standing over their own corpses like they aint sure what to do next. It's awful, seeing something that nobody would understand and feeling like you can't help."

"You're the kind that likes to help?"

"I was," Carson said with a sad smile, before taking another long drink from the flask. "But then it all got too much and I just left my fellow man behind me. Since then, I been looking out for myself and nobody else."

"You're like me in reverse. I always been looking out for me and me alone. Had little choice in it really, thanks to the gift my folks left to me. But since I found out I'm gonna be a father myself, that's changed things. Made me want to do what's right, so I can be there for my kid."

"Sure hope you find what you're looking for, Boone."

"I already have, old man. And I thank you for it." Boone tipped his hat. Carson frowned, not quite understanding what Boone meant. His vision blurred slightly, causing him to rub his eyes to clear the haze from them. It didn't help, and now there was a ringing in his ears. His balance departed from him and he slumped sideways on the log beneath him. Sleep took him completely before his head even hit the dirt.

"There he is," said Boone, leaning down and looking into Carson's face as he opened his eyes.

The older man winced as his eyes struggled to open, but then suddenly opened them wide as a searing pain struck him. It was coming from his right hand. Carson tried to scream but couldn't, his mouth stuffed with a torn sheet of cloth making a crude gag. His feet were tied at the ankles, and his hands tied before him at the wrists. Looking down at his right hand to see the source of the agonising pain, Carson could see that on the spot just below his thumb joint was a darker patch of skin bearing the pentagram mark.

It hadn't been burned or drawn onto his skin, though. In

fact it wasn't even his skin. A separate patch of skin had actually been cut away from its source and then stitched onto his own hand. To confirm this, Carson looked up at Boone and saw that his own right hand was now bandaged and bleeding.

"Little crude, I know. And I didn't have much liquor left to numb it, for either of us. Sorry about that," Boone explained. "But you drank most of it."

Carson remembered the flask Boone had given him. Drugged, evidently.

"See, you said you wanted to help me, and now you are. You offered to break bread with me... or beans, at least. The food itself is incidental. As is the wine we shared. We sat under the moon and shared our stories, you let me share your home, such as it is, and then finally you said,and I quote, 'if I could help with your burden then I would.' Which I thought was real nice."

Carson screamed into the gag in protest.

"Now, I know what you're thinking. That was just a figure of speech, not to be taken literal or nothing. But see, that's the funny thing about these rituals. They aint too good on the particulars. The laws and statutes they follow are anything but fair. I mean look at me. I never signed no Devil's bargain. I never took part in no Black Sabbath. That was all done before I was even born, before any of us kids were. But we still had to pay the price. That ain't no more fair than what I've done to you. But life ain't fair, is it? We both know that. And perhaps if things were different, I'd be content to live out my burden until time caught up with me. But I'm gonna be a daddy. And that changes things.

"That was true, you know. I didn't lie to you about that. Didn't lie to you about much at all, in fact. The only lie I told, was when you got a little scared and I said that the shadow thing was plenty far behind me. That weren't exactly true. See, I've been getting a little desperate. I ain't passed no streams or crossroads for a few days, and I'm slowing. I knew it was going to find me tonight, and I was going to have to accept what was coming. But then I met you, sitting by this fire, and your humanity offered me another way. And I am sorry, old man, I truly am."

The night wind picked up, carrying with it a chill so strong that the empty tin pot Carson had cooked his beans on was now immediately covered in a coating of glistening frost.

"Time I was gone, I reckon. I ain't its target no more but I'd still rather not be here when it shows. Probably holds something of a grudge that it's liable to act on if it sees me," said Boone, straightening his Stetson and standing up.

Carson screamed again into his gag, struggling uselessly against his bonds.

"Let me give you one last piece of advice, such as it's worth," said Boone, turning one last time to look at Carson, who flopped around on his side like a helpless fish. "Don't scream. I once heard one of the Pleasance folk say it likes the taste better when they scream. Don't go giving it that satisfaction."

With that, Boone tipped his hat and walked away. Carson pleaded helplessly, inaudibly for him to come back, tears streaming down his face. Boone was soon gone, out of sight in the darkness as the full moon slipped behind a cloud. Carson closed his eyes and sobbed, opening them again when he felt a teardrop freeze against his face.

The roaring fire before him blew out suddenly, the shallow pit in which it had burned immediately covering with frost. A shadow spread across the floor, surrounding the prone Carson in a semicircle and then rising up from the floor. Two blazing red eyes burned near the top of the dark shape, and a clawed finger slowly stretched out and pointed at him. Carson screamed and begged into his gag for God to help him. Nobody replied.

Inspired by The Housemartins "Caravan Of Love"

He pushed his thumb and forefinger, cracked and calloused from years of turpentine and splinters, against the handle of his chisel, driving the blade across the surface of the wood. He trusted the sycamore. Could feel its every bend and groove, knew when it would warp, when it would break. His hands, so deft and sure despite their looks, caressed the wood. He ran his little finger with the lightest touch along the ridge he had just carved. It was smooth, with not a snag or jagged edge.

He kept his tools sharp.

Gripping the chisel firmly, he took the point back to the start, carving another line which swooped alongside the first. A delicate curl of wood formed under the blade, like a snail shell.

Carve. Swoop. Curl.

Carve. Swoop. Curl.

Carve. Swoop. Curl.

Soon, the form of a bird began to rise from the timber. Then another. A pair of turtle doves, feathering their nest. He

always carved his motifs in pairs, it was his signature. He
used his own unique blend of linseed oil and powdered oxide,
fiercely guarding his secret recipe from the other waggon
builders.

He knew all about secrets.

Contrary to what most non-Gypsies, or *gorjas*, believe,
the building and decorating of waggons was one of the few
talents the travelling folk looked for outside their own tight-
knit communities. The caravans, or *vardos*, were not just their
homes and modes of transport, but symbols of wealth and
status. A life on the road did not allow for many possessions,
particularly those that did not serve any practical purpose. So
the practical became the beautiful, and they paid men like my
father to carve and paint ornate patterns on the bodies of their
trailers. This soon became a competition, and when the
families would meet at summer fairs, they would show off the
gold-leaf on their wheel spokes and the intricate lining-out in
grassy greens, buttercup yellows and chalky whites, and
wooden bunches of grapes that looked so shiny and juicy, like
you could pluck one off and pop it in your mouth.

I remember the first time my Pa took me to Appleby
horse fair. It was like landing on an alien world or in some
exotic, far-flung country. I was surrounded by men shouting
in fast tongues I did not understand, by bartering and hurly-
burly. Dark-eyed women stared out from trailers. Shirtless
boys, younger than I was, rode huge ponies, driving them to
wash in the river. I dodged steaming piles of horse dung and
dogs and small children. The smell of cooking mingled with
the sweat of men and ponies made me light headed. Pa set up
his trailer, gaily painted with the words Collins and Son,
Waggon Builders.

Then he took me to my first bare-knuckle fight.

"Don't tell your Ma," he said, handing over a few coins
to a round man with a book and pencil. "If you come to a fight

and don't put a wager on, you're nothing more than a ghoul."

I had no money, could make no bet, but I knew I was no ghoul the moment I heard the first crack of knuckle on jaw. The scarlet arc as teeth connected with bone and the spray of blood that splattered my boots. I pushed my way through the crowd, back into the thick wood-smoke and meaty mist of the camp. That was when I first saw her. Just a kid then, like me. Her face lit from below, those heavy, serious brows and blue-green eyes that danced above the firelight. She held up a morsel of food in her hand, without smiling, but still in a gesture of welcome. I ambled over and she passed me a tiny leg of hare. I could taste the grass under its feet as it coursed through the meadow. I could taste the sunlight on its ears and the spring rain dripping from its waxy fur.

"Your first fair."

It wasn't a question.

"Yes. How did you know?"

"You got the look, is all, got the smell."

"Talking about smells? How can you smell anything other than horse shit?"

This made her laugh.

"*Gorja* boy. You live brick, you don't know The Way."

"What's your name?"

"Elvie."

"I'm Jack. Jack Collins."

"I know," she said, pointing to the side of my Pa's waggon.

"Have you been to Appleby before?"

"I was born here, *gorja* boy. In that waggon, right there."

We talked for a while, warmed by the fire. I had a hundred questions for her, but my Pa soon came running along the muddy path. As he got closer, I could see his cheek starting to swell up and grazes on the backs of his hands.

"It turned into a brawl, Jack. Bloody great brawl, everyone swinging punches and hooting and yelling."

He didn't look frightened though, he looked alive. His good eye glinting and twinkling like the stars above our heads, the other starting to close and turn purple. He put his arm around me and we skipped and swayed back to our trailer.

I turned to look for Elvie, but she was gone.

The curved point of the veiner pressed down like a long metal fingernail, creating a half-moon shaped scallop. Lifting and pressing created another one, and another and another. A fish-scale pattern emerged, getting harder to see as blood seeped through the deep slices.

He kept his tools sharp.

Next was the slant chisel. Into the flesh, straight down to the bone. Unlike sycamore, this canvas was not so strong. It moved under his fingers, it tensed, it struggled. He did not know where it would bend, when it would break.

But he could learn.

A carp leapt from the skin, caught in a crimson lake. His hook was embedded in the roof of its mouth, and he pulled and pulled, carved and cut, until he landed his prize fish.

He set to work on the other straight away. He always carved in a pairs.

In the years that followed, we attended many fairs; Stow, Seamer, Priddy, Brough. But I longed to return to Appleby. Ma said it was too big, too dangerous. The year we went, ten people got crushed to death by a stampede of startled ponies, including some children. But in my fifteenth year, almost a man by then and a head taller than her, she could no longer forbid me to do anything. I'd started living outside in Pa's trailer all year round, cooking on the fire, sleeping under the canopy of stars. I didn't want to live brick anymore. All the while, I was learning how to bend ribs, whittle spindles, carve, paint and gild.

I don't know why I was so certain I would see her there again, and why it hadn't occurred to me that she would most likely be at the other fairs, as they by their nature attracted travelling folk from around the country. But in the same way that I knew how to mix the right varnish that would bend but not crack, I knew she would be at Appleby and that she had been there every year, looking for me, the same way I was looking for her now. Pa had pitched up on the same plot as before, but in the few short years since my first visit, the field was now crowded with painted waggons, some of higher quality than others. I spotted a few of Pa's builds and even some of my own fledgling paintwork.

I recognised her family *vardo* straight away. It was painted with cherries and summer blossom, with golden pears and apples adorning the doors.

She was a woman now, of that there was no mistake. But I recognised her all the same.

"Jack Collins," she called to me. "How's brick life?"

I pulled myself up to my full height, puffed my chest out and willed the few downy hairs on my lip to bristle with manly pride.

"I don't live brick no more."

She narrowed her eyes and beckoned me closer.

I came over to where she sat, on the steps of her waggon. She curled her finger, calling me closer still. She leant towards me and took a deep breath through her nose, inhaling my scent.

"You might sleep under the stars, Jack Collins, but you'll always be a *gorja* boy."

She touched my cheek and the corner of her lip lifted, ever so slightly. "And that's no good to me," she sighed.

Movement in the waggon behind her made us both look up. A face appeared in at the glass, scowling under a shawl.

"You'se be off with yer now," Elvie shouted, shooing me away. Just before I turned to leave, crestfallen, she whispered,

"Meet me at the river, down the bottom of the meadow. I'll be there at sundown."

The door to the wagon swung open, and I caught a glimpse of treasures unknown. Dried herbs, shiny kettles, wild flowers, and right at the very back, a bed big enough for two.

It was the waiting he couldn't stand. Wood didn't make him wait. But flesh was delicate, unpredictable. It had to heal before he was sure the carvings were true. And, unlike wood, there was only so far he could cut, only so deep he could pierce, only so many layers of skin and fat he could slice before he reached the bone. Bone was useful, to be ground down into a fine dust and used as a stabiliser for his colours. But bone was not, in his eyes, beautiful.

Once the gouges had healed, once the scabrous skin had peeled and flaked, and raw scar tissue presented itself to him, only then could he paint.

He painted freehand, whatever the canvas. He had no time for stencils or tracing. Natural ox-hair gripped in a tiny quill. If he was painting ponies, a single hair would be used to line out every stroke in the horse's mane. If he was painting fruit, he would use big, juicy swooshes of colour.

Today, he was painting a pair of eyes. Blue-green eyes that would forever stare at him, accusing, blaming, pleading.

Eyes that looked into his soul and found only shame.

I stood in the shadow of a tree whose branches hung low over the river and watched the sun go down. Somehow I knew I mustn't be seen, that our meeting was secret, shameful even. And it thrilled me. Every now and then I heard splashes of laughter, a fiddle playing, a dog barking. When night came at the fairs, it was time to dance, to drink, to love, to fight. Humanity at its most basic and glorious. Tribes have gathered in the firelight to sing and share stories and satiate their lusts since before time began.

I waited. The sun had fully dipped behind the horizon, taking with it all the warmth of the day.

I waited. She wasn't coming. It was a trick. Silly *gorja* boy, falling in love with a gypsy girl. I imagined her bragging to her cousins, telling them how she had left the fool down by the river, waiting for a sweetheart who would never come. I imagined they were watching me, through the hawthorn bushes, stifling laughter behind their hands. I turned away from the riverbank to head back up the hill towards camp, when I heard a thud of footsteps and a jingling of tiny golden bells.

"Where do you think you're going, Jack Collins?"

"Come to tease me some more, have you?" My voice was bitter as crab-apples.

"Tease you? I've been trying to get away. My brothers, they won't let me out of their sight."

I wavered. Should I believe her? I pictured those same brothers, hiding just over the ridge, waiting to jump out and push me in the river, hold me under and drown me in horse piss and spilled beer.

"Well, ain't yer gonna talk to me now, Jack Collins? I thought we was friends, you and me?"

"Are you alone?"

"Course I am. You know what else I am? Cold."

She moved towards me just as the clouds parted, letting moonlight spill over her face, illuminating her skin so that she looked unreal, like a figure painted on a waggon. Her hair drawn in single strokes of charcoal, her lips stained with orchard fruit. She pressed herself against me and I rested my fingers on her bare shoulders.

"My brothers... if they catch us, they'll kill me. Kill both of us. Do you ever wish you were someone else?"

"All the time," I whispered into her hair. "All the time."

The pliers were heavy in his palm, carrying much more weight than any of his other tools. There was nothing special about these brutes, they had one purpose and one purpose only.

Gold.

He yanked and twisted with all his strength, both hands around the grips, jamming his knee into the bed. A neighbouring tooth cracked and hot blood welled up over his fingers. With a final pull, the gold was extracted from the cavernous mouth-mine. He held the tooth up, marvelling at the length of the roots. Gelatinous blobs of spittle and gore plopped onto the bed. He turned the tooth upside down, so it now resembled a tiny, golden crown.

"Jack Collins, King of the Gypsies," he laughs, but the words come out as a mangled mess.

Those days at Appleby were the greatest of my life. Rolling and riding under the cover of night, catching stolen smiles over campfires. Our secret love blossomed, as only the love between two young people can in less than a week. My father and I still had business to do, and we were trusted by the travelling folk, as much as they ever trusted *gorjas*. I wanted Elvie to tell me everything about life on the road; the turnpikes and traditions, what they ate, how they slept, what they did when they were sick. I wanted to know The Way.

"I'd give anything to be that free," I told her one night, my hand cupping her naked breast, our skin still slick and sticky.

"I'll never be free."

"Come with me," I said, the thought thundering through me on horses' hooves. "Come with me tonight. We'll take my Pa's trailer and go, live together on the road. I can learn The Way..."

"You don't understand, Jack. This way, this life, it's not for you."

"I want it to be, please Elvie, I want it to be so much. Why are we so different?"

She sat up, gathering her clothes and brushing herself free of grass.

"I'm not a pony, Jack. You can't come to the fair and take yourself home a little piece of The Way and think it makes you one of us, it doesn't work like that."

She wrapped her shawl around her shoulders and ran.

I wish that had been the last time I saw her.

He never did learn The Way. So he made his own Way.

He kept his tools sharp. He looked for beauty in a dark world.

Travelling, living the life of his dreams. But all he had left were nightmares.

Then one day, his chisel slipped, carving a perfect line into the crease of his thumb joint. That feeling of metal cutting through flesh, as soft and satisfying as catching an eel with his bare hands. He stared as the blood pumped itself out, flooding his palms.

And felt no pain.

He could smell wood smoke and summer blossoms on a night time breeze.

He remembered her, how she was.

Then, the pain came.

This was His Way.

It was the last night of the fair. Pa was packing up so we could leave at dawn. I was gathering my tools, thinking about Elvie. I couldn't leave it like this, I might not see her again until Appleby next year. I swung my satchel over my shoulder and went to the meeting place, hoping she would be there one last time, despite our fight.

As I crested the hill, I heard screaming. No-one in the camp would have heard it over the noise of the fair, but down here her voice rang out over the river.

I started to run towards her, but then more voices joined in.

"*Gorja* with *gorja*, Rom with Rom," they growled. I skidded low to the ground and hid behind the hawthorn.

There, next to the moonlight dappled water, was Elvie, being held from behind by someone I couldn't see. The arm around her neck showed it to be a man, I guessed it must be one of her brothers. She struggled and kicked, trying to reach who I assumed was the other brother. He lifted a muscular arm and hefted his palm into her face. Her whole head whipped to the side.

I wanted to leap up, to run over there and save her. I had my bag, I kept my tools sharp. But instead, I lay there, a coward, hiding in the bushes. Elvie lifted her head, a thin line of red trickling from the corner of her mouth, the mouth that I had kissed not more than a few hours ago. Her eyes went over her brother's head, straight to where I was cowering. She couldn't know I was there.

But her eyes showed. She knew.

"*Tomberon!*" he shouted, spitting in her face. I knew this word. It was the worst thing you could call a woman, that she was nothing more than a hole for men to fill. He drew his arm back and punched her again and again. When she was flopped so far forward that she had to be held around her waist to stop her falling to the floor, the fists stopped. He nodded to his brother, and Elvie dropped to the ground like a bunch of rags.

That was when the kicking started.

Gilding always came last.

He had worked on this creation for so many years, so much pain, so many scars. Yet it was never enough. He wanted beauty in a dark world. Beauty through his own suffering. Every slice was both punishment and blessed relief.

Every cut reminded him he was a spineless coward, weak and ashamed.

He had pulled out all his own teeth. At first for the gold fillings, then just because they were there and he didn't deserve them.

The eyes carved into his forehead were hers. Every day he painted them with leaded paint, hoping the headaches and sickness would not bring death by poisoning before he could finish. She stared out at him when he looked in the mirror, full of hateful silence and disappointment.

His tongue had been hard to cut out, but he no longer had a use for it. Life on the road demanded only the essentials could be carried. Any dead weight must be discarded.

He made his own crucible from clay before he ripped each of his fingernails out with pliers. The crucible was now nestled deep in the fire. The gold fillings melted down, along with his mother's wedding ring and one of the tiny golden bells he found on the ground when Elvie's brothers had finally finished with her and rolled her into the river to wash up at a village downstream. Just a murdered gypsy girl with no name.

But he knew her name.

"Here's to you, Elvie Lee."

He toasted her through raw gums and ragged tongue stump as he lifted the burning clay cup from the flames with iron tongs.

"Here's to you, my one true love."

He opened his mouth wide as the liquid inferno poured over his face, searing his throat. Molten metal forced its way down his gullet and burned his organs with filigree branches.

He had finally found The Way.

Inspired by Blue Oyster Cult "Don't Fear The Reaper"

The October sun was almost too hot to bear as Claire leaned in towards Hiren and touched her lips to his. Claire's breath tasted of cherry soda to Hiren. Hiren's tasted like a church to Claire: a dizzying blend of spices, incense, and strange secrets.

It helped them forget about the game, and about Tilly.

They sat surrounded by staffs of barley, lost to the blissful rush of their kisses. The other kids' voices were distant whoops and laughs, and in the vast blue above the field, frustrated birds of prey screed at the children whose boisterous presence reduced their chances of snatching a tasty morsel.

Hiren's sensitive skin itched with excitement. For the first time in his young life he wondered what death was like. Was it peaceful, like this? Had his Grandfather slipped from his body and emerged in a sunny field, where he would relive his first kisses for the rest of eternity? Hiren hoped so.

Claire smiled at Hiren's dopey expression. He was her friend and, now that they had kissed, she supposed he was also her first love. While the others tore through the barley field, screaming their freedom to the yellow gods of the autumn sun, Claire and Hiren savoured their silent privacy. Sat beneath the barley's wavering ears, they tasted each other's breath and sweat, and each time they parted they sighed with satisfaction.

Claire and Hiren found comfort in their wordlessness, because the other children's shrieks told them that Amy was growing restless, and that the time to play Don't Fear The Reaper was approaching. Neither of them could forget what had happened to Tilly, and the sounds she had made as they carried her to the well. That had been Corn Day; now, it was Barley Day.

When they had first sat before each other to kiss, Claire had yelped when the edge of a pebble had poked her behind, so she'd slipped it into the front pocket of her dungarees as a memento. They had started off brushing lips and pecking, and swiftly moved on to thrusting their sloppy tongues out as far as possible, clashing their teeth and filling each other with grossed-out giggles. Claire had even blown a raspberry into Hiren's mouth. Now though, their curious kisses had become tender, and while they would go no further (and couldn't have guessed how to anyway), their intimacy was real.

"It's playtime!"

Amy's cry rang out across the field. A breeze rustled the barley, and on the distant horizon of their hearing Claire and Hiren made out the low, fizzing rumble of the famished Reaper. They'd known it was coming, but foreknowledge did not lessen their dismay. Still sitting, they parted and looked at the ground.

Hiren's face was pleading when he looked up at Claire; eyes wide, lips knotted, brows urgently raised. He was asking if they could run in the opposite direction. Surely they could escape to the back of Claire's mum's house and climb the trees where the air smelled of flowery fruits, and they could slip inside for a taste of freshly-made ginger beer whenever they chose. But while he was technically right and they *could* dodge playing the game today, they were worried what might happen if they did. The pair were afraid of both Amy and the Reaper, but they were just as afraid of what the repercussions would be if the game was discovered by their parents, their teachers, and the police.

Hiren and Claire had hoped that what had happened to Tilly would dissuade Amy and the others, but if anything it had increased the game's importance, locking them all behind the bars of a shared secret. It was now no longer solely a game, but a ritual, too.

So Claire shook her head and rose to her feet, offering Hiren a hand that he batted away irritably. The others were nearer than they'd thought, stalking the golden crops just a few metres back. When Claire and Hiren stood up, the others ended their search. There were four of them aside from Hiren and Claire, but Amy led the group.

The drone of the Reaper was rising, and when Claire and Hiren turned they saw the monster's approach. In the distance, it was a pale, far-off shape that made Claire think of a baby's face chewing and spitting out food, and Hiren think of a monster from one of his father's books about Greek myths; a manticore, maybe.

"There you are!" Amy said, smiling toothily. The others – Sanj, Eleanor, and the boy with the lazy eye who Claire and Hiren thought of as Squint – grinned in silence.

The hot wind fluttered Amy's red hair. Amy, two school years higher than Claire and Hiren, was a farmer's girl and often dressed in baggy, shapeless clothes. She'd told them that her father had once let her watch him slaughter a pig for their Christmas meal, and she had snuck back into the barn to dip her fingers in the bucket of blood.

Claire remembered how Amy had dipped her fingers into the red, bony spot where Tilly's leg had been, too, before they had dropped her into the well.

"Have a nice time banging, guys?" Amy asked.

Both Hiren and Claire blushed.

"You're so nasty, Amy," Claire said.

"Whatever. I got it on film. Gonna upload it to Pornhole."

Sanj sniggered, his eyes and forehead glittering. "Yeah! To the animal section, 'cos you guys are chickens!"

"Shut up! We weren't doing anything!" Hiren yelled. He hoped that Claire couldn't hear his shame.

"It's the first day of the barley harvest," Amy said. "Barley Day."

Amy's parents owned the fields, and Don't Fear the Reaper had been her idea. She'd told the children that her family had played the game for many years in many different forms, and it was now up to them to carry on the tradition.

"We don't want to play, Amy," Hiren said, thrusting his hands into his pockets. "It's stupid and no one should have to."

"You'd rather we showed your raggedy old mum what happened to Tilly then, would you? She'd have a heart attack and die on the spot!"

Squint guffawed and laid a hand on his chest, grimacing and howling. His lazy eye pointed at his nose as he fell to the ground. The others laughed. Claire and Hiren didn't.

"And what would *your* mum and dad think?" Hiren asked.

At Hiren's question, Amy's smile gained a harder edge. Hiren thought of one of his father's favourite phrases: "Cruel eyes, cruel heart".

"Where do you think that Tilly's mum and dad went after we put Tilly in the well?" Amy asked.

Hiren was confused. Tilly's parents had left town to go and look for their daughter. Amy had told them. Claire knew how to read between lines, though, and a frightening image came to her: Amy's parents dragging two more people through the corn field towards the well at the edge of the farm.

"My ma and pa always say that it's important to stick to tradition," Amy said. "We've had this farm for a long time, and my family says that Don't Fear the Reaper is the only reason we're still here. My sister used to play the game every year until last autumn. Now she can't play anymore, so I've got to. And you were all here on Corn Day, *so do you too.*"

While Hiren once again saw no deeper than the surface of Amy's claims, Claire's tummy squirmed at the words, "she can't play anymore…". Her mind went even further. Had Amy's older brother been prepared for what had happened to Tilly on Corn Day? Maybe that was why he'd had those black sacks ready with him, and had been so quick to help gather up Tilly's wet and broken pieces. Perhaps that was how he'd stayed calm when he'd cradled her largest part and carried it alongside the kids, the lame form in his arms making those slopping sounds that Claire still remembered at night.

"Come on," Amy said, finally. "Positions."

With Hiren feeling helpless and Claire coming to understand how dangerous things were, they did as they were asked. The Reaper sounded hungry as the children crouched with their heads below the line of the barley, the monster's stomach growling in their ears. They grouped together like six pips on a die: Hiren and Amy at the front, then Claire and Sanj, followed by Eleanor and Squint chuckling at the back. It looked like the start of a playground game, but the whirr of the Reaper in the distance, and the silence that gripped them, felt reverent. They would once again race towards those blurred spinning teeth, and the child who ran for the longest time and dared to step closest to the Reaper would win.

Amy and Tilly had been at the front last time, and both Claire and Hiren had seen the satisfaction on Amy's face when she had announced herself the Corn Champion. Claire hadn't been able to speak in the wake of Tilly's fate, but a small part of her had since wanted to tell Amy that technically, although she was no longer with them, Tilly had won Corn Day.

Crouching beside Sanj, Claire could only see Amy's back and the swishing barley. She felt nervous and sick, and would rather lose the game than risk getting too close to the Reaper's flashing metal.

Hiren glanced to his right. Amy leered back. It was a look he often saw on the faces of kids who pointed at an injured child staggering to the school medical room but did nothing to help. It made him feel small, but also made him want to wipe that horrid look off her face. The only way he'd do that would be by beating her at Don't Fear the Reaper.

"*Now!*" Amy shouted.

And they ran.

Hiren launched himself through the barley, limbs electrified. He tore ahead of Amy with a whoop, the barley whipping his legs as his feet pounded the soil. When he looked straight ahead he almost froze; the Reaper seemed so close.

Claire saw Hiren's immediate lead but tried to focus on the rhythm of her sprinting legs. Something thumped against her chest. Sprinting beside her, Sanj made hacking noises of determination. She had no way to guess the distance between their group and the Reaper, but she thought it would take less than a minute for the race to end. It glowed yellower than the barley – almost as yellow as the burning sun – and the crops bowed before its gaping mouth as it chewed and swallowed and shat waste in its wake.

Amy was laughing behind Hiren, but he dashed faster than he had on Corn Day, filled with determination. He would beat this nasty girl at her own dangerous game. It was important. His parents would fly into a rage if they knew what he was doing, and he supposed that Claire would too, but as the field shot by and Hiren led the pack closer to the Reaper, all he wished for was to reach the beast first.

Fear climbed Claire's throat. Hiren's reckless pace told her enough: he was wrapped up in the game, and while he was no doubt doing so to relinquish Amy's control over them, she felt that it was also his competitive nature that drove him towards pain or worse. She stumbled over a rise in the ground and although she managed to right herself she dropped behind the others. Squint cackled as he passed and Claire almost lost her footing again.

Up ahead, Hiren ran full pelt. It was a short sprint and he was one of the fastest runners in his class. Although Amy was older and bigger than Hiren, he was confident that if they were heading for a finishing line he could have won without a problem – but they were aiming for a moving, lethal target, and Hiren was close to losing his nerve.

From the back, Claire felt her legs slow. She'd twisted her foot when she'd staggered, and while it wasn't a serious injury she did not want to keep going. She had to, though. Hiren was paces ahead and Claire had the dreadful idea that it wasn't solely the Reaper endangering him; it was Amy, too. Claire panted as she ran, remembering the smoky taste of Hiren's breath on her tongue. The Reaper was so much closer now, and Claire could make out the face of Amy's older brother through the sun-streaked glass. Through the glare, she saw the white of his grinning teeth.

Nerves and terror filled Hiren with doubt. Even if he won, would Amy *really* declare him Barley Champion? Would it make a difference, either way? The churning teeth of the Reaper looked more ravenous than ever, like some enraged Greek god demanding sustenance. Hiren could safely run for a few more seconds, but the desire to come first was draining away as he realised how pointless victory would be. He was about to stop when he felt a pair of hands gripping his shoulders.

Claire's heart lurched when she saw Amy reach ahead of her: the older girl was shoving Hiren towards the maw of the Reaper. The weight Claire had felt against her chest moments ago hit her again.

Amy's laughter filled Hiren's ears. He tried to veer off course and away from the formidable Reaper's path, but it was as though Amy was not only pushing him but *carrying him* too, so that even if he stumbled or lunged sideways he would remain on course. He was moments away from the whirling metal edges that would devour him whole, just as they had devoured Tilly.

Claire was not a runner like Hiren, but from a young age her father had instilled within her a love of cricket. The stone which she had placed in her front pocket to remember her first kiss had a familiar curved shape. It evoked memories of passing and catching her father's cricket ball. She stopped, took aim, and hurled.

Ten paces from the Reaper, Hiren felt Amy's grip leave his shoulders. He placed all his weight onto his right foot and launched himself to his left. The Reaper's spinning steel seemed to bear down on him as his body struck the ground, so he clenched his legs against his stomach and covered his eyes with his arms.

Standing still and breathing hard, Claire saw Amy trip, reeling from the stone that had shot like a missile into her back. Amy landed on her knees before the Reaper, holding out one hand in a traffic cop's "stop" pose. The driver's white grin did not falter behind the windscreen, even as the crop lifter dragged Amy's outstretched arm into the jagged incisors of the vehicle's cutter bar. She flailed and struggled as her upper body turned a wet new colour.

The Reaper coughed and halted. Its teeth stopped spinning. Amy's shrieks made Hiren think of a fox's gibbering howl in the dead of night. The Reaper's cabin door opened and Amy's tall, wiry brother leapt down onto an unshorn patch of barley. To Hiren, his grin looked angry.

"*Now* you've gone and done it!" the brother yelled.

Hiren and Claire were frozen by the screams of the broken girl and the furious smile of her sibling.

"You *knew* it didn't want another family member, didn't you? You clumsy bitch!"

Amy kept wailing.

"Can it, Amy," her brother said over her cries. He turned to the children. The smile remained on his face, taut and strange. It did not reach his eyes. "Come over here and help me with her." He beckoned impatiently with his arm. "Come on."

Sanj, Squint, and Eleanor went to him.

Claire started to move, but Hiren pulled himself to his feet, rushed towards her, and grabbed her wrist.

"Ow," she said.

Hiren held her firm.

"What do you think you're doing?" the brother demanded. "We've got to take her to the well."

"No!" Amy said. "The hospital! The hospital!"

"The game's over, Amy," her brother said. "And you know it."

"It doesn't matter about the game," Amy said.

"It matters more than anything," her brother said, and the smile drained from his face at last. He reached down to Amy, who managed to raise her unwounded hand into the air. Her brother's fingers passed hers and came to rest on her other shoulder, which was now barely attached to her mangled arm. "It matters, because of the Reaper," he said, and with a sound worse than the slopping of Tilly's ruined body, he wrenched Amy free from both the combine harvester and the remains of her arm.

Hiren gasped and looked away but Claire, finding her courage, said, "The Reaper is just a tractor! The game is just a game! It doesn't mean anything!"

"Wrong," Amy's brother said. "Wrong in *every* way. The game means that my family can keep living here. It's about feeding the Reaper, every harvest day. And this vehicle is *not* the Reaper, you stupid girl. If you help me take Amy to the well, to where the Reaper can eat, maybe we'll avoid…"

The ground shuddered.

"Oh God – we're too late," Amy's brother said, and that grin, stiff and awful, returned to his mouth. He dropped to his knees and lowered his face to the soil. "Please don't be angry."

Claire took Hiren's hand and they ran. Behind them, the other children howled in pain or terror. The wall at the other side of the field seemed like miles away.

As they went, Hiren couldn't resist glancing back.

Something that dwarfed the farm vehicle had burst from the earth: a twisting black column higher than an apple tree, its frame so thin that its very shape seemed to demand nourishment. The summit of the shadowed form bore the only details that were of a different shade: a shifting mass of white teeth, chomping and chewing and clattering together. Those gnashing rows reminded Hiren of Amy and her brother's callous smiles.

Dozens of dark, sweeping appendages protruded from the wormlike body, cutting through the air with the sound of swishing swords. Before Hiren turned back to pick up his pace, he saw those black blades slice the air low to the ground *en masse*, and the children and Amy's brother vanished behind a spurting crimson cloud.

The sound of the true Reaper's roar was that of a beast who had been disappointed one too many times, whose sacred ritual had been disrupted, and whose endless hunger must always be sated.

Inspired by The Beatles "Here, There and Everywhere"

From a book, from a story, from hearsay, a boy was born. From tales of the past, an accumulative product of every author his parents had ever read, or ever would, came a new person, an invented distortion, a perception of the perceived. Words are important. They get everywhere. Watch what you read — and be careful what you write.

Frank was an over-ripe grapefruit. Five feet nothin' and almost as wide, the man had arms as thick as thighs and mottled, pocky, porridge-skin that was a stranger to the sun.

With no time for a proper diet, he favoured an improper one instead: cheap coffee, cheaper noodles, the occasional donut or six, and a floppy pair of greasy pizzas whenever the two-for-ones were on. Which was every other day, really. And they were sad-looking things, too. Cheap cheese, overdone onions, and something billed as a crispy, home-made base was essentially prefabricated crap which soaked up all the flavour. If bread could be stupid, this pizza base was an imbecile.

This was how Frank had always grown, and how he would always grow. With every junky meal, his leg-like arms became even leggier, and his boobs boobier. Despite the evidential lack of self-care, and despite that which all those clichéd protagonists and overloaded tropes might suggest, fatness was not a metaphor for self-loathing. Not in this case. Frank wasn't one of those chaps; quite the opposite, in fact. It's just that he went about things a little differently. And he liked being weird.

Who wants to conform, anyway? This was the very question he would ask his front-facing smartphone camera six times a day. Even though he couldn't quite fit his entire face into the frame, Frank was content to analyse himself bit-by-bit: he quite liked that one eye on the right, and the top of his left ear. Just there.

Conveniently, the guy was a writer. Sort of. Thing was, though, as he'd long since broken up with exercise, so had he fallen out with stories; the day job had put paid to that. The last time he'd produced *anything* of value was when he'd cobbled together the most mind-numbing report for the boss-of-the-boss, all cold stats and dull numbers: risk assessments this, business plans that, fire drills galore.

As Health and Safety rep for his local branch, the chap realised the irony of his girth, his unhealthy state not exactly reflecting the principles of his professional position. Frank hadn't been this big when they'd hired him, and they were too afraid to deny or demote; his employer had just been awarded some equal ops accolade or other, so they could hardly take any drastic action or make any fattist decisions.

It wasn't just a case of missing out on a lifetime of diet and exercise – Frank's brain just wasn't in the right place for that self-improvement lark. Never had been. He was more than wrong – he was, to put it mildly, *not right*. And there's a world of difference.

Whilst he was usually too out of breath to walk to the doctor's surgery, health food stores didn't sell anything Italian, and the gym was where all the people were. Yuk:

people. The big grapefruit didn't fancy mixing with the rest of the fruit bowl.

And like any decent wannabe-but-neverwould, Frank had dreams of making it big(ger). If he managed five hundred words a day, even, he could get that novel of his finished in a few months, tops. But he was fed up to the back teeth — which, in fact, due to his dentist-dodging ways, he no longer owned — with his colleagues asking how the book was going. Because it wasn't. That's what he deserved, he supposed, for mentioning his outside interests. It meant he had to contend with know-it-alls who had an idea for a book, or people whose auntie's best-mate's brother-in-law's cousin was *also* a writer. Same old story: everyone had a novel in them. *Yawn.*

Frank logged out of his workstation for the day, dropping his pen onto a crumb-covered carpet, where it would have to stay until the cleaners came. He had a hell-dwellin' snowball's chance of bending down for it, which wasn't exactly a shocker considering you can't bend a grapefruit in half.

Giving up, going downstairs, and being well and truly goosed by the time he arrived at the underground car park, Frank squeezed into a vehicle which looked just like him, with its podgy rear bumper and squinty headlights. The car — shiny and gruel-coloured like its owner — had been adapted to suit Frank's own personal bigness. The standard level seats were recent replacements for the factory-fitted bucket ones whose sole purpose was to squash you in and squish you up, when, in reality, you needed to hang over the sides a little more. What was *with* that? Stupid seats. Like his existence, they made no sense, those things.

An automatic gearbox allowed Frank to concentrate on other things, though, like singing along to his guilty pleasures album on repeat. And, truth be told, he had quite a decent voice. Sang at the office, sometimes. But *then,* he'd be regaled with tales of people whose brother's wife's sister's kid was also a singer.

Arseholes. It was always about them. They *always* made it about them. They were why he hated people, for the most part, and why he tried to only ever see the unavoidable ones. One might say he was a bit of a loner. Kept himself to himself. Loved his mother. That sort of thing.

Narrowly avoiding at least two potential road rage incidents along the way, Big Fat Frank arrived home in one big fat piece, which was more than could be said about the pheasant he'd sped up to kill. It would've been cruel to just maim it a bit and leave it to suffer, and there was no time to stop, no room to swerve. The car was now adorned with a resultant splash of bird-goo, but it'd wash off.

Greeted by an overfed house cat, BFF set about his boring chores. Coffee pot on, check. Pre-heat the oven, check. Feed the cat, get the prefabricated dinner out of the freezer, check-check.

Felix was content to remain curled up, his human slave having prepared a veritable heaven for his imminent night's sleep. Fresh water, cat-jerky (not made from felines but *for* them, you understand), and a bowl of crunchy treats sat beside a fluffy pyramid tent-bed thing which had never seen the inside of a washing machine and consequently smelled of cat's arses and a little bit like cheese. His human wasn't the cleanest of folk, you see, what with his particular breed of OCD being limited to order only, avoiding cleanliness and bypassing hygiene altogether. Books and DVDs were alphabetised, and everything was in its place, including filth. Wherever it landed, it would remain.

Before Frank could flop onto his concave mattress, it was message-checking time. Most of the e-mails were either junk from junky places, or spam from Nigerian kings who promised to SWND YO SIXY MILLON DOLARS. There were marketing ploys and casual annoyances here and there, and one genuine e-mail from the bank. The remaining thirty-seven of the day's intake were a pleasure to delete.

ATTN: WRITERS - SUBMISSION CALL was pretty intriguing, though:

Would you like to be part of an exciting anthology? Read our submission guidelines below.

He clicked on the link with a big fat click of his big fat fingers.

Do you love horror - real horror?

He did. He really did.

As we are looking to promote new talent, we are looking for previously unpublished authors to submit. The one rule? Your work must contain a piece of YOU. Put your stamp, your voice, your VERY SELF into your story. We want to know who you are. We want to know YOU.

Frank grabbed a slice of coffee (it was *that* strong) and a bowl of pizza (it was *that* slimy), slippered his feet, scratched his nethers, and sat down at the computer on a leatherette chair with one wheel missing: wonky, damaged - and slightly dangerous. He thought of the day job, and backminded all the backstabbing that went on there. This could be his OUT. This could be his escape. No more being treated like a sixth, seventh, eighth-class citizen.

He would write something so controversial, so unique, that one of the big publishers would be bound to pick him up. Talent-spotters still ran in literary circles, didn't they? Was it the Big Five, now? Or were they up to number six? At what point did a small press become a big 'un in any case?

Frank climbed inside a pair of psychotic boots, walked around in them, and began to write words which came unsurprisingly easily. As he sucked on slabs of cheddary-pineapple through the gap in his two remining front teeth, the whole pizza sagged with fruit juice, serving as a reminder why those two things *do not* go together. Chalk and cheese should be jealous.

A couple of thousand words later, probably only two

hundred of which were any good, a rather-satisfied Frank decided he deserved a coffee break. He bounced into the kitchen past a sleeping ball of purring fur, refilled his mug, and necked two out-of-date habitual pills whose purpose he'd forgotten. Then, he and his words continued their dalliance a little longer before hay-hitting time.

His bedtime routine included the most unusual ablutions and omitted all the necessary ones; right there in his bathroom together with unlathered soap and a superfluous toothbrush was the most despised mirror in the universe. Because that's what protagonists do, y'know. Self-awareness via reflection of their...*erm*...reflection.

Being told –daily– of his worthlessness for the first two thirds of his life, their opinions might well have become his. Instead, every night, at the same time, he fought against them: his parents, schoolchildren, colleagues; all reflector-folk who had it coming. Fat though Frank may have been, he had to stay small for now; by letting it all out, he made sure to keep himself in. Self-loathing was for losers, so he continued to let the others hate him, instead. He was very hateable, after all.

"You're just too fucking FAT!"

"Why don't you do us all a fucking favour and just go to your room, and leave US some fucking food, ya fat fuck?"

"You'll never fuckin' amount to NOTHIN!"

One good ol' dose of hater-hatin' later, and Frank was ready for bed. A quick swill of Listerine, and his mouth was clean again.

***

Frank woke way ahead of his alarm clock, coffeed himself up, fed the mog, and went straight to his story; there was still time to get a few hundred words down before he had to leave for work.

As he pulled up the document, the *ping!* of an e-mail alerted him to his inbox.

Thank you for your submission. We loved what you wrote, and would like you to continue.

With a *what-the-fuck* face, Frank checked his sent items: empty. And in his documents sat the unfinished story he'd started the night before. The e-mail must have been a glitch; he wouldn't respond to it, in case he appeared confused at best, antagonistic at worst. After craning his podgy neck around to satisfy himself that he was, indeed alone, a relieved Frank shrugged off the illogical notions that had been bothering his noggin. Nobody was in the room, around him, or behind him, except for maybe that creepy bastard arachnid in the corner, staring him down with its far-too-many eyes.

It didn't matter what he wrote, or whether it was any good, he could edit it later. Even writing bad rubbish was still writing. And writing was something he hadn't done in forever, it seemed – he was too busy doing other things.

Coffee.

As his esophagus filled up with a scorching mugful of Kenyan, his document increased by a minute's worth of words. Nonsense, mainly — he was typing out loud.

More coffee.

"She sits in the grass, cross-legged. Her hair flicks in time with the nods of her head - I wonder what band she is listening to..."

He made a correction: "*which* band..." and continued.

"Perhaps it's rock. Or metal. Oh, the way she taps her feet. Her hips sway even though she sits — I'd give anything to be running my hands through her hair — " He seemed to recall every tiny detail of this make-believe girl. "She's incredible. She's poetry. And she will be mine."

More coffee. A scratch of the crotch. Yet more coffee. Stale donuts whose aged jelly refused to ooze.

"I walk. Slowly. But ensure I am not creeping. The difference between stealthy and stalkerish is quite a fine line; I shan't cross it again. *Hello,* I say. *Good day.* She says hello right back and smiles as if she knows me. This is great! I couldn't ask for more. Perhaps there will be more tomorrow. I shall see. We shall see."

Coffee. Work. He could finish this later. He didn't know where the words were coming from, but at least they were coming.

In the lift - which had ten floors to go - Frank made elevator conversation with weather-talkers. Rushed indoor discussions were had about the windiness of the wind and the wetness of the rain outside, even though a quick look at all the soaked folk with their windswept hairdos already told the story.

"Still raining out, Barb?" Terribly Dull Derek from finance was flirting with the Area Manager again. Peopley people. Were they *really* that unimaginative? As he ignorantly scratched a left-wrist itch, Frank resigned himself to the fact he would have to leave all the interesting conversations to the inside of his head. Again.

Stepping out of the lift with a ho *and* a hum, Frank chirped up. There were only eight hours to go until he would be back home, polishing off chapter one. This would be an easy day to get through - meetings went quicker when he took notes; now, as he planned to ignore the business side of things and concentrate on his real passion, he had specific notes to take.

He scratched the itch again and made a crap coffee from the crap granules in the crap communal kitchen. It'd do: soft, hot, and wet. Just like his memories.

The itch was becoming progressively more scratchworthy throughout the day. Once the final meeting was over, Frank and his itch nipped to the bathroom and made a beeline for the cold tap. A chunk the size of Peru had been gouged out of the side of his wrist. What the hell? Of course, this went straight into the accident book.

Details of incident:
Surface injury to left wrist and hand. Apparently self-inflicted, due to over-scratching. May be due to an allergy - subject has been in contact with detergents in communal kitchen this morning.

Description of injury:
Bloody wound, approximately 5cm by 2cm and an estimated 4mm in depth. Parts are turning green/yellow; infection apparent.

Action:
Ensure Hazardous Substance posters are on display in kitchen and arrange refresher training for all staff. Affected colleague to see GP immediately.

Frank escaped work early with swift permission from his line manager, who'd ushered him out with a horrified *don't-even-think-of-coming-back-until-that-thing's-been-seen-to* face.

Whizzing down to the walk-in centre, Frank controlled the steering wheel with just the one hand. As he pulled up, the wound seemed to be taking on a life of its own - or a death, more likely. Like a roadkill pancake, this red mass promised a noseful of disgusting smells if he didn't have it sorted soon. And the pain was getting quite intense, so he popped a couple of whatever the red tablets were that he'd found in the glove box.

The grossed-out receptionist took his details and sent him off to the doctor immediately, bypassing the usual triage procedures. Numbing injections were administered all around the area; this thing was going to need stitches. He couldn't have done it by scratching, they said, unless he had shovels for nails. So, apparently, he had shovels for nails.

Four stitches, an iodine dressing, and a big fat bandage later, and Frank was good to go, along with a prescription for antibiotics and painkillers and a follow-up appointment at his GP's surgery in a week's time. He could self-certify an absence from work for a week without needing a doctor's note, so he'd use the time to write. This could be a good thing after all.

Home. Drugged up, stitched up, time to put his feet up.

But first - caffeine. The wooziness from the medication needed to be offset so he could stay awake long enough to write.

"I saw her again today. My mouth was filled with my heart, yet all the words were gone from it. A look was all I could give."

Frank knew this wasn't exactly the most ground-breaking of stories. Yet. So far, all he'd done was yak about meeting this girl he fancied, drip-feeding his own self to the reader. He had to hook 'em in, , or they'd lose interest. Better add some drama, or comedy, or something, quickly.

"Suddenly, a rabid man appeared, jaws gnashing..." *No. That's shite. Delete.*

"A creepy-looking weirdo, watching from the bushes..." *Oh, for fuck's sake, Frank. Must do bette*r.

He'd have to have a rethink. Writing for an audience was never his forte. He'd rather be let loose. Perhaps he should do a Hemingway and write pissed, edit sober. He didn't know what he was writing half the time anyway, and whilst he didn't quite buy into the idea of automatic writing, he was well-aware his words weren't exactly conscious, either. He reached for the scotch, something he knew didn't mix well with painkillers, but the man was all out of fucks. He needed this gig, having promised his beloved mother that if he wasn't published before she snuffed it, he'd at least be published before *he* did.

Four glasses, and he was out. Five hours later, and Frank was miaowed out of a bed he couldn't remember having gotten into, and he and Felix sauntered downstairs like a pair of odd zombies with fleas.

Coffee.

"Come over, my dear, and show me what you've got there. What are you listening to, my love? She handed over one of her ear buds: just the one. It played a tune I didn't know. But the unleashing came too soon. It could neither be restrained nor postponed, and the voices became too loud. It took over, over, over, until it was me and I was *it*. Screams. Blood - mine and hers. Tearing, sharing, gnashing and gnawing. Imminence. Persistence. Until - nothing. Until calm. Calm. Until … sssh."

Words. Words which had come from somewhere, about someone, in some place or other. From here, from there, from anywhere and everywhere. He didn't have a clue what any of it meant, but he supposed he might be able to knit a horror story out of the threads. But first things first: after starting a sentence with "But," he went to check on the bandage. It felt kinda wet. Did he spill booze on it last night?

He unpeeled and unravelled, and unravelled and peeled – picking off the iodine dressing was going to be the hardest part. It was probably going to be stuck to the wound like an Elastoplast. But underneath, there was nothing. And I don't just mean there was no *wound*. The entire once-was-injured part had gone. No thumb, and the hand was two inches narrower. It didn't even hurt. There was no blood, no goo, no *nuffin'*.

Perhaps Frank was still asleep. A punch to his face should advise him accordingly. Nope: definitely awake. *Shit.* One thumb down, one aching face - these must be some strong fucking drugs (note to self: get some of those). He reckoned he'd better try the local GP instead – he couldn't wait a week. Goodness knows what the hospital had given him.

"There's no record of any injury, Mr -"

"No record of any injury? I was at the out-of-hours clinic only yesterday. The walk-in centre at St. Cath's. Did they not send my records over? And – HELLO – I HAVE NO FUCKING THUMB!"

"The so-called injury you mention — well, your records show you were born this way. Did your mother take Thalidomide? Perhaps you're having a mild delusion. Have

you been taking any medication, Mr — "
"I'm NOT fucking delusional! I was at work yesterday, and I had this motherfucker of an itch, and — " *Work*. He should contact work. Legging it out of the doctor's office to her delight (she couldn't be doing with all that fucking swearing), he jumped into a cab and ordered it to the workplace. There was no way he could drive, now.

His line manager boomed across the office, making drinks wobble and paintings vibrate. "Frank! Where the hell have you been?"

"I rang in yesterday and said I was going to be off for a week. I've only come back to check something."

"What're you talking about? You don't have any leave booked."

"No, I know. I'm talking about the accident. The *injury*, I mean. It's all there in the accident book." It *wasn't* there, of course. Just like his thumb.

After a bit of persuading and a promise of an extensive report on the new business model for the North West area, the boss allowed Frank to take the rest of the week off. And so, with his tail between his legs, he buggered off home: thumbless, thin of hand, and thinner of brain. Maybe his computer would have the answer. Or AN answer. Anything would do.

Thanks for your latest submission instalment! We really love what you are doing – keep it up, and we look forward to reading the next part.

Again, there was nothing in the sent items folder, and no sense to be had. Perhaps he should talk to the publisher. Maybe some interaction might get him out of this current nonsense and re-set everything.

I didn't send you my submission yet, so I was wondering if you could explain the relevance of your e-mails?

Nothing passed. No time, no space. Not even a second,

nor a heartbeat, before the reply came in.

We are reading your work, and we are loving it. Please continue.

Was that *it?* It didn't even answer his question and was more than a tad creepy. Mind you, Beryl in accounting was talking about algorithms only the other day – how parts of the internet can contact other parts of the internet, or something. You can type SOCKS into a browser and suddenly your e-mails are filled with advertisements for shoes and bunion relief products, or tights and heel grips and Stilton and anything else that was even remotely feety. Maybe this was a similar thing.

Best to take advantage of the break: business as usual. Well – I *say* usual, but you know – as usual as business *can* be with the absence or omission of body parts.

"Her eyes don't see me, and her ears no longer hear, but I'm not sorry. I can't be sorry. How can you be sorry for something you intended to do?"

Four painkillers, seven hot drinks, and six hundred words later, Frank dragged himself over to the sofa for a kip. Felix joined him, the finest furry heater for his legs. He switched on the TV, as daytime-sleeps were best taken with background noise. Listening to Jeremy Kyle yelling at benefit cheats and crap dads was really rather soothing when you didn't have much of a life.

On waking with ideas for the next paragraph, Frank jiggled his feet to gently suggest the cat away, but Felix wasn't going anywhere on anyone's say-so. Too comfortable. His human sat up and reached forward to flick his furry arse down from the sofa, but a freshly-missing hand told him that'd be an impossibility. *Well, fuck.*

You know how they say illnesses piss off as quickly as they arrive? And by "they", I do of course refer to illogical old wives whose scaremongering has never made a scrap of sense — well, this was the sort of mentality Frank was employing right about now. Maybe this would all just go away - as in *come back*. Maybe his bits would reappear as suddenly as they'd vanished. Maybe. But honestly, he considered himself somewhat fuckeder-than-fucked.

Shifting to his equally knackered chair, he picked up the story where he'd left off. Words were typing themselves onto the document. The automatic dance of the keyboard played clicks and clacks into his nearly-gone ears. No hand, no hands, no arm, no arms. Dying legs, dead legs, gone legs.

"I couldn't help it." CLICK.

"She struggled, but not much." CLACK.

"It was over as quickly as I could possibly make it — after all, I did love her. Why would I want her to suffer?" CLICKETY-CLACK.

Despite the pickle he was in, and notwithstanding the likelihood of inevitable demise, Frank the Torso was a writer to the end, and wondered how he might describe his fading self in a story. He might say both arms were not there, or that neither arm was. Perhaps he would allude to his rapidly-disappearing state with the omission of letters, as he became Fran, Fra, and Fr.

Screams would have been screamed and shouts shouted, had there been a mouth to make them happen.

F.

Stabbing pain. Then none. Itching sides, then no sides at all. No skin, no wounds, no scars. And no pain. Not now. There wasn't enough left of him to *feel*. Frank stared at the monitor, no mouth to cry out and no hands to type. If he were able to, this would be something for the accident book, for sure.

The screen came to life with a message. Luckily, he still had eyes with which to read. Or, more accurately, the eyes had him:

Thank you for your continued efforts. We do not usually accept staggered submissions, as we prefer to receive

<u>finished documents, but your technique is intriguing. We are</u>
<u>enjoying your work, and it's clear you are really putting</u>
<u>yourself into this story.</u>

As the room gradually became Frankless, so the document's words increased. No midsection: a hundred thousand. No torso: a hundred and ten. As the head vanished from the room and took Frank's eyes with it, a novel was complete. One-hundred-and-sixty-thousand words. After all, he was a big bloke.

What seemed like a lifetime but was more than likely a deathtime or two later, an old woman who smelled of cats and stale cookies browsed through an even older bookstore that smelled of childhood. Picking up a battered book, Mrs Johnson started to read the introduction, something she always did before committing to purchase.

This edition was initially intended as an anthology of different voices, as we were aiming to champion previously-unpublished authors. But we received one story which, quite simply, blew us away with its realism. Never had we seen horror depicted quite so honestly, and it is unlikely that we shall see the likes of it again. We were unable to locate or contact the author after he submitted to us, so, after extensive consultation with our legal team, we found a way to publish this work anonymously.

Mrs Johnson had always been a horror fan; a passion she'd shared with her daughter until they were suddenly, due to life, death, and all the everywheres in between, unable to share anything else. Melissa would have loved this book, with its prison-bars cover art and claustrophobic title, although the old lady wasn't so sure. A graphic murder, depicted either viscerally or, more likely, *eviscerally*, might restore memories of the undesirable kind.

The young lady's sharp, unsolved exit was still raw, and as fresh as yesterday, although her mother would probably never find the answers she needed. There'd never been any viable suspects, and there were no precedents or repeat incidents. No – her daughter had been a one-off for an opportunist, an experiment for the irretrievably hungry. An itch someone just had to scratch.

She probably shouldn't buy the book after all. Best to forget the things they'd shared, and to keep on moving on until it was time for her to stop. Yes – she should return it to the shelf and leave it for somebody else. Mrs Johnson had had enough horror to last her until the end, which was something she prayed would come soon.

She'd had enough of horror since what was left of her daughter had been found in the park. She'd had enough of it since she'd learned of Melissa's eaten-away fate, piece-by-piece, until all that remained was a blood-soaked pair of ear phones. And she was pretty sure that until she was reunited with her girl, she was never going to find closure. All this book would do is remind her of the dreadful things dreadful people do in dreadful ways.

The old woman recalled her daughter's music, and wondered if Melissa was somewhere else, listening to the same old tunes. She needed music. Sweet, soft music – although these days, this was something she could only hear in her head. And if she wasn't deaf, she'd have heard the book scream as she slammed it shut, crying out to the nobody who was listening, and to all the everybodies who weren't.

From a book, from a story, from hearsay, a boy was born. From tales of the past, an accumulative product of every author his parents had ever read, or ever would, came a new person, an invented distortion, a perception of the perceived. Words are important. They get everywhere. Watch what you read – and be careful what you write.

Inspired by The Pogues "Rainy Night In Soho"

"Hey, Cliff, what's the name of the band playing tonight?" I asked and the fat fuck ignored me, too busy chatting up a skank in a short skirt at the other end of the bar. Fuck it, I just wrote 'LIVE MUSIC' on the chalkboard above the till and tossed the chalk in a pint glass with pens and shit in it. Cliff handed the skank a drink and tapped the bar. Another one 'on the house'. I wonder what his wife Doris would make of it. I felt like telling her but I hated her even more than her husband. They were assholes and meant for each other. They owned The Soho and I had the misfortune of having to work there to make ends meet.

"Hey, you, baldy?" said a cunt from behind me. Before turning, I gazed briefly at my reflection in the dusty mirrored wall of the bar. I wasn't bald or at least not totally. 'Thinning' was what I preferred. I turned and asked the drunk cunt what he wanted.

"Two pints of lager and two pickled eggs, ballbag," he slobbered, nudging his equally dumb mate beside him. I shook my head.

"Look, no matter how much you crave a ballbag right

now, we don't serve them here," I replied.

"What?"

Yeah, that response summed up the general intelligence of The Soho. I popped two eggs in a paper cup with a sachet of salt and then told the guy there was no lager allowed in the bar today.

"There you go, don't choke on them all at once. And yeah, only serving Guinness today."

"That black shite? Fuck that stuff. Give us two voddies and coke," said his mate, the nudgee.

"No can do, Guinness or soft drinks only. Try it, it might expand your cultural horizons."

"What?"

They took their Guinness back to the poker machine and sucked eggs while losing their Job Seekers allowance in Cliff's rigged machine. I wiped the bar as more and more punters arrived in various shades of green clothing. It was St. Patricks Day and probably the busiest day for The Soho. There was racing on the television but Cliff had the sound down because he said it killed the 'ambiance' in the bar. I wish he had something to kill the stench, the rot and the constant air of vomit in the place but I kept those opinions to myself. He was dumb as pig-shite but too big a fucker too annoy. I would have checked my phone for the time but I didn't own one. Fuck those things. Fuck all that social media and shit. After what happened on St. Patrick's Day last year, I gave up on all that stuff. I had my musical career to think about, my identity and my dreams.

"Hey there he is, Mr Irish. Guys and gals, meet Jimmy. How goes it Jim?" said Mince. I hated that guy. Flash bastard and his 'hoe' train which consisted of two skinny sisters he was banging and both of them too dumb to realise. They giggled in that gooselike way they did.

"Hi, Marvin," I replied, careful not to use the 'Mince' title everyone knew him by. "What can I get you?"

"Well, definitely not a rendition of that song you sang last year, I mean, that was a one-off. How many views has it had now on the Tube thing?"

I had no idea the music video was still up there and I never ever found out who recorded me singing that night. I had my suspicions but nobody ever came clean.

"Jim? Still with us there?" Again the geese giggled. I looked up from the bar, focused and smiled. Forced one at least.

"What are you having? Just Guinness today, mind?" I said, hoping the hoes would hate Guinness.

"Yeah, that will do, one pint and two halves of the glorious black stuff, please, Jim and one for yourself."

"I'm good thanks, haven't drank since, well, a year ago, I'm sure Cliff will take one though,"

I left Marvin talking with Cliff, popped the money in the till and went for a pish. I didn't need one, I just needed to get out of the lounge for a minute or two. It wouldn't be long before Doris started her shift too and being behind a bar with those two was hell at the best of times, but on a busy St. Patrick's it was going to be shite. I sat in the middle cubicle and lit up a smoke, leaning back against the freshly cleaned cistern, freshly cleaned because I had just wiped the shit and piss stains off it with a good fistful of bogroll. The smoke was what I needed. I knew it was wrong to smoke because they say it damages your vocal chords and those were my lifeline. I had practiced for a year, really practiced, none of this having a few beers and pulling out the guitar at a party. Proper singing and given time, people would come to realise how much that event last year had inspired me.

The door to the toilets opened and I heard shuffling feet on wet floor, a belt being wrestled and the fallout out from a drunk arse in the cubicle next to me. He reeked whoever it was, and complimented each splash with a groan or a sigh as if pleased with himself. I stubbed my ciggie on the door among the phone numbers and obscenities and made my way back to work.

Doris had arrived and was already barking orders at Cliff, who was red-faced and looked to be on the verge of a stroke or something. The thought of it pleased me. I'd love to watch that fucker wriggle on the floor all drooling and sweaty.

"Jimmy, get the fuck behind this bar and get serving," screamed Doris. I squeezed my way through the crowd and eventually got to work. The orders flew in, glasses were banged on the bar, impatient bastards all calling for more of the black stuff. My mouth was as dry as a nun's cunt and I grabbed an orange juice from the shelf. It would have to do. Cliff poked me on the arm. "I saw that, you'd better pay for that later," he said walking off, smug as fuck.

Three guys were waving from the door. I guessed they were the entertainment for the evening. Good luck pleasing these drunk fuckers. Doris parted the crowd like a Chanel smelling Moses and showed them to the corner where they began to set up their instruments; a guitar, a bodhran drum and a Irish whistle. Doris approached me from behind and with breath like roadkill she spoke in my ear.

"Get the band some Guinness and take it down to them, Jimmy. On the house but don't tell Cliff, okay?"

"Yeah, no problem."

I poured three nice pints, put them on a tray and made my way through the crowd, the singing, dancing, fighting fucks that they were. The band were polite and took their pints from the tray. I wipe the tray, popped it under my arm and nodded to the three of them. That's when I heard something familiar. My spine froze.

"Turn the volume up, this is a classic," screamed somebody from near the fire. More cries for volume rang out. I couldn't turn around, my legs wouldn't let me. The three guys from the band were looking around me to see the television.

"Well, here he is, our very own barman Jimmy, stepping in to

help us out since the band haven't arrived yet. Big round of applause, folks,"

Those words had haunted me for a year. Last year the band didn't show up on time and the punters were getting uneasy and a little violent. Cliff had told Doris that I was a musician and she grabbed me from the table I was at with my mates. I needed a pish. I was wankered but when Doris asked you to do something, you did it and although it was my night off, I kind of felt obliged. She was my boss and something inside me, maybe the alcohol, told me that this was my chance to show this bar and this town what I could do. I was ready. The toilet could wait.

I turned and watched the rest of the video. Marvin had streamed it from his phone onto the television and the entire bar were now engrossed in the footage.

"Hey, how are you all doin this evening? Nice to be here and gonna kick things off with an Irish classic, 'Raglan Road'. Hope you enjoy."

I started okay, strumming the first few chords in time and almost perfect, but it went downhill from there. I started in the key of C and that was way too high. I hadn't thought it through but I continued.

"On Raglan Road, of an autumn day, I saw her first and knew..."

After those two lines, I felt a horrific twist in my stomach. It hurt. It hurt like fuck but I sang on. I wouldn't let such trouble get in the way of my moment. The crowd seemed to like it. I sensed it. What I didn't sense was what was yet to come.

"That her dark...hair...would, the enchanted share..."

That's when it happened. I farted. I thought I could multi-task but I wasn't that strong-willed enough. I kept singing even though my arse had just evacuated itself into the base of my jeans. I felt the warmth. I sang on. My singing was on point. A few heads were nodding. That was enough for me.

I actually moved. I turned and walked through the crowd as they watched my demise on the television. I had nothing to offer. Let them have their fun at my expense. It meant nothing. As I passed under the television it had reached the point in the video were the crowd had noticed the smell. Laughter and screams rose around me. I wanted to die. I didn't want to live that moment again. I could hear my voice above the laughter. I sang on. Music and performing were all that mattered that night.

After putting the tray underneath the bar the first person I saw was Marvin. He was red-faced and smiling. I hated the bastard. I wanted to bury a pint glass in the side of his neck and watch him bleed out all over his two bitches. He spoke, wiping his mouth of sweat as he did.

"Jimmy, lighten up, man, remember, you're among friends here. If someone else had had such an elaborate musical debut, you would have seen the funny side. Let me get you a drink?"

I bit my tongue. The laughter had died and Marvin had stopped streaming the video. The band were warming up and apart from a few fart noises being made here and there around the bar, it was a bit more comfortable. "Okay, just an orange, then," I replied. Marv looked up the bar at Cliff.

"Hey, get this guy an orange, think he deserves it."

As Cliff poured he sniggered to himself. I knew he had something to say.

"Does that orange not give you the shitters?" he blurted, out along with some snot to accompany his childish humour. A few people did laugh but their attention was drawn to a fight near the poker machine. It seems the 'eggy' boys had fallen out over a gamble and were knocking fuck out of each other. Then Doris screamed from the back of the bar.

She came running out, pale-faced and frightened. "Fuck, fuck! Bastard thing was just staring at me. Cliff, come here, for fuck's sake."

Cliff waddled over and I heard her tell about the rat in the back cellar. "No fucking way, I hate those things. Here, Jimmy, Doris has a job for you," he said. I pushed past them and made my way out the back.

The cellar was freezing but the peace and quiet were most welcome. The light was dim but it was enough to let me change the Guinness keg. It was the large one at the end. I looked around for the rat but he or she was nowhere to be seen. Rats were okay, I kind of liked them. I just wished he had bitten Doris on the leg or something. That would have made up for tonight. I kicked the keg and it was indeed empty. I wiped the sweat on my jeans and removed the coupler. It was stinking, all moldy around the handle. I tried to wipe it but it was encrusted. I looked around hoping to find some cleaning spray or something. That's when I saw the wee fucker, big fucker actually. He was standing up on his back legs, staring right at me. I laughed.

"Aren't you the handsome one, what's your name then?" He didn't answer. He didn't need to. I still liked him. As I approached him, he ran off under a shitload of discarded cushions and upholstery from the bar's last renovation. I walked over to where he had stood and there was a cabinet against the wall. It opened with a little force, rusty as fuck. Inside were all manner of cleaning materials and chemicals covered in cobwebs and dust. On the top shelf was the rat poison. I looked at it and smiled, shaking my head. That would be cruel. Let him live. I got to work, taking my time and making sure I had changed the keg and everything was up and running before I left the cellar.

Doris hugged me, actually fucking hugged me. "Thank you, Jimmy, I hope you got rid of that thing. Oh, I'm still shaking thinking how close it was to my foot. Dirty bastard shitting all over the place,"

"Yeah, they do that when they're nervous," laughed Cliff. Doris punched him in the gut. He wheezed and his glasses fell halfway down his big fat nose.

"Shut your hole, you, at least he was man enough to go in there. Jimmy get yourself a drink and go for a break, long as you like. Place is settled now that the band have started."

I took another orange, a fizzy one this time, grabbed my hoodie from beside the dartboard and made my way out the back. I sat with my back against the wall with only the wheelie bins for company. I rolled three smokes just in time because the rain started, nice at first but got heavier as I enjoyed the first soothing draws of my ciggie. I stepped back under the canopy and pulled my hoodie up, like a cloak of sorts and inhaled deeply, eyes closed, hand in pocket.

"Hey, you okay?" said a voice, somehow in the distance but close enough to be in my own head. It wasn't. I looked up and there was this girl standing above me. I got to my feet.

"Yeah, I'm good. Shit, I must've fell asleep. What are you doing out here, it's staff only?"

She laughed and stepped closer, the security light highlighting the flow of red hair. She was quite stunning and I'm sure she wasn't a regular in The Soho. "The rain got real heavy so I stepped in here for shelter. I thought you were dead, sorry,"

We laughed and she smoked a cigarette with me. "Are you coming in for drinks?"

She laughed again, stubbing her cigarette on the wall. "Nope, I'm the singer. A bit late but better late than never, hey?"

"But I thought the band were already here, they're playing away in there."

"I told them to go ahead because I was running late. You sing too, don't you, Jimmy?" She asked. I held my cig inches from my face, dying for that last draw but confused as to how she knew my name.

"Don't worry, I've heard you sing. You're good. Maybe you can do a number with me near the end of the night. You know, make up for your last big moment. If you want, like?"

I think I loved her right from that moment. I sucked the life from my cig and opened the back door for her. The rain followed us in, really bucketing down now. I shut the door and heard the rattle of keys in the lock. I turned them and put them in my hoodie pocket. Nobody would be going out in that weather. At least I didn't think so.

"By the way, what's your name?"

"Ginger,' she replied and I followed her in. Nice to have a real lady in the bar.

Cliff was coming back from locking the front door. The place was heaving and nobody else was welcome. It was a tradition in The Soho. Once you were in you were never getting out until the band stopped playing and the Guinness stopped flowing. And it did flow. As soon as Ginger took the stage the place went mad. They couldn't get enough of her. It was new. They seem to forget about the past and were enjoying the future more. Some of them even sang along.

Ginger almost floated behind the microphone, her voice light but full of passion. A punter actually fell at her feet and didn't even try to get up, just squirmed around the wooden floor in some weird exotic dance. Others joined him, holding their stomachs and dancing in that Celtic fashion that was standard for the day and the celebration. Others just coughed into their pints. I watched. It was glorious.

Cliff fell just below the dartboard and Doris tripped over his vast frame on the way to the bathroom, face ashen and broken. The 'eggy' boys had lost their fight and hung onto the low hanging seat of their trackies as their stomachs evacuated. Ginger sang louder, screaming tradition down each and every one of their throats. They lapped it up, Well, those that could until it took them too, the pain first, then the cramps, the swollen throat and an array of feels.

Eventually the band members stopped playing, lost in awe of the Ginger lady, laying down instruments and stumbling for help. There was no help. There was no way out. Cliff was lying dead on one set of keys and I had the other. No, they would stay and watch the show, to the end, whichever end that would be.

Ginger began her last song, a slow one, an Irish version of the Unchained Melodies. No music, just a voice so spiritual it brought silence to the crowd. Her only accompaniment was the sound of distant sirens coming from town. They were a long way off and there was time for a smoke. I asked Ginger if she would accompany me but she was gone. I didn't fret, I didn't search. I knew a woman that strong would be back.

I stepped over some bodies, slid my way through pools of vomit and blood, sometimes a mixture of both and towards the front door.

It was locked of course so I sat with my back against it and watched the last remaining punters drown in their own sick, shit fire from their arses and crawl over each other like the poisoned rats they were.

It was probably the best smoke I ever enjoyed. That's when the front doors knocked. They banged and my whole body shook with every thump.

They made it in eventually. I can't recall but I think it was the firemen who finally made it through. I was shoved aside as the ambulance, police and fire crews swarmed past me. They helped those who could be helped. I watched for a bit but I knew my time here was done. Ginger had shown me the light. I got up, tossed my ciggie into the chaos and walked out of The Soho for the last time. It was still raining.

I never returned to Trinity. I spent the next few weeks trying to get gigs in bars up and down the coast. It wasn't easy but I knew it would all work out when my Ginger lady showed up again. I often wonder what happened to all the girls and boys from The Soho?

I stopped into a little newsagents in Blackhaven and the

lady behind the counter eyed me with disdain. I was used to it, I had left Trinity with only the clothes on my back and a few quid in my hoodie. I had enough for one more pouch of tobacco and that was it. I needed a break and as she pulled my pouch from behind the rolling doors of the tobacco cupboard I saw it. My chance to shine once more.

Open Mike Night in Macgowan's Bar and Grill. First Prize £500

It was a light in the dark. I paid the old bitch fifteen pounds and walked out without my change. I wouldn't need it. I rolled one just outside the shop and this guy came walking by, all up in his phone and flicking the screen with his thumb.

"Hey, which way to MacGowan's pub, mate?"

He pointed me in the right direction and, with a smoke in my mouth, I made my way to my destiny. The £500 would be enough to buy a guitar and that was all the honest to God musician needed.

The MacGowan wasn't as packed as I would have liked but I made my way to the bar and didn't order a drink. There was half a pint just along the way so I grabbed it and nursed it as my own. The barmaid was wiping down a slight spill and I clicked my fingers to get her attention. She walked over, all sullen and hating her job.

"Hey, where do I sign up for the open mike?" I asked. She shrugged. Thought about it and replied.

"The only other two entries have just finished. It was between them two but if you want to get up, go ahead, I don't really care."

"Okay, folks well that just about wraps up tonight's open mike, no wait, hold on, what have we here?" said a skinny guy with the worst mullet I've ever seen. He looked at me as I approached. Stepping back a little for some reason as I took a foot onto the stage.

"Are you for singing then" he asked. I nodded and he

passed me the mic. I took it and removed my hood, arranged myself and reached into my pocket.

"Hi, ladies and gentlemen, my name's Ginger and I'm here to entertain you. I hope you enjoy."

Inspired by Belle & Sebastian "Funny Little Frog"

It was cold in the overgrown bushes behind the apartment building; a pre-dawn chill. I had been waiting for over three hours, only partially protected from the intermittent rain. Midnight had long since come and gone. I only had a few hours left before I'd have to give-up, driven away by the early risers of the neighbourhood. The previous three nights had also been wash-outs and, if tonight followed the trend, I'd have to wait at least another week before trying again. I work shifts and I'm nowhere near popular enough to get someone to swap their days for my nights.

The building wasn't large, only three storeys with eighteen one-bed units. It was low-rent, like the surrounding neighbourhood. Paint was flaking from the walls and weeds grew through cracks in the courtyard. The outdoor pool, a selling point when the place was first built, was half-covered by a mat of dead leaves. In daylight the water looked slightly green. I hadn't seen anyone use it once during my stakeout, or the weeks before I spent casing the place, not even a stray dog tempted for a drink. The days had been hot enough for it, only the nights were cold.

Most of the lights were out but I was only interested in the third floor, middle right. Apartment 3E had been dark since I arrived and I knew I had got there before the girl – the current face of my enemy. I'd left her in a beach-front bar with her friends, too poor to buy another drink or catch a cab. My clothes were still wet from the downpour that had started and ended with my walk through the streets and alleyways.

Wherever she was, she hadn't come home. It had been the same story all week, and the same every other time I had tried to catch her over the last few months. She was young and, whilst not beautiful, pretty enough not to pay when she went out – she certainly didn't make enough in tips at the diner to pay for herself night after night.

The delay in completing my task had been frustrating, nothing more, until this week. I'd simply gone home, content to carry on with my life as normal and wait for the perfect opportunity to arise. Patience has always been essential to what I do and I have learned to take disappointment calmly. I've waited years for the right moment to come around in the past. It's no big deal.

This time was different; I didn't have the luxury of patience. For the first time in thirty years I'd discovered an active enemy agent, living in the city at the same time Charlie was home for a prolonged period. After several intense years, filming across the world and cementing her place in the firmament of Hollywood, my idol and twin was taking a break. The gossip rags were asking if her time was over, now that she was nearing forty and her looks were fading, but I knew better. She was as glorious as ever and would remain so when she decided to return to the game, if I could keep her safe.

I heard a car approaching, silently willed it to be a taxi bringing the girl home, preferably alone. It didn't even slow

down before disappearing into the night. It began to rain
again and I hunkered down as far as I could, the hood of my
cheap plastic raincoat pulled down to my eyes.

Charlie – Charlene – and I were born on the same day,
only minutes apart. People say there's no way I can know that
for sure, even in the internet age the exact time of a star's birth
isn't on public record. When I was younger I would answer
that I simply knew we were, because we were twins. It was
cute until I was seven or eight years old, when it suddenly
became annoying, stupid and childish. I learned to keep it to
myself, even managing to laugh at myself when people
brought it up again, years later. That didn't stop it being true
and I'd apologise after every time I mocked our connection,
burning the insides of my thighs as penance.

I know that we aren't genetically related; I'm not crazy.
She has Latino blood and I'm as white as they come, but the
connection is there, more real than anything else in my life. I
was only five the first time I saw her, a small part as a bratty
sibling in an otherwise forgettable comedy, and didn't
understand what I was experiencing. If anyone had asked, I
would probably have said that I thought she was funny or
cool, something like that. It would have been true, and not just
for me. Her turn as a wisecracking brat in that film started her
career, made her a star before she hit puberty.

It took me until my own teens to fully understand how
deep the connection is, for my own mind to mature enough to
start grasping anything beyond the immediate. Before then all
I needed to know was that I liked anything she was in, no
matter how soft or girly it was. My father and three brothers,
all older, hated them just as much but my mother supported
me, possibly just so she herself could get a break from the
relentless diet of action and monster flicks, at least to begin
with.

As I grew older she joined the chorus urging me to be
more manly, to stop pretending I had a secret connection with

a starlet I was never going to meet, even if we both came from the same city.

I put the first posters of Charlie up on my bedroom walls as much to convince my mother I had a normal crush, the kind that inspired my brothers to pin glamour girls to their walls, as I did because I needed to see my idol if I was to talk to her properly.

I have never kept a diary, although I sometimes wanted to in my early teens. I had my own room by then, moving into the smallest bedroom in the house after my eldest brother left for college, but I knew my other two brothers and at least one of my parents came snooping when I wasn't there. Instead of a journal, I spoke to Charlie.

My room wasn't large, most of the wall space taken up by my bookcase and wardrobe, ailing flat-pack things I'd inherited from my eldest brother, along with the room. The only spare space was beside the door and I filled it with pictures of Charlie, carefully cut from the teen-gossip magazines I never brought home, until she got old enough to pose in swimwear – that made the difference in my family's eyes, although I've never seen her that way.

I'd pour my heart out to her, finding all the words I never could when I spoke to anyone else. I never said any of it aloud, even when I was alone I could never get my tongue to twist around the words without stuttering or lisping. Thinking it was enough, and I have always said what I want to far better inside the confines of my mind.

She didn't start to speak back until we were sixteen, not long after I replaced the magazine cut-outs with a large poster of her, wearing a halter top and denim shorts, looking back over her shoulder.

My father said she looked like a slut, but he seemed happy that I had a picture of a pretty girl on my wall – my brothers teased me about what I did when I was alone and looking at it. I think they would have teased me more if they knew that all I did was talk to her, neither of us saying a word out loud.

In my head she has the accent she was born with, the same one that I still have but was drummed out of her before she was ten by voice coaches, replaced by something far more generic. One of the first things she told me was that she had been forced to lose her true voice, threatened with violence and worse if she didn't. I was, and still am, the only person she can sound like who she really is around, be who she really is, even though we live in different worlds and only the most innermost parts of her soul and mind are aware of the connection. She told me about other things as well, and gave me my life's mission.

There are people who want to capture Charlie, drain her vitality and soul, everything that makes her unique, powerful. Working in shadows, far beyond the most crazed fantasy of every conspiracy nut, they want to do the same to everything and everyone that is pure and good in the world, replacing their victims with half-alive automatons. There are hundreds of thousands of others they want to claim; Charlie is not the only one, but she is the only one I care about. She is the only one I am linked to, the only one I am sworn to protect.

I think I took the path before I was born, it doesn't matter. I have reaffirmed it countless times over the years, been true to it no matter what I have to do or endure as a result.

I have no regrets, only pride.

The girl came home as I was preparing to leave, checking my watch for a ten minute countdown. She came through the side gate, the same one I had used earlier. She was carrying her heels in one hand, her pantyhose reduced to rags – essentially barefoot despite the cold and rain. Her micro-dress was dirty, one shoulder torn, and even in the dim light I could see that there were cuts and bruises on her face and arms.

She was limping and her shoulders drooped. For a second or two I thought about taking her there, but it was too exposed. She looked like she had already fought her way free once that evening and I didn't want to take the chance.

I counted to ten before slipping from the bushes and following her. She let herself in through the outer door and started up the stairs so slowly that I only just had time to catch it before it closed without being seen. I lingered at the bottom of the stairs until I heard the faint echo of her apartment door closing, then I ran after her, my training shoes making no sound on the concrete steps.

My heart began to pound and my throat tightened as I approached her door, the way they always did. I had to pause for a moment to get my breathing under control, subdue the rising panic attack before it made me start to rush, get sloppy and make mistakes.

They thought I had asthma when I was a child, the doctors and my parents forever wondering why the inhalers seemed to have no effect. In my teens, when I was better able to describe what was happening, the doctors worked out that I was having panic attacks, seemingly at random. I was in my twenties before I realised that they strike whenever Charlie is at risk, or when I am about to remove one of those risks. When I don't keep them under control I end up barely able to breathe, my voice reduced to a croak. One day my mother, trying to ease the tensions, joked that I had a frog in my throat – the joke was a bullseye and, until I cut all ties with them, my family and a handful of acquaintances called me 'Frog'.

I used to hate the nickname; it was demeaning. A few years ago I heard an obscure song with the word in the title, lyrics about talking to pictures in a magazine – at least that is how they seem to me – and now I like it; it is how Charlie and I have always, will always, talk. I am Frog, if only to myself these days.

Breathing controlled I took the pepper-spray from my

coat pocket and approached the girl's door. My heart was still in my throat and my stomach was twisting, my breath coming in short little gulps, but I stuck to my plan and pounded on the door. I could only hope that it sounded official, like a policeman's and not a psycho's. It hurt my knuckles, even through my leather gloves, and I was relieved when the door opened a crack just before I was about to knock again.

"What?" the girl said from behind the chain, her East Coast twang more evident now she was tired than earlier at the bar. "Who are you?"

I only got one of her eyes through the narrow crack but it was enough to make her fall backwards with a scream. The flimsy security chain broke on the second shoulder barge and I was inside her apartment. She was still on her feet, getting ready to defend herself, so I sprayed her again, getting both her eyes. She staggered backwards into the cramped living room, catching her legs on the coffee table and saving me the bother of knocking her down.

I closed the door and caught her as she was trying to rise, blinded and terrified. I'm not a monster, I felt some sympathy for her fear and pain in the hour that followed, but she was an enemy of Charlie, an enemy of all that is good. I only did what I had to, and it doesn't matter if I enjoyed parts of it or stayed until after the blood that gushed from her throat began to congeal and her glazed eyes started to whiten.

Charlie was waiting for me when I got home, just like always. Our surroundings have changed, I left our hometown for Los Angeles as soon as I could – I haven't been home since. I rent this place, it's cheap and I make enough. I don't have many outside interests.

There aren't as many pictures on the walls as when I was young, or in the succession of apartments and hovels I called home before buying this place. Each room only has one, but they are all framed, high-quality. In the hallway, kitchen and bathroom they are quite small; she never speaks to me much in those rooms. The ones in my living room and bedroom are larger, blown-up headshots from her early twenties and thirties – when she was still just a comedy actress. In the spare room, my office, I have an almost life-sized picture of her sitting in a chair, legs crossed and looking classy. It was taken a few years ago, when she was finally starting to get the serious roles her talent deserves. I had to have it custom made, using a picture from her website, and it is the one I talk to most often these days.

I told her about my night as I stripped off my bloody clothes, shoving them all into a bag I'd throw into the ocean later. There were some deep scratches in my cheek – the girl had fought more than any I'd taken before – and I asked Charlie if I needed to go back, take the girl's fingertips so they couldn't get any DNA from under her fingernails. There was no response, to that or anything else I said. She hadn't said a word to me in weeks, not since she came back home for her break.

The first time I killed for Charlie was almost accidental, not premeditated in detail although it was in desire.

I was approaching nineteen, just finished high school and gearing myself for college. I wasn't happy with it, my father deciding when I was young that, if I was going to be a faggot, I'd at least be a clever one. My eldest brother landed an Ivy League sport scholarship, and the next youngest was in the marines – I was going to be the brains, make my parents proud that way, pay them back for everything they'd given me. I had a third brother, between me and the other two – he was a mechanic, still lived at home.

College held no appeal for me, there was nothing that interested me enough to take on that level of studying, but I could see a way to escape from home. Charlie was equally ambivalent – all she wanted was for me to move to LA and be close enough to protect her from the circling enemy. All I wanted was to please her, and a car of my own to give me the option of just leaving. I believed her when she said all I needed to do was be near her for everything to click into place.

I did what my father wanted, threw myself into study with as much enthusiasm as I could manage. He wanted a doctor, someone as high status as the sport star and army hero, but had to settle for an engineer when I just couldn't get the Biology grades. If my final summer at home had gone differently, I would probably have gone to college, continued trying to please my father and only able to watch Charlie from a distance.

My father was a bully, ready enough with his fists when he was angry or drunk enough, but my brother, the mechanic, was meaner, bigger. Working as a grease-monkey and living at home were not signs of success in my father's eyes and, for a while, my brother had been as terrorised as the rest of us. Then he learned to fight better, nastier, than our father, adding a few extra inches and several pounds to the advantage. It took a couple of fairly savage fights but, in the end, my brother won, putting the matter well beyond doubt. When he chose to stay at home, rent free and openly waiting for the day the house would be his, my father acquiesced and, like all true cowards, became my brother's biggest fan and defender.

Most of the time, I didn't see much of the mechanic. He only came home to eat and sleep, and often spent days with his deadbeat friends, or one of a shifting cast of skanky girlfriends. During term, I could go days, weeks sometimes, without seeing him. The extra study sessions and full range of extra-curricular clubs and activities made it even easier.

During the holidays it was harder, worst of all when he took his own holiday, invariably spent hanging around the house, drinking and playing video games. In the evenings he'd sit on the porch and smoke weed, keeping it outside the house in a small concession to our mother.

I had graduated and already knew which college I would be going to, somewhere small but respectable, only a few hundred miles from Charlie in LA. Somewhere closer would have been better, but I didn't make the grades to pick and choose. The place I was going came the closest to offering a full scholarship, and the courses I could live with the easiest. Charlie wouldn't be that far away, far closer than she had been ever since she moved from our hometown. I even started to feel motivated, spending that summer in my room, getting a head-start on the reading, and talking to Charlie. I only left for my job, a few hours every week stacking shelves, and the driving lessons my father had finally agreed to, even paying part of the cost himself.

Everything was fine until the second week of my brother's holiday, the start of August. He had spent the first week with his friends at some music festival and bumming around, until his money ran out. Bored and penniless, he made himself felt around the house. Both our parents worked and he always found enough money, or a party to crash, to occupy his evenings – I took the brunt of it.

The bookworm jibes were nothing new, and I knew better than to try to keep studying when he chose to saunter into my room. It didn't stop him taking my books and notes, throwing them around the room, but protesting, or ignoring him, were only goads. I did my best to humour him, we even played video games together a couple of times. In retrospect, I should have given him what he wanted, let him see that he was getting to me, but I might not be who I am today if I had. I could be just another nobody, with nothing more than vague dreams.

I was at work the afternoon he trashed my room, already so drunk he spent the evening after passed out in his own room. Dimly aware that it was the best way to get me out of his life he left my college stuff alone, except to pile it all in one corner and pour beer over it. Then he pissed on my bed, at least I imagine he did that first. Leaving my computer, second hand and elderly, on was my own mistake, and not one I've ever made it again. For a couple of hours he watched porn, leaving stains and empty beer bottles on my desk. Before he left, he tore Charlie from the wall, ripping her to shreds and leaving them on my piss-soaked bed.

My parents never knew about the desecration. I cleared the mess and aired the room before they got home, torn between anger and grief as I put Charlie's ruins in a waste bag. The internet history was easy to clear, his tastes simple and aggressive. It was the first time I fully realised just how dangerous my enemies – Charlie's enemies – were. I knew it was only a poster, not having it didn't stop me feeling her, hearing it, but it was a statement of intent.

I don't know what I intended when I followed him from the house the next day. He had his own car but the police knew it, and him. Sometimes, depending on his destination and errand, he chose to walk. I saw him entering the woods from my bedroom window and followed on impulse, guessing that he was on his way to his friend's house – the woods were a shortcut, only a mile or two across. When we were younger, I'd played in the woods with all my brothers, and their friends. Other than Charlie, I've never really had any friends of my own.

A small river cut through the woods, before it was diverted underground to the other side of town. The banks were steep and high, studded with outcrops of bedrock. A network of paths ran through the trees and there were two bridges over the river. It was popular with joggers and dog-walkers, the occasional mugger or rapist.

That day there was no-one, just the two of us, and he thought he was alone. As he walked, earphones in, he smoked a joint and drank a beer. He seemed oblivious to me, following less than fifty feet behind, heart pounding, right until the last.

One of the bridges was much higher than the other, almost thirty feet above the river at its highest. The banks were steeper and higher than anywhere else, one side an almost bare wall of cracked rock. Rocks were strewn across the riverbed and, for a short distance before disappearing underground, it ran in a shallow, violent rapid. The bridge had been placed for the view, and was only just wide enough for two people to pass.

My brother was standing on the middle rail of the barrier, right in the middle, and pissing into the river when I came up behind him. He'd been drinking since he woke, far earlier than usual because he'd passed-out so early after trashing my room. He was laughing, spraying the arc of urine from side to side, joking to himself about horse bladders.

He saw me as I reached the end of the bridge, swaying as he half-turned, still pissing. He said something I couldn't understand over the thud of my own heart, and his drunken slur. It made him laugh and he turned back to his piss, the stream finally slackening. Shaking the last drops free made him sway again, except this time he was too drunk to control it. As he began to fall back, I ran forward.

I think I meant to catch him at first, but then Charlie spoke. He was much bigger than me, far stronger, and normally I would have just bounced off him. Drunk and off-balance, feet still on the middle-rail and grasping for support with his hands rather than jumping down, he was easy to tip the other way. I bit the fingers of the hand he managed to get on the top rail, saw the surprise on his face as he fell and split his head open on one of the rocks below – it was sharp, split his skull almost in half.

I went home and said nothing, even though my mother was home that day. She made me lunch and I went to my room and studied until dinner. It was quiet without my brother, and I saw how broken and pathetic my father was. It was the first time I didn't feel scared of him.

My brother was found the following morning, long enough for a rat or two to take a nibble on his face. I went back to my room after the police told us, pretending to be in shock. Downstairs my mother sobbed and my father went out to get drunk. From the start it was treated as an accident, the sort of thing that was likely to happen to my brother. There were no real questions, and no-one seemed to care.

Except Charlie. She was pleased with what I'd done, told me how I'd saved her without knowing it. Everything she said those first couple of days made more sense than anything I had ever heard, even when she told me that she was Charlie's subconscious, reaching out to her guardian – the waking Charlie, the actress I adored, was safely oblivious, kept perfect by her ignorance.

I left home three days after my brother died, sneaking out before dawn with a single bag and the contents of my mother's purse. Terrified I'd get stopped, I drove two hundred miles straight in my brother's car before I dared to stop and empty my account through an ATM. With my mother's money included, I had a few hundred dollars.

It was enough.

Charlie has gone silent on me before. It happens most often when she is physically a long way from me – when she films on the other side of the world I can barely feel her, let alone hear her. There have been times when she's been close as well, when I've done something to fail or anger her. I have never been shunned for more than a few days, never for longer than a week.

Her silence this time has lasted for months. There is no consolation in knowing that it isn't just me that she's excluded. Her social media accounts are ghosts, still officially active but silent. There has been no scandal, no public announcements, and her last film did well. She has simply withdrawn inside the confines of her mansion in the hills, requests to her PR given stock 'working on several projects' answers.

I have tried to believe that is the truth, if only because I haven't wanted to admit what it means if it isn't.

Charlie is a star. A natural. I know her better than anyone else ever can; I know what she is in the core of her soul. She would never withdraw from the lights, never stop finding a way to be in the public eye. She brings too much joy to ever withdraw; it isn't something she'd ever do to the people who love her. It isn't something she *could* do.

Something terrible has happened, and it is my fault. The party-girl in the cheap apartment wasn't the only active threat; a double attack something I've always known would happen but still wasn't prepared for. Whilst I was congratulating myself, eyes half-closed to bask in my own glory, the other threat had slipped past, and now the enemy has won.

Charlie is dead. That is why I haven't heard her in so long, why she has withdrawn from the world. I'm the only one who knows, the only one who ever can. The enemy has replaced her, the way they have with so many others. Where there was light and hope, there is only darkness and imitation.

No-one will ever notice, except on the kind of roles she'll increasingly play, the new menace in her eye they'll give awards to. She'll never be less than a star, just not the kind the world needs to have shining. Not the kind she was born to be.

It is cold in bushes outside her window, the only one still lit in the entire mansion. I came over the perimeter wall an hour ago, been waiting since then for the help to finish in the kitchen and retreat to their own homes – quaint little guest-houses on one side of the property; luxury slave-quarters.

Their lights have just gone out, and I'm raising the nerve to do what I need to – what must be done. I'll find a knife inside; it doesn't matter if I get caught, as long as I succeed first.

I killed nine times after my brother to protect Charlie.

Now that I have failed, I owe her two final sacrifices – the imposter's and my own.

I want to scream. There's something itching in my throat.

Inspired by Carole King "It Might As Well Rain Until September"

Each raindrop bounced off the garden shed with an almost military impact. Pops and cracks ricocheted off the tin roof, filling the night air with an unceasing and deafening din.

Behind closed curtains Martin slept unencumbered. His sleep was deep, his dreams uninteresting, but most importantly he was dry.

Martin toyed with his mother's umbrella. The almost foreign object was the centre of so many lives, yet it was one Martin never had need for.

At fifteen years old Martin was an unassuming character; short mousy brown hair, clear skin and a slight dusting of facial hair littering his top lip. He stood at only 5' 6" making his ability to blend into a small crowd a time mastered ability.

And yet at fifteen years old, not once had he seen rain.

"Martin!" His mother's voice barrelled down the hallway with incredible force.

"'I'm by the front door."

Martin stood, bringing his mother's umbrella with him. Her worried face poked around the kitchen door.

"Oh sorry, I thought you were upstairs."

"No Mum, its two o'clock, time we left."

Holding out her umbrella with one hand, he took her jacket from a nearby hook with the other.

"Sorry baby, don't worry, we will still make it."

Martin's mother had spent her whole life apologising. She held herself responsible for what Martin was going through, despite not knowing what it was she actually did wrong.

"Its OK Mum, let's just get a move on."

She took her jacket and slid it on with an effortless grace. Stopping before Martin's outstretched hand, she looked down at the umbrella. "Do I need that?"

"No, no I guess not." Martin put the umbrella aside and opened the door for his Mother.

"Sorry," she said once more.

"MARTIN TUIL!"

The receptionist called his name and scanned the room despite Martin and his mother being the only ones present.

Martin stood and walked towards the only door other than the exit. Through a metal-laced glass panel he could see a corridor of closed doors. Always closed, never left ajar.

"I'll just be out here baby," his mother offered.

"I know," he muttered.

"Sorry," she added.

The corridor always reeked of antiseptic, the sharp smell scratching his nostrils.

He stood before a door. Raising his hand for the

doorknob, he paused.

Dr Gene Ralphs

The door to the right displayed another name.

Dr Liz Hearth

He stepped aside and entered the second door.

"Good afternoon Martin."

Dr Hearth stood to greet him, her arm extended, her palm flat. Martin shook it limply before sitting on the vacant sofa.

"You've moved offices."

"Yes Martin, is that OK?" Dr Heath sat opposite him picking up a clipboard to her side before scribbling a short note.

"Yeah, yeah, its fine, just talking is all," Martin spoke into his chest. He had been coming here for the last seven months; twice, sometimes three times a week. He still felt awkward, that would never change.

"So Martin, it rained last Friday at 3pm, did you see it?"

Martin shifted on the sofa, the leather creaking beneath him.

"No" his answer was deliberately short. She made a point of reminding him of the week's weather every session, it always rained at night, it occasionally rained during the day.

"I was asleep."

"Oh that's a shame Martin, it ended with a beautiful rainbow."

"I know, I saw that."

Martin arched forward, slipping a handful of mints into his sweaty palm. The bowl sat at the centre of the table before him, he referred to it as the "Mint Bowl Paradox"; no matter how many sweets he took, the bowl seemed to remain full. He chuckled to himself softly.

"Good, it's good to laugh Martin."

Martin sneered, he looked up in a weak attempt to show her his disdain but she was busy scribbling more notes to herself.

"Martin, I would like it if you told me more about your dreams."

"Martin, I would like it if you told me more about school."

"Martin, I would like it if..."

"Martin, I would like..."

"Martin..."

"Martin..."

Every question was the same, only the subject matter changed. And like every one of her conversation starters Martin had a sure fire way to shut them down.

"I want to die."

He had said that very phrase nearly a year ago, it had no real meaning then, just empty, hollow words. But then he said it again, and again, and again, each time the words spoke to him with more substance, each time it added more purpose. He had always wanted to die, it was just he had never given it much thought, only after he first verbalised those words did he truly understand.

"I want to die."

Wanting to die and trying to kill yourself are two very different things; no matter how many times he told his mother, his therapist, or even his teachers they couldn't understand it. Martin wanted it all to end, that was for sure, but not at his own making. Whether it was fear, or even a lack of confidence, he really didn't want to do it himself.

He would daydream of buses swerving off the road crashing into him, tiles from rooftops dropping down and crushing his skull. Every way was quick, every way was relatively painless, but what was important was it wasn't by his own hand. However, recently that was becoming less of a concern.

"Martin, we've covered a lot today, you've done really well. You should be proud of yourself." Dr Hearth clasped her hands together in praise; for a split-second Martin was sure she was about to clap. She did that once, she actually applauded him for bravely telling her he wants to end it all. What a fucking joke.

Martin pushed himself from the sofa, from the corner of his eye he could see her rising too, her hand outstretched for a parting handshake. He ignored her attempts to humanise herself, she was a shrink, a literal garbage bin for the mentally inept to vomit their worries and concerns into. Martin worked it out a few weeks back. He hated Dr Hearth, he hated her attempts to explain everything, to see the good in it all. Sometimes life was shit, he got that, he accepted that, but people like her made him want to take on more than his fair share. Someone had to feel bad, why not him?

Martin left the room and quickly made his way back to the overbearing fluorescent lights of the waiting room. One bulb in particular always caught his attention, the shrill buzzing which no one else noticed despite his complaints. He was sure it was there just to spark a reaction which would then be dissected by the shrinks. If it was a test he was sure he had failed.

"Everything OK, Honey?"
Martin's mother stood so quickly the receptionist jumped.
"Sorry," she whispered.
"Yeah, all good Mum. Come on, lets head off, this place depresses me."
Martin bit his tongue. The D word, no matter how often it came up, was obviously a delicate subject. His mother

paused slightly, like a rabbit unsure of the speed of a fast-moving car. He could see her eyes measuring the distance, her muscles tightening, ready to leap forward. He'd only seen her crack a couple of times and he really didn't fancy another. No matter what, he loved her and hated the pain he was putting her through. She relaxed, he watched her chest sink before grabbing another deep breath; the rabbit had crossed the road safely.

Martin hadn't gone to school for the last couple of weeks. The teachers that once cared had grown tired of his complaining, being drowned in his self-pity. They seemed relieved when he stopped bothering them; a breath of fresh air from the toxic waste dump that was Martin's mind. It started with the odd afternoon, followed by the odd day, no one seemed to mind so eventually he just stopped going. Martin thought that the absence of school would help, after all, all of this, all of this broken, fucked up hatred of himself came from them. He sought comfort from Mrs Dancer, confided his biggest fear in her and she fucked it all up. *She* was the reason the school councillor got involved, *he* was the reason Martin had to dissect his feelings, and *they* were the feelings that made him crumble into the psycho he always feared he was.

Martin kicked a nearby pebble, watching it skip and dance across the tarmac before submerging itself in a brown puddle, a puddle from last night's rain.

Rain that had been coming down in quantities never seen before; rain that filled the night air *every* bloody night. Rain that Martin had never seen.

He gazed at the muddy ripples that emanated from the sunken stone. This was as good as it got; wet fucking floors.

The evidence was there for all to see and yet no one believed him. Every night it rained and every night it rained while he slept; the only time it rained during the day was again, while he slept.

His mother tried to blame global warming, something about air currents mixed with the cool night air. Even the news took her side, they called it 'Nocturnal Rain Influx'. Some idiot actually got paid for coming up with that!

Shit name or not, the world had noticed but they couldn't figure out why.

But he knew.

It was Martin, he was the reason.

It came to him a few years back. It took a while for him to fully accept it, but all the evidence was there. It only rained while he was asleep, as if it was him the rain was avoiding.

For some sick reason Mother Nature had chosen him to suffer. Mother Nature wanted to hide the beauty of rain from Martin and despite the seemingly trivial quality of rain it truly pained him. It ripped him apart to know that something so vast, so ineffable, wanted to punish him.

This is why he was depressed, this is why he saw only the negativity of life. If Mother Nature wanted him to suffer she had truly succeeded. With one tiny action she had destroyed him. Martin took a while to admit it but what followed was acceptance.

Of course, the doctors called him mad. They claimed that one boy cannot be singled out by an unknown force, that one boy cannot decide the fate of the world and its soggy nature due to his sleeping pattern, that one boy couldn't control the weather.

When he challenged them, pushed them for another reason for the rain falling only while he slept they all had the same answer, "you're not the only one who sleeps when it rains". And there, and only there, they were right; but others could choose to stay up late and watch the rain, others could choose to wake up at 3am and watch the rain, others saw the rain during the day when only Martin slept, others had seen the rain at least once in their life; Martin had not, not once.

When he was a child his Mother claimed that the sun always shined for him, that every time he awoke the rain would stop and the sun would come out. It happened so much that his family would joke about it. His grandfather called him the sunshine boy, his jumpers adorned with smiling suns and rainbows, everything about it was a blessing, a nonsensical blessing.

But as he grew older he realised it wasn't the sun that came to greet him, it was the rain that left him. Somehow, it was Martin who was causing the rain to stop.

He tried to think positively, to look at only the good in it. When he was awake people were happy, no one likes getting caught in the rain, everyone would rather stay warm and dry inside. But by making the rain come only when he slept he was ensuring millions of people had the best opportunities to enjoy their day. He was the reason for their happiness. But that kind of knowledge can only go so far.

Martin liked the rain, or at least what he knew of it. He watched 'Singin' In the Rain' hundreds of times, rewound the ending scenes of 'Shawshank Redemption' with a smile on his face, a happy refrain would wash over him whilst Forrest Gump trekked through Vietnam. Soon he realised that he was missing out; whilst others were happy, it was all at his expense.

He had taken to showering fully clothed, as idiotic as he felt it was a strange comfort being rained on, even if it was indoors. He dabbled with the temperatures, a warm summer drizzle cascading through his mopped hair, thunderous downpours that washed over him blinding him with their incessant yet tepid flows. But his favourite was perhaps everyone's most hated; the steady freezing deluge that penetrates your very being, the kind that makes you wince as damp clothes brush against your skin while you walk. The one that makes your bones ache and your muscles tingle; yes, this was his rain.

He had tried to analyse it once. He thought of it as a punishment to himself, a necessary evil to balance out his ill nature. But now he just accepted the truth, anything other than freezing was just having a shower with your clothes on, the icy water made it feel like *real* rain.

Martin's alarm erupted into life. The shrill shriek pierced his deep sleep, wrenching him into the darkened room. He liked to test the rain every now and then, to see if he could catch it as it turned to flee. He would set alarms throughout the year and then forget about them. Perhaps if he didn't know when he was going to wake then the rain wouldn't know either. Even as he set the alarms he didn't believe it. After all these years it had never worked.

The window to his side gave him a clear view onto the garden, once more the eaves trickled fresh rainwater to the ground below. Every night was the same and every night Martin prayed for something different; every night his prayers went unanswered.

He propped himself up against the window ledge, his hand pressed against the cold glass. Beyond he could see the twinkling of every drop as it made its final run off the leaves to the ever-waiting grass. Every lawn was lush and full of life, weeds spread their roots far and wide so not a single patch of soil lay bare. Martin tried to focus. The world was green because of him.

Shifting back into bed he closed his eyes, that brief moment of calm before he remembered what sleeping meant he was missing. His mind battled with itself *"it's only rain"* rung out from one corner, *"who cares if you miss it"* from another, *"think of all the good your sleep does to the world, who else can claim that they save lives in their sleep"*. As always, the darker voices would bellow into his skull replying with their anguish. They started as soft whispers many years ago but as time went on, their words held further resonance. Each comment dug its way in deeper and deeper, a deadly infection spreading with every syllable.

"But if it's such a little thing then why can you not have it", *"it's not fair that others benefit from your pain"*, *"they don't even believe you, they don't even want to be grateful for your sacrifice"*.

Where there once was resistance now came a wave of acceptance, he found comfort in their words, they truly knew how he felt. And then it came, the one voice that has become louder than all others: *"It's ok to give up."*

Martin's eyes grew heavy once more, he was tired, tired of fighting, tired of being told he was crazy, tired of watching every word, every movement around his mother.

Yes, Martin was tired.

It seemed silly when he really thought about it, to end it all over rain, but that was exactly what Martin had to do.

He sealed the envelope before him, a brief but loving note to his mother. No matter what, he knew she was going to hurt. The pain she would feel would never subside. He had to convince himself that she would understand, that she would take comfort that he was finally free. He knew that deep down there would be a tiny speck of relief, a quick gasp of release that she would no longer need to worry for him. She would, of course, hide it, buried in the furthest, darkest depths of her soul; but it would be there, a miniscule glimmer of selfishness. Martin smiled to himself, he was proud of her for having that little ebb of humanity.

Martin turned to his computer and hit play. With his vast collection of music, he was sure fate would take control and play something meaningful as he prepared for the end. Tsunami by Manic Street Preachers began to play.

Despite his music now openly mocking him, he left it to play.

Opening his bedside drawer, he pulled out a small metal lock box. Martin had left it deliberately unlocked. Again, if fate was to play its hand then someone would have found the box by now and put a stop to his plan, yet no one had. Inside Martin ran his fingers through an assortment of pills.

He had been saving any pills he could find and put it inside this box, waiting for today. Anti-depressants, Imodium, migraine relief, Ibuprofen; all over the counter medications but together they would have the desired effect. He marvelled at his collection, pastel pinks, whites and blues littered like pebbles on a wonderous beach. He had only been collecting for the past month but already he had easily one hundred pills before him, each one meant to do good but now, in his hands, they would serve a much higher purpose.

Martin took a handful and swallowed them, washing them down with a stale bottle of water from under his bed. He took another handful, repeated, burped and then picked the remaining pills from the box. He stopped and inspected the pill between his fingers, it was one he had found on the floor one day. A little baggy tossed into a siding by a stranger, normally people wouldn't eat unknown pills from unknown sources; Martin however loved this little pill. He had no idea what it was or what it could do to him, worst case scenario is that it killed him, and that was perfect. This pill was his little cherry on top of a very dangerous sundae. He swallowed it with the dregs of the water.

Inside his chest his heart began to beat a little faster. Martin was unsure if this was the drugs taking effect or the excitement, either way he liked it. He took off his shoes, tucked them under his bed and then lay down atop the duvet.

Martin had played this day over and over in his head and knew that there would only be one problem; guilt. Guilt would now bleed from every pocket of his consciousness as his body struggled to survive. His brain's only weapon against the impending death is to now persuade him that he is wrong. He laughed at the irony; his mind concocted this whole thing, fed his fears, drove his decision and now, when it finally was getting what it wanted, it scrabbled to survive.

He pictured his mother finding his body lying still in his bed; her hands running over his neck as she prayed for a pulse. That damming realisation that he was gone, all her effort, all her love wasted as he now lay lifeless before her. Her wails torture all those that hear as she buries her only son; years of her life lived without friend nor lover, dedicated to Martin and this is his empty reply. She grows old, lonely and fragile, struggling to find meaning to it all, she carries with her the never ceasing pain of a son lost.

No, *he* has been the hinderance, *he* has held her back. Without him she would have led a full life; she would have been able to be selfish, to think and care about only herself. She was a good person and she *will* get through this, she will find love again, she will laugh, she will smile. Martin couldn't remember the last time he heard her laugh and that was on him. His depression was a disease, an infection that had spread and was taking hold of his mother, sucking the life from her, feeding on her innocence. With him gone she will live, she *has* to live.

His head began to swim, little specks of light danced rhythmically before him, each one bouncing along to the lyrics playing through the air. He tried to concentrate on the song, to focus on the words, his shuddering mind now failing to lock on to anything specific.

Martin's stomach began to cramp, just a little at first but it soon grew into something much more fierce. He held his gut and gritted his teeth. He knew that whatever the pain he must ride it through, he wanted his mother to find him and just assume he fell asleep, she didn't need to know if there was any pain. He mustn't die curled into a feeble ball.

A fog washed over him. Unsure how long he had lay on the bed, he knew that soon it would all be over.

The music stopped, a moment of silence before Carole King's soft voice filled the room. He knew this song, he knew it well, he had listened to it many times and for some reason it comforted him when he was truly low; fate had delivered.

His eyes felt heavy, the room had stopped spinning and instead now began to close in on him, a strange and warming comfort. He knew with all his heart that this was the right thing to do. No matter the pain it will cause others, it was only a fraction of the pain he had lived with all these years. He had carried on as far as he could, this wasn't selfish, this wasn't cowardly, this was just his final act; after all even fate had chosen *It Might As Well Rain Until September* to carry him through.

Even fate was on his side.

The rain wasn't heavy, but it was constant, it had been since the day he died. Martin's mother stood by the open grave and watched as the sodden soil began to fall onto her sons' coffin.

Only a few mourners had come to pay their respects, most of her family had already left town due to the flooding. Her sister entwined her fingers with her own, her neighbour's hand rested on her shoulder. Her father, despite his age had insisted on helping the gravedigger, in fact without his help the council wouldn't have permitted her son's burial due to lack of staff.

A bitter wind whipped through her, drawing her tears away as they joined the rainwater streaming from her hair. The last thud of soil covered Martin's grave, even as she stood above it she could still sense her son below her.

"It's best that we leave now," said her father, dirt running through his beard as he held out his hand. She took it gracefully before falling into a deep embrace, she felt his chest shudder as he held back his tears.

"The town is being evacuated in a few hours, we need to leave," he managed before inhaling sharply to stifle his tears.

She looked out across the town. The council had approved Martin's burial due to the height of the hill. Below her the streets rippled with water. The lower High Street was under five feet of water whilst the playground was already fully submerged.

"Martin, would have loved this, no matter what it is doing to the town he would have finally seen the rain." Her sister wiped the drips from her face with an already saturated sleeve.

Martin's mother stiffened, it all fell into place at that very moment. Pulling her father close she wailed into his chest.

Finally, she knew what it all meant.

Martin hadn't missed the rain, he alone was holding it back.

hat music means to...
Rob Lane – Bassist

There was an art to the perfect Mixtape.

It wasn't just a collection of favourite songs, they needed a theme, a purpose. You had to get it just right. Much like your number one album, you had to plan the ups and the downs, the highs and the lows. Come out all guns blazing followed by the secret favourite song. Maybe three or four songs in, slow down the pace a little before bringing things back up again. Be careful though, you've got to know your running times or you're gonna cut a song before that killer guitar solo or go to the other extreme and end up with two and a half minutes of dead air before you can flip the tape - no one wants that!

Mixtape's became friends as much as an actual band's album which you'd brought from Woolworths on the High Street. These tapes were truly yours, crafted and created in your own time to suit your own moods. Long walks with your trusty Walkman when you knew which song you'd lined up when you flipped the tape - and damn, you were ready for it. No instant skipping if you got bored, there was no chance of that - you'd thought this sucker through to avoid that.

I never met that girl though who I could give a Mixtape

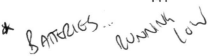

* BATTERIES... running low

to. CDs came onto the horizon and it just wasn't the same anymore.

I wonder what she would have thought?

Rob Lane is a dreamer, constantly hitting the rewind button to his favourite memories of a happy childhood surrounded by 1980s Pop Culture, Horror VHS tapes and trips to the local cinema on a Saturday afternoon. All of that culminates into his nostalgic power pop project STRAIGHT TO VIDEO.

He has also played bass guitar for more bands than he can remember - performing all over the world with the likes of Bulletboys, People on Vacation, Let Loose and most recently Ryan Hamilton & The Traitors.

Em's foreword

Music is everything to me. I cannot imagine living without it. I'm a grunger, I'm a raver, I'm a rocker, I'm a joker, I'm a toker, I'm a midnight smoker. But I digress. I was raised on reggae and Motown, I love musicals, I listen to classic FM, I dance around my kitchen to Willie Colon and Manu Chao. I love to see live music, I love to read about music, I love to sing (badly). I even had a tattoo of an EP cover from my favourite band Red Aunts (who have only written the foreword for this very book. Cue teenage me screaming loudly forever).

I had no idea what flowers I wanted at my wedding, chose a basic wedding cake and barely thought about menu choices, but the playlist was all consuming. I walked down the aisle to Amy Winehouse singing To Know Him Is To Love Him, we walked back as a couple to Marvin Gaye and Kim Weston singing It Takes Two.

My first music festival was Phoenix 96, aged 15. It was a vintage year for the now, sadly, discontinued four-day festival. The weather was positively Mediterranean, the line-up was astounding. Prodigy played twice, Foo Fighters were on their first UK tour, The Sex Pistols headlined on Sunday night, Massive Attack, Cypress Hill, Beck, Skunk Anansie, The Flaming Lips, Super Furry Animals...the list goes on. It really was the pinnacle of 90s music. And the Saturday night headline act was Bjork. I had been a fan of Bjork since her first solo single, Human Behaviour, and was so excited to see her. Alas, the festival gods were not shining down on me and I got stuck in inside a two-man tent after taking too many legal highs. The recklessness of youth. It is one of the few regrets of my life.

Isobel - I could have chosen twenty Bjork tunes, I love her that much. She is a genius, and I don't mean that in a hyperbolic sense, she is one of those rare creative souls who walk a different path to the rest of us. I chose this track because I love the feel of it. It makes me think of secret jungles and caves hidden by waterfalls.

Lady Grinning Soul – Perhaps the greatest of those rare musical genius types is, of course, David Bowie. Believe it or not, at the same festival that I missed Bjork, I also missed Bowie. (I know, I know, what an idiot. Teenagers, eh?). My mother instilled a love of Bowie in me from a young age, and some of my earliest and favourite memories are of listening to cassettes in my mum's car. This is my forever favourite Bowie song, it takes my breath away every time I hear it.

Rain Dogs – I'm a relative late-comer to Tom Waits I will admit. I know him more as an actor than a singer. His turn as Renfield in Coppola's Dracula, one of my all-time most loved films, was fantastic. I could never really find an "in", his back catalogue being so vast and variant. Then someone recommended Mule Variations as a good place to start, so I worked backwards from there. But I chose Rain Dogs, as it is classic Waits.

Hanging on The Telephone – I got a Blondie Greatest Hits tape at age 12, and I fell in love with Debbie Harry, as many young girls do. Young boys fall in love with her too, but the love girls have for Debbie Harry is different. She was, and still is, the coolest woman on the planet.

Mountain People – We all have our exes. Some we stay in touch with, some we wouldn't wring a damp flannel on if they had just been napalmed. One thing all my exes have on common (apart from me) was being introducing me to new bands, and in one particular break up this was more literal than figurative, as I kept all his Super Furry Animals CDs. The best thing to come out of that relationship was SFA. This is everything I adore about SFA, who I would say are my favourite band. I love how this song starts as a lush, hippy-dippy sweeping ballad and ends in a mad techno rave. Perfection. Might be my all-time number one cannot live without song.

Maps – Karen O is a cool chick in a band. And I love cool chicks in bands. I have always found myself drawn more to female fronted bands and female artists, and Yeah Yeah Yeahs followed in a long line of inspirational women. I chose this song in particular because of its beauty, and its obliqueness. I wanted to see what a writer could do with it, and I was not disappointed.

Down By the Water – Another bad-ass female singer song writer. Hugely inspirational and unique, PJ Harvey never stays still, never releases the same old thing. She is the only artist to have won two Mercury awards, and should be regarded by everyone as one of the greatest British song writers.

Hot Knife - Fiona Apple got me through some tough times. I read a quote once that said "I used to think there was a Fiona Apple song for every occasion. Turns out I was just clinically depressed". Well, I think there most definitely IS a Fiona Apple sing for every occasion, and far from being miserable, I often find her joyous, raucous, vital. Hot Knife is such a unique song, it could only be by Fiona Apple.

Indigo – I have very fond memories of the early 2000s that are wrapped around Moloko and the album that this is taken from. Although most people think they one hit wonders from the club track Sing It Back, they are actually much more mental and avant-garde than that track. Roisin Murphy is another inspirational female artist who always takes an unexpected route.

Gold Dust Woman – It's the Mac. What else do I need to say? Stevie Nicks is the queen. This song is the pinnacle of her dark, witchy, wild persona, and it is the perfect topper on the perhaps the most perfect album of all time, Rumours. It just goes to show what mountains of cocaine and multiple love-triangles can do for your creativity.

I hope you grow to love these songs, and stories, as much as I do,

Em x

July 2019

hat music means to...
Polly Phluid – Singer

A relic from the past, a romantic and otherworldly device that saw the young me through romances, friendships and a rocky, literally, road to new music.

Or so it seems now.

Stripping the plastic wrapper from a pristine C90 was the start of a quest that led to hours in front of your hi-fi, surrounded by scattered vinyl, tapes and magazines – pulling tunes from your head and slapping them down, in real time, on magnetic particles whizzing past your eyes at 2.4 cm per second.

It was a labour of love, in more than just name! You poured your time, energy and soul to creating the perfect mix of music for your friends, lovers and acquaintances – meticulously scrawling the name of the track, and band, on each tiny line the cover afforded you.

I miss it. It required commitment, belief and love – all things music may start lose in this fast, easy world we now live in.

* stock up at poundland

Don't let that happen, make a mix tape – even if it's a Spotify one – let the music you love explain how you feel.

Polly is the lead singer in DIY, underground rockers The Idol Dead. He makes music for the people who don't need rock stars to tell them how to live. He also shouts his soul into the abyss with industrial metallers Blood For Bones and plays a little bass in The Spangles. He likes his music, it defines him and he's cool with that.

Inspired by PJ Harvey "Down By The Water"

My heart was ripped from my body. In truth my love grew its own arms and legs and stumbled into the world years ago; crying and screaming through a premature birth. I named her Jean after her great grandmother. My beautiful Jean.

But after watching her grow for sixteen years, after watching her strong spirit flesh out into a dazzling personality of compassion and creativity, I find myself watching nothing but the flow of the river Stour. Every evening I come down here and sit underneath the bridge, listening to the trains hurtle past above me and think of the times she used to sit beside the reeds; her toes in the water, daydreaming of all the things a teenager would. Of seeing her favourite bands, of a career as a famous artist, of meeting the man of her dreams; of a future that was so cruelly and inexplicably ripped away from both of us.

I try not to think about it. Keep my mind focused on the memory of her happy smile. But every day is another day I grow further from her. The gulf of time continually expanding until it becomes a chasm I cannot see across. My memories are only echoes of my own thoughts, bouncing back to me in ever distorted form. Decreasing. Decaying. Disappearing.

They found her downstream, taken by the current until she was washed up on the embankment, where the river bends by the town library. Of all my memories, that one remains the most vivid. That bloated, pale sack I was called in to identify. That was not my daughter.

The coroner concluded she had been beaten. Bruising suggested that she'd been attacked prior to entering the water. Her wrist broken. Her hair pulled from its roots. Traces of semen found on her clothes.

That was not my daughter.

My daughter is free in a way I have yet to fully understand. But I am learning. As I watch the sunlight glint off the backs of the swimming fish, I catch a glimpse of her smile. A subliminal flash of her liminal presence. Her laugh resonates behind the susurration of the flowing river and I laugh along with her. Only, not too loud; I'm frightened I'll scare her away.

The more I visit, the more I am able to perceive of her new form. Her body snaking over the cracks in the river bed. Her breath sighing through the archway of the bridge.

On a clear day I can watch her fingers, more like tendrils now, wave lazily to the influence of the current. Her long, flowing locks have become a dark shade of green, but are still just as vibrant. I miss the days when I used to sit her in front of my dresser and run a brush through her gorgeous, blonde mane. But it pleases me to watch the fish gently nibble at the ends; grooming her with a tectonic patience that only nature can possess.

When the sun begins to lie low in the sky I am able to make out her halo just above the running water. The faint iridescence tells me she has found peace, like those of the saints. I wonder if she communes with them?

It's at this time of day I can watch how she's grown artistically. Lying on my back, I stare upwards to the heavens. The streaks of red and brilliant purples. I watch her handiwork in a rapture that only Jesus would understand. As my eyes trace the contours of her brushwork I allow tears to roll down my cheeks and I whisper words; encouragement to my little princess. I tell her how proud I am. I tell her how much I love her. I beam with a secret smile that only she will ever see. And I feel myself relax into a spiritual embrace.

I close my eyes and listen to her soft, birdsong lullaby; allowing the influence of its lilting melodies to ebb away at my consciousness. As I drift through a blank mind, tonight, three months after she became one with the water, I am truly at peace.

She is all around.

And she is within.

She is beautiful.

This is my daughter.

I awake to the strangely soothing rumble of distant thunder. Grass is stuck to my cheek. My skin is sticky with perspiration, brought about by the intense humidity. There's a storm approaching.

Night has fallen, and my eyes take a while to adjust to the silvery glow of the moon's illumination. A splash of water and I soon realise it was not the far distant clap in the night sky that had pulled me from my peace. I roll to my side and follow the commotion.

As I sit up I hear a panicked voice.

"Help."

I stand and he reaches out for me, thrashing wildly in the water.

"Help," he calls again, his voice cracking in terror.

I judge him to be close to my Jean's age. Maybe a few

years older. From the width of his neck and size of his shoulders, the boy looks well built. The river should be no challenge for him.

"Pleash, help." I hear the slurring effects of alcohol, and I can't help but judge, despite his predicament.

What was he doing down here?

Had he been here before?

Had he met my Jean?

I kneel on the embankment and stretch towards him. As our hands clasp I lean backwards to pull him out, and that's when I notice them. My daughter's fingers, slithery and black in the ghostly glow of the moon. They slide across the boy's body, caressing him to start with, but the more I pull him free from the river the tighter they squeeze; entangling and wrapping themselves around his muscular chest, and pulling against me.

As I release my grip he cries and falls backwards, landing in the water with a loud splash. For a moment there is silence, but the peace is fleeting. The boy breaks the surface and tries to scream, only to choke on the water. Under and up, under and up, he continues to struggle, thrashing his arms in an attempt to keep himself afloat. Each time he rises above the surface I see my daughter's fingers wrapped around his torso and growing in number; more and more each time he reappears.

She wants him, but I'm not sure why.

At first I worry it's something sexual but as she releases a roar above me, I realise it's anything but.

A flash across the night, her anger splitting the sky in two, and another roar as I watch the boy tire. The fight quickly leaves him and he sinks below the surface. Black water dances in excited waves as I imagine my daughter doing the same.

I smile as I sense her happiness.

And at last I understand. Every young girl needs friends her age.

I blow her a kiss and make her a promise.
A mother must provide.

Inspired by Yeah Yeah Yeahs "Maps"

As with a great many other platoons in the United Nations Expeditionary Fleet, Blight Squadron had a motto. It was in Latin, a language as dead as most of the squadron itself, but they could all recite it from memory.

If not with fire, then with swords. If not swords, then fists.

The sentiment was clear; Blight Squadron would fight until they had nothing left. Until this moment, Sergeant James McIntyre had never really considered the weight of that statement. It was a motto he'd lived by. But now, as one of the few members of Blight Squadron left standing, holed up in the mangle of collapsed walls they once called a base, the empty ammo counter on the last remaining rifle told him it was a motto he'd also *die* by.

As a child, he'd dreamed of travelling into space. He hadn't anticipated that living this dream would mean him dying in battle on the slopes of *Mons Hadley*, one of the largest mountains on Earth's moon.

"It's been a great honour serving with you, Blight Squadron" said McIntyre, throwing the useless rifle to one side and pulling out his boot knife. "Every single second we can hold off The Morass, we buy a chance for our families up there."

He pointed the tip of the serrated blade at one of the many holes in the ceiling, where Earth hung overhead like a beautiful blue-green marble. Its surface was clean and unblemished, untainted by the black tendrils of the Morass corruption that had engulfed every other world in Earth's solar system.

He looked about himself at the handful of soldiers left under his command, an array of tired and scared - yet still defiant - faces staring back at him. He paced up and down the row of beleaguered troops, trying to exude a confidence in them he wasn't sure he was feeling himself.

"The Morass's primary target will be the shield reactor. They won't risk a bombardment, so they'll be visiting us in person. Remember; go for the nerve ganglion on their necks and they'll go down like a sack of..."

He stopped, distracted. There was an unusual sensation in the room – they all felt it – like the pressure had increased, as though time had frozen, the fighting outside brought to an abrupt halt. Motes of light hovering at the corners of the room rushed to meet, dancing and spiralling like shoals of fish. The image reflected from half a dozen visors, white-hot particles forming a humanoid shape. The gathered soldiers had to hold their hands in front of their faces, the polarization filters on their helmets failing to shield them from the blinding brilliance.

A subtle shift again, the world restored to some semblance of normality. A woman suddenly stood there amongst them, unsteady on her feet, unmasked and gasping for air. She looked to James, an arm reached out. She was dressed in no kind of outfit James recognised; a baggy, segmented, white coverall, like the spacesuits of old, albeit covered with an array of electronic devices that pulsed with light, each of them affixed with a thick fabric strap.

James had the rebreather detached from his belt before she'd even started to fall, catching her before she concluded her slow-motion descent. Her eyes flickered, and a moment of recognition passed between the two. He'd never met her, but the feeling began to overwhelm James, who found himself still staring into her eyes even as The Morass flooded into the base, the room erupting into brutal melee.

Composed now, but with tears in her eyes, she briefly lifted the rebreather away from her mouth.

"You're not him," she said mournfully. Her body jerked, and, with less ceremony than she'd arrived, she vanished. James' arms were empty. Whatever had happened, however, there were more pressing matters. In the few seconds left to him, James leapt to his feet and towards the nearest Morass warrior, vicious blade ready to plunge into the alien bastard's neck.

It was the spark in his eyes that first attracted him to her, that flash of light across the azure of his iris whenever James became excited or enthused. They'd worked together for months without the slightest hint of a spark between them, but that had changed the first time they'd ever met outside of work.

The reason had been innocuous enough; a few drinks to celebrate the first anniversary of the formation of their team. Darren, their team leader, had brought them to the local bar but had expressed a single rule – that none of them could talk "shop". Melissa had never liked to think of herself as a stereotypical scientist unable to exist outside of her lab work, but they'd all spent much of the evening drinking in awkward silence. Cho, the lab tech, was the most uncomfortable of all – he literally didn't seem to possess any kind of life outside of the lab.

Until James had happened to hear something said on a nearby table, accidentally eavesdropping on a group of three smartly dressed lads in their twenties. They all looked like they'd come here straight from the office, and James, without a word to anybody on his table, suddenly stood up, strolled over, and joined them.

James appeared to be trying to explain something to them, and within minutes they were smiling and laughing like old friends. He gestured for Melissa to join them, which she did. Cho barely looked up from his Coke Zero as she left his side.

"These guys are in marketing," James explained. They all smiled at Melissa, and then turned their attention back to James, hanging off his every word. "They're working on a campaign for a new version of a piece of software and I heard them use the expression 'Quantum Leap'."

Melissa smiled, knowingly. James was clearly in his element.

"I was just explaining to them that people commonly think a quantum leap is a huge distance, whereas quanta are the smallest – the *minimum* – amounts of energy needed for something. Quantum mechanics is a theory that describes nature at the very smallest scales."

Like Melissa, James was a scientist specialising in quantum theory. At first glance, it would be easy to mistake James' enthusiasm for arrogance or condescension. However, after just a few seconds in his presence, it was clear that it was anything but – he talked about it with a passion she'd rarely seen in any other, a genuine love for the subject and a selfless need to pass his passion on to others. As he continued to explain his chosen field of science (at one point using salt and pepper shakers and a bottle of Tabasco sauce for a demonstration), the business-suited lads were spellbound by his every eloquent and fervently delivered sentence.

And so was Melissa, finding herself lost in his words. To

hear him was a delight. Looking back on it, she'd fallen in love with him at that very moment.

They'd joked in the early days at how their fledgling relationship was an experiment, of sorts. Initial and continued observations were that being in each other's company was preferable to their scientific state of being single. Potential conflict (in this particular case a noted individual preference from each party for Star Trek or Star Wars) was resolved amicably, and ongoing observations and feedback were looking favourable.

During the day they studied many-world theory - an interpretation of quantum mechanics that posits all possible alternative histories and futures are real – and by night they argued over hypothetical conflicts between the Enterprise D and a Star Destroyer, pulled apart the science in lazy B-movies, and made love.

It's possible to find statistics relating to the average time from the beginning of a relationship to getting married (twenty-five months), but, being a less legal and formal event, the same data isn't available for the length of time before getting engaged. It was a little over eight weeks for James and Melissa, which they both imagined was *way* less than the average.

As they lay in the park, the empty bottle of champagne at their feet, Melissa stared at the picture postcard star-scape that hung over them. *If there are an infinite number of Melissas (Melissae?) out there in the multiverse,* she thought, *none of them are happier than me at this moment.*

The experiment was now at an end, they agreed. The conclusions would, however, be a continuing work in progress.

James stared through the viewfinder of the thermo-binoculars for the third time in as many minutes. He was relieved to see that the three necropolice left to guard the mausoleum entrance remained on low alert, their heat signatures still a shifting pattern of navy and cyan.

He was concerned. Despite all the reconnaissance and intel, it struck him as odd that they'd leave what was supposed to be a major hive so lightly guarded. Something wasn't right.

Still, no going back now. Switching his visor to a direct feed from the first of the drones, he guided the hovering contraption towards the mausoleum entrance. He had to remind himself to breathe as the tiny joystick guided the explosive-wielding robot. It was responding sluggishly, thanks to the weight it was carrying, and this made navigation difficult.

If he moved the drone too fast, the necropolice would hear the automaton's rotor. If he collided with any of the labyrinth of walls and stonework that lined the mausoleum entrance, the game would be up. The necropolice would spring into full alert, their heat signatures a violent pulsing blur of whites and yellows. They'd track James down in seconds, and he'd be as dead as the last guy they sent out do to this job.

So far so good. The necropolice remained dormant, undisturbed. A tiny bleep, increasing in speed from an intermittent electronic whine to an almost solid screaming tone, indicated the drone was above one of the structural weak points of the mausoleum – provided the intel was accurate. With a deft flick of his thumb, the drone froze in place. With another, it began to slowly descend to deliver the first gift from its payload.

An unexpected sensor was triggered; a proximity alarm. James' instinct was to glance at the necropolice, but they were, thankfully, still inert. A bright light at the corner of his vision saw him turn to face it, the light enhancement abilities on his visor temporarily blinding him and painfully stamping the after-image of a humanoid form on his retina.

A catastrophe of alerts; a myriad of calamities. As his vision slowly restored, the first thing he saw were the colours warming on the necropolice. Blue and cyan warmed to dull orange and green as the cyborgs were activated, servo-motors sparking into life, life-giving ichor pumping into necrotised veins as the guardian corpses were hastily reanimated.

The figure that had triggered it all stood there, bewildered. She stood on the dead plains, seemingly completely unaware of the havoc she'd unleashed. At first, he'd thought her one of the resurrected, but her outfit marked her more as tech-caste. The heat signatures of the necropolice were now aflame with white and yellow and they were all fully alert.

The woman stood between James and the mausoleum. He was faced with a quandary; he could detonate the explosives now, which would destroy the necropolice and spare the woman but leave much of the mausoleum undamaged. The alternative was to leave well alone – let the necropolice do their work in killing the intruder, after which they'd return to a dormant state.

He owed this stranger nothing – if anything, she'd potentially jeopardised the entire operation.

But there was something about her, something he couldn't place. An adulthood of fighting the Dead had left him cynical, jaded, and mostly unhindered by standard morality, but this woman…

His hesitancy had taken the decision from his hands. The necropolice had hurled themselves away from the mausoleum, powerful mechanised legs propelling them in an awkward yet hasty gallop towards the stranger. His thumb moved away from the detonation controls, and he went to turn away. He'd seen what the necropolice did to their victims a dozen times, but he'd never get used to their barbarity.

A volley of shots leapt from a pistol in the woman's

hand. The weapon itself was no larger than her fist, but the silent, yellow bolts that spat from it made short work of the necropolice, leaving nothing but hissing pools of molten metal and flesh dotted about her. She stared at the gun in her hands and threw it at her feet.

Who *was* she?

He switched off the electronic camouflage dome that surrounded him, revealing himself to her as its shimmering form quickly faded away. They tentatively stepped forw ard, both carefully studying the other. They drew close, and she raised her hand to his face. He flinched, but some strange compulsion kept him in place. Her hands brushed against the metal side of his face, a mesh of scorch-marked chrome and steel plates that held it together.

Tears welled in her eyes.

"You're not him," she said, in a voice he felt he recognised. Before he could respond, her hand had moved to her belt. With a faint click, her form flickered, and she was gone, only the faint sensation of her touch lingering in her wake.

Traditional couples finish each other's sentences, James and Melissa finished each other's *experiments*. They'd been a formidable force before they'd gotten together, but now they were unstoppable. It was as though something powerful had been released, something that made them more than the sum of their parts.

The progress on Project Panorama had already been impressive, easily justifying the considerable expense that had been ploughed into it from several governments and wealthy private parties. With James and Melissa working on full flow, every month saw a dramatic new breakthrough.

Panorama had a lofty aim; to prove the existence of alternative realities. Of an infinite number of universes, all occupying the same physical space but separated across dimensions. Each reality had its own quantum signature, a distinctive combination of a resonation of frequencies and energies that could uniquely identify each one.

The team would talk long into the night, hypothesising over strong coffee and, much to Melissa's chagrin, too much Hawaiian pizza. James would often joke, as Melissa carefully deposited each strand of pineapple carefully at the side of her plate, that her ideal reality would be one where the occupants had all universally decided that it was a *really* bad idea to put fruit on pizza.

Cho would invariably always default back to theories about Hitler, having read and watched way too much science fiction in his thirty or so years of existence. There were realities out there, he'd posit, where Hitler had won WWII, and ones where WWII had started even though Hitler had never progressed beyond a painter struggling to sell pictures and postcards. James would chide him for his lack of ambition – what about even more extreme realities where Hitler had led the allies to victory in the war, or ones where Hitler himself had been raised a Jew?

Infinite realities, infinite possibilities.

The theory was that for every decision made, for the outcome of every event, a new reality was born. As realities deviated more from the standard path, the more chaotic the quantum signature – it was possible to tell, at a glance with software, how *different* each reality was, just from this pattern.

There was no *true* reality – billions sprung to life at every moment, and each was as real as any other. All they could do with Project Panorama was use *this* reality – the one that James and Melissa occupied now – as a control. The more different the quantum signature of any alternative reality from the 16,823-character-sequence of text that uniquely identified our own, the more different the reality would be from what they *knew* to be real.

It was late one evening, when James and Melissa were sitting against the outside wall of the lab, staring up at the stars after one such pizza and coffee session, that they completed their last sentence as a couple. Not so much a sentence, more two halves of a formula, but one that stopped them both in their tracks, neither of them able to fully comprehend the enormity of what they'd just calculated.

The local pizzeria had run out of pineapple that evening and perhaps it was the absence of fruit on the oft-imbibed combination of yeasted flatbread, tomato, cheese and caffeine that provoked the inspiration that Melissa and James had both sorely needed. In another reality, perhaps there'd been no such scarcity of pineapple and the essential progress would never have been made.

In hindsight, across a billion realities, that would have been preferable.

Even through the padded thickness of both of their gloves, Melissa could feel James' hand squeezing hers so tight as to threaten to cut off her circulation. They turned to face each other, only their eyes visible through the narrow visors, illuminated from the array of LED displays lining the inside of each helmet.

Melissa checked the oxygen mix display for the third time in as many minutes, convinced from the bitter tang at the back of her throat that there was something wrong with it. Still unconvinced by the read-out, she closed her eyes and took a few deep breaths in a futile attempt to calm herself.

The narrow part of James's face visible to her was dotted with beads of sweat, shining like baubles of magnesium in the artificial light. She could read his every emotion in those blue eyes, the apprehension and excitement about what they were able to achieve.

The EQA – Extra Quantum Activity - suits had been the

culmination of four more months of frenzied activity. They were a means of allowing the wearer to travel between the quantum realms, to map and explore every reality, every elsewhere and elsewhy. They'd originally conceived of the technology as a chamber, a room capable of transporting the occupants, but that had proven fatally flawed and had been abandoned.

The same impulsive nature in James that Melissa loved was not without its downsides. In the later days of the project he'd become over-confident, reckless and impatient. Their funding had been put on hold whilst their backers sought a means of proving the technology without endangering human life, but James could not wait. He knew it worked – in his mind, there was no way it *couldn't*.

Which is why the two of them were here now, tightly squeezing each other's hands in an unauthorised out-of-hours test drive of the EQA suits, as the batteries in each suit continued to gather enough residual energy to breach the theoretical membrane between realities. The batteries were ridiculously over-engineered, but critical for journeys into the unknown, recharging from the sun and even the electromagnetic charge in the atmosphere itself. Both James' and Melissa's suits were synchronised; where one went, the other would follow.

The date for this experiment was significant. A year to the day since they'd fallen in love.

As the displays in their helmets counted down to zero, their hands squeezed tighter together. A physical tether of sorts, to accompany the electronic one that bound their suits together for this simple test drive to a reality with a signature very close to our own.

"Just a quick drive around the block," he'd joked, barely convincing himself, let alone Melissa.

A loud bleeping indicated they were fully charged and ready to go. A solemn nod between the two, and they both pressed their buttons, the controls to push their EQA suits into another reality.

James faded from view, his features losing definition until he was vanished completely. Several things suddenly happened at once; there was a quick glimpse of Darren, their team leader, as he burst into the room, his face registering horror and shock. The read-out in her helmet showing James's vital signs suddenly spiked, a worrying array of red numbers flashing up. Panorama lab vanished from sight as reality spat her out elsewhere, alone.

She emerged into a maelstrom, a cascade of energies. She was sent flailing, spiralling out of control into the ether. However, the training he'd drummed into her kicked in and, ignoring the impossible concepts that flitted past her visor, turned her attention to one of the sets of control boxes strapped to her arm. It was as though she'd been caught at the cusp of an explosion, forced to readjust her quantum signature to match the reality in which she'd been deposited.

The danger adverted by her quick thinking and training, the entropic energies faded. The world faded into place around her, like tuning into a channel on an old television set.

She was alone.

The indicator in the helmet flashed a bright red defiant SYNC LOST legend at her. The suits had, according to the system logs, been disconnected before she'd shifted across from the lab. It looked likely that they'd simply emerged into different realities.

Simply. An inappropriate word, given the circumstances. He could be in any one of a trillion alternate realms, and she had to find him. From the brief glimpse she'd had of his vital signs before their suits had become separated, he could be injured. Or worse.

Think, girl, think.

She looked about herself. Not unexpectedly, given the figuratively short hop they'd made, she was in a lab very much like the one she'd left. The Panorama logo was in a darker shade of red with a thicker black outline, but still quite recognisable. It was late at night, and the lab was deserted, the only illumination in the room coming from a scrolling, blue, cloudy sky screensaver on a huge monitor fixed to one of the walls. Confirming from one of the many environmental read-outs dotted around the periphery of her vision that the air was breathable – she couldn't *assume* such things anymore – she flicked the release on her helmet and it hissed noisily open.

The first journey should have been followed by elation; a sense of amazement and relief that they'd both survived. Then the awe of realising the experiment had worked and that they were in a different *reality*.

Not distress, not this sense of overwhelming panic. The feeling of being absent from a man who she so loved the bones of, she'd miss him if he popped to the corner shop for milk. And now they were separated by a gulf larger than any physical space the two of them could ever have imagined.

It would be so easy to drift into despondency. But she was a scientist, and she had means. She could *track* him.

Both James and Melissa, like the realities they inhabited, had their own quantum signatures. With the aid of the computers in the lab – which luckily weren't that different from the ones back home – she began to chart a course to him, focussing in on his unique pattern. A path to him, calculated from the realities available to her at each step of the journey. The suits couldn't simply leap from reality to reality unguided; at every step, there were a limited number of pathways available. However, now she'd charted a passage through the quantum that would take her to James– a *map*.

Inexorably, as sure as pineapple is, at best, a substandard

pizza topping, each step would bring them nearer together. Each reality would be a stepping stone closer.

The opening steps were treacherous. Like when you're trying to guess a number when you're only told whether the value is higher or lower than your prediction; you start at the extremes, and zero in. And, despite the onboard computers, there was always the possibility you'd end up somewhere *slightly* different than expected. It seemed as much down to luck as science.

Every arrival was greeted by the same explosion of energies, but over time she'd gotten used to them. In those initial tentative steps, she'd felt threatened - but now she'd familiarised herself with adjusting her controls to cater for them, they'd lost their danger. If anything, they'd began to feel like strong winds, pushing her towards her destination.

Realities of widely contrasting signatures, mind-boggling vistas defying the laws of nature and physics, opened to her. She was forced to stay for a little time in each as her batteries recharged, wandering on the desolate plains of abandoned Earths or hiding in the ruins of buildings whilst sanity-wrenching goliaths blocked out the skies.

She'd zero in on *that* reality's James as she arrived, never quite prepared for what she'd encounter or whether – however unlikely - her map had guided her to *her* James.

They varied wildly; many were scientists, like the man she loved. Others were on wildly deviated paths; a grizzled soldier in an alien war, a pirate captain on a drowned Earth where advanced technology was forbidden, a bionic priest fighting a war against cruel cyborg undead.

She noted that, as she was growing more anxious and impatient, she was becoming increasingly careless. She'd nearly met her maker (or that reality's one, anyway) when she'd forgotten to seal her helmet and nearly choked upon arrival on a chemical-cloud saturated Earth.

Gasping for air and struggling to find the control to hermetically seal the EQA suit, she'd saved herself quite by accident. With a slight adjustment to her controls, she learned she could shift the suit out of phase, suspending her in some kind of limbo state. She could observe the realities without interaction, and without danger. An invisible ghost.

She now only appeared when she felt like doing so. Every now and then a shift between realities would see her encounter a piece of technology of use to her, and little by little her inventory improved. At one stage, despite her hatred of firearms, she'd gathered a weapon. She'd even used it, in anger, in a way. She'd been threatened and had opened fire. The artificial intelligence software on the pistol had done all the work, targeting each threat with pinpoint accuracy. Still, it had made her look quite the sharp-shooter. Sadly, it had depleted the weapon's power-cells and the only technology capable of recharging it was several realities in the opposite direction, so it had been rendered useless.

Melissa wandered still, following the sometimes-erratic course suggested by the ever-changing map. She stood on the cracked rocky shores of an Earth where invertebrates had never progressed beyond leaving the sea, and on the desert plains of a world where mankind had mastered space travel hundreds of years before, long having departed for the stars.

She passed through realities so like our own as to be almost indistinguishable. A world where they'd never progressed beyond paper pound notes or where the gravity was a fraction lower, as well as a myriad of worlds where there were both a James and Melissa but whose paths had never crossed.

There were moments of despair when she almost felt tempted to return home, but that would be folly. They'd both used the equipment without authorisation, and if she went home, she'd more than likely be arrested - fired at the very least. They'd take the experiment away from her, and James would never be found.

No, they'd face the music *together*. That said, growing more homesick the further she got from her own reality, it would have been so tempting to stop on one of these worlds and never leave. To meet that reality's James, and to fall in love all over again.

But, observing invisibly, they were different to the man she'd fallen in love with. They were petty or cruel, or slovenly or neurotic. None of them were her James, so the journey had to continue.

She'd all but given hope, feeling that every step along the map was so small as to be insignificant, when it had happened. She was on one of many of the worlds where bloody warfare had wiped out the populace several decades before, sitting on the edge of a rusty pier in Belgium and waiting for the batteries to recharge. It was of great scientific interest to her how many worlds had died before they'd even reached their twentieth century, fallen to pandemic or war – the surviving humans of all the twenty-first centuries didn't realise quite how lucky they *were*. She'd almost missed the faint bleeping from her helmet over the soporific lapping of the oceans against the rusted iron struts of the pier, but a warning light caught her eye.

Without her needing to quantum travel, James's signal had gotten closer. Only by a fragment, but closer nonetheless. This was the first time this had happened without her doing, and it could only mean one thing.

He was alive, and he was looking for *her*.

It had been months since James had been out in one of the OmniStriders, but the knack of operating one never left you. "It's like riding a bike," Bernard constantly pointed out, the only Bioperative in the colony still old enough to remember what a bike was.

This particular OmniStrider, named Silver after a famous horse from one of the old Two-D cable shows, was one of James's favourites. As an older model, Silver was slow to warm up, especially around the rear joints, but once the old boy got started, he was the fastest of them all.

James glanced at the view outside the cockpit set in the OmniStrider's head, never failing to be captivated by the beauty of the long dead city. Vegetation had flourished where humans could not, long since adapted to the chemical soup that was the toxic outcome of multiple failed terraforming attempts. Thorny, oak-brown vines as thick as a man's waist hugged the skeletal remnants of skyscrapers and tenement buildings like a drunk clinging to their bottle, fractal patches of primary coloured moss dotted in haphazard patches on walls and ground alike.

Piloting the OmniStrider was so much fun, it was sometimes easy to forget he was at work. The trio of orbital sensors that hung above the American eastern seaboard had picked up a life-sign in the heart of the dead zone, the first such sign in nearly eight months, and James was next on the rota to investigate.

Having spent his whole life in the cramped confines of the *Pax Sanctorum*, one of the few places on the planet still inhabitable, he envied humanity for when they'd had the opportunity of living in cities such as this. There was so much damn *space*. Most of his ancestors had all died horribly and suddenly in cities such as these across the globe, but they'd at least done so with room to spare.

James careered around the corner at West 58th Street, hurtling down 6th Avenue towards Central Park. Without man around to tend it, it had grown beyond its confines, with fronds of vegetation creeping across the surrounding roads and thick tree roots cracking through warped and heat-blistered concrete.

With a flick of his controls, James switched the OmniStrider into bipedal mode. To the onlooker, the mech would have resembled a mighty beast rearing up as though to attack, before its metal-muscled forelegs shrunk and retracted, now closer to human arms in appearance.

James manoeuvred it into the park, guided by a pulsing life signal on his heads-up display. He ducked it under branches and carefully moved aside obstacles that blocked his way, inching closer to the source of the signal.

The official designation for the lake at the south-east edge of the park was The Pond. It was a title that had never done it justice back in the day, let alone now, at least a third bigger than it ever was on the maps.

She was sitting on one of the remaining sides of a bridge, dangling her feet over the edge. She was wearing a large bulky suit, something that looked like the spacesuits that they'd worn on that moon landing in '73. She was oblivious to his presence, the audio-enhancement equipment on the OmniStrider picking up the sound of the woman singing.

He turned up the volume up, trying – and failing – to place the song. The mood of it, however, was clear – chords draped with loss and longing.

He approached her slowly, the OmniStrider knee-deep in the teeming waters of The Pond, slow steps dragging ripples in its wake. The stranger finally looked towards him, seemingly unfazed. As he leaned in towards her, he pushed the opacity controls slider down to the minimum setting.

Melissa, convinced that none of the creatures in this reality's version of Central Park could pose her any real threat, allowed herself the luxury of a few moments of relaxation. The last few destinations had been fraught with danger; a chaotic, volcanic wasteland spraying geysers of white hot lava, a desiccated world thrown from its orbit to be dangerously close to its sun, a flaming asteroid field of what remained of that reality's Earth.

Compared to those, this dead version of Central Park was an oasis of sanity. She'd seen a number of worlds such as this – where, in man's absence, Mother Nature had flourished. She'd been sitting on the edge of a decayed bridge, absent-mindedly singing a song whilst watching the carp and sunfish dart about in the sun-specked waters, when she'd heard it arrive. The fish, alerted by the presence of the stranger in their waters, darted for the cover of shadows in an explosion of gold.

A large, beige-coloured, bipedal automaton, was slowly wading through the waters towards her. It was tall and sleek, the word "Silver" inscribed in military stencilling down the things left-hand side. She'd at first suspected it sentient - like ones she'd met on two previous occasions across other realities - but as it drew closer, its head became transparent, revealing the tightly-belted pilot within.

Leaning in so close that they were almost face to face, separated only by the transparent shell of the mechanoid's head, she recognised him instantly. They were so close on the map now, but this still wasn't *her* James.

A reassuring sight though, nonetheless.

"James," she smiled.

The occupant of the automaton looked surprised, even the robot he occupied recoiling back in shock by accident, as James brushed against one of the joysticks. Composing himself, he leaned back in, his response sounding metallic as it echoed through the external speakers set into the suit.

"How did you know?"

Melissa leaned back, half-closing her eyes and breathing in the sweet nectar from the abundance of fauna and flora that had invaded and captured the park.

"I've met a thousand of you, James. Possibly more. Every time I arrive, you're nearly always the first person I see. Coming to help. Coming to investigate."

"I'm not sure I understand."

"I'm going to repay the favour, James. I'm going to find *you*. And after such a long time, I think I'm going to find you *soon*."

Melissa glanced down at the battery meter she'd duct-taped around her right forearm – fully charged. She took one last look at this James's face, marvelling at how like hers it was. She'd seen every variant – bald, hirsute, scarred and plastered with cybernetic implants – but this James was so much like her own. He looked innocent and kind. Perhaps this reality, despite its apparent absence of people, wasn't that bad.

"It was nice speaking to you, James."

Her outline rippled and convulsed, and she was gone.

In a futile gesture, the giant mechanised hand of the robot prodded at the space where the girl had been. She'd vanished.

Briefly alarmed, he checked the environmental sensors. Her existence could only have been a hallucination, a mental aberration caused by psychotropic pollen making its way into Silver's filtration systems, no doubt released by some of the more evolved plants that lived in the park.

Nope – all clean, indicating that the vision must have been real. His already addled brain had only just begun to contemplate the enormity of that, when a variety of other sensors began to scream at him. Emergency lights that he'd never even been taught the meaning of, flared into life, burning away the thick dust that had clung to them for years.

Something was very wrong, although James would never get the opportunity to learn what.

They were now two ships caught in the midst of a whirlpool, both caught in the maelstrom but spiralling towards each other on a collision course. With every step, James and Melissa grew closer.

The worlds flitted by without regard, beautiful or terrifying tapestries now of little concern, awe and wonder relegated to their pursuit of one another.

As Melissa stood on an Earth reduced to a flat plain of blackened glass set against a violent cloudscape spitting out electromagnetic flashes, there was only one place left unmapped.

The countdown of her battery charging crept downwards at a crawl, Melissa feeling as though she could see the slow pulse of every light-emitting diode as they flicked from one number to another.

Zero.

Trembling fingers jabbed at the control to send her onwards, and the EQA suit powered up.

James – *her* James – suddenly appeared in front of her, inches away, close enough to touch. As their eyes briefly met, they filled with tears. Their fingertips briefly touched, a spark between them more powerful than the blazing conflagration that lit the skies.

And then she was gone, moved on to where James had just left.

After compensating for the inevitable explosion of energies upon arrival, she chuckled to herself. What were the chances? They'd overlapped each other, each arriving in the other's reality.

This empty reality.

Melissa was floating – or was it *falling* – through an empty blackness. No, not blackness – an absence of *anything*.

Her suit read-outs were all going haywire, dials spinning without reason, digital displays flickering with rapidly changing random numbers or flashing up a variety of incomprehensible warnings and errors.

She felt nauseous, as though she were spinning or falling

haplessly into a void, but with nothing to see, it was impossible to know the truth.

The battery countdown seemed to take forever to inexorably count to zero, but not for the previous reasons – this wasn't excitement she felt now, but sheer terror. As though at any moment she'd slam into a wall or the ground, or simply *cease to be*. Trying to concentrate on the job at hand, she entered the coordinates into the EQA suit – to take her back from where she'd just left, back to James.

Zero.

No eruption of energies this time, just the sensation of movement as she closed her eyes tight shut, that familiar feeling of moving between realities.

She feared the worst when she opened them, and her fears were confirmed. She was still in the void.

No. She'd just been here. James should be here. James should be waiting for her here. She must have entered the location wrong, hurled herself to the wrong reality in her panicked state.

But she hadn't. She was in the right place. It was just *gone*. A whole reality, wiped out.

Trying to hold back the tears, the crushing gravity of wracking sobs that threatened to overwhelm her, she set the coordinates to a few stops back, somewhere to calm her nerves and try to figure out what had happened.

No explosion, just the void. The all-encompassing, all devouring void. A realm where even entropy had died of starvation.

Over time, it dawned on her. As she retraced her steps, she quickly learned to predict the outcome of the next – or rather *previous* – point on the map. Gone.

Something with the suit, something wrong with the calculations. Perhaps something they could never have anticipated relating to the side-effects of travelling between realities – perhaps something they *could* have anticipated had they not rushed headlong into the final testing phase.

The explosions were clear now – not random bursts of energy, but the shockwaves from the reality she'd never left – the residual energies erupting from its destruction.

Every place she'd left, she'd destroyed.

The enormity of it – the term genocide barely did it justice. A universe extinguished for each careless whim, the lifespan of each determined by the ticking of a recharge clock.

And, more selfishly, it had destroyed James.

He'd have had no time to react to what had happened, caught in the detonation of a dying paradigm.

The fact that it would have been quick was no consolation.

To travel further was to doom a cosmos.

She wept. She wept for James, for the ones they'd erased on their journey towards each other. Some pity for herself, too, at the end.

It was only her suit that was preventing her from being ripped apart by the same forces she'd damned others with. To flick open her helmet would be enough, to expose herself to the tumult of forces that man was never supposed to be amongst.

Her finger hovered over the helmet release control.

A thought flittered across her mind, a lone fragment of rationale.

"You don't have to do this," she mused. "You doom a place when you *leave* it. Travel somewhere – *anywhere* – and abandon the suit. Never leave. Live your life."

"No," came the counter-argument, strong and resounding.

"You don't deserve to."

As she flicked her helmet open, she hoped that, in an infinity of realities, a James and Melissa out there would stand a better chance than they had.

In the final moments she had before even thought itself

was lost, she felt something. The evidence-based rational scientist in her had always disputed the existence of God, thinking Him to be the stuff of superstition and a way to placate mankind's inherent fear of death. However, here, at the very end, she struggled to think of a scientific explanation for what she felt.

Reality opened before her like an unravelled map, and for one moment, she could see the interconnectedness of it all. Every soul – every James, every Melissa – every loving glance, every stolen kiss. She'd once selfishly hoped what James and she had was unique, but it filled her heart with gladness to find that she was quite wrong.

There was the map, in its entirety. Yet despite that, with bittersweet irony, this Melissa was forever lost.

"Hi," said James, reaching out a hand to shake hers. "Welcome to Prospect Labs."

She smiled back. She'd expected her new colleagues to be one of the stereotypical nerds she'd worked with her last job, all neckbeards and Tank Girl tattoos, but James seemed different. He was handsome for a start, a glint in his eye that she found herself staring at for an uncomfortably long time. Probably a little *too* long, but he didn't seem to mind or care. Truth be told, he seemed reluctant to give up the handshake.

"I'm Melissa. I'm happy to be here."

Inspired by Moloko "Indigo"

1975

Drinking wasn't paramount, this was all about the music and the moves. The proprietor was a fanatic and saw the club as an extension of his love for disco culture. He was at one when surrounded by his people on the flashing dance floor, at one with the gyrating throng of revellers, at one with the pulsating beat that drove his limbs and body. Sweat peppered his mahogany brown skin, moistened his short black beard and soaked into his lilac suit but he span and span with the grace and stamina of an Olympic athlete.

A screeching scratch of needle gouging vinyl cut the music off mid-beat and the crowd stumbled to a halt. A voice came over the speakers, it was easier to reach the owner amidst his people this way.

"Yo! Rameses, you need to come to the office immediately."

No sooner had the disc jockey made his announcement when the first shrieks of 'fire!' reached him. Instinctively the edges of the crowd made their way off the raised dance floor towards the exits. Rameses' deep baritone was heard shouting at the panicking partygoers to keep calm.

A loud crack came from above his head. Colossus, his pride and joy, swayed in its fixtures. He had built it himself purposefully to make sure he held the record for the biggest glitter-ball on Earth and now he saw endless images of his own terrified face as the spinning globe came loose from its moorings.

The ball fell, crumpling Rameses like a paper doll. It hit the hard floor and exploded. Fragments of mirrored glass engulfed the dance floor, piercing people's skin like shrapnel. One lean young man had jumped from beneath the falling sphere but on its impact with the floor, Colossus showered his back with silver. Disco was dead.

2018

Mason studied the bartender's back when he twisted round to snatch the glasses away. Randomly placed flat freckles of what appeared to be metal covered the man's lower back, and Mason and his little brother Andy had been trying to decide whether they were some odd transfer or genuine body modification. The barman took off and Mason leaned over the table to his brother.

"They're totally stick-on."

Andy wasn't having any of it, he shook his head vigorously then immediately stopped. He hated the way his flabby neck wobbled when he did that. He looked across at his older brother and wished to hell he could swap bodies.

Andy wasn't really into the nightclubbing scene, but his brother and his friends were. Mason was three years older than him and girls buzzed around him like flies around shit. They thought he was The Shit, The Bee's Knees and The Dog's Bollocks. Their mum had been a goer back in her day and judging by Mason's dark-skinned, black-haired, chiselled masculinity, she had copped off with some hot Cypriot bartender twenty years previous. Andy thought about his dad, Barry the fat taxi driver from Ipswich, who looked exactly like someone had tried to carve a voodoo doll from pork-pie meat, and wondered what had gone wrong with their mother.

"They're real man, I'm telling you," Andy protested referring to the bar man's obscure body jewellery.

The barman was one of the faces of the island, everyone they had spoken to had asked if they had been to Blue Roy's Bar yet. They hadn't until this, their penultimate night. The bar wasn't amazing but the drinks were cheap and like Mason, girls seemed to flock to it. Blue Roy was definitely a sight to behold, a completely hairless six-foot man who seemed to be made out of solid muscle. Andy was reminded of Drax the Destroyer from Guardians Of The Galaxy. Blue Roy was called Blue Roy because his skin was predominantly blue, every exposed centimetre of skin being covered with tattoo ink. Maps in intricate detail decorated his skin, separated by seas and oceans, the place names barely legible unless you got really close. The map of Africa that covered his back was the most impressive. The Cape of Good Hope curled down into the top of his arse crack which was always on show above the waistband of his camouflage shorts. The unusual metal shrapnel made South Africa glitter in the bar lights.

"Think about it, this guy's a badass tattooed dude. Why would he go half measures on the body mods?"

Mason rolled his eyes and smirked maliciously, "Okay then, ask him."

He revelled in the way Andy's fair skinned complexion suddenly flushed, his skin blooming as red as his short-cropped ginger hair. The thing about his brother, Mason thought, was that he needed the gift of the gab, like him. Mason knew his brother had little going for him in the looks department and no one really liked gingers but that shouldn't stop him. Take his mate Bez, for example, Bez was just as ginger as Andy except he got himself ripped like Vin Diesel, plus he had a way with words that even the most stubborn knickered of girls fell prey to.

Mason wished he had come away with his mates rather than just his brother but it was something that needed to be done. His crew back home all liked Andy but they'd had words about his coming out with them. The rest of Mason's mates knew how to act around girls, knew how to have a good time and they told him that Andy cramped their style. Mason had promised them that he would take his brother away and bring back a party animal, educate him on the best party island in the world, or die trying.

Andy was determined not to be undermined by Mason, so what if he was God's gift to womankind? Most of the women he went with had fewer brain cells than a Tamagotchi. Andy liked reading for fuck's sake, something their mum openly encouraged and bragged about to her mates, even though they usually responded with a sympathetic grimace. He didn't want to shag a plethora of women, he would be happy with just one girl if she was the right one. He always tagged along with Mason and his similarly good-looking friends, loaned them money when they had spent all theirs on girls, drugs and booze. He was reliable and knew deep down he was just there as a failsafe, someone to get the rest of them home. Someone to be used and abused. Andy didn't drink much and didn't take drugs really, though once he took what someone said was an E and it just made him sweat loads and have the complexion of a beetroot.

Andy was about to boldly go where he had never gone before and summon Blue Roy to not only order another drink but also quiz him about his enigmatic accessories when he noticed his brother casting his ever successful winning grin across the bar and carefully watching the trajectory of the mermaids he'd caught on his line as he reeled them in.

Great, Andy thought at the prospect of experiencing yet another pair of uneducated TOWIE bimbos slithering over each other to be the one to receive Mason's affections, even though he would probably shag both of them whilst Andy tried to sleep in the dingy hotel room with a pillow wrapped around his head to blot out the grunting.

He heard their voices before he saw them and knew his expectations were right. Essex girls were Mason's favourite.

"Alright mate," said the first to appear at the table, a skinny blonde who seemed to be mostly comprised of tits, arse and legs. Her skin was the colour of tomato Cup -a-soup which for some reason really turned Andy's stomach.

"Hey beautiful, I'm Mason," his brother said holding her hand lightly. "What's your name?"

The girl giggled, instantly smitten, "I'm Amy, spelt A-I-Y-M-E-E-E."

Mason's eyes went wide, "Wow, exotic! So many E's."

"Ooh, speaking of which have you had one of those pills that they've got here..."

Andy mentally switched off from their cringesome banter and turned to shrug in embarrassment at the girl's friend, no doubt a carbon copy who would proceed to either ignore him entirely because he was fat and ginger, or speak to him grudgingly after insisting he wasn't her type before he'd even said 'Hi.'

Andy was shocked when her friend appeared and seemed equally uncomfortable as he did.

She was a big, broad girl, wide at the hip and shoulders, with an amazing bust and thick, strong looking arms. Andy thought she looked like a female Viking, a warrior princess, like she could wipe the floor with any man in there and match them drink for drink. She was beautiful and natural, she wore glasses that were instantly a hit with Andy and had her naturally dark blonde hair scraped back into a ponytail. She was like an arse-kicking heroine hiding behind her librarian day job disguise. A small triangular symbol that Andy instantly recognised sat in the webbing between her thumb and index finger and the magic wand she had tattooed up that finger confirmed several things to Andy in that lingering but oh so fleeting moment, that she was a Harry Potter fan and quite possibly that meant a reader, of books. Andy felt faint in the presence of this Valkyrie. The fact that she blushed slightly when their eyes locked almost made him fall from his bar stool. The goddess was called Freya, and even though she had a similar accent to Aiymeee he was thankful that she made an effort with her pronunciation. Within five minutes Aiymeee was sitting astride Mason's lap, painting their faces and the bar walls with the whitewashes of a thousand selfies.

"I can't believe you're related to him," Freya said sipping at what Blue Roy had referred to as a *virgin cocktail*.

Here's where it turns sour, thought Andy, where she begins to tell him all about how gorgeous his brother is. He'd heard it all before, knew what she was about to say and an unusual bout of presumptuous attitude came over him.

"Yeah I know, we take after our Dads. Unluckily for me mine is everyone's image of a fat man called Dave." He rolled his eyes and downed the rest of his lager.

Freya burst into hooting laughter, which too seemed to be a rare occasion. Her hand deftly fluttered over her mouth as though she was ashamed of what Andy thought was a perfect smile.

"You're a funny guy, I like you," Freya said, flushed a little and rapidly changed the subject. "How are you liking the island?"

"It's great, beautiful place. It would be nice to actually see something other than pubs, clubs and beaches," Andy said before adding, "Not that there's anything wrong with those things. Either way, I'll end up going home with a brother who looks like an Italian movie-star and me looking like a lobster who's just come off the boil. I've just noticed there's an older part of the island and really hoped I'd get to check it out before we leave."

Freya nodded with enthusiasm, "You definitely should, it's amazing. I went there yesterday morning whilst Tit-Face over there was still shit-faced. I don't drink you see, wastes so much time and," she lowered her eyes and her voice, "there are other reasons that I don't really want to go into." She sipped her drink and brought a smile back to her face, "but the Old Town is wonderful. The buildings and stuff are beautiful, it's like being in Venice or something, not that I've been but I'm always watching holiday programmes you know, thirty minutes of somewhere different from bloody Chelmsford."

Andy was impressed but at the same time worried about her vow of alcoholic celibacy, did she frown upon others that drank, like him? What secrets was she hiding?

"If you want we could go have a wander around tomorrow?" Freya said, startling him.

Andy nodded over enthusiastically and jolted when someone came into the bar slamming the door open against the wall.

"Jesus Silvio, open the fucking door why don't you?" Blue Roy boomed from behind the bar at the newcomer. A black man wearing wraparound mirrored shades, shorts and a sleeveless fishing jacket grinned a mouthful of silver-capped teeth at the barman and greeted him like an old friend.

Aiymeee squealed like she had set eyes on a major celebrity and flapped her hands beside her face in excitement. "O.M.G. It's only bloody Silvio."

"The Silvio?" Mason said wide-eyed, enjoying the way Aiymeee was grinding on his lap. He didn't know who the fuck Silvio was but she obviously did, an air of jealousy surfaced as he wondered if he had competition.

"Silvio!" Aiymeee shrieked across the bar waving frantically.

Mason watched as the famous (to Aiymeee at least) Silvio winked at Blue Roy, shared some complicated handshake and strode towards their table.

"Silvio's one of the best DJs ever!" Aiymeee said, addressing Freya and Andy for the first time since joining the table, as the man moved towards them. "We saw him at Flava last night and his set was epic, and I mean totally epic, weren't it Frey?"

Freya nodded, her smile as fake as her younger cousin. "Totally epic."

Aiymeee noticed the whispered words between her and the fat ginger boy, and the mutual sniggers but didn't care as one of her idols stood by their table.

"Ladies," Silvio said and shone his twinkling smile at Aiymeee and Freya before quickly sizing up Mason and Andy, "and gentlemen."

"We was at Flava last night, me and my cousin Freya, your set was totally amaze, I caught a bit of the vinyl of the last song you played when you smashed it at the end and I'm going to treasure it forever," Aiymeee blurted out, her Essex accent flowing as freely as the alcohol she had imbibed.

Silvio nodded gratefully, and surveyed them all from behind his sunglasses.

"You all need to come to Indigo tonight for a bit of retro boogie."

Aiymeee frowned. She'd not seen it on any of the socials, not Twitter, not Facebook, nothing.

"What's that? Are you going to be there?"

"Yes, I am pretty lady, and you four should be there too. A musical education is what Indigo is, it'll take you back in time to when your parents were kids, and hey the prices are as cheap too."

"Sounds epic," Aiymeee said laughing excitedly.

"Club Indigo is a very special place, only one night every ten years man!" Silvio said, the glittering smile never seeming to leave his face.

"What the fuck?" Mason blurted out. Surely this big event would have been advertised everywhere and then he had a flashback of an insanely hot girl who was naked save for yellow glittered body paint handing him a purple diamond-shaped flyer with simply the word 'Indigo' and a date embossed on it. He reached into the back pocket of his shorts, pulled out the flyer and gasped as Aiymeee, Freya and Andy did the same.

"Woah... I've never seen this in my life!" Freya said, dropping the card to the table like it burned, as a hazy recollection of a tall attractive bearded man with glitter on his cheeks and a cute smile surfaced like a long forgotten memory.

Andy nodded in agreement, "Did you plant this? Some kind of sleight of hand thing?" Then he too questioned himself when he remembered a shy looking girl in a pink vest and shorts handing it to him the previous night.

Aiymeee chuckled, "Oh yeah I remember now, some big bodybuilder guy in a thong gave it to me at Flava last night, he'd got glitter everywhere," she cackled at Freya, "and I mean everywhere."

"You remember for sure Aiymeee," Silvio said with a leer. "You'll probably be pissing glitter for a week."

Mason roared with laughter as Silvio's obscenity unravelled itself in his head and Aiymeee slapped the guy jokingly on the forearm.

"Oi, you dirty bastard."

Silvio smiled and he turned to watch Blue Roy vanish through a door at the back of the bar. "Now, I want to make sure you kids have the time of your lives." He slid two fingers inside one of the many pockets of his fisherman's gilet and dangled a small transparent bag containing four small, violet tablets with a little stick man on each. "These are Colossus..."

"They're the ones I was telling you about," Aiymeee said

to Mason, clapping her hands. "The ones that last for like nine hours with no come-down!"

"No, thank you," Freya said politely and turned to look at Andy, hoping he would decline. Not for her benefit but because she hoped he was better than that and wanted him to go out with her the next day.

"Nah, I'm alright, cheers," Andy said sheepishly.

"How much?" Mason asked and was amazed at Silvio's reply. He fished into his wallet and handed the euros to the man. "Let me buy all four."

Silvio's eyes went wide and he became serious, threatening even, "Now don't you go thinking you're Bertie Big Bollocks and taking more than one of these things like you would back at home, brother. These babies are not your bog standard backstreet MDMA you understand?"

Mason nodded, even though the older man had scolded him like a teacher would a schoolboy. "For tomorrow, like."

"Tomorrow?" Silvio said in disbelief before his regular happy demeanour returned, "For tomorrow, okay." He snatched the notes from Mason's hand and whispered into his ear whilst shaking his other hand.

Silvio stepped back and pointed at the four them.

"I'll see you all later. Indigo opens at midnight, don't be taking them until at least eleven forty-five, do you hear me? Go play, have fun, do what you young folk do best, then come find me at Indigo." With that, the mysterious Silvio left them.

"I don't care, I'm not taking one."

Andy heard Freya shout at her cousin as they walked ahead of him and Mason down the street towards the beach. He felt Mason elbow him in the ribs.

"Hey bro, you and Freya seem to be getting on alright," Mason said and appeared genuinely happy for him.

Andy smiled, "She's fucking amazing man. I really, really like her but I kinda don't want to at the same time in case this is just some holiday shit."

"Chill man, I don't think either of you two are like that, and if it is then it is. Take it as it comes. Trust me." Mason put his arm around Andy's shoulders and blew sweet marijuana smoke into his face.

Most of the bars had closed, encouraging the traffic to flow towards the island's major clubs if people wanted to continue their night.

The multitude of revellers seemed to be migrating towards the beach. Up ahead Andy could make out the green fishing jacket of Silvio as he no doubt sold more drugs and hustled people to come to the once in a decade event. He saw the DJ-come-drug dealer throw his arms about wildly as two men grabbed him and dragged him into an alleyway between two sand-coloured buildings.

"Dude, I'm going to get us all a beer to take out," Mason said and vanished before Andy could point out the incident.

"Oi! Leave him alone!"

Aiymeee had obviously seen the commotion as he watched her race ahead, her stiletto heels clacking against the road.

"Aiymeee!" Freya screeched as her cousin vanished around the corner and into the dimly lit alley. Freya's taste in footwear wasn't as loud on the cobbles as Aiymeee's and the way she bolted after she suggested they weren't as awkward to move in.

Andy stood, momentarily frozen, transfixed and terrified. His gut told him to be a man and give chase, to assist in any way he could but his brain encouraged him to stall by filling his head with no end of potential street crime scenarios. He rubbed his sweating palms over his podgy red cheeks and across his ginger stubbled scalp, gritted his teeth against the fear threatening to overwhelm him, shouted, "Fuuuuuuck!" and raced after the woman of his dreams.

He was out of breath by the time his squeaking shoes hit the corner and he honestly thought his heart was going to exit his chest in the style of everyone's favourite Ridley Scott extra-terrestrial.

"Sweet baby Jesus!" Andy exclaimed, hands grasping his knees as relief washed over him like a welcomed rain shower after a heatwave. "Thank fuck for that."

Whatever the reason for those men accosting Silvio in such an abrupt manner, it wasn't violent. The two men were crouched around a third who sat on the alley floor propped up against the wall. Silvio stood before them smiling uncomfortably at Aiymeee and Freya.

Andy walked towards them, taking a look at the three guys. They were just party goers, young like the rest of them, nothing dodgy about them. The guy on the floor was mumbling to himself, his pink shirt plastered to his chest like a second skin, drool foamed and dribbled from the corners of his mouth.

"Shit, is he okay?" Andy said, directing the question to no one in particular.

"No, this geezer sold him some shit gear." A greasy looking boy with bleached hair said, his eyes frightful.

"I'm calling an ambulance," Aiymeee said, whipping out her mobile phone before looking doubtfully at Freya and Andy. "Do they have ambulances here?"

"Of course they fu..." Freya began but Silvio waved his hands about in the air.

"Now everybody calm down, alright. Everything's okay and under control."

"How can you say that when our mate is having a fucking fit?" the other lad said in a prepubescent squeak.

Silvio grinned and turned to Freya and Andy, singling them out as the sensible ones they were. "Guys, this happens all the time. Why do you think I told your mate back there not to take more than one Colossus? These babies aren't your regular E, man, you get me? I told you." He turned back to the two boys and gave them an expression that was half-sympathetic, half-angry, "and I told you, boys, too."

Freya barged past Silvio and the two boys and crouched down to get a closer look at their semi-comatose friend.

"She did a first-aid course once," Aiymeee bragged proudly. "She's well clever, my cousin."

Silvio winked at her, "I can tell it runs in the family."

Aiymeee snickered and Andy moved away from the sickening display of flirting passing between the DJ and the girl to see if he could do anything.

The boy's eyes were half-closed and he had a stupid, happy grin on his face, despite the trailing saliva. His lips moved lazily like they were made of rubber and he laughed groggily and muttered something indecipherable about crabs and waves.

"Jesus man, he's tripping his balls off, big time," Freya said to Andy, in a voice that made it sound like an official diagnosis. Andy agreed even though he didn't have a clue as to what that would look like.

"Rameses colossus," the boy whispered and a large wet patch appeared on his khaki shorts.

"Urgh, he's pissed himself!" shouted one of the boy's mates.

"Chill, bro. Listen, this stuff is relatively harmless, the guy is just having a massive, massive good time right now like you wouldn't believe." Silvio said putting an arm around each of the two boy's shoulders. "Wouldn't surprise me if that isn't even piss if you get me?"

The two boys laughed, then recoiled in horror.

Silvio hugged the boys closer and took a more serious tone, "Listen, it's not long now until Indigo starts, get your mate up on his feet, keep him upright, try and get him to drink some water. Bring him to the club, yeah? They've got medically trained peeps there, better than the hospital here, but truth be told he'll be fine in the chill out room. They'll look after him, trust me."

All eyes radiated towards Andy and Freya, the sensible ones. Andy shrugged and even though she seemed doubtful Freya sighed and said, "Well, they can't be any worse than the rumours I've heard about this place's hospital." She looked at the two boys. "But it's your call, he's your mate."

The two boys exchanged glances and the bleached one took a deep breath.

"We're taking him to the club."

"Alright!" his friend said, punching the air.

Silvio clapped his hands together.

"Right you guys, get him on his feet and get him to the club, yeah? I'll see you all there."

Andy grimaced beneath the semi-conscious boy's sweaty armpit. One arm trailed over his shoulders and the other over the squeaky-voiced kid who said his name was Joe.

Mason appeared out of nowhere, the necks of four bottled beers between his fingers. "Took fucking ages to get served. What did I miss?" He noticed the three other boys and his brother helping to prop one of them up.

"Rameses colossus," the coma kid spluttered before his head flopped onto his chest.

"Took the words right out of my mouth mate," Mason said and shoved a beer bottle in Andy's free hand, watching proudly as his little brother necked the contents in one go.

They left the three boys on a wall at the beach side with promises of finding them in the queue at Indigo. The semi-conscious chap had perked up a bit but still seemed a planet away, muttering gibberish about the colossus tablets.

"I'm glad we fucked them dudes off," Mason said, absentmindedly staring at Aiymeee's butt as she walked across the sand beside Freya, shoes in one hand, beer in the other.

"They were alright," Andy protested, "I just don't think that guy should have taken the pills is all. I think you should throw them away Mace, you don't want to end up like him."

"I don't know," Mason reflected, "he looked kinda happy to me. Anyway, chillax bro, I'm an expert at taking drugs, no one handles them better than me."

Andy shuddered, a spliced video of one of the worst presidents America had ever elected crossed his mind where the piggish, small-handed boar in a wig made of piss-soaked straw bragged about himself, almost every line taken from numerous speeches contained the phrase "no one does... better than me." He hoped that Mason wasn't going to end up in a bad way, like he hoped Donald Trump would.

Ahead of them was a gigantic bonfire, the tiny silhouettes of people milled around before it. They had decided a refreshing walk on the beach would stimulate their minds enough naturally to face whatever festivities Indigo had to offer. The fire was stacked high and as they got closer they could hear the sound of merriment and celebration. A few of the local islanders, dark-haired and deeply tanned nodded at Mason and called out greetings in Spanish or French. Andy found this hilarious as his brother clearly didn't know what they were saying to him, although neither did they, obviously assuming he was local due to his complexion.

They could feel the heat from the flames and began to make out finer details, people with portable barbecues handing out bottled beer, a tractor and trailer was parked at a safe distance from the fire and people were hurling what looked like clothes and luggage onto the pyre. They quickened their pace, hoping to score some free food maybe before the long night ahead when a familiar figure jogged towards them. Blue Roy.

"Hey, kids how you all doing?" he said in his strangely inappropriate voice. He sounded like a Shakespearean actor.

His breath smelt of fish and rum. "You guys having a good night?"

"It got a bit weird earlier but it's cool now," Aiymeee said leaning forward and hugging the muscly bartender. "That Silvio sold us some..."

"Tickets," Mason blurted out, remembering that the dealer DJ had waited for the barman to be out of view before he touted his wares. "He sold us some tickets for Indigo."

Blue Roy slapped his hand over his mouth and closed his eyes, Andy noticed what looked like a map of the island on his right eyelid and felt queasy at what that must have felt like being tattooed.

"Listen, you seem like good kids, you don't want to be hanging around that Silvio, he's dodgy as fuck. And you don't want to be going to Indigo either," Blue Roy said with genuine concern.

The group couldn't deny the suspicions about Silvio but Mason wanted to know what was wrong with the nightclub and it's once in a decade event.

"Why shouldn't we go? This is a once in a lifetime event."

Blue Roy shot a look at the islanders behind him, nodded a greeting to an old couple who made their way to the fire carrying a picnic hamper and waited for them to leave before answering. "Indigo is only here once every ten years or so."

"And?" Mason said, finishing his beer.

"It's cursed."

"How can a nightclub be cursed?" Aiymeee asked, wide-eyed.

"Back in the seventies was when the nightclub scene really picked up on the island, all night parties and all day hangovers. The sun seemed to sweat it out of you, especially if you had a fair dose of carbs. I still swear by my hangover preventative, you kids never listen but one day if you try it you'll see I'm right." Blue Roy rubbed a hand with a detailed

map of an unfamiliar island on its back across his face.
"Mashed potato. At the end of a night's drinking force yourself
to eat mashed potato." He smirked at Aiymeee's disgusted
face and dry retching. He continued his story.
"There was a club run by some fella from God knows where
called Rameses. He called it Indigo..."
   "Woah!" Andy blurted out, "that's what that out-of-it
dude kept saying remember? Rameses."
   The others nodded and began to listen to Blue Roy's
story more seriously.
   "Oh, most people here know about Indigo, it was a
world-famous club back in the seventies. It was the place to
be, full of cheap booze, cheap pharmaceuticals and even
cheaper people. Disco was big then and the music was so loud
that you could feel it rattle your bones. Purple lasers would
pass over the beaches nearby like spotlights, it seemed to
draw people in. Other clubs began to crumble whilst this place
flourished and bloomed like a fucking orchid. Obviously,
some people don't like healthy competition and a couple of
the big players who ran the other clubs teamed together and
destroyed the place.
   "Now, the owner of Indigo was obsessed with disco
music and the dancing, he was always on the dance floor each
and every night, was famous for it. The clubs that plotted
against him wanted to finish him, and his club. Someone
started a fire, I forget whereabouts, and they rigged up a trap
to see the owner off. Every night he would be below the dance
floor's centrepiece, the world's biggest glitter-ball. He called it
Colossus."
   Andy shook his head smacked his brother in the ribs,
"Dude, colossus!"
   Mason tried to disguise his mutual shock at yet another
familiar word but put it down to the lore of the island. If
everyone knew about this infamous club apart from them then
it was probably common knowledge and no doubt where they

got the name for Silvio's wonder drug.

"There's a couple of bars on the island called Colossus," Blue Roy offered, noticing that the word seemed familiar to them, "and even a bloody road. All named after a great big old glitter-ball.

"I was there when it happened, people were shouting fire and somebody cut the music. Everyone, even Rameses, froze when they did that, right beneath the glitter-ball. Then the fucking thing dropped from the ceiling and squashed Rameses and everyone underneath it. When it hit the floor it went off like a bomb." Blue Roy smirked at the rapt teenagers. "And that's how I've got this on my back." He span round and displayed the metallic shrapnel Andy and Mason had argued about at the beginning of the evening. Freya laughed drily, she didn't believe Blue Roy's story. The likelihood that the remnants of a thirty-odd-year-old glitter-ball would still be in the barman's back was ridiculous.

"Didn't they take the glass out of you when you..."

"Now, I know what you're thinking," Blue Roy said, seemingly oblivious that Freya had spoken, like this was all rehearsed. "Why have I still got the glass in my back? Like I said I don't know anything about Indigo's owner but I'm suspecting there was some weird voodoo shit in his background as every time I've had the glass removed it's come back."

Andy let out a laugh and instantly went cold under the man's angry stare.

"You ain't heard the worst of it, mate. Every ten years to that night, the nightclub appears, like some fucking glammed up Brigadoon, and it attracts people like yourselves with its fancy lights and promises of a good time, and the next day there's several hundred missing people. It's got to the point where the authorities here just keep it quiet, say the missing were seen leaving the airport, there's always that many connecting flights from here to anywhere anything could happen. But the kids are still missing."

Freya frowned at Andy in mild amusement, trying to see if he believed any part of the weird barman's story, whilst Aiymeee huddled terrified beneath Mason's arm.

Blue Roy cocked a thumb over his shoulder at the people who were throwing stuff on to the bonfire. "All that stuff is your belongings from the islands' hotels and hostels."

Aiymeee shrieked and pulled away from Mason and stepped towards the fire. He grabbed her arm and squared up to Blue Roy, shoving him with one hand. "He's taking the fucking piss!"

Blue Roy was momentarily stunned. He circled around Mason, the light from the fire illuminating his face, chest and stomach.

Andy felt his legs go weak, there was no way his brother could hold his own in a fight against this man, he was fucking huge, a giant. A colossus.

Mason's stare was venomous, he hated feeling that people were mocking him. He had heard similar far-fetched stories about the party islands before, locals abducting teenagers and chaining them up in warehouses like in those Eli Roth films, for rich people to buy and torture. It was scaremongering, locals trying to have a laugh at their expense.

"Bullshit," he said, losing confidence now he could feel the effects of the Colossus tablet he had secretly taken when he went off to buy beer begin to work. The waters of Blue Roy's tattoos began to swirl and swish, minute waves crashing against tiny, permanently inked shores. He could see seagulls the size of sand grains hovering over the man's skin.

Shouting from the crowds at the fire broke the awkward silence. Blue Roy turned towards the silhouettes of several people gesticulating wildly. Their words were barely decipherable but had an aggressive tone. Andy saw Blue Roy's face take on the look of a scolded schoolboy before he turned back to stare at his brother. Blue Roy stepped back and bellowed with laughter so loud a few of the islanders behind him turned in their direction, tears fell over his cheeks as he hugged Mason against his broad chest, "No flies on you is there mate?"

Andy breathed with relief, "Jesus, I thought you were going to kill him."

Blue Roy assumed that he had been addressing him, "Nah don't be daft mate, I'm a pacifist me. Right," he pointed behind them back the way they had come, "be off with you, your night's only just started."

The four turned around and stared in awe at wide purple laser beams that came from somewhere on the seafront, passing over the beach in slow motion like Wells' Martian death ray discolouring the people's faces.

As they made their way across the sand, Andy noticed most of the revellers that had previously been at smaller gatherings dotted about the coastline dropped what they were doing as the light passed over them. Along the beach side street people spilt from other clubs and the few remaining open bars, as Club Indigo drew them in.

They saw the three boys from before. Andy and Freya called out to them, racing up the sand spattered steps leading up off the beach but the boys seemed oblivious to their shouts. The lad who had been semi-comatose before shuffled along ahead of the other two. The fact that he was walking unaided gave both Andy and Freya reassurance.

Freya waited at the top of the steps for Andy and the others, arms folded across her stomach. Andy smiled as the purple rays passed over her, she looked like a warrior princess against an alien landscape.

"I hope they turn these fucking lights off soon, they're doing my head in," she said as Andy approached her.

He momentarily squinted as they lit over him. "Once we

get on the streets if we walk the same side as the buildings it should be okay, more sheltered like."

"Good thinking, Batman," Freya smiled at stole a glance over his shoulder. "What's keeping your brother and Aiymeee?"

"Oh, he was going off on one about Blue Roy's tattoos moving and then him and your cousin started rolling around in the sand and I didn't want to get too close if you know what I mean?"

Freya chuckled and muttered something under her breath.

"What? What did you say?"

"I said 'lucky Aiymeee'." Freya grinned and turned her face in embarrassment.

I knew it! Andy thought as the bottom dropped out of his world, yet another poor soul defenceless to his brother's incredible good looks. He tried to hide his crestfallen, shattered emotions but it wasn't enough to fool Freya. She smiled apologetically at Andy. He hated that smile, it was the same on all the previous girls' faces just before he was well and truly shoehorned into the friend zone.

"I'm sorry," Freya began but Andy had had enough, he didn't want to hear the spiel again, not from her. He had let his own defences down and had foolishly thought he may have had a chance with her.

"Just forget it!" Andy snapped, totally out of character but it was either anger or sobbing that wanted to come out of him and he felt like he had cried enough in front of girls. He pushed past Freya and jogged across the road, narrowly missed by a couple on a moped.

"Andy!" Freya called, wondering what the hell had gotten into the boy.

"Ey, if you're not going to drink that I will!" Aiymeee's voice screeched in her ear and she grabbed the full bottle of beer that she still held in her hand.

The realisation of what she had said and what Andy must have thought sunk in and Freya found her own temper boil.

"For fuck sake!" She snatched the beer bottle back out of Aiymeee's hand, saw the sparkle in her eyes and the smudged lipstick over Mason's gurning mouth and jammed the bottleneck between her lips and thrust her head back.

Aiymeee watched in horror as her cousin drained the bottle's contents without pausing for breath before hurling the empty at the beachside wall.

"Alright, Freya's got her game on!" Mason cheered bringing an eventual smile to Aiymeee's face.

Freya whipped a hand up behind her head, pulled her hair tie out, shook her dark blonde locks over her shoulders and into the hot night air shrieked her war cry, "Let's go fucking disco!"

It sounded like the battle-cries of an approaching army or the chanting of die-hard football fanatics. The shouting was rhythmic; one, two -break- one, two, three, four. It filled the narrow streets as the mob ascended the hill through the town. A solitary feminine voice shrieked a command, "Let's go!"

Her followers replied in unison, "Fucking disco!"

Andy sat staring at the bend in the road where the noise was coming from. Any second the lynch mob would come around that corner, flaming torches held aloft as they prepared to storm the fabled discotheque. Then she appeared, fist punching towards the stars, hair billowing out behind her as she led her people. Boudicca had nothing on Freya the Fantastic.

"Let's go!" She screamed, her face raised towards the passing purple lights.

"Fucking disco!" cheered the crowd at her heels, Mason and Aiymeee followed closely behind their leader making sure they were kept in the highest of ranks.

Andy was all things at once but mostly horrified and horny. What the Hell had happened to his Freya?

She ploughed her way through the few bemused people in her path and grabbed fistfuls of Andy's soaked black shirt. Two buttons hit the air, exposing a bit more chest flesh than he was comfortable with. Freya's startling eyes bore into his as she thrust her face towards him like she was going in for a head-butt. "I fucking want you," she roared majestically and Andy waited for a variety of expected phrases to follow.

"I fucking want you... to fuck off!"

"I fucking want you... to eat shit and die!"

"I fucking want you... to fuck off, eat shit and then die!" Delete wherever applicable, but no more words followed, only something that made his heart stop, sphincter clench and penis soar.

Freya crushed her lips against his in one of the most viciously passionate kisses he would ever experience in his life. The strength of Freya's embrace felt capable of cracking ribs and he fucking loved every second of it.

Freya's army cheered; the three boys they had helped earlier, dozens of other party goers, and then silence befell the group at a raise of her hand.

Andy faced the throng wide-eyed, his lips throbbing from Freya's kiss. They were waiting on him, his reaction, whether he would help lead them in their victory or run to the hills with his erection pummelling against his flabby thigh. Andy fought the urge no longer, felt the power of Freya's gesture flood him and explode from every pore.

"LET'S GO FUCKING DISCO!"

As they reached the crest of the hill, their chants alternating between *Let's go fucking disco* to *Rameses, Colossus* as suggested by the previously comatose kid, they beheld the holy grail of their heroic quest.

Club Indigo.

It sat embedded into the cliff like a gigantic white shell, a smaller less pointy version of the Sydney Opera House. Two long antennae jutted from the curved white roof, each shining over the town and beaches below.

Bright purple letters hung above a dark, oval entrance bespeckled with scintillating pink and violet lights. Humongous speakers that throbbed with disco beats framed the entrance whilst twin cannons shot bombs of exploding glitter over their heads.

Silvio stood in the doorway wearing a hideous lilac suit with bell-bottomed flares. Surrounding him was a legion of helpers; men who were built like Trojans, women like beautiful ethereal sirens.

"Welcome," he boomed, his voice bellowing from the twin speakers, "to Club Indigo." He whipped off his mirrored sunglasses and bright silver lights shone where his eyes should be.

"Now that's fucking cool," Andy heard Mason shout before everyone went wild.

Silvio laughed and picked up on the chants of Freya's crowd, "Rameses! Colossus!" He turned his glowing eyes away from the people and entered the club, his entourage of staff vanishing ahead of him.

They walked across plush, purple carpets, the crowd hooting with excitement. Freya squeezed Andy's hand, mischief in her eyes. Small versions of the glitter cannons shot gold and silver glitter into the air and something somewhere pumped in the intoxicatingly sweet scent of Parma Violets.

Silvio stopped before the entrance to a huge dancefloor, his eyes now glittering with contact lenses that covered the whole area of his visible eyes.

"Now my groovy young things, everything you see here tonight is free, free to you all. We have drinks," he waved a hand towards his crew of helpers who reappeared carrying silver platters of champagne flutes filled with purple liquid and bowls filled with what looked like Colossus pills. Andy wondered whether the whole drug thing was a con, whether they were just placebos or sweets, another one of the islanders' gimmicks to draw them to the club. A glance at his brother told him otherwise, there was no way his brother and Aiymeee, plus numerous members of the congregation, could be this deliriously happy without drugs.

"The club is now closed. It has reached its maximum capacity. Take what you want, it's all yours," Silvio crowed. Andy craned his neck and looked through the people behind him and saw that the doors were now closed. Well, that wasn't quite right, he couldn't actually see the doors, whether it be due to the lighting or the dry ice being pumped into the air, the entrance wall was just a misty blur.

"Come on, let's go get a drink," Freya said leading Andy a huge muscular man wearing nothing but silver glitter and a thong. The music began the moment Silvio climbed onto a small stage at the front of the dance floor. Freya gestured to the drinks and held up two fingers. The server's expression was blank, almost robotic, as he lowered the tray. His eyes showed twin reflections of her and Andy. She took two glasses and gave one to Andy.

"Woah, did you see that guy's eyes?" Andy said, bewildered as he held the flute's stem between thumb and finger.

"Yeah," Freya started, pressing her mouth closed to Andy's ear to be heard. "Crazy contacts aren't they?"

Andy nodded, wondering if he had imagined the blood surrounding them or whether it had been some macabre makeup effect. He sniffed his drink with suspicion and tried to get another look at the man.

"Quick," Freya blurted and dragged him across the dancefloor spilling the majority of his drink over his wrist.

A spotlight shone down onto the figure of Silvio on the

stage, where he stood Christ-like, arms outstretched and beamed his silver-plated smile at his adoring crowd. The trick contact lenses shone brighter, with an intensity that seemed impossible. People squinted through drug-blurred eyes and persistently hollered in celebration at the light show.

When Silvio spoke again his voice had changed, become sultry and dark with the velvet tones of someone who serenades romantic diners, Barry White laced with spiced rum and dark chocolate.

"I am Rameses. I am Colossus. I am the Discohead."

Andy squeezed his eyes closed as the light from Silvio temporarily blinded everyone, a few panicked squeals were heard before the glare lessened and everyone gasped in wonder.

Where Silvio's head had been sat a rotating glitter-ball, its many-faceted surfaces raining a myriad of light motes over the people, mosaics of silver painting their faces.

"I am the Discohead." This time the voice came from everywhere. Andy watched as the crowd fixated on the stage, spellbound by Silvio's magical transformation. They appeared drugged, which they obviously were, people had been cramming themselves with the proffered free Colossus pills and hypnotised by the spinning, orb-headed entity on stage.

"Rameses! Colossus!" The people cheered, their mouths working in unison, jaws moving in perfect synchronisation, their faces completely expressionless like the glitter covered drink server.

"Let's boogie," the Discohead said and the sudden pow-pow of disco music that matched Andy's racing heartbeat drowned out all other noise. On the stage, the Discohead began to dance.

The glitter-ball on the Discohead's shoulders span, fleeting patterns of light tripped over the already drug-addled eyes in the crowd, everyone danced in time, the same dance.

Andy thought it was weird, staged. They weren't just copying the guy who led them, their motion was too fluid. They stared blankly at the dancing vision and mirrored his moves with perfect mimicry like he was a fitness guru.

Andy pushed his way through the people, their empty expressions unnerving him. "Why's everyone acting so weird?" Freya clutched at his hand and tugged on his arm.

Andy was glad he wasn't the only one that seemed unaffected by the strange choreography. He thought back to the pills everyone had been taking and Silvio's precise recommendation of when to take them. "It's gotta be the Colossus pills."

The crowd moved as one, their backs to Freya and Andy as they all ducked and swirled in synchronisation. "This ain't right," Andy said as they searched the back of the dance floor for an exit.

"We need to get the others and go, this is some cultish, mind-control bollocks and has to totally be illegal." Freya let go of Andy and scoured the crowds for her cousin and Mason.

Andy followed apprehensively, using his hand to shield his eyes from the glitter-ball's lights. If he looked at it for too long it made him feel queasy. Freya pushed through the people.

"It's like they're in a trance or something, look at them." She spotted a dimly lit doorway and made her way towards it still searching for Aiymeee and Mason. She stopped suddenly, Andy slamming into her back.

"Andy," Freya said stepping aside to show him what she had spotted. "They've let little kids in here." Andy saw them then, whole families dancing together in the crowd. The lack of any kind of health and safety or security added to the perplexity of the place and he knew he wanted out even more. Surely they've not let the children take the drugs? Andy considered the craziness of what was happening and what taboos would be broken if that was the truth.

"It's the lights!" Freya shouted back at him and pointed to the sparkly headed figure.

Andy spotted the silhouettes of his brother and Aiymeee and a sudden burst of adrenaline took over.

"Come on I've seen them."

Freya let him take lead and they jostled the zombified dancers out of their way.

Andy grabbed Mason by the shoulders and tried to spin him around to face him but he shrugged him off with unnatural strength.

"Mason!" he shouted and shouldered a couple of people out of the way to stand in his brother's line of vision. Mason's jaw sagged, his expression different from the others. Drool ran over his designer stubble and his pupils were wide, absorbing the lights from the Discohead. Andy slapped him hard across the cheek, instantly fearing rebuttal but welcoming it nonetheless. For a second Mason's trance wavered and he moaned, "Go."

Andy pulled on his brother's arm but Mason used the current dance move to swerve, pirouette and fling him to the floor.

Andy wriggled on the floor, dodging stamping feet. A stilettoed heel came down hard on the webbing of skin between his thumb and finger, he screamed as the dancer span around.

Freya shoved the woman aside, knocking her into two other people but none of them broke their step.

"Come on, Aiymeee's as fucked as your brother, let's go."

She pulled Andy to his feet. He looked at the bloody hole in his hand and agreed that they needed to get out, regardless of anyone else. A hand shot out of the crowd and clamped around his forearm, he turned and saw his brother's face, an horrific mask of agony.

Mason fought against the urges, the driving force behind the perpetual trance, everything was betraying him, his body and his brain. All he wanted to do was dance and give into the exquisite bliss that bloomed behind his eyes but he knew it was wrong.

He struggled with the pull the Discohead had over him, knew the combination of the drug and flashing lights were somehow manipulating him. Andy was okay, he had a chance of getting away if he avoided the lights.

He hadn't taken the Colossus pills, Mason hadn't spiked his drink, Andy's was the only one he hadn't. He forced his face back around as his body jerked away from his brother.

"Get away!" he spat the words out through lips that tried to defy his order. "I'm sorry about Freya."

Andy barely understood what his brother had said but could see that he was trying to refuse the hold the Discohead had over him. He spat more words out before his body jolted as though electrocuted and he whirled away into the crowd.

"Andy!" he heard Freya shriek, as the whole dance floor erupted into an explosion of silver light. The music stopped and the dancing with it.

The light came from the dancers. Everyone in the club now stared blankly through mirrored eyes.
Freya dragged Andy through the statue still people towards the doorway she had noticed earlier, the lights from the crowd's eyes making it clearer.

On the stage, the looming presence of the Discohead beckoned them.

"Andy, Freya, don't leave me this way," he crooned, from the walls surrounding a backing track of synthetic drumbeats and guitars that went whacka-whacka filled the spaces between words.

Andy and Freya looked at each other incredulously and quickened their pace towards the doorway.

"Don't be crazy like a fool. Come back to funky town."
Freya elbowed the motionless partygoers out of her way,

their scintillating stares following them as she walked through to the darkened doorway.

"Andy, come on Daddio, come back in and feel the love."

The disembodied voice came from all around them. They entered a dim corridor, ahead two female glittered staff members appeared from out of nowhere. They danced before Andy and opened their eyes. Twin tiny mirror-balls spun where eyeballs should be, light emanating from within, hypnotising and seducing him at the same time.

"Feel the love, Andy, feel it. We have it all here, baby. Dance with us, know ecstasy like you never would believe. Let your young heart run free."

Andy was spellbound by the glitter girls' sensual movements, their glowing disco-ball eyes flickering over his blue, dilating his pupils and making him look drunk.

"Oi, slag!" Freya roared in frustration and swung her handbag around into one of the gyrating girls. The bag struck the girl's head and it exploded like glass. Sharp splintered particles flew everywhere. Freya shut her eyes instinctively and felt fragments pepper her cheeks and chest.

The sound of the girl's head breaking shook Andy from his haze, he gawped as the decapitated corpse gave out a pathetic solitary spurt of glittered blood from an otherwise clean neck stump and fell to the floor. The remaining girl thrust her fistful of pills at Freya's face, the big girl let out a choked yelp as she felt half a dozen pills slide down her throat.

"Nooo," Andy yelled and threw the first punch he had ever thrown at the back of the girl's head, the silver platter of pills crashed to her feet. His hand disappeared into the explosion of flesh coloured glass, tearing his skin to shreds. He screamed and shoved the girl's falling body away from him. Without stopping to check her state, he grabbed Freya with his good hand and ran.

Andy pressed his hand against the dark walls and recoiled at the vile sensation. The walls were warm and sticky and squished beneath his touch like flesh. The passageway he had run down tapered off into a dead end. Freya staggered, zombie-like, beside him.

"Rameses. Colossus," she muttered through sagging lips, thick frothy spittle flowing from her mouth.

"Andy, come on groover don't be a drag."

The voice reverberated through the floor.

Andy dug his fingers into the soft texture of the wall and felt it give way into fibrous strands. He forced his fist into it and felt the warm sea air on his skin. With renewed vigour he yanked at the substance, even using his bloodied hand.

"ANDY!"

He spun around at sound of the voice.

The Discohead stood behind Freya, brown hands caressing her shoulders. The ball atop his shoulders whirred, hundreds of tiny images of Andy's frightened red face in the spinning mass. Behind the Discohead stood all the dancers, glitter-ball pupils mimicking their God.

"There is nowhere to hide Andy. My followers are as many as the fragments of the original Colossus. When that glitter-ball smashed I forged them out of blood and glass. The site on which we stand was once a shrine to The Great Crustacean."

Andy heard the Discohead's head spin slower, the lights flitting through the thin membrane of his closed eyes.

"For years I kept Him sated by ritualistic dancing and cavorting, the vibrations soothed him in his sleep beneath the rock." The whirring began to slow, even more, the flickering fading. Andy opened his eyes and faced the surreal entity holding the woman of his dreams, his glitter-eyed minions poised behind him. Something round and silver lay by his foot.

The Discohead continued his story, the once spinning

globe now still.

"But now The Great Crustacean roams and only The Map knows where he's going next."

Andy threw the metal platter like a Frisbee. It flew across space between them and struck the Discohead's glitter-ball head. A loud crack resounded and everyone apart from him, the Discohead and Freya fell to the floor screaming. Sickly pink light seeped from a deep fissure splitting the glitter-ball in two.

Andy leapt forward and pulled the semi-comatose Freya towards him and thrust himself against the disintegrating wall. His arm burst through the fibrous wall, scrabbling around for something or someone to help free them from this insanity. A powerful force tugged him back into the club and snapped his arm at the elbow. He thought the Discohead had got him at the last second but as he was thrown to the floor he saw him cradling his cracked sphere, the partygoers shrieking at his feet as blood poured from their eyes and they screamed out for help that would never come. Freya gazed down at him, his twisted arm clenched in her fist, she lifted her eyelids and twin glitter-balls whirled where her eyes should be.

The Discohead pushed the pieces of his fractured cranium together, the pink light helping it meld. He stepped towards Andy, carefully avoiding the injured dancers like they were important and meant something to him. Andy screamed and begged for his life as he saw his brother clawing at his own gore filled eye sockets.

The Discohead stopped and raised a dark brown hand to him as if to offer assistance.

"All you've managed to do is save yourself and everyone here a blissful, euphoric death. We are Colossus. Colossus is us."

The Map, otherwise known as Blue Roy by the locals, stood on the edge of the beach with the islanders and stared up at the oval hump of Club Indigo shimmering against the rocks. The letters of its sign bled into one another and absorbed into the two antennae. Two purple orbs opened out on each end. The shell-shaped building rose from the rocks on eight segmented legs the length of buses and coated in a mottled orange armour.

It never failed to fill him, or any of the islanders, with simultaneous fear and wonderment. His tattoos burned, the edges of the depicted continents and islands stinging like freshly injected ink. The waves of a multitude of oceans and seas, some familiar, some forgotten, all real, churned on his skin as The Great Crustacean crawled its crazy-legged dance down the cliff-side across the sands towards the sea.

He winced as a tiny replica of the crab-god forced its way out of his right tear duct and crawled away from the small island on his eyelid and entered the waters of his cheek.

Blue Roy and the islanders combed the beach for any remnants of the clubbers, although they knew that all would be contained within The Great Crustacean. He spotted a severed hand, the skin freckled and fair, and was amazed that someone had almost found their way out, he had never known The Great Crustacean to have weaknesses before.

The islanders sighed with relief when the monster vanished beneath the waves, grateful that there had been enough souls on board to satisfy its hunger.

As the tingling sensation of The Great Crustacean's journey beneath Blue Roy's epidermic ocean slowly began to move down past his right clavicle, Blue Roy, The Map, a human map of a God's progress, wondered where Rameses would take his club next.

Inspired by David Bowie "Lady Grinning Soul"

In the end, he couldn't stand to watch me burn. Reclined among the rocks like Venus in flames, a gutful of sleeping pills, a breadcrumb trail of personal effects scattered around my charred body like offerings to a blackened god. The smell of petrol was sharp in my nostrils as I lay down, thick-headed and dizzy with the pills. Overwhelmed with the desire to close my eyes and accept the offer of oblivion, sweet and numb: *sleep now; you'll never feel a thing.*

He sobbed as I lit the match. He was such a sweet boy.

Pain is a necessary condition of any transition; it is the trigger point for change, that intensity of sensation; so strong, so unbearable that the soul's answer is to tear itself free of the flesh. For most people, this is the moment of death. The soul transcends, naked and trembling, a damp-winged butterfly unfurling from its chrysalis. The trappings of mortality are greatly overvalued.

The pills had gifted me a pleasant haziness, like strolling through thick fog; looking down at one's own hand and seeing only a vague suggestion of a limb. When the fire overcame me, the pain felt strangely distant; the sound of a faraway siren, urgent in its persistence.

He was there, somewhere; I could not see him, but I felt his presence, a ghost in an adjacent room.

The drugs swaddled my brain. I forced myself up, through, fingers clawing at the filmy membrane so that I might feel it: skin shrunk and crackling like a pig on a spit, the animal smell of burning hair, and pain, bright and insistent as sunrise, glorious in its intensity; my nerve endings were shrill with it, singing high and loud. I reached raw fingers to the sky, liquid with heat shimmer, and I opened my mouth as far as my scorched and splitting skin would allow, and though the words were lost beneath the roar of the conflagration, I spoke them all the same: *thank you.*

A bar in West Berlin, that first time. I knew he was far younger than me by the smooth, unlined skin around his eyes, dark and huge as an animal's; narrow body clad all in black as though he were a shadow. He could find anything I wanted, he said, like I was naïve of West Berlin's capacity for reckless decadence. Nobody slept in that city; they drank and danced and sang from the moment the sun dipped below the horizon to the moment the streetlamps guttered in the pastel-hued morning chill, and still they would keep going: the leather-boys and the drag queens, the queers and the artists stumbling out of Chez Romy Haag at five am, veins pumping black coffee and white powder. I knew about all of it, but I let him think I was innocent, gasping at each revelation. This wild, uninhibited city, this inspired island. I played a stranger in a strange land, and he was charmed by it. He took me to Ku'damm and we took turns to stand on the spot where Rudi Dutschke had been shot years before. I was not a Marxist or a revolutionary but I felt my blood buzz as I stood there, staring out into the river of traffic. I could almost feel the kiss of the muzzle against my temple, the thrill of cold steel. They would kill me, if they knew, without a second thought.

What should I call you, I asked him, emerging from a

closet-tiny Schöneberg bar into the star-dappled September
night. He smiled. Thought for a moment, calculating the
specifics of his identity. I had seen that look before, a hundred
times; my own furrowed brow before a mirror, practicing my
name, my age, my place of origin. We were of a soul, I think,
and I let myself grow attached to him in spite of my better
instinct. He was not a beautiful boy, not in any traditional
sense, but from an artist's perspective he was a marvel; stark
Art Deco lines, marble and obsidian in contrast, flat planes as
smooth as glass. It was the era of Bowie; to be splendid held
far greater power than to be beautiful, and he was so splendid.

My name is Sasha, he said at last. He didn't ask mine. I
would give it to him freely, when the time was right. Artifice
bound us, inextricable, though we had known one another
only a day and a night. In Berlin, time was fluid; the rise and
fall of the sun delineated nothing when you flitted between
underground bars and closed-door clubs. A subterranean
existence where every last abject body was perfect in the dark.
An island paradise for the strange and the different and the
lost. But I was not lost.

I brought him to my hotel room and told his fortune. I
lay out the cards on the bed as we sat and smoked, and he
eyed me with sceptical interest as I described his journey.

The Tower, I said, placing it in the centre of the bed. I
sipped blood-dark wine; the imprint of my lipstick was half a
heart on the rim of the glass. A troubling card. Sudden change
is coming. You cannot hold on to things as they are. You may
have to abandon truths you have held dear all your life.

He took a long, slow drag. You tell a good story, he said,
flicking his cigarette into the crystal ashtray. Smoke emerged
from between thin lips. When he smiled, I saw neat little teeth.
Not a poor boy, this one, not with his expensive suit and silk
ties, oddly formal in spite of the reckless bohemia of his
surroundings. Long fingers and sharp Florian Schneider

haircut, the aggressive jut of his nose, a cultivated severity. As I poured him more wine I realised he might have been Stasi. I knew he was only masquerading as German; his accent was not quite right, though I could not place it. Perhaps it wouldn't have troubled me at all if not for the fact that I too was playing at being German.

Change cannot come unless the Tower is destroyed, I told him. Only when it is ashes can you welcome the new. But the Tower is a prison. It is built on rotten foundations. It does not serve you as you think it does. Better to let it burn.

I'm not afraid of change, he said, and his eyes were liquid fire.

He might have been Stasi, I told myself, as I knotted my fingers in his shirt, pressed his mouth on mine; bitter smoke and sharp wine and hard teeth. I swept away the cards with my bare foot, let them scatter. I felt his hesitation, the sudden tautness of his body even as he came to me, and I unbuttoned his shirt, one by one, slow, so that he might refuse if he wanted; I would not blame him, would not think him less of a man. I knew I was suspicious; I held on to a semblance of cover with the tips of my fingers and I knew he could smell it on me, deceit sweeter than any cologne. It was unlike me, to let my mask slip so readily.

I tugged his shirt aside, ran an exploratory hand down his torso. The curve of his shoulders was smooth, delicate; bandages tight around his chest, pressing his breasts flat. Slender waist, the tell-tale convexity of hips. Such a fine-boned boy. I tugged at his belt buckle, looked him straight in the eye: *yes?*

He burned with shame, with desire. He must have thought I'd revile him when I reached between his legs. He must have thought I'd reject him, a freakish thing, a boy in girl's skin. It did not matter; flesh is so temporary. *Yes*, he answered, and though the words never passed his lips, his warm, eager body spoke so eloquently on his behalf.

I was good at disappearing. Resurfacing somewhere new, as someone new, shedding the skin I'd accumulated in my previous life. My previous self, sloughed and discarded. In time I would be forgotten, except perhaps as a shadow on the fringes of a memory; a transient figure who came and went as though in a dream. I took nothing with me from my previous life; I removed packaging from cosmetics so nobody would know their origins, cut the labels from my clothes. I kept my external accoutrements untraceable. And though I accrued lovers in each of my incarnations, I made certain they could not follow me when the time came for me to leave.

I left Sasha sleeping. Slipped out one night, a windblown, directionless thing moving silently through the Berlin night. I followed my instructions as always. New name, new passport. Suitcase emptied of all but the most essential items, even those things I had carefully anonymised; I could replace those in Norway. Somewhere on the Danish border I had been reborn. Those weeks in West Berlin had belonged to some other woman; I had never set foot in that city in my life, had never turned dizzy circles in the blue-black shadow of the Wall, cognac buzzing in my blood and bitter laughter on my lips. I had never fallen in love.

These were the rules that had kept me alive. Burn everything. Leave only ashes behind.

Sasha was the only mistake I ever made.

In hindsight, I made it easy for him. And perhaps there was a part of me that had orchestrated the mistake; perhaps it had not been a grievous error but a quiet act of self-sabotage; some part of my previous self lingering in the recesses, a stain I had not been able to scrub out. Perhaps I had wanted Sasha to follow me all along.

He found me in Bergen. A pale face reflected in oil-black

espresso. I looked up and met his gaze, so soft despite the anger in the thin line of his mouth, the set of his jaw. For a long moment, I didn't recognise him. He was someone else's memory, the centrepiece of someone else's love story; a boy I had seen in passing, perhaps, in some town square somewhere, a face I had briefly appraised as a work of fine art. He wrapped long fingers around my knuckles, and his skin was so familiar.

Ana, he said. Ana, I can't believe I found you.

I was not Ana. I did not look like Ana, did not move or speak like Ana; she had been a flickering flame of a woman, fated from the first to burn out quickly. White-blonde wolf in blood-red lipstick, she would eat a man alive and spit out the bones. Ana would tell dubious fortunes in gaudy hotel rooms, sip rum cocktails in neon-dark clubs where the bass ran through her like a second heartbeat. Of course Ana would have been utterly disarmed by someone so sweet, so earnest. But I was not Ana.

My name is Claudia now. Murmured, so that nobody would overhear, though the coffee shop was almost empty, and nobody seemed interested in either of us. Sasha was not the sharp-edged boy Ana had left sleeping in a Charlottenburg hotel; he was dressed casually, his hair feather-soft, cigarette smoke for cologne. He might have belonged anywhere. I shouldn't have been surprised. Hadn't he been blending in for years?

I brought him back to my hotel. Buried my face in the conch-delicate curve of his clavicle, inhaling the warm nicotine scent of him. I played Ana for him; the illusion was fragile, brittle as old ice, but he swallowed the lie gladly, and if neither of us spoke the words aloud perhaps we could go on pretending that nothing had changed. That we were the same people we had been in Berlin. That we always would be.

Afterwards, I lay my cheek against his unbound breast, running a soft thumb across the angry red lines scored into his

white flesh; the scars by which he had earned his manhood.
His heart was a metronome ticking in time with my thoughts.
He slept like the dead. I wondered how I would fix my
mistake. Ana's mistake. I wondered if it mattered at all that I
did not want to.

It was only a matter of time before they caught me. I was
not surprised when I got the call, though I was appropriately
contrite. Ana was dead, but her lover lived on. They had
specified that Claudia should travel solo. The information she
sought was not that which could be gleaned from beautiful
boys, or hedonistic girls; a companion made her more visible,
and what was more, a companion was privy to the same
things she was privy to. I did not bother to tell them that
Sasha hadn't been in Stavanger, nor in Trondheim, where I'd
found them everything they'd wanted to know; that Bergen
was a bust and the only thing worth writing home about was
the coffee. They could not be reasoned with. I had disobeyed
them, and they would have my head for it if I did not perform
the proper penitence.

I had always been the model of obedience. Performed
my role with a professionalism so crisp it seemed I'd been
born to play the part. Maxim's voice was as perturbed as it
was angry; my first and sole transgression, and for what? For
a *boy*? They must have thought me a machine, an automaton
that fucked and drank and lied, everywhere, to everyone, but
did not *feel*; did not dream someday of a life in which she
might shrug on a new skin for the final time, construct piece
by piece a history she might be allowed to keep forever.

We have no time to make preparations, Maxim said. His
voice was tinny on the end of the phone, immersed in static
like the roar of a distant ocean. You will source a new
disguise, and you will return home. *Click.* The plaintive whine
of the dial tone. An order, then. A punishment.

I had seen Maxim only once, and even then I could not be sure I had *seen* him; the man inside the shell was Maxim, but it was impossible to know whether the meat and bones he'd couched himself in were his own. He was just like me, after all.

Sasha sensed my unhappiness, ever the empath. He knew what I was, though we'd never discussed it; I'd never spoken the words aloud, and he seemed not to need my confirmation. We took one another at face value. I wonder sometimes if I was the only lover he'd ever had who had accepted him without question; who had seen and touched and tasted his body and understood, still, the truth of his maleness.

You're in trouble, he said.

I'm always in trouble, I replied, and lit a third cigarette. Ash formed a perfect mound on the hardwood desk. I pressed delicately with the pad of my pinkie finger, cloud-soft, leaving a divot in the ash; a shallow caldera at the summit of a long-dead volcano. My dry throat ached for whisky.

He pulled bare legs to his chest, propped up against the headboard. Long and thin, like a greyhound, and dog-loyal; a canine eagerness to please that was untrainable, a gift he gave so freely. A gift I did not deserve, but accepted as though it were my due. Is it my fault, he asked, a little sullen.

There was no reason to protect him, except that I knew he would run if he thought he had put me in danger. I had already risked so much to keep him with me. No matter what Maxim said, no matter how he threatened me. I would die before giving Sasha up, because if I did, they would kill him. He knew too much. He knew nothing at all.

I pushed my thumb into the ashes. Smeared them out across the dark wood, into the grain. I wanted to tell him he was an angel. That in all the lives I'd lived, in all the men and women I'd had, I'd never once felt so understood.

No, love, I said. Not your fault. Never your fault.

I longed for West Berlin, its gleeful sleeplessness. For the hot, dark bars and the low throb of bass, everywhere, all the time, cleansing the mind of useless thoughts. I could have been Ana forever. I could have lived my whole life in the shadow of that wall. Gone, now, like so many other lives I might have lived.

Becoming Claudia was simple. Dye stains on hotel towels; padding at the hips and breasts, the illusion of fullness. A new speech pattern, a new gait. Changes I had made a hundred times before. That was not what Maxim had meant.

Usually, there was anaesthetic. They would pick the form into which I would be moulded; their meticulous research might necessitate a diminutive, voluptuous blonde, or a red-haired waif; a Genoese *contessa* or a Czech prostitute. Whatever their extensive research dictated was necessary. Such an extravagance, to wake as someone brand new, to run hands down unexplored flanks, an alien topography. This time, I would have no such luxury.

When I told Sasha I would have to die, he was inconsolable. Dramatic, in that way the young and the vibrant are; those who consider death a distant, terrifying prospect, a long and terrible silence. I held him as he sobbed and begged, though I was calm; death had long been my due, and I understood how strange it must seem to him that I would simply walk towards it with my arms held wide.

Either I die on my own terms, or they will kill me, I said. It was always going to end this way. You should be glad, Sashenka. People like me don't get to choose very often.

I held him until he slept. I lay awake, feeling the thrum of his pulse, the cool silk of his skin. My body had outlived its purpose, but his was just beginning to understand its potential. I buried my nose in his hair, inhaled the clean scent of him, the delicate curve of his skull perfect beneath my lips. I had thought him Stasi, but he was far too pure, too honest. His was a body that had never told a lie.

Let's go walking tomorrow, I told him, when he woke a few hours later. His cheeks were fever-bright, his eyes still raw. I want to die somewhere beautiful, I said. You don't have to come with me, of course, I'll understand-

No, he said, defiant even in his despair. I won't let you go alone. You deserve better than that.

There are many stories told of Lake Svartediket. The little ghost girl who roams the woods, bleeding dark ink from her open mouth. The humpbacked midwife with her basket of unwanted infants, their cries echoing out across the lake as she drowned them, one by one. It seemed fitting, then, that I should pass by on my death-march. It did not seem a cursed place; bright sun on steel-blue water, the surrounding forest cast in autumnal vermillion, the gentle chatter of unseen birds. A sharp wind, abrasive, scouring the city from my lungs.

The valley I chose to die in was secluded enough that I felt sure they would not find me for days, perhaps weeks. They would find me; they were too good at tracking, too clever for me to evade them for long. But it would be enough time for Sasha to get away. The fire served this purpose admirably; charred flesh obfuscates, it muddies the waters. Until they identified me with certainty, they would not look for him. And by the time they did, I hoped he would be long gone.

He could not watch me burn. I would not ask it of him. I had asked so much already.

Before Maxim perfected his technique – before anaesthesia and morphine and grim-faced teams in stainless-steel rooms – the only way to transcend was to harness the pain. To cloak oneself in it, engulfing the body like flames, on and on until there was nothing else in the world but pain, so sharp and so exquisite that the only way through was out; peeling the flesh away like petals, struggling weak-limbed and exhausted to that singular point of light, the wide-open cavern of a screaming mouth. And that moment of pure freedom as the soul transcends: weightless, immaterial, no longer tethered to its flesh-anchor. My old body – Claudia's body, Ana's body, Genevieve's body – an empty, smouldering thing in the valley below, pig-flesh stink and cracked skin, arms drawn in like a boxer ready to lash out. It cannot last, though; the soul must always seek shelter.

Maxim would never tell me whether usurpation caused harm. I suppose he had no way of knowing. In those days, there was no precise science to it; as an art form, it was rudimentary at best. I did not want to think that Sasha might suffer when I slipped into his body. When he found himself trapped in mine. I had stuffed my former shell full of sleeping pills; the smoke must surely have turned the lungs black, filled the blood with poison. If he felt anything upon waking in that ash-choked prison, it must only have been momentary. That is what I told myself as I flexed unfamiliar legs, the rush of hot blood into strange limbs, a gait I would soon come to think of as my own. I knew his body intimately; I would adjust soon enough. It was not the first time I had lived as a boy.

I did not look back as I walked away, out of the valley, away from Norway; away from Maxim's all-seeing eye and the body he had gifted me, so perfect for the job. Away from the only life I had ever really known. I did not look back. I would honour Sasha's refusal like a final request. I would not watch him burn.

Inspired by Blondie "Hanging On The Telephone"

Roy Jones was eighty years old and he was so tired, and his phone was ringing. This wouldn't have been out of the ordinary had Roy not been without a telephone since his wife, June, had died just over three decades ago. The day of her funeral, he had returned to a house that was finally quiet, and then he had proceeded to smash the telephone to pieces.

He had never been much of a one for phone calls. He had always believed that if something was worth talking about, you ought to do it in person. Now June, on the other hand, she had loved to talk on the phone. She incessantly called everyone and kept them talking (or listening, as was most often the case), for as long as possible. Roy had never understood the fascination with a hunk of plastic that just sat there waiting to bother you. Every time it rang, it was likely a telemarketer or someone with some bad news. But it was after he and June separated that he really started to detest the sound of the phone ringing.

Over the years, June had left Roy on several occasions. In the thirty-one years since they'd wed at the age of eighteen – quite normal in their day – she'd left him once a year, usually around Christmas. It was like clockwork. She was unsatisfied, she always said. Didn't feel like Roy made enough effort, didn't feel like he was in love with her *enough*. Didn't feel appreciated, didn't feel special. You name a vague grievance of that nature with no solid examples of why or how, and Roy had heard it.

Of course, she always changed her mind within a month and came back home. There had been many times when she'd claimed it was 'for good this time', and she'd even moved her belongings out and started talking about selling the house during one of her many episodes. But she always came back, in the end.

It was the last time, thirty-one years ago, that had changed everything. There had been some silly argument about the dishes and that had been that. June had stormed out, muttering that their marriage was a shambles. A few weeks after Christmas, she had tried to return, and this time Roy had said no. For him, that last time really was 'for good this time'. He just couldn't face the thought of having to go through yet another Christmas sat at home alone, crying over June, desperately hoping that at any second she would walk back through the front door. It had become too cruel. No matter how happy she seemed, her leaving again was inevitable.

Every time she left him, he lost a piece of himself. Some self-esteem there, some contentment there – he hadn't been his whole self for quite a long time. He could never fathom what he'd done to warrant such a reaction, to deserve to be abandoned. They'd been childhood sweethearts; neither of them had ever had another partner. Once upon a time, they had been so in love that people thought them quite mad, but also adorable. They were a testament to what true intimacy and respect was. Roy had loved June since the first time he laid eyes on her, and had loved her a little more every time he awoke next to her.

The first year into their marriage, at the beginning of December, was the first time she'd left. She was only gone for a few days, though Roy struggled to remember why, all these years later. What he did remember was that those few days had been the worst of his life. He'd been confused and hurt, and angry with himself.

Their relationship was his entire world and it was quite a world indeed. Realising that for June, something was lacking, that the feeling wasn't quite mutual, was devastating to him. He vowed to do better for her, for them. But nothing was ever enough, and so each year, she'd go.

It got worse the older they got, because Roy became exhausted trying to better himself. He had no real idea what he was doing wrong, because he had no real idea what the actual problem was. He would just be relieved and grateful each time she came back and they'd discuss it and argue and then sweep it under the rug and go about their lives until the next time. The longer it went on, the more anxious and depressed Roy became. He grew to expect it, to fear it. Would this time be the time she never walked back through the front door again? He couldn't bear it.

After their son, Adam, had grown up, June would stay with him, which meant that Roy was utterly alone over the holidays while his family were together elsewhere. A deep, gnawing hollowness finally rooted itself in his core, and once he realised that actually, he couldn't stand it, he knew that the next time would finish the marriage.

June, of course, was shocked. She even laughed at first, thinking that Roy's refusal to take her back was just one of his jokes she'd never quite understood. She'd called him to let him know she needed to be picked up with her suitcase, and Roy, through tears, told her that he thought it would be better if she just stayed where she was for now. There'd been a stunned silence, followed by laughter, followed by a rage in June that Roy had never seen before. What did he mean, she couldn't come home? It was she that had decided she needed space, who was he to tell her that she wasn't welcome to come back? She'd given him that space to think about how to make her happier, not decide that he wanted out of their marriage. Did he not love her? Did he not care that it was her house too, that she wanted to come home and sleep in her own bed? How dare *he* do this to *her*?

Despite insisting they speak in person – this was their marriage after all – June refused to see him until he 'came around'. As a result, Roy had spent a good few hours on the phone to her that night, trying to explain, mostly through choked, agonised tears, that he'd finally figured out their problem. It wasn't him that wasn't 'in love enough'. It was her.

She'd never loved him the way he'd loved her. She was a dream, but he wasn't quite enough. When they'd married, Roy had felt set for the rest of his life. But June had wondered if there was something more for her out there. Maybe not someone, but something. Something else that wasn't her life with Roy. He had everything he could ever want, but she had settled. That's why she'd pick a petty fight and find an excuse to walk out, because she was frustrated with her life, and no amount of effort on Roy's part would ever change that. Her heart just wasn't in it.

It took a long time for Roy to give up on his marriage, but in the end, it was self-preservation that did it. Her leaving him was a kind of torture that he'd grown to expect. Roy's feelings of inadequacy and failure had seeped into their relationship the way that black mould seeps into a house. At first, it's just in one corner of one room, but a few years down the line, the whole house is rotting.

June had not taken kindly to being on the receiving end of feeling rejected, and she had most definitely not been happy with suddenly losing control of their relationship. She'd pulled out all the stops in a bid to make him change his mind, but alas, Roy was resolved in his decision, despite the pain it caused him. She hated him, then she loved him. She'd tried to convince him that he was crazy, being unreasonable, cruel even. Then she'd apologise and beg him for a chance to put it right. She'd promised never to leave again, but that was a promise she'd broken time and time again already.

She'd threatened to divorce him and slander his name to all that knew them, then she'd cried and told him she couldn't live without him. She'd told him she would see a counsellor, and then in the next breath accused him of having an affair. That particular idea was the most preposterous to Roy, for he could never have imagined loving anyone else at all. In her most desperate and low moments, she had even tried to convince him to make love to her one last time. Roy, throughout all of this, had been an emotional wreck, but he'd known her long enough and well enough to know the difference between sincerity and tactics, and unfortunately, her most sincere moments were the hateful ones.

They'd 'talked it over' a thousand times through the years. She just wasn't happy, and Roy couldn't stand another stomach churning moment of feeling responsible for that. They were in their mid-forties when they officially separated – no spring chickens – but with plenty of life left to live, Roy thought. He figured that despite June not taking the separation well initially, she would be thankful one day to have been released from the burden of their marriage, and he hoped she could find whatever she thought was missing from her life.

It was just when Roy thought that June had accepted the separation that she started calling him in the middle of the night. He would never forget the first call. He answered, half-asleep and groggy, concerned that it was past midnight, and the first thing out of her mouth was, *'please, I don't know what I might do'*. It was a phrase that she would repeat every time she called, every day, for the next week. It was a phrase that had repeated in his mind every day since she had passed. At first he hadn't realised what she was getting at, but then she had made it quite clear that if he didn't take her back then she could not, *would* not, live without him. *'You'll be sorry when I'm gone and it's your fault,'* she'd told him. At first, he'd felt sick.

She'd make some vague threat of that manner and then hang up before he could respond. Several times in the first few days, Roy panicked and drove to Adam's house, only to find his disgruntled, sleepy son confused by it all because by the time Roy got there, June would be tucked up in bed, and sleeping like a baby.

Roy wondered if June's threats to her life weren't just her last attempt to manipulate him, to make him feel guilty, to emotionally blackmail and torture him for finally standing up for himself. He began to see June in a whole new light, and it was then that he started to hate her, but only on the surface. Hating her helped him stick to his guns and follow through with what he thought was right, which was only imperative to him because he thought he was doing what was ultimately best for her.

For days, every time the phone rang, his stomach would twist and knot and he'd sweat and feel sick. He'd lie awake, frantically trying to call her back, only to eventually reach Adam and be told that June was quite all right, actually. That there was no need to worry, that he needed to stop calling, that he needed to stop pandering to her drama.

So he'd stopped answering the phone. It would ring and ring all night and day and although it kept him awake, Roy had found some satisfaction in knowing that June's spell over him was broken. On the fourth day of refusing to answer, he'd simply taken the receiver off the hook. He left it that way all day, and only put the hand piece back in the cradle when he was about to go to bed, figuring that she surely would have given up.

It had rang immediately.

He'd closed his eyes, feeling a tension headache set in. He would answer, and he would tell her that was enough now, she had to stop calling. For a while, she could reach him through Adam if she needed something, but he would no longer take her calls or put up with her rants. He answered the phone.

'*Roy, I don't know what will happen if you don't come,*' she'd cried. Roy's heart had broken. Despite his pain and his anger, he could never stand to hear June cry like that. But he had to stay strong. This had to end, for both of them, and it would only end when she accepted that she could no longer control him. And so, that's what he'd told her.

'*Please, I've taken something. I don't know what will happen if you don't come.*'

Crying, Roy had told her to just go to sleep, and that he would speak to her in the morning. Then he'd hung up. The instinct to panic and run to her was almost overwhelming, but she'd said things like that before, and she'd been lying. Roy had gone to bed but hadn't managed to sleep much. He'd ignored the flood of calls the next morning. It was only when Adam turned up at the door demanding to know why he hadn't answered his phone all morning that he'd known.

June had told him. She had called and told him and begged him to go to her. And he'd told her to 'just go to sleep'. And she had. She had overdosed on the painkillers prescribed for her back pain, slipped into a deep sleep, and then gone into cardiac arrest. Roy had always thought, but never voiced, that she'd ultimately died of a broken heart.

The guilt had been eating him alive for thirty-one years, and now, on the thirty-first anniversary of her death, the phone was ringing. The phone he had smashed up in a fit of grief and shame all those years ago. It was sitting on the windowsill, where it had lived before, ringing and ringing like it still belonged there. Ringing like it had never been gone at all, like she had never been gone at all. He supposed that in a way, she hadn't. Even when it was gone, he'd never stopped hearing that phone ring. Roy wondered, as he stared at it, if he had finally lost his marbles.

With a hand that shook with both age and nerves, he lifted the receiver and pressed it to his ear. "June?"

'Please, I don't know what I might do.'

Roy fell to his knees, hurting himself but not really noticing. He clutched the phone, pressing it too hard to his ear, and sobbed silently with his eyes closed behind his glasses, and his mouth hanging slack.

'I don't know what will happen if you don't come.'

"Oh, my darling," Roy wept, barely audible. He'd wished to hear her voice just one last time for all these years, but now that he heard it, it was unbearable. His pent up guilt, grief, misery, and love for June all went crashing into him at once, catching his breath and tightening his chest. "Oh, my sweet darling."

It went quiet for a moment, and that was even more unbearable than hearing her voice. Here he was with an opportunity to put it right, but his throat was closing around his words. "June? June, my love, are you there?"

'I don't know what will happen if you don't come.'

"Oh, my darling, please don't, please don't," Roy begged, his voice strained to a whisper. He pressed his free hand to his heart. "I'm so sorry, so sorry."

'Please, I've taken something,' came the reply. She sounded exactly the same as she had before, like a recording. Roy had never been able to get her last words out of his head, but to hear them again was far worse than anything his memory had ever served him. He winced.

"Sweetheart, oh please don't. I'll come to you, where are you?"

'I don't know what I might do.'

"June, I'm so sorry, I should have come. I love you so much, my darling…" Roy stopped to breathe in. His chest was so tight. Speaking was a struggle. "I never wanted to be without you, I was just angry, I..."

'I don't know what will happen if you don't come."

"Please, don't... please stop saying..."

'Just go to sleep.'

Roy's breath was running out. Her words were knives. His words were too. His chest hurt so much. His heart hurt more.

"I should never have... I didn't mean... my darling, I didn't know..."

'Just go to sleep, I'll speak to you in the morning.'

Tears of anguish slid down Roy's contorted face and the receiver fell and clattered to the floor as he let go of it to grab his left arm. He clutched it, keeling over from his knees onto his side. He could feel sixty years of love and heartache swelling in his chest. The pain was intense and loud, but he could still hear her as his own heart broke and failed him.

'Just go to sleep.'

ACOUSTIC CASSETTE   N.R.I   ☐IN ☐OUT

B *Mountain People - C. L. Raven*

Normal Bias 120µs EQ   A|60

Inspired by Super Furry Animals "Mountain People"

Sion sharpened his knife at the kitchen table, the metal glinting in the candle's flame. A speck of dried blood clung to the blade, so he scratched it off with his thumb. Blood ruined things.

"I'm going hunting," he told his sister, Leri, as she chopped vegetables, saving the peelings for the sheep and hens.

"Be careful, there's a storm brewing. I'm not coming out looking for you. I'll leave you for the wolves."

"There are no wolves left in Wales."

"I meant the human kind."

Sion frowned. "They don't come up here after dark. They're more scared of us than we are of them."

Leri rubbed her swollen belly. "You know that's not true. Besides, they hunt in a pack."

"I'll be back before the storm." He crossed to her and kissed her on the forehead, tucking her long black hair behind her ear. "Maybe I'll get lucky and catch a wolf."

"Make sure it's a plump one." She smiled. "There are

three of us now. I'll get the sheep into the barn."

Sion sheathed his knife and left their grey stone farmhouse. Night had cast its cloak over the sky, turning the beautiful mountain into a deadly wilderness. The large oak tree that guarded their family graveyard looked like a monster, its twisted limbs reaching to snare anyone who came too close.

The wooden swing swayed beneath the wind's invisible hands, its rope creaking. He heard Leri calling the sheep. Sion crept down the mountain towards the woods that led to the village below. Lanterns glowed like sirens' eyes, luring him to his doom. Part of him hated the villagers. Part of him feared them. Part of him pitied them.

They never knew freedom. They only thought they did. Sion entered the woods and stopped, listening to the sounds of the night.

Rustling, to his left. He held his breath and unsheathed his knife. Footsteps. Crying. Rabbits didn't cry. He edged closer, the trees bathed in an eerie silver light, allowing him to see. A woman darted out of the undergrowth, stumbling in front of him. She stared at the blade, her eyes wide. Tears streaked her face. Her dress was torn.

"No," she whispered.

"You seem lost."

The woman screamed and fled, leaving one shoe behind like a frightened Cinderella. But Sion was not her Prince Charming. Sion chased her, the trees reaching out to slow him. He and Leri spent their childhood exploring these woods, learning to hunt, learning to survive, learning to kill. He turned off the path and circled around, hoping to cut her off before she reached the stream. She wouldn't see it in the dark. He waited, his ears straining to pick up her footsteps. She might have turned off the path and got herself lost in the undergrowth. No, they never left the path. They were more sheep than wolves.

He stepped out in front of her. She screamed again and turned to run away but lost her footing. She collided with a tree and slumped down onto the leaves. Sion stood over her, sheathing his knife.

"You villagers never learn. Don't come up here after dark. Danger roams these woods."

He scooped her up and carried her back through the woods. Sheep grazing on the mountain gave him a cursory glance then continued snatching mouthfuls of grass. His legs and back ached by the time he reached the farmhouse. It had been a while since he carried someone up the mountain. Village folk didn't come this way much anymore.

He let himself in through the stable-style door and found Leri cooking a vegetable stew in a cauldron over the kitchen fireplace.

"Back already?" She asked without turning around. "Did the rabbit just surrender?"

"No rabbit stew for us tonight. I caught a wolf."

"Carys is missing!"

People in The Black Sheep Inn turned to stare at Owen as he burst in. Wind rushed in after him, extinguishing a candle and howling for flesh to bite. The door slammed, silencing it.

"She went out hours ago and hasn't come home. She's always home by dark. She knows it's not safe."

The Innkeeper, Griff, stepped out from behind the bar. A tall man with grey hair and beard and a slight paunch from too much beer. "Maybe she's visiting a friend and hasn't realised the time. You know what she's like. Once she gets riled up about something, there's no shutting her up."

"It's midnight, Griff. She should've been home hours ago."

"Where did she go?"

"To take food to Mari in Crow Cottage. She hasn't been

well."

The Inn fell silent. Griff glanced back at his wife, Alys. She fumbled as she put a tankard down, spilling ale over the bar.

"Have you asked Mari?" Griff asked. His voice didn't sound so steady now.

"Aye. She said Carys left at eight. It doesn't take four hours to walk back from Crow Cottage. *They've* got her!"

"She might have fallen over and hurt herself. She always was clumsy. Remember when she tripped over the stile and had to have five stitches in her forehead? Let's go look by Crow Cottage. But check your house first. She's probably sat at home, wondering where you are. In five minutes, she'll be round here, giving me a row about letting you drink."

"They've got her tied up and they're probably killing her and cooking her flesh right now!"

"Owen, calm down. You're no use to Carys in this state. I'll get my coat."

Owen paced the Inn, looking out the windows for Carys. He was in his late twenties, slender with brown hair. The villagers turned away, their silence and downcast eyes telling Owen what he already knew.

The mountain people had her.

Griff appeared with his coat and hat on, carrying a brand. He stuck it in the fireplace until it ignited, the flame casting weird shadows over their faces and turning men into monsters. They left the Inn, the door banging shut behind them, banishing the cold and the darkness. Owen hurried on ahead. Griff struggled to keep up, the wind turning his flame into a dancing puppet. They passed pretty stone cottages, the blacksmith's where Owen worked, the post office and local shop that sold products from the neighbouring farms. They looked out for their own in Rhai Hynafol. Owen rushed into his house, shouting Carys's name. The house was empty, its silence mocking him and filling him with dread. Returning outside, he shook his head at Griff. Griff sighed and they continued through the village.

Past Riverside Farm was the stile where Carys had her accident, falling over it trying to catch her wayward dog. They climbed over it, the stream flowing beneath, and followed the path leading to Crow Cottage. The lights were out and there was no sign of Carys.

Griff knocked on the door. After a few minutes, he heard shuffling then the door opened a crack, an elderly woman peering out.

"Sorry to disturb you, Mari, but has Carys come back?"

"Sorry, love, I haven't seen her since she left at eight."

"Thank you. Go to bed now. You need your strength."

Owen stared at Mynydd Bran that loomed above them; the black throne of the gods. Crow Cottage sat at the base. The last defence between the mountains and the village. Thunder growled in the bellies of the clouds, hungry for destruction. Lightning flashed as the rain fell.

"She's probably already dead!"

"Why would she go up into the mountains? It makes no sense. Maybe she called in on Seren."

"No. *They* have her. Maybe she heard a scream and went to help. Even on her days off she can't help being a nurse. Or she saw an injured sheep. Our house is full of strays and injured wildlife she's rescued."

"Aye, my niece is a good woman. Stubborn and willing to take a risk but a good woman. When we go back, you'll probably find a sheep by your fireplace. We'll find her, Owen."

Owen jogged up the mountain. Bits of slate decorated the soft terrain. Sheep grazed in the dark, some sleeping, others watching them. Three ran when they saw the flame, startling the rest of the herd who chased after them, leaving the men alone on the mountain.

Owen and Griff returned to The Black Sheep. Candles gave the inn a warm, fiery glow. It was usually closed at this hour, but nobody wanted to miss any news. It had been a year since young Tomos vanished after the farm boys saw him playing in the fields. Griff shook the rain from his coat.

"Any sign?" Griff's wife, Alys, asked.

"No. We'll start the search in the morning."

"We can't wait until morning!" Owen said. "They could be killing her right now!"

"If we go out in this we'll be washed down the mountain."

"Griff, *please*."

Griff sighed. "Alright. We'll search the woods. If anyone would like to join us, fetch coats and torches and meet here in twenty minutes. Be careful. I don't want anyone getting hurt. There's a storm coming."

The inn emptied as the villagers went home to prepare. Carys was one of theirs and if the mountain people had her, they were going to bring her back. There had been rumours about the mountain people for as long as the eldest resident could remember. They were there before the village, living in caves or huts before their descendants built a house to seem civilised. They lived off the land, coming to the village only to buy provisions or to sell vegetables, eggs and wool. They barely spoke and they didn't go to school. Rumours hinted generations had only bred with each other. The uncle's face was hideously deformed on one side; huge and misshapen. The mother had a club foot and barely left the house. That's what happened when you mixed the same genes.

There was just the son and daughter left after their parents died in an accident. Nobody knew what the accident was. Some people believed the children killed them because they ran out of food during the harsh winter two years ago.

Ffion, the post mistress, said the daughter looked a little plump in the belly the last time she saw her. As they didn't socialise in the village, there was only one man who could have got her with child. Some of the boys who had been playing in the woods ventured up Mynydd Bran, to the farmhouse. They said they saw bones hanging from trees and weird symbols painted in blood. Then Tomas vanished. The word 'sacrifice' had been whispered in the village. That was the only explanation for how they grew vegetables up there, when most of the mountain was devoid of life.

If they had Carys, the villagers were going to bring her back.

The twenty minutes dragged. Owen imagined each ticking second was Carys's heartbeat, and he waited for the ticking to stop. The door opened and the villagers arrived in pairs or threes. This wasn't a backwards village where the women stayed home and worried. Everyone was an equal part of the village, so everyone was going to help.

Griff and Alys's daughter stayed to guard the inn, in case Carys came back. One of the farmers entered with his rifle and his border collie.

"I don't think the gun is necessary, Rhodri," Griff said.

"Best to be safe. Who knows what roams those woods?"

"You have nothing to fear from badgers."

Others held various weapons – knives, a shotgun, a fire poker, a pitchfork. The blacksmith had his hammer, the woodcutter his axe. Owen wished he'd fetched a weapon. The mountain people were known to hunt with their bare hands. Going unarmed was suicide.

Griff eyed the weapons uneasily. "This looks less like a search and more like a witch hunt."

The door opened and the village police officer, Dai, walked in. People hid their weapons behind their backs, until he pulled his wooden truncheon out and nodded at them.

They left the inn and headed towards Mynydd Bran.

Crow Mountain. The atmosphere was charged with excitement, worry and fear. Nobody went up the mountain after dark. Mari was silhouetted in Crow Cottage's window, watching them pass. An uneasy thought rippled through Owen: how many would come back?

They reached the edge of the woods and stopped. Dai explained how to conduct a search. But they already knew. Carys wasn't the first to go missing on the mountain.

The others had never been found.

They walked through the woods in a line, their brands dancing through the dark. Owen's heart pounded. Carys had to be alive. But why would she come here after dark? There was nothing but sheep, the farmhouse and ruins of the old stone huts. The mountain people must have grabbed her as she left Mari's. They must have been watching her.

A whistle disturbed Owen's thoughts. He ran to where Dai stood, his lantern casting writhing shadows over the ground.

"Two sets of footprints," Ieuan, the game keeper said. "One male, one female by the looks of it." He rose and walked on, following the footsteps. "His set goes off here." He pointed into the undergrowth. "Hers continue along the path. Could be the brother and sister."

Griff stooped and picked something up.

Owen's stomach churned. "That's Carys's shoe. Those are her footprints."

Owen followed Dai along the path, his mouth dry, dread plaguing him. Had Carys snuck off to meet a man and lost her shoe in the dark after undressing? No. She wouldn't. But if she had, why had the footprints separated? Was he hunting her?

The villagers followed the path in nervous silence.

"Looks like she was running," Ieuan said.

"From what?" Owen asked.

"Or who?"

Trees encroached as the path curved up the mountain; a

stony bandage wrapping around the mountain's old wounds. Gnarled wooden fingers reached to snag their hair and slap their faces. They kept their torches low so as not to set fire to the trees. Though a fire might cleanse the mountain of its evil, expose the final resting places of those it had taken and release the souls it had swallowed.

The stream gushed in the dark and they stopped. Ieuan explored the area, holding his torch to the ground.

"The man's footprints are here." He moved towards a tree stump and crouched. "Both sets stop here." Reaching out, he touched the trunk then offered his fingers to the flame. "Blood."

Owen gripped his torch. "They killed her!"

"There's not enough blood for that. Likely she hit her head." Ieuan continued scouring. "Only his footprints lead away. Unless she got into the stream and swam away…"

"He carried her."

Ieuan nodded, a pained expression creasing his face. Silence cast a heavy cloak over the villagers. Some glanced toward the mountain then swiftly lowered their gazes. Sickness pummelled Owen's stomach.

"It doesn't mean she's dead." Griff placed a hand on Owen's shoulder. Carys's shoe dangled from his other hand. The only thing left of her.

Owen shook it off. "There's *blood*, Griff! He carried her back to his cave to rape and skin her. They will eat her flesh and make clothes and shoes from her skin! Or keep her to breed with, like a prized mare so they can have more deformed offspring roaming the mountains and taking our people."

"Owen, you're being ridiculous. It's time those rumours died. On the rare occasions I've spoken to them, they've been very shy but polite. They know they're not welcome in the village."

"People have *disappeared*, Griff! For *years*, people from

the village have gone missing and have never been found. Why? Because there's *nothing* left to find! One of our own wouldn't do that. We weren't raised by savages like they were. The sister is pregnant by her own *brother*! They are depraved and evil and I'm sick of us all living in fear of them. It has gone on for generations. It ends, *tonight*. They can live on another mountain and practise their sacrifices far away from here."

Griff turned to Ieuan. "Where do the footprints lead?"

Ieuan crossed the stream then pointed up the mountain.

Dai stepped forwards. "Form a chain. Keep your links in sight. If anyone sees or hears anything, whistle and we'll stop. I will come and investigate it. If we find the brother and sister, wait. They are uncivilised and could be dangerous. They might not understand our language. We don't want them to harm Carys or us out of fear or hatred."

The villagers glanced nervously at each other then formed a long chain. The stream swallowed their footsteps, the cold biting their flesh through their clothes. They climbed higher, the trees becoming dense. Even the moonlight didn't want to be seen on Mynydd Bran.

Heavy silence stalked the group. They were afraid to speak or even breathe in case the mountain people found them and dragged them off into their sepulchral lair before they had a chance to scream. Rumours said the mountain people were quick and didn't always walk upright. They masqueraded well as civilised people when they visited the village but once they were back on their mountain, they reverted to their feral ways, running on all fours like wolves and climbing trees like monkeys. Barely human.

A twig snapped. Owen whirled around, his flame dancing menacingly above his head. Rustling. Nobody moved.

A badger stuck its striped face out of a set, saw the group and froze before darting back in. The group released their breath.

The mountain grew steeper as the trees thinned. They emerged in a clearing, the rain attacking them and their flames now they'd lost the trees' protection. The villagers looked at each other. The farmhouse sat at the top of the darkness, flames glowing in its windows. It stared down at them, daring them to approach.

"I thought they lived in a cave," Ffion whispered.

"Just because they live in a house, doesn't mean they aren't animals," someone replied.

Owen gripped his brand and stepped forward. He couldn't save Carys if he was too scared to leave the woods. The rest of the villagers followed, grouping together, rather than staying in their line. They were safer in a pack. Owen slipped on some slate, but Griff caught him. Fear surged through his veins, making it difficult to hear anything over his thundering heart.

Owen stopped at a large oak tree. A wooden swing hung from the lowest branch. Wooden crosses protruded from the ground. They didn't want to live among the villagers, so they weren't allowed to be buried among them. Their sinful bodies rested in unconsecrated ground. Some said the crosses were stakes and pierced the dead's hearts so they couldn't rise and feast on the villagers after dark.

It seemed to take forever to reach the house. Owen stopped at the front door and hesitated. Griff stepped in front of him and knocked.

Owen could almost taste the tension as they waited. The top door creaked open and a frightened female face peered out. She was quite pretty for a monster. Owen opened his mouth to speak when Rhodri pushed him aside, slid back the bolt on the bottom door and forced his way into the house.

The girl stumbled back, startled. "What do you think you're doing? Get out!"

"We know you've got her! Give her back and we'll spare

your lives."

"What's going on?" A young man stepped into view, his hands stained with blood.

"He's killed her!" Owen pointed.

"Murderer!"

"Monster!"

"Inbred beast!"

The villagers burst into the house and dragged the young man out into the rain.

"It's rabbit blood!" he protested.

Ffion picked up a wooden horse that stood on a table. "That's Tomos's!"

"Sion found it in the woods three months ago," the girl said. "He brought it back for my baby."

Someone grabbed her and forced her out too, her pregnant belly huge and grotesque.

"Filthy whore!"

"You hurt her and I'll kill you!" the brother threatened.

"Let us go!" the girl begged. "We haven't done anything!"

"They *can* talk like proper folk then," a farmer said.

The brother broke free and punched the nearest man. As he reached for his sister, three men punched and kicked him to the ground. The sister dropped to her knees to protect his head until she was dragged away.

"Stop it!" Griff yelled. "You're behaving like savages!"

Owen was swept out with the others and watched as they bound the mountain people's hands behind their backs with twine from Rhodri's hay bales. Griff tried to wrestle the farm boys off the sister as they grabbed her breasts, laughing. Owen pushed through the crowd and stared at the pair. They didn't look inbred. They looked like frightened teenagers. The girl was sixteen, her brother eighteen.

"Where's Carys?"

"Who?" The brother asked, blood trickling from his

eyebrow and lip.

"Carys! My betrothed! You took her from Crow Cottage. Where is she?"

"I didn't take anyone from Crow Cottage."

"Liar!" Owen struck him in the mouth. "What have you done with her?"

"The wolf," the sister whispered. "Tell him, Sion, or they'll hurt us."

"She's inside," Sion said.

"Hang them!" Someone shouted.

"We've done nothing wrong!" The sister protested. "Sion found her hurt in the woods and brought her here for me to heal." Tears streaked her face, forming fiery trails under the brand's flames.

"See?" Griff said. "Let them go. Let's talk about this like civilised people."

Someone punched him in the face, knocking him to the ground.

"Griff!" Alys rushed to him.

The villagers dragged the siblings to the oak tree that stood between the house and the woods.

Owen ran inside. "Carys!" He checked the living room and kitchen. Nothing. His terror grew. A cheer erupted outside. "Carys!" He burst into a bedroom and found Carys curled up on the bed.

What if she was dead? He couldn't bear to know. He edged forward, his shaking hand reaching for her. He gently shook her and she jumped.

"Owen!" She sat up.

"You're ok! Have they hurt you?" he swallowed. "Touched you?"

"No. There was a farm boy outside Mari's. He… grabbed me. Tore my dress. I managed to get away and ran into the woods. He chased me and I got lost. The brother found me. I thought he was going to kill me, so I fled. I must've hit my head because I woke up here and the sister was tending to my wounds."

"They didn't hurt you?"

"No. I was terrified, but they're nice. Shy. They fed me vegetable stew and said they'd bring me home in the morning when the storm passes."

"But they're monsters."

"No, they're not. We were wrong about them, Owen."

"Their uncle was deformed, from the inbreeding."

"From a facial tumour Dr Llewelyn refused to treat because of who they are. I was there when he turned him away."

"She's pregnant with his child!"

"It's not his." Carys's cheeks reddened. "I... I saw the farm boys drag her from the market seven months ago. She was screaming and begging for help but..." She looked away. "...she's mountain people."

Dread festered in his gut. Owen cursed and ran outside. The mountain people hung from the oak tree, their legs kicking uselessly. He fought his way through the crowd.

"They didn't hurt her." He shoved people aside. "Cut them down! Carys is fine."

"They're inbreds!" Someone shouted. "He impregnated his own sister!

"She was raped! By three of you. The only monsters here are us."

The crowds' shouts faded to uncertain whispers.

"Dai! Cut them down! This isn't justice, it's murder!"

"It's too late." Dai's face turned ghostly grey.

Owen stopped below the branch. The swing lay discarded on the ground. The mountain people's lifeless bodies swung gently, the creaking rope the only sound.

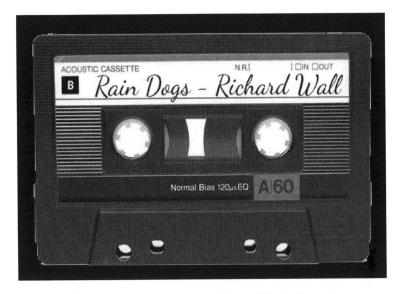

Inspired by Tom Waits "Rain Dogs"

Are you sitting comfortably?

Then I'll begin.

Once upon a time, in a tumbledown cottage in a field in the Gloucestershire countryside there lived a couple called Joan and Bob.

A lifetime of indolence and a fondness for the wrong types of food had crafted Joan's physique into a shape that Bob, in his braver moments, likened to a furious version of Penfold from Danger Mouse.

Of course, he never said that out loud, because it would propel Joan into a seething, spitting, cursing rage, as many things often did

Bob was of slight build, with a mousy comb-over that was turning grey. A quiet, ineffectual man, he bore Joan's frequent wrathful outbursts with apparent fortitude. He would never react, or shout back, which would infuriate Joan, who would then escalate into a screaming fit that could be heard three fields away by their neighbour (a farmer who kept prize sheep).

Thirty years previously, when they bought their tumbledown cottage, it was an idyllic country home with views to die for.

One morning, not long after they first moved in, Joan asked Bob if he could put up some bookshelves. Bob said that he would do it that very evening, if Joan could tidy the room up a little so that it was ready for him to start when he came home from work.

Joan's apoplexy that day went into the record books, for length, content and originality. Spittle flew from her lips as she screeched invectives that questioned Bob's parentage, the size of his genitals, his physique and his general usefulness to mankind. The summary of this diatribe was Joan's assertion that it wasn't her effing job to clean the effing house.

Bob replied calmly that in that case, it wasn't his effing job to put up the effing bookshelves. Neither would budge from their position and there then followed a thirty-year Mexican standoff during which neither of them made any effort to clean or maintain the house ever again.

Nowadays, the views were the same but their tumbledown cottage was a shithole. A stinking, festering, dilapidated shithole.

Every room was piled high with cardboard boxes, bin-liners, books, clothes, magazines and newspapers, all coated in a thick layer of dust. The only visible floor space was a pathway of cracked and worn linoleum that connected the filthy, defeated, dog-hair-covered armchairs in front of the TV to the equally filthy and defeated kitchen; in which grease-stained work surfaces supported unwieldy towers of dirty crockery. Congealing food waste covered the floor and rats lived in the cupboard under the sink.

Bob couldn't remember the last time they'd had visitors.

Joan and Bob also kept dogs. Six large German Shepherds who lived in cramped wire cages stacked in the corner of the living room. The cages were lined with months-old newspapers that were stiff with dried urine and dog slobber, all of which contributed to the overall aroma of the house.

When friends used to ask how they could live in such chaos, Joan's mouth would tighten with prim sanctimony.

"I have better things to do," she would say. "And besides, tidy people don't make the same exciting discoveries that I do."

"Tidy people don't live in stinking squalor," thought Bob.

But of course, he never said that out loud.

Joan didn't have a job. Instead she preferred to sit at home all day, either reading cheap paperbacks (25p for 10 from a charity shop) or at the keyboard of her ancient PC, dispensing her advanced internet-wisdom (Joan was NEVER wrong) among internet forums, chat-rooms or Facebook groups.

In the parlance of Oscar Wilde, Joan knew the price of everything and the value of nothing. An avid frequenter of charity shops, she particularly enjoyed browbeating the hapless staff (usually elderly volunteer workers) to "get a better deal". Her favourite story was the time she bullied a 75-year-old retired teacher (a smiling, good-natured, grey haired old lady) into slashing £1.50 off the price of a manky leather handbag, which was marked up at three pounds. The ferocity of Joan's malice, intimidation and general nastiness that day was such that the elderly lady gave up volunteering, developed acute social anxiety and never set fought out of her house until twelve months later when she was taken into care suffering from early-onset senile dementia.

When Joan returned home victorious she threw the handbag on top of the pile of rubbish in the back bedroom, never to be touched again.

"It was a bargain," she declared. "That's how I roll."

Joan was particularly fond of attacking anyone who was

unable to fight back. Years ago, when Joan and Bob used to socialise, restaurant waiting staff were her targets of choice. Joan would often boast about reducing a waitress to tears with a foul-mouthed diatribe regarding some non-existent food complaint in order to get a couple of pounds knocked off the bill.

All that ended when they stopped going out to restaurants. Friends drifted away because of Joan's behaviour towards them. She would be openly critical, firing off cruel, spiteful and sarcastic barbs with the intention of inflicting the maximum amount of hurt and upset. If anyone tried to counter Joan, or criticise her in any way, she would rant about it for weeks, every slight stored away in her elephantine memory of grudges, and relived time and again through internal dialogues which would end with Joan crushing her foe with a vicious verbal slap-down.

Very soon, Joan and Bob had no friends.

"People don't like me," she would declare. "Because I tell it like it is."

"People don't like you," thought Bob. "Because you're a spiteful, loudmouthed bully."

But of course, he never said that out loud.

Bob was a travelling salesman. He knew his stuff, and away from Joan he was a different person, animated, articulate, charming and persuasive. His patch covered the whole of the UK and he would spend hours, sometimes days on the road.

When he got home, often late at night, it was his effing job (according to Joan) to let the German Shepherds out into the muddy, dog-shit-ridden wasteland that in days-gone-by had been a thriving vegetable patch. After that he would sit in front of the TV with a large tumbler of cheap blended whisky (supermarket own-brand, in a plastic bottle. Bob still shuddered at the memory of Joan completely losing her shit in the middle of a busy Tesco Express when he'd had the temerity to pick up a bottle of single-malt).

Bob liked watching DVDs of Formula One highlights. If he didn't fall asleep in the chair (which most nights he did), he would climb into bed next to Joan, and lie awake listening to her snoring as he tried to remember why he married her in the first place.

One day, Bob was with a client in Cumbria. It had been a long day. He'd managed to secure a very lucrative deal but it was late afternoon before he was able to get away. At first, he planned to go straight home, but the radio warned of a band of gales, thunderstorms and torrential rain, which was forecast to sweep the country. Furthermore, local traffic news told Bob that the M6 Southbound was closed due to an accident near Preston. Bob made a rare decision, pulled into a service station and booked a room at the Travelodge.

Bob rang Joan to tell her that he wasn't going to be home that night, and that he had another site visit in Nottingham the next day, but assured her that he should be home about teatime.

Joan snorted her disinterest. "What-effing-ever," she said. "As long as you're here to let the effing dogs out."

Bob said that he would see her tomorrow.

"Eff off and die," snarled Joan as she slammed the phone down.

The next day, driving conditions were horrendous. At the Manchester bottleneck the traffic on the M6, hampered by driving rain, spray, reduced visibility and several accidents, had slowed to a crawl. Bob rang to cancel the appointment with the client, and then called home. Joan didn't answer and so Bob left a message telling her that he might be late, but would be home as soon as he could.

Eleven hours later, Bob was three miles from home, driving along a single-track country lane. The storm had worsened, battering the car in a deluge of rain that the windscreen wipers had no hope of clearing. Tired and disoriented, Bob came around a bend just a little too fast, failed to register the flood marker and ploughed into four feet of standing water.

The engine died with a bang. The electrics expired soon after.

In pitch darkness Bob fumbled into the glove compartment, pulled out a large torch and emergency hammer, and then grabbed his waterproof jacket from the back seat. As he contorted into the jacket, rainwater cascaded from the surrounding fields, pushing the flood higher around the car until the bonnet was awash.

It took several blows with the hammer to smash the sunroof glass and Bob was breathing hard when he eventually clambered onto the roof. Kneeling down, crouched against the wind, Bob switched on the torch and then gasped. The flood stretched for at least fifty yards in front of the car and was rising fast to cover the road behind. The torch revealed that the grass verges on either side were still just above the waterline. Bob got to his feet, steadied himself against the wind, took a deep breath and jumped.

He almost made it.

Landing on the grass verge, Bob grabbed the hedge and then howled in pain as a large thorn impaled itself deep into the palm of his hand. Jerking his hand away, he lost balance and fell backwards into the flood. Hitting the side of the car kept Bob on his feet, but the shock of the sudden chest-deep immersion in freezing water forced the air out of his lungs in a single explosive gasp. Lightheaded, frightened and panting, Bob panic-splashed his way to the rear of the car and managed to wade clear of the flood and back onto the road.

When he'd calmed down, he forced his hand into a sodden pocket and retrieved his phone. It was waterlogged and useless. After a few moments of taking stock, Bob thought he knew where he was and planned a route home across the fields.

Backtracking along the lane, Bob found a metal farm gate, grabbed the top and howled again as his thorn-damaged hand gripped the rusty barbed-wire wrapped around the top bar. Cursing as he straddled the gate, he cried out again as his foot slipped, and as he pitched headfirst into a patch of mud and cow shit he felt the barbed wire slash deep into his trailing leg. The field was on the side of a steep hill, at the top of which was a footpath which would lead eventually to the tumbledown cottage.

As Bob scrambled to his feet the field lit up with a brilliant phosphorescent glow, followed by an explosion of thunder directly overhead. Following his torch light, Bob set off up the hill.

Almost cresting the hill, Bob was fifty feet downstream of hundred-year-old oak tree, around which a torrent of surface water poured down the field. As Bob's foot splashed into the water, a lightning bolt hit the oak tree and arced along the stream. Bob saw the flash, felt the punch of a steam hammer and then everything went black.

When he regained consciousness, Bob found himself lying face-down in cow shit. His joints ached with every movement, his teeth hurt and the stench of scorched hair filled his nostrils.

He finally arrived home three hours later, drenched, bleeding, caked in mud and shivering violently.

As he searched for his door key, Bob could see Joan bathed in the glow of her computer screen, her face distorted by the rain on the outside of the window and the thick layer of grime on the inside. Bob tapped on the glass. Joan looked up, mouthed an invective and then returned to the screen. Eventually Bob found his door key and let himself in, the familiar wall of stench hitting him in the face.

"Where the eff have you been?

"I drove into a flood," said Bob. "I had to walk back across the fields. I was struck by lightning."

"Teatime, you said."

"No, I called you after that," said Bob. "I left a message on the answerphone."

"I didn't get any effing message."

Bob looked over to the base station of their cordless telephone, where a large, green, '1' flashed brightly in the gloom of the cottage.

"I gave your dinner to the dogs," said Joan.

Bob felt his pulse twitching in his temple.

"Did you renew my car insurance?" he said.

"What?" Joan didn't look up.

"My car insurance," said Bob. "You said you would ring them up and get it renewed."

Joan shrugged. "I don't think I did."

"I gave you the renewal letter," said Bob. "I asked you to call the insurance company and get it renewed."

Joan stared fixedly at the computer screen. "It's not my effing job," she said. "To follow you around wiping your arse for you."

"The car's waterlogged," said Bob. "The engine's fucked. If it's not insured we're stuffed."

Joan shrugged again.

"Not my problem," she said.

A nerve twitched beneath Bob's left eye. "I'm freezing," he said. "I need a shower."

The bathroom was toxic. A thick, grey, tidemark ringed the inside of the cracked, plastic avocado bath, above which black mould was spreading up the damp wall with ceiling ambitions. The floor mat around the toilet hadn't been lifted in years and was crusty with all manner of bodily excretions. The toilet itself looked like someone had filled a shotgun cartridge full of shit and fired it into the pan. Bob pressed the flush lever with his foot, closed the pan lid, wrestled himself out of his sodden clothes, and then stepped into the shower.

Half an hour later, dressed in pyjamas and wrapped up

in a thick tartan dressing gown, Bob sat down in front of the TV, opened a new bottle of whisky, and filled the glass tumbler as he pressed play on the DVD remote.

He woke with a start in the early hours. The whisky bottle was empty, but his head felt surprisingly clear. Bob stood up, switched off the TV, and then went upstairs. Not bothering to get undressed, he lay on top of the bed and fell asleep to the sound of Joan snoring and the rain battering the windows.

At 3:30 am, Joan shook Bob awake. "I heard a noise in the kitchen," she said. "It might be a burglar. Go and check."

Bob doubted that any self-respecting burglar would be out in this weather, and even if they were he didn't think that they would stay very long in this stinking shithole of a house. Much less root through the kitchen.

But of course he never said that out loud.

Next to the bed, propped against the damp, mould-stained wall stood a baseball bat. It was heavy, made from hickory and had the words 'Louisville Slugger' burned into it. Bob had bought it the last time they visited America in September 2001. He remembered Joan kicking off at the airport staff because their flight home had been cancelled due to the attacks on the Twin Towers. Joan had spent the rest of the day pointing and sneering at weeping Americans.

Bob picked up the bat, made his way downstairs and paused to listen.

The house was quiet.

Bob stepped softly towards the kitchen, pushed the door open and switched on the light. A six-foot rat was sitting upright on a chair, leaning on the table and gnawing on a three-week-old chicken leg.

The rat looked up.

"Hey Bob," said the rat. "You and I need to have a little talk. Why don't you let the dogs out and then pull up a chair."

A wall of rain hit Bob as he opened the front door, the

dogs almost knocking him over as they bolted into the darkness.

Bob returned to the kitchen, sat down and soon he and the rat were putting the world to rights.

When the police arrived they found the front door wide open, and Bob in the kitchen sitting at the table talking to an empty chair and gnawing on a half-eaten rat. He was covered in blood and spattered with brains and other human matter.

They found Joan in the bedroom, her head beaten to a pizza-like mush from which a lake of blood had spread across the floor like a cartoon speech bubble. Next to her, the baseball bat lay broken in two, its splintered end matted with blood, hair and brains. Joan was formally identified by her teeth, some of which were embedded in the bat, the rest scattered across the room.

The coroner called it a vicious and sustained attack.

The police had been called by the neighbouring sheep farmer, who had woken up to the sounds of animals in distress. When he reached the field, the farmer dropped to his knees. His entire flock was dead. Savaged by Joan and Bob's German Shepherds, who were now feasting on the carcasses.

The farmer went back into his house and returned with his shotgun and a leather bandolier filled with cartridges. He shot all six dogs and then called the police, sobbing uncontrollably as he tried to explain what had happened.

Bob was found guilty of the murder of his wife, and was sent to Broadmoor Psychiatric Hospital. He has a room to himself, which he keeps spotless.

Bob is the model inmate, and hopes that he never has to leave Broadmoor. It's the best place he's ever been and if he's ever released then he has decided that he will probably go out and kill some more people, just so that he gets sent back.

Bob says that out loud, at least twice a day. And because of that he lived happily ever after.

ACOUSTIC CASSETTE   N.R.|] ☐IN ☐OUT

B *Pick Your Path and I'll Pray - Jessica McHugh*

Normal Bias 120μsEQ A|60

Inspired by Fleetwood Mac "Gold Dust Woman"

He's in pieces again.

When a distant cry wakes Elmer Wray that evening, he has to assemble himself like a marionette with sweaty strings. Untangling his arms from the pillow and unslinging his legs from the sofa's edge, he's a sticky knot tumbling across the floor to retrieve his head. It sits like a swollen plum at the bottom of the whiskey bottle, but he ties it on with a belt of hot backwash that cinches his muscles, sharpens his thoughts, and allows him to stumble to the window facing the Bodie Hills.

It's probably another fire that started the hollering. The drought of 1881 is still taking its toll on the California town, and blazes are getting as commonplace as the mining accidents of old. Elmer's certain he'll see flames swell up from a neighbor's barn any second, red and orange fingers reaching for the heavens, followed by the hands of would-be heroes swinging lanterns out into the night.

But there are no flames fixing to kiss the sky, no tell-tale smoke tinged with corn and molasses, or whatever goods the miners turned to when the hills went dry. And though the screaming persists, not a single citizen rushes to investigate. The buildings remain dark and their occupants quiet while Elmer's heart aches under the pressure of the woman's wailing.

Yes. He believes it's a woman.

And not just any woman.

It doesn't make sense. The people of Bodie love a good distraction. Celebration or calamity, it doesn't matter as long as it helps them forget their own desolation for a while. And considering how much they despise Elmer Wray, the entire town should be lapping up his misery like mother's milk right now. They should be gathering at his porch like bees on a piece of warm licorice, eyes like full moons looking down on the man whose wife disappeared without a trace nearly ten years ago.

The warped wood beneath the window groans as he sinks to his knees, the planks long ago weakened by years of Jenny rocking from foot to foot, watching Elmer set off for the mine, waiting for him to find his fortune in the hills instead of in her.

Whiskey sloshes in his skull as he curls up in the cradle she left behind, and when he touches the secret notch in the wood, the house falls in on him, the walls thudding closer and closer, threatening collapse. But they're not kind enough to splatter him like an egg yolk. They stay far enough away for Elmer to breathe and move, but never find comfort.

The place was bigger when Jenny was there. She had a light about her that created space wherever she went. From crowded church services and marketplaces to the confined wagon that carried them from Brooklyn to Bodie all those years ago, Jenny had an energy that... opened. She was much like the untamed west: a grand expanse of fortune and salvation, cool water and prism light, changing men so gradually that Elmer didn't realize he was in love with her until they reached Wyoming.

A woman like that doesn't deserve to suffer, and if the good people of Bodie won't help her, Elmer will have to scrape up the courage to face her himself.

He throws back another belt and gulps so hard it hurts. It's been five years since he walked the path to his former claim, three years since he left his porch, and sixteen months since he opened his front door. In all that time, the back window's been his only portal to the outside world, and his only true-blue connection's been a barrel-chested teen named Chet. Although their exchanges revolve solely around the boy's food and whiskey deliveries, he likes to think Chet's there for more than payment. He's not deluded enough to believe it, however. The boy's gaze is constantly moving, darting, searching the house's interior for some sign of the gold he earns from Elmer each month. He'll never find it from the window though. He'll have to come inside.

But he won't. There's the smell, for one. And even if it had the reassuring sage aroma of the old days, the last time Chet made a drop-off, a neighbor spotted him talking to the crazy old shut-in and he took off like a shot. Hasn't been back since either, and the whiskey's running low.

It takes some muscle, but he forces the brittle door open, and the acidic air of an alien world rushes into his lungs. The night is a leery stranger, the summer air thick as the sweat that ran like congealed mud between his eyes after a day in the mine. A gritty reality stings his eyes, and he has to put on his goggles just to endure the view from the porch.

The stiff rubber cracks when he tightens the strap around the back of his head. He expects it to feel strange, but the strap settles right into the mushy ravine that divides his scalp into opposing ecosystems. The swampy roll of flesh under the strap cascades into a freckled tier of dry flesh that pours down his back. Jenny used to rub liniment on his scalp at night, and he paid back the favour those months before she disappeared, when the baby stretched her skin tight as a drum.

It squirmed and rolled when he did that. When he circled her bulbous belly-button with liniment, the baby kicked his hand and did somersaults that made Jenny giggle in a way she hadn't before the pregnancy.

Elmer holds onto the memory of that laughter as he fixes his trusty Davy lamp to his knapsack and steps off the porch.

Is the ground softer now? He twists his boot in the dirt and furrows his brow. Yes. It feels like wet sand, so much he's tempted to kick off a shoe and scrunch his bare toes into the earth.

The indulgent thought instantly fills him with shame. Opening his knapsack, he shakes out a canteen of whiskey and takes a gulp large enough to drown any happy notions to come.

It works. The scream sounds like an infant now. The colicky cry of a child who might've never drawn breath strikes him deeper than Jenny's wails. An organ he didn't know existed throbs with the insistent bawling and wrenches him faster down the path. It's like the dent in his scalp — well trod and waiting — and though he made that trek for years, back and forth, away from Jenny, to the mine he worked with Billy, the journey was never so painful as tonight.

Elmer looks back at his home, dark and small on the edge of a dim planet. Though he feels the footprints of his former self beneath him like pencil marks chronicling growth on a childhood wall, it's the prints beside the trail that grant him an ounce of comfort. It's as if she chased after him instead of standing at the window, day after day, the floor bowing beneath her as her belly grew nearer to the glass.

She was especially anxious the day she died. The physician predicted labour within the week, and Bodie was in the thick of the worst drought in a decade. But they were too close to let up now. Every day the claim yielded more flour and flecks; it was only a matter of time until they struck the big one, the jackpot, the vein from which all the little droplets broke free.

"You'll see, Jenny. Once we hit the mother lode, everything will be different."

Billy agreed, condescendingly patting his little sister's head. "That's right. Then you'll have enough money to whisk yourself and the little whelp off to Europe and leave us to our work."

It was barely playful the first time her brother said something like that, and by the ninth month, it had become a threat. As much as he loved his sister, Billy made no secret of loathing the pregnancy. He made jokes about drowning the baby like a rat or using it as bait to snare the yowling mountain lions that prowled the outskirts of town.

But Elmer wanted the baby. Every day before he left for the mine, he kissed Jenny's belly and said, "I love you, little girl," because he hoped against hope that the baby would emerge a tinier version of the woman he loved. Beautiful and strong. Obstinate, too. But only because, like Jenny, she would almost always be right.

No one in Bodie appreciated the breadth of his adoration. All they saw was his morning desertion, and how distressed his wife seemed at the window suspecting her husband preferred spending his sweaty days in a cave with her big brother. Nobody said it outright, but there were accusations in their eyes as he and Billy made the long walk through town to their claim, where the pair had been mining since they were twenty.

Billy should've been a suspect in Jenny's disappearance too, and Elmer assumes he would've been the first person questioned had Billy not gone missing the same day.

He was the reason Elmer didn't tell Jenny he loved her 'til the wagon reached Nevada. Billy had been his best friend since they first met. The only child of a deadbeat father in a dilapidated Brooklyn tenement, Elmer had nothing to offer the boy with the freckled cheeks. But for reasons Elmer never understood, Billy welcomed him into his life with such unbridled joy that Elmer swore to him a silent vow of loyalty.

As they grew, their relationship deepened and Billy became more than a friend; he became a saviour. When Elmer slept through the night, it was because Billy let him sneak into his room and doze in his lumpy twin bed. When he went an entire month without a black eye, it was because Billy whipped up the perfect plan to keep him away from his dad. And when Elmer arrived in California at seventeen with a dream of striking it rich with his best friend and a heart full of newly blossomed love, he had Billy to thank for convincing his family to let Elmer join their westward journey.

Admitting he'd fallen for his best friend's little sister, and Jenny's confessed reciprocation, seemed a vicious repayment for Billy's kindness.

So they hid their love. He stole nights with Jenny just as he used to steal nights with his friend back in Brooklyn. All those evening brawling in the streets, sweat and blood speckled boys, skin on skin in the sticky violence of puberty, or on the trail when the nights were too hot for clothes and he and Billy lay out naked under the stars: they belonged to Jenny now.

They were one year into mining their shared claim in the Bodie Hills when Billy finally discovered the tryst.

He wasn't angry.

Elmer wanted him to be angry.

The pain rises in him like it did then. It's been ages since this path forged mountains in his lungs and ran rivers from his eyes. He wants to hold onto the thought that it might lead him to Billy again, but it's too slippery to grip. It's hard to catch a breath too, like trauma had stolen the oxygen from around the adit, and Elmer's head swims with the fog of regret.

He's stumbling when he passes the last cluster of

limestone that marks the place he once considered another home. Another life even, apart from the easy love he shared with Jenny.

He imagined it sometimes, that Jenny had chosen to stay in Brooklyn and marry one of her many suitors. Elmer would've still gone with Billy. They would've still had the claim. He would've drank the same whiskey, got into the same types of trouble, still sweated out days of shit-creek sickness. And all that without the guilt currently shredding a hole in his gut.

The screaming is all at once a man and his pickaxe. The noise tugs him faster down the path, the canteen again at his lips, pouring gumption down his aching gullet. It's the last place Elmer saw him draw breath. Is it so hard to believe he might still be there?

The word "help" forms like a pregnant raindrop in the peals, and Elmer stops in his tracks. He sinks slightly into his footprints, like the earth locks him in place, has always locked him, maybe even kept him on the edge of the claim these long years while Jenny waited in her cradle. The "help" echoes inside him, and his wonder grows like a tidal wave that rushes him into the crumbling castle where the Brooklyn boys once reigned.

It was long ago condemned, but he sidesteps the barriers and sinkholes, and with the lantern flickering memories across the broken ledges, he's finally able to fill his lungs with musty air. Relief is short-lived when the screaming begins again. It's like a rubber ball within the mountain, a deafening mosaic of voices with no definite origin.

Elmer drops the lamp, claps his hands over his ears, and shouts, "Jenny!"

It doesn't feel like it comes from him but her name slides out smooth and wet and dampens the noise.

Silence. Then, almost disbelieving, a voice: "Hello?"

He presses his hand to the rock and feels breathing

behind the wall. "Yes. I'm here."

The voice is high-pitched and tear-choked, and words come like a downpour.

"Oh thank God, please help me. I'm trapped, my leg— please you have to get me out."

"How'd you get in there?"

"Please, I can't breathe!"

He rights the lamp and grabs his pickaxe with a grace he thought long ago fled his muscles. It's as if no time has passed—and, perhaps, neither has Jenny. It sounds like she's on the other side of the rock, needing him, begging him to free her, give her air again, to give her life again.

The axe splits the stone as easily as the day they hit the mother lode. The mighty whack that made Elmer and Billy the richest men in Bodie now reveals a woman floured in golden dust, pouring from the mountain in weeping gratitude.

Patched in grimy yellow and red, she buries herself in his chest and grips his shirt like she hasn't touched anything but her tattered dress for a hundred years. Her neck is raw from it, glistening wet down her back and arms. The cloth is as rough against Elmer's exposed skin, like burlap and pumice loomed into an irritating torture chamber of attire, but he lets her dot him with crimson kisses and burrow herself deeper into his embrace. Only her right leg remains outstretched, the calf shredded and flesh like gilded ribbons curling down her ankle.

"Jenny, what happened to you?"

She whimpers an apology and lifts her head, her hair like a dirty bridal veil. It's too pale to be Jenny's. Pushing it aside, he also finds a face too round and lips too small.

"You're not—"—His voice catches. "Who are you? How'd you get in there?"

"Water. Please."

He swipes a thumb across her brow and inspects the glistening powder in his swirled fingerprint. Gazing into the chasm where she was trapped, he sees only dirt and stone. Not a crumb, not a fleck of gold anywhere but on the strange woman's skin.

She grasps his hand and bears her dirt-encrusted teeth. "You have to help me. I can't walk."

"Don't worry, I'll get you some help. I'll fetch the doctor."

He tries to pull free, and her arms lock around his neck. "No! Don't leave me!" she wails. "I can't stay here alone! Not one more minute!"

Elmer's chest aches with regret. Jenny's gaze said as much each morning and he still turned away. The woman may not be his dead wife, but she is still a creature in pain. And the gold in her skin compels him like it did the last night he was in this mine, when he walked the path more than a dozen times, transporting both flesh and gold.

Tonight he will do it once more.

She isn't easy to carry. The pain makes her coil and uncoil around him like a restless dragon. Angry breath pelts his skin, which her dress scrubs like a porous stone. Each step shears a little more until he is raw and red and damp as a Brooklyn summer by the time he reaches his cracked porch. Agony tears through him like wildfire as he deposits her on the couch, but he doesn't stop to feel it. He fetches her water. He fetches her bread. He brings her a wet cloth to clean her wounds.

But when he returns to his living room, she's no longer on the couch.

"It's a beautiful view," she says from Jenny's warped spot at the window. "She must've loved it... at one time."

Elmer gulps. "She?"

The leg wound affects the gold-dusted woman's balance as she turns, but pain isn't what gives her a stooped and prowling gait. It's simply how she moves—her head low and shoulders hitched, and her fingertips curled as if preparing to hand-dig a grave. But she crouches in Jenny's divot instead and unfolds her fingers against the floor.

"What were you doing in that mine?" he says.

Looking up at Elmer, she smiles wryly and taps the boards with one nail.

"Who are you?"

The tapping sets his teeth on edge and drums his nerves raw, and as her pinkie moves closer to the notch in the floor, her breath fills the house with cold air that chills his eroded flesh. He shivers so violently, his knees soften and surrender under his weight. He collapses beside her, his muscles shuddering as he smacks her hand away from the notch in the floor.

She retreats to the wall and pulls her legs to her chest. She fits perfectly in Jenny's basin, and her eyes are just as tearful with worry. She squeezes them closed and whimpers.

"Did she die here?"

Guzzling the last of the knapsack whiskey is the best answer Elmer can give. Fact is, he doesn't know where Jenny died. Or where she delivered — if she delivered. For Jenny's sake, he hopes she did. Every night since she disappeared, he's prayed that she got to hold her child and hush her with songs unsewn from maternal fabric, the kind of music only mothers know, before they both went to sleep. But for the baby's sake, he hoped they were still one, that she was safe and warm when their last night came.

When Elmer finally arrived home, the massive puddles and smears of blood were old enough to have acquired nests of flies, and though the people of Bodie confessed to hearing mountain lions brawling in the hills, no one saw them come to town. No one saw them slip into the Wray's house and tear the pregnant woman limb from limb. No one saw them carry her back to their den in pieces like Elmer does in his dreams.

"What took you so long?" asks the gold-dusted woman. "What kept you so late at the mine that night?"

She crawls to him, her scapula oddly jutting from her back and the dusted fuzz along her arms looking like golden spikes in the moonlight. Pinning him against the couch, she unrolls her spine and looks down on him the way Billy once did. All the fury, all the remorse, all the desperation that drove his best friend to raise a pickaxe and threaten to split his skull roils in her enormous yellow eyes. Her lips move, but it's Billy who speaks.

"You promised me," he says. "All these years, putting it off, waiting for the mother lode, and here we are, Elmer. It's time."

Something like hot wax drips down either side of his neck, and when he reaches up he finds his ears soft and sloughing down his face. He screeches and barrels through the woman to reach the whiskey in the kitchen cupboard, but she catches hold of his ankle and curls her claws deep into his flesh. The skin peels too easy, and her grin stretches too wide.

Elmer howls as his flesh falls in flanking piles and he squirms to the stuff that'll set him right. It'll put him back together and shut them all up. She lets him make the journey and watches in fascination as he rifles through empty bottles and canteens. He tosses them across the kitchen, his lips like dried up slugs by the time he finds a flask with a splash remaining. But his fingers are too loosely attached to unscrew the cap.

"That can't help you anymore, Elmer."

He flips onto his back and wails at the woman creeping closer. "Why are you doing this to me?"

Her wheezing laughter is a collage of voices. Billy, Jenny, the baby he never heard: their screams pour out of her like vomit that drenches Elmer in all the questions his wife and best friend hurtled at him on their last day together.

"Why weren't you here?"

"Why can't we leave?"

"Why didn't you look for me?"

"Why don't you just die?"

Gold dust gets in his eyes. His tears thicken it, texture it, and despite his mad rubbing and scraping, it encases the organs in the blurry yellow nightmare he's been having for the last ten years. The woman's back appears broken, her limbs bulging and reversed as she crawls to the cradle under the window and stares at the notch.

"Why didn't you look for me?" she whimpers. It's Jenny's voice again, but it sounds strained, even choked, as if she's been calling for hours and her throat is filling up with scabs and loose meat from the brutality of being forgotten. "When you came home and saw I was gone, when you saw the blood, why didn't you search the hills with the others? Why did you walk that path over and over until morning? Why was gold more important than our lives?"

Aurous tears scald his cheeks and fill the air with a meaty stench that prompts the woman to lick her chops.

Billy's voice rolls out then, a low rumble that hits Elmer like arrhythmia. "But it wasn't the gold that kept you."

His head's too cumbersome to shake, and salty golden stalactites form on his cheeks as it hangs limp, his chin to his throbbing chest.

"I didn't want it to end," he says. "The business, the partnership, everything we had."

"That was the promise we made, Elmer. When we struck the mother lode, you had to choose. Me and the gold, or her and the kid."

"It was too late. I couldn't keep that promise. But I couldn't let you leave with the money either. I couldn't let you leave."

The gasp is Jenny's — as is the sorrow, the rage, and the devastation at now knowing that while she and her child died like worthless meat in the hills, Elmer was murdering his lover in their mine.

"You killed him," Jenny whispers shakily. "My brother."

"He attacked me when I told me I was choosing you! He was going to kill me!"

"So you killed him," she repeats. "My brother."

"If you only knew how much he hated you — "

"No," Billy says gruffly. "I hated you both. I hated that you broke your promise. But I told you, Elmer. Pick your path, and I'll pray. I did my part."

"There was no other path, Bill."

"I know. No matter how much you loved me, you were always going to choose her."

"But you didn't," Jenny says, her voice as distant as the scream that roused him. "If you chose me, you would've been there to save me. The beasts took my arm and my eye and my toes, but I was alive for so long, Elmer. We both were. But I couldn't hold onto her."

When the woman shivers, phantasmic wails pour like hungry beetles from her body, skittering invisible but deafening about the room. While Elmer cowers in torment, the cries push her closer to the hole in the floor, her fingers outstretched and bones shifting under her flesh. He tries to stop her, but she rears back and slaps him with curled fingertips that smash the tear-shards to golden dust and pluck rubies from his cheek.

The woman presses her face to the notch and inhales deep.

"You couldn't carry him back with you," she says and glances over, saliva dripping down her chin. "Not in one piece."

Hooking a finger into the hole, the dusty woman releases an animalistic scream and rips the plank out of the floor.

He pulls himself to the opening, where she looks down, mouth agape, at what's become of the Brooklyn boys' claim. Though it still shines sometimes in Elmer's dreams, it looks like piles of yellow shit beneath the floorboards. Smells like it too, even years after the insects stripped Billy's bones. They're scattered throughout the treasure, many still lumped with the same gold that made the trek from the mine to the house all those years ago. While the people of Bodie searched the mountains for Jenny Wray, Elmer marched the path in the dark, back and forth, carrying both fortune and curse in his aching arms.

The golden woman looks down at the bones and gold and releases a heavy sigh. Favouring her injured leg, she faces Elmer with her scapula arched high, her head low, and her mandible dropping slowly. Her skull stretches and splinters, and her beauty drains like a stopped up sink, gurgling brown and clotted before running clear.

When Elmer finally sees the golden creature for what she is, he knows he will not walk the path again.

The man and the lion regard each other: two wounded beasts desperate to escape but only one looking to get out alive. Her amber eyes gleam in the moonlight, and her tail twitches a warning, but even as she prepares to pounce, Elmer Wray doesn't move.

She fills her belly and slumbers in the cradle beneath the window, rising only when the sun beats hot upon her golden fur. She can't carry much, and she has to walk the path slow, but she's on her way, almost home, to her hungry children screaming in the hills.

Inspired by Fiona Apple "Hot Knife"

"Dannie, are you coming? We need to be there at least 10 minutes before the movie starts so we can get good seats and have time to buy Lemonheads."

Dannie waived her roommate away

"Gimme a minute, Abigail, I want to hear this." She was focused on the pleasant baritone of a handsome news reporter running down the lurid details of the Hot Knife Killer. The story spilled from the television while Dannie brushed her hair.

"The Hot Knife Killer was believed to have last struck two years ago. There are usually several years between these murders. But, the authorities believe he is on the prowl once again. The Hot Knife Killer's MO is always the same; he stabs his victims, just once, with a sharp object that has been heated to a very high temperature. Wound cauterization is only one of the telltale signs that identify The Hot Knife murders, and some of the more shocking detailse have been held back by the Police working the case. The killings have been so sensationalized, that his methods have spawned three copycat killers. But unlike the original, they've all been apprehended, convicted, and proven to be unaware of some of those closely held details. The Police know they have not been able to halt his killing spree."

"C'mon, Dannie. We're going to be late. Get ready already. Christoph is more interesting than this crap, and he's probably already there. I love his exotic accent, and how he calls the movies the cinemascope. If you're not interested, you can always dump him and send him my way."

Dannie waved her friend off again, but said, "Okay, okay, I'm coming. And for the record, I'm not dumping Christoph so you can pick up the pieces. He's too good looking for the likes of you, and he has a job. You only like ugly dudes with tattoos and prison records, like Derek."

Abigail leaned over to retie her boot and grunted, "Derek is currently in between gigs. Not that Christoph is much better. His job is processing medical insurance claims out of his basement at night. He might as well be unemployed."

Dannie cut off the conversation by pressing the button of the remote and throwing it on the couch. The action shut up the reporter and her friend. She refused to be upset and sang, "Off to the cinemascope we go," while skipping towards the door.

They arrived with barely enough time to buy snacks and were standing in line when Dannie picked out Christoph waiting patiently for them. It always surprised her how beautiful he was, like he was carved instead of born, with steel blue eyes, and jet-black hair. Christoph was easy to spot, he was almost a head taller than everyone else in the lobby. But that height was perfect for her; when he hugged her, it put her head right against his chest. So far, hugging was the most intimacy that she had experienced with him. They hadn't kissed yet; he was always the gentleman and told her not to rush. That made her want to kiss him even more, and go even further still. She felt like she was falling in love with him. Maybe tonight was the night. Maybe tonight she got her first kiss. Maybe tonight, she got more than a kiss.

Derek had already gone into the theatre, abandoning Abigail for a good seat up on the back row. He waived when the three of them entered, but didn't join them. The theatre was packed and they ended up having to sit on the front row and crane their necks to see the film.

Dannie leaned over to Abigail, sitting alone, and said, "Your boyfriend is an ass. He didn't even save us a seat."

Abigail whispered back, almost drowned out by the soundcheck, "I probably won't be home tonight. We have a hotel reservation."

"Geez, Abigail, maybe you would get better fish if you spent more time actually fishing."

Christoph leaned in with his eastern European accent, "The cinemascope does not allow talking," smiling so they knew it was a joke. Sarcasm doesn't carry well with an accent, and without the smile, Dannie would have thought he was dead serious.

While the coming attractions spun across the screen, they previewed a dark tale of vampires, and a thought occurred to her. Christoph looked exactly like a vampire, at least what she thought a vampire would look like, his accent being the icing on the cake. So she playfully asked, "Christoph, are you one of the undead? Are you a vampire?"

He laughed and responded with, "I'm here to suck your blood." He leaned in, nipped playfully at her neck and followed with, "You have seen me in the daylight. I do not sparkle."

He didn't even need to preface the joke with a smile for her to get that one. They slid down in their chairs and she leaned her head on his shoulder to take in the show.

"I'll see you. Don't wait up!" Abigail grabbed Derek's hand and headed off in the opposite direction, leaving Christoph and Dannie alone outside the theater.

Dannie leaned in, "Do you want to come to my place? I make a mean cup of coffee."

Christoph hugged her, making the leather of his coat squeak around her shoulders. "I would love that. Coffee is a temptation that cannot be passed up."

They walked slowly, commenting on the people on the street, their breath making frosty vapour clouds when they laughed. The wet cold of the city's winter could not dampen their mood.

Dannie pulled out her key at the front door of their apartment building, and both were surprised by another tenant elbowing his way past to get into the lobby.

Christoph reacted with, "Well, excuse us fine sir."

The stranger turned suddenly, brandishing a knife. "Gimme your money and jewelry, or you both die."

Christoph smiled, and his voice came out measured but gravelly, "I am not one to be trifled with."

"Okay, bitch, trifling it is." The man lunged forward, stabbing straight out towards Christoph's stomach.

Dannie gasped, and started crying in anticipation of holding Christoph's head in her lap as he struggled for his last dying breaths. But her fear was unfounded. She had never seen someone move so fast. He side stepped the thrust of the knife, slid his left hand down the attacker's arm until he clamped down on the wrist, and then stepped forward, twisting the robber's knife hand up behind his head, while simultaneously throwing a right elbow that connected with the man's nose. Dannie heard the nose crunch under the blow, and blood sprayed out like a small explosion across his cheek. The brutality of the elbow strike knocked the robber, now victim, down to the ground. Somehow, Christoph now possessed the blade, twirling it in his hand. It was the most fluid, most violent thing she had ever seen. Dirty, sensual thoughts about the man in front of her jumped unexpectedly into her mind.

Christoph spoke, his voice untouched by fear while pointing the knife at the thief. "Go, go. You know not what you do. Don't ever come back here, though, or I will not be so forgiving." It amazed her that he could remain so calm.

The robber, who had been intent on murder only a moment before, scrambled to his feet and rushed out of the foyer of the building, trailing blood on the linoleum floor.

Dannie wiped the nervous tears from her eyes. "Are you okay?"

Christoph smiled, a twinkle in his eyes, and said, "How long does it take to make coffee?"

The adrenaline of the moment made her shake uncontrollably. She leaned on Christoph for support, and he was an unwavering rock.

They didn't speak at all while she ground coffee beans and flipped on the espresso machine. Dannie finally broke the silence as she brought two tiny cups on matching saucers to the living room couch. "Christoph, I thought I was falling in love with you. But I realised I have no idea who you are. In fact, you don't really know anything about me either."

Christoph's mouth twisted up in a knowing smile, "I will tell your secrets, and then share mine."

"No, no, Christoph, your English didn't come out right. You're supposed to tell me your secret, and I will tell you my secret."

"I have spoken correctly." Christoph brought his ankle up to the opposite knee, took a sip of the hot coffee, and then nestled the saucer in the crook of his lap. "First, I tell your secret. It will make my secret easier to share."

Dannie shrugged, "Okay, have it your way." She leaned back on the couch and sipped her coffee, intent on his secret, curious if he could guess at her closely guarded information.

"I will not, as you say, beat around the rose bushes. Your secret is that you are very, very ill. You have cancer, or as my people call it, the Wasting. I would guess by your aura that it is pancreatic cancer and you probably have three to six months to live."

All the emotion she had been holding inside for months burst forward in a flood of racking sobs. "Christoph, I haven't told anyone. Not even Abigail, not even my family. You can't know this."

"But I do know, which leads me to my secret. I have an inherited talent, what some people would consider to be supernatural. It is not truly supernatural, because it is in my people's genetics, in our blood. It comes down from my mother's side, an uninterrupted bloodline back through time to a group of travelling gypsy healers. My people translate this talent as, the Sight. It is my duty to travel the world, looking for those that suffer the Wasting, and to do what I can." He sipped at the espresso, the small cup clinking against the saucer.

"So you only dated me because you felt sorry for me?"

Christoph shook his head and raised his hands in supplication. "No, no, not that at all. I dated you to see if you were worthy of the help of my people. You were more than I could have hoped for. Beautiful, caring, thoughtful and trusting. There are lots of people with the Wasting, but not all of them deserve help."

Tears ran freely down Dannie's cheeks. "Christoph, until tonight, I was just trying to live out the rest of my short life. The doctors cannot cure what I have. It cannot be operated on, radiation will not destroy it, and chemo will just speed up the process. I did not mean to get involved with someone that I would fall in love with. I just wanted someone that I could have fun with, before I died. You have turned out to be both, someone to have fun with, and someone that I can't help but love."

Christoph leaned in for a soft kiss, and while he had been a rock during the attack, he trembled while their lips met. It made her knees week and she was grateful she was sitting on the couch. She leaned in again, kissing his neck, and he shuddered with an indrawn breath that rushed through his clenched teeth.

Christoph pulled back abruptly, "I must stop you. I do not want to stop you, but I must. I cannot partake in this...feistiness."

Dannie felt rejected, and started to cry again, "I'm, I'm sorry. I thought...I don't know what I thought. I just wanted to share everything with you."

"I wish to share everything with you as well. But I cannot. My talent will not allow it. If I do, you will be lost forever." Christoph gently separated their faces and wiped a tear from her cheek.

Dannie nodded, "Most men wouldn't turn down a free roll in the hay."

Christoph gently caressed her hand, running his thumb over her wrist, used his other hand to push a stray hair back behind her ear, and then whispered, "I am not most men, and I am fated to either cure the woman I love, or watch her die. I cannot satiate our desire unless you are cured."

"You keep talking about helping and curing me. How exactly do you do that? I had already come to terms with my illness. I was ready to die Christoph."

"It starts with the Sight, but there is also an ancient ritual." He looked down, almost like he was ashamed of himself.

Dannie needed him to explain more, so followed with, "And?"

"There is also danger involved with the ritual. It will

either cure you or kill you. It has something to do with faith, with belief in the process. If you do not believe, if you do not trust in the ritual, you will be lost." Christoph wrung his hands and then ran them through his hair. It was a nervous tick that Dannie had never seen him perform before.

"So, when can we do this ritual? The ritual will bring me the possibility of a cure, right? If I don't do it, I will definitely die. What do I have to lose?"

Christoph explained, halting after each statement. "The ritual does not work one hundred percent of the time. Because of this, we must break up, and wait to hold the ritual until one month from now. Everyone must think I am no longer in your life."

Dannie bought into the idea but asked for a little more detail. "What am I to tell people about our breakup?"

Christoph already had the answer ready, "Tell them of your illness. Share with them that you have cancer and that it is terminal. Tell them that you couldn't break my heart when you pass, so you broke it off. Tie up any loose ends, finalise your Will, and give as much closure to your friends and family as you can. Do not mention me after the break up; not in email, or in conversations. Maybe even go on a few more dates with other men. The connection must be severed. After all of this, we will perform the ritual on the day of Saint Valentine." He quickly jotted down an address in the industrial area of the city. "We will meet here in the evening."

Dannie thought about the ritual he kept referencing. "Will it hurt? I mean the ritual, not my feelings."

Christoph cringed. "It will definitely hurt. It could kill you. It could kill me as well. But it's worth the chance. It may also save us both. I will give you details on the day we perform it. If you are too scared, we will call it off."

Her laugh was laced with nervousness "Scared of an ancient ritual? I'm scared of dying."

Christoph smiled, lightly caressed her face again, leaned

in and kissed her deeply. They were both out of breath when he pulled back. "Until the day of Saint Valentine."

Dannie watched the back of his leather coat as he walked out of the apartment. He turned briefly and said, "I am shutting door on our relationship."

She giggled at his grasp of the language and blew him a kiss before the door clicked shut.

Sergeant Collins rubbed his eyes. He was exhausted.

Agent Becker leaned in past the doorframe and asked, "You want a refresher?" wiggling a ceramic coffee cup imprinted with the FBI badge.

"Please." Collins was going through the case file of The Hot Knife Killer with the fourth FBI Agent in as many months. The previous three had all been retired, and willing to work cold cases. Becker was still active, which gave her additional access to the Bureau's files, and as an added bonus, she was easy on the eyes.

She walked through the door, with two cups of cheap, black coffee, and set them down on the metal table. She spun her chair around, straddled it, and said, "Why don't we start from the beginning? There's got to be something we're missing."

Collins indulged her. The Sergeant pulled the first box of evidence and started by spreading pictures of the victims on the table. There were six killings that they knew of. He pointed to the first; Karla Jamison, aged 24. His finger followed the pictures as he read off the victim's names and their ages, Maria Sanchez, 22; Kathleen Peters, 31; Christine Smith, 58; Holly Barringer, 36; and Felicity Washington, 29. There are no physical similarities with the victims. They are of diverse ethnicities and ages, different colours of hair and eyes. But they are all women. This is all public information. What the public doesn't know is that every one of his victims were dying. They each had some form of terminal cancer. The cauterized stab wound was directly over their cancer. This is how we were able to distinguish between the copycat killers. None of the copycat victims were terminally ill."

Agent Becker focused on each picture, hesitating on each victim's face before moving to the next. "What did the profiler give us?"

Collins rustled around in one of the boxes and pulled out a laminated sheet of paper and started reading, "White male, early thirties, possible ex-military, where he would have had medical triage training. If he's not military, he could be a nurse, or someone that dropped out of medical school. The wounds are precisely over the affected organs, but crude in their application. Probably has a working knowledge of several languages. Very smart, very charismatic."

Becker snickered, "Sounds like someone I would date."

Collins sneered, "I thought you were a lesbian. Clearly, I wouldn't make a very good profiler."

Agent Becker snorted at the chauvinist ribbing and retorted, "Maybe I go both ways." Men had been giving her a hard time since her first day in the academy, and she usually just ignored it. She wasn't going to rise to the bait, so she asked her next question. "Boyfriends, family members, acquaintances? There's got to be some connection."

Sergeant Collins shook his head, before taking a sip of his coffee. "There's nothing. We've interviewed everyone in their inner circles, and there is nothing that ties them together with any of the other victims. They don't mix with the same people, they don't go to the same restaurants, they don't live or work near each other. No similarities, no ties, nothing."

"Okay, so what forensics do we have at the scenes? I need any similarities, any common threads. Do we have DNA?" She had to repeat the questions as he had gotten lost in a photo of one of the victims.

"There is some sort of ancient text written in a ritualistic pattern around the corpses. And then the sharp object used for the stab wound is incredibly hot. It's not just hot, the knife would have to be cherry red. So he would have to have some sort of forge near the victim to get it to that temperature. And no DNA. He's very careful, almost like he disinfects the area." He shuffled through some more evidence in the boxes and pulled out a picture of one of the crime scenes.

The FBI Agent hovered over the new photo, taking in the scribbles and pattern around the body of a young Hispanic girl. "What language is that?"

The police sergeant had already run that lead down as well. "We're not entirely sure. It looks like a variant of Romanes. An ancient language spoken by gypsies from Romania and the surrounding area."

Becker nodded her head like that wasn't the first time she'd heard of the language. She's gotta be a lesbian, Collins thought, a full of shit lesbian.

She broke into his thoughts with, "That word there...it means, faith?"

"Damn girl, how do you know that? It's the one word that is repeated throughout the inscriptions more than any other. It took us years to figure out what it meant." The FBI agent was turning out to be full of surprises.

"I'm a linguist. I specialise in Eastern European languages, their origins, and the development of language through culture. That's why the FBI sent me. That, and the previous agents were male. They thought maybe a female viewpoint would help."

"Well, do you spot anything else in there? Faith was the only real thing we got from the writings." Collins jumped at the chance to learn something else, anything else, and pulled a stack of detailed photographs, close-ups of the ritualistic writing.

The agent spread photos out and nodded several times before she spoke. "This is all conjecture, and I can't make it all out, but it seems like this is wasting, while that is sight, and this is fires of Hell to open the gates of Heaven," all while pointing at different words on the table. She hesitated in thought before saying, "He fervently believes these writings. It's his religion."

It felt like the first headway they'd made in years and triggered him to run down a different avenue. "How is he finding these women? How does he know they have cancer? You think he works at a doctor's office, maybe as an orderly at the hospital?"

Becker pointed at him and had a decent thought of her own. "Maybe he's a hacker. Maybe he goes online, hacks into the standardised medical records, and identifies his next victim based on their cancer. Maybe he thinks he's doing it for their own good."

The nagging feeling that they were really close, but not quite there, pushed Collins to ask, "Then how does he go through with the stabbing? It seems like he's abducting them at random, because there are no ties to the victims." He rejected that thought immediately and said, "No, that seems too sloppy; someone, somewhere would see the abduction and give us a lead."

Agent Becker leaned in, the light of discovery in her eyes, and in a hushed voice gave him the answer, "It's because they are helping him. They want to be his victims."

The day was finally here. It seemed like an eternity, but it was an eternity that she hadn't succumbed to her cancer and had lived her life with hope. She was in constant pain now, and the doctors told her that it wouldn't be much longer; maybe a month or so. The dull ache in her abdomen would continue to grow as the cancer festered, and soon she would be obligated to use heavy doses of opioids. But, it was the Day of Saint Valentine, and she was ready to be cured.

Abigail had once again rented a hotel room for the day's festivities, but the boyfriend had changed. Dannie hadn't even bothered to find out his name. Abigail gave her a pain killer and winked at her as she left for the evening. Dannie waited for Abigail's key to turn in the lock before she jumped out of bed, fully dressed, and ran to the window. She waited impatiently while Abigail jumped in to a stranger's car and sped off into the night.

Once she knew she was on her own, she smoothed the red dress over her hips, slipped on her running shoes and grabbed her jacket. Dannie plugged the address into the GPS on her phone, then lit the handwritten paper on fire in the garbage can. As soon as it burned completely, and she was sure it wouldn't light the rest of the apartment on fire, she hurried to the rendezvous with Christoph.

It didn't take her long to walk the mile and a half to the abandoned warehouse. She knocked on some plywood that replaced a broken pane on one of the chained doors and heard shuffling inside. A large bay door, further down the block, rolled up, clanking and rattling to reveal a dank, old processing plant and Christoph's lean outline.

Dannie ran, hopped the concrete loading dock and embraced him. They held each other for several seconds, and she said, "I've missed you so much."

"I have been missing of you as well, Miss Dannie." The strength of his embrace was intoxicating. She felt drunk and happy, forgetting the dull, but constant pain of the cancer eating at her. It was only for a brief moment, but she cherished it.

She pulled slowly away and grasped his hands. "Let's get started. I want this finished so we can be together again."

Christoph smiled a radiant smile. "Yes, I have been preparing."

He allowed the bay door to slam heartily to the floor and shut out the rest of the world, slapping a rusty padlock on to ensure their privacy.

"This way." He led her to the back of the building to a windowless room and slid open a barn door to grant them access. "This is where they kept the animals. It is dark, to keep them calm before they were slaughtered." He gave her a lighter and instructed her to light candles around the floor of the room. "They must be placed exactly at the point of the stars, and intersections of the lines. The drawing, inscriptions, and candles are the base of the ritual."

Dannie carefully placed each one, revealing more of the inscriptions with each candle. When she completed her task, she could see a large design of intersecting circles, bathed in an eerie, wavering light. It reminded her of the drawings she used to make with a toy when she was younger, each circle a slight deviation from the one before to create a mesmerizing design.

Christoph grew serious. It scared her a little. "I spoke of the danger of the ritual before. Now I must show you so that you understand. I will operate on your cancer and attempt to transfer it into my body. I am immune because of my genetic nature. If I fail, you will die from the operation, or you will retain the cancer and it will consume you. If I succeed, we will be rid of this horrible disease and will walk out of here. We will have an unbreakable bond, forged this night, to span the rest of our lives."

Christoph walked over to the wall and opened a valve on top of a gas canister. He then bent over and quickly lit a small, ceramic box. The fan on the bottom of the ceramic box blew life into the flames, and there was a devilish glow that overpowered the candles. "While the furnace heats, we must change. You must remove all other articles; the ritual attire must rest against a naked soul." He grabbed a paper wrapped package and gingerly placed it in her open hands. "I will not look."

Dannie watched him open his own package and then

turn his back. She turned and stripped down. She kicked her shoes over to the corner of the room and pulled her dress over her head. She lay her dress on the cold, concrete floor, dropped her bra, panties and socks into the bundle, wadded up everything like she was swaddling a baby, and threw it into the corner to cover her shoes. The delicate paper of the package tore easily and revealed a bleach white, sleeveless robe. She pulled it over her head, blinded for a moment while she struggled to pull the robe down over her torso. The robe was a mini dress with an open midriff.

Christoph questioned over his shoulder, "Are you ready? Please turn."

"Yes." She turned slowly, letting Christoph drink in her shape.

There were tears in his eyes as he said, "You are beautiful."

She had been so intent on his reaction, that it took her a moment to register his ritual clothing. He was wearing ballooned, blood red pants, an intricate golden belt, embroidered with red symbols similar to the concentric circles on the floor, and no shirt. The sight of his chest was shocking, and unexpected. Old burns twisted his scarred skin from his collar bone all the way down past his belt. The overlapping burn scars looked like melting caramel slowly cascading down his chest. "Christoph, the pain...how...why?"

"These are fifteen years of burns and scars, ever since I took responsibility from my mother for the Sight and the cure for the Wasting. This is the price I pay for curing the people I come to care greatly for." He turned her shoulders and walked her to the centre of the candles, then turned her to face him. "You must stand here."

He walked back to the forge and using blacksmith tongs, removed a spike attached to a metal base. It looked like a sinister, sharp candlestick, glowing red and radiating hatred and heat across the room. "Now is the time. If you believe, you can be cured. If you do not believe, you will die. You must have faith or you are lost. The operation is performed by pushing this hollow spike into your cancer, and resting the base against my skin, opposite the puncture. We will embrace for eight seconds, and then pull apart. If the operation is successful, the cancer will travel down the crucible, and into my raw burn, to be destroyed forever."

Dannie was certain of his belief and tried to project her own. "I believe. I want to do this. I want to live, Christoph. Will it be quick, or seem like forever?"

Christoph smiled at her bravery. "It will be quick but painful. Like a hot knife through butter."

Dannie giggled, "That saying doesn't quite fit the situation, Christoph."

Christoph returned the chuckle, and responded, "Are you ready to be my little pat of butter?" His mirth faded quickly as he focused on the task at hand.

"Yes, Christoph, I believe."

He grabbed a thick leather glove, picked up the cherry-red spike and strode forward. He set the hot knife against his chest, accompanied by a sizzle of burning flesh, and embraced Dannie. The embrace pulled them together, punching the spike into her abdomen, duplicating the smell of seared meat and skin. Her natural reaction was to jerk backwards, but Christoph's embrace held her strong and unyielding.

Eight seconds was a lifetime. Her body fought against the pain, fought against the searing agony, while her mind struggled to have faith. She found herself concentrating on the smell of bacon in the air, her brain trying to cling to fond memories and shut out the trauma. Her mouth filled with saliva like some lupine experiment. Finally, it was over. Christoph stepped back, and removed the knife, kneeling and setting it gingerly off to the side. Dannie expected the sound of suction as it slid from her abdomen, but it sounded like two dry sticks rubbing together.

"Is this it? Am I healed?" She could feel the death of the cancer in her body. She knew it was no longer there.

Christoph looked up, tears running down his face, and said, "I have taken it into myself. It is gone."

"Then why are you crying?" Dannie's legs chose that instant to give out, their strength robbed by the ordeal. He sprang into action, a mirror of the speed shown during the mugging, and caught her before she hit the ground. One arm cradled her around the small of her back, the other held her neck to stabilize her lolling head.

"I am crying because you will not survive the ritual. Of all the ones that I wanted to survive...I wanted you to believe." He watched the dying light in her eyes as she slowly slipped away. The rattle of her last breath sounded like thunder in his ears, accusing, appraising his faith, and passing judgement.

"Come down here, quick. He struck again, and the kill is only hours old." Collins' voice waivered with anger and regret.

Becker responded, "Send me the address. I'm on my way."

Becker arrived shortly after, lucky that she didn't live very far away. She donned her paper suit to avoid cross contamination of the crime scene and shuffled in on paper booties. Only two other people were present in the slaughterhouse, both hovering over a body in the middle of a familiar pattern drawn on the floor.

Collins looked up and introduced her to the attractive man squatting down and taking photos, "Becker, this is Christopher, the best crime scene technician on the Force."

He turned, standing up, and looking down from his imposing height, responded, "Good to meet you, my friends call me Chris."

"I can't quite place your accent, Chris. Where is that from? The South?"

His steel blue eyes twinkled as he proclaimed, "New Awlins."

Inspired by Bjork "Isobel"

Her name was Isobel. Not Izzy or Iz or Bel, or any other variation. Just Isobel. And that was how she wanted to be known.

From as far back as she could remember, Isobel had always corrected anyone – other children *and* adults alike – on this, and the resolve had only gotten stronger each year. But never delivered with petulance or tantrums, only iterated with calm surety. It had begun with her mother, who used to spit 'pet' names with sneering derision. Yet even *she* eventually capitulated when it became clear this was not a subject her daughter would budge on.

Ah, Isobel's mother. Something else that was clear to the girl from a young age was that this woman – a person who should have been her protector, her nurturer, her first and best and closest friend – could barely tolerate the only child she'd brought into the world. It was there in every spiteful glance, in each dismissive word. Isobel's father was a dark, lumbering presence, a grumbling, vague shape to be avoided as much as possible, but the real menace was her mother. Though her regular attacks had remained verbal in nature so far (though no less cutting and hurtful for that; worse, it might be argued), Isobel suspected it was simply a matter of time before that changed.

But those thoughts – and other heavy, grey musings – were far from Isobel's mind on this particular day. For she was currently sitting in class, waiting with barely restrained patience for the final school bell to ring.

Today was a special day for Isobel; one of her favourites, in fact. Most afternoons, she was required to go straight home from school, lest she risk the ire of her mother. However, this was the one day of the week when the flat would be empty until later in the evening. Isobel's mother had a part-time cleaning job, and on Thursdays she always went to the same office block with two or three others. Though it wasn't strictly legal to allow an eleven-year-old to be left alone in the family home, the money was needed; for alcohol, mostly, but still considered a necessity. Her father never arrived home before 9 pm, preferring to spend his after-work time in the pub When he *did* roll in, it would be surrounded by a hazy cloud of stale beer, and he would either stagger off to bed or engage in verbal combat with her mother.

And so, this afternoon, Isobel intended – as she did every Thursday – to attend the local library. This was *her* vice, her addiction, one that was infinitely less harmful and more nourishing than those her parents were beholden to.

The teacher, Mr Bleak – and everything about him embodied that name, from his sagging, grey-tinged skin to his washed-out old suit – droned on, oblivious to the restlessness of his pupils. They either flicked continual glances at the ticking clock on the all above Mr Bleak's desk or stared through the grimy windows at the promise of freedom beyond. A few were kicking the legs of their desks, the mounting, arrhythmic drumming a portent to the stampede to come.

Isobel herself was fidgeting with a pen, her fingers twisting and manipulating the implement. At one point it skittered from her overly-tight grasp, skidding across the table and nearly dropping off the end of the desk. She caught it in time, looking around, but no-one was paying attention; all were lost in their own eagerness for the school day to be over.

She went back to staring at the clock, trying not to let the pen fly from her hands again.

Usually, she would be invested in whatever it was Mr Bleak was saying; even though he wasn't an especially inspiring teacher, Isobel still paid polite attention to the lessons. But this afternoon, she would have been incapable of repeating what they were being taught. Not that it mattered much; she was at a level beyond most of the other students anyway, though she kept that side of things hidden and mostly pretended to be learning along with them, so she wasn't singled out as a swot or teacher's pet. Isobel had few friends and none who were especially close.

Without warning, the bell sounded, making her – and the class – jump in their seats. It trilled a deep, vibrating ring that seemed to go on forever, and the mumble of whatever Mr Bleak was saying – the tatters of his lesson, admonishments to leave in an orderly fashion – was lost in it and the tumult of two dozen children bouncing to their feet and rushing for the door.

Isobel waited until the class was nearly empty before getting up and leaving herself. By then, the whole school was almost bled dry of children, streams of them having poured from the exits to swamp the streets outside. She emerged into fresh air, the chatter and laughter of other kids echoing and fading behind them.

Even though it was early October and quite chilly, Isobel still liked to linger outside. Part of it was the avoidance of home, which these days was beginning to feel like a prison, grim and grey. But another part was that she loved this time of year, as the days grew shorter, as the temperatures dropped, as the colours in nature changed. She loved seeing her breath fog in front of her face, loved the different smells, loved the afternoon lights of the town coming on early as the night drew down earlier and earlier. Something in the season spoke to her; a whisper on the growing wind, a delightful touch from the icy air. It was like coming home or meeting an old friend.

She wandered down streets which would eventually take her to the library. The building was located in the opposite direction to where her parents' flat was, otherwise Isobel might have been able to visit on other days, also. But even once a week was enough for her.

As she walked, she looked about, taking delight in the world around, even in things most might find mundane; after all, it wasn't often she got to experience them. On the other side of the road stood a small, stone church, its cracked walls snaked with ivy. Though her family weren't religious in the slightest, she longed to go inside, to soak in the divine hush she was sure it contained. Maybe she'd see an angel or hear the voice of God Just beyond that was a little park, its overgrown greens cut in two by a meandering pavement. There was a tiny playpark inside the grounds, too, empty and – to Isobel – forlorn. One swing rocked ever so slightly, as though some unseen child had just vacated it. The thought made her feel a little sad, though she couldn't say why. Perhaps it had been a ghost, hiding and waiting till she'd gone past so he could come out and play again.. And up ahead, on the other side of the town's main crossroads was a modest shopping centre, a rather garish construct of glass and steel, housing a supermarket, a music shop, and various assorted clothes and electrical stores. Isobel never went that far because the library was on *this* side of the crossroads, but again, she wished she could go in and wander around. Not because she was especially interested in shopping, but because again, it was something different, something unusual to her normal routines.

Perhaps one day.

But for now, she had books to browse.

Picking up her pace – but not hurrying *too* much; though her blood sang to her to rush to the library, she held herself in check, savouring the delightful tingle the denial of haste gave – Isobel marched onwards. Even so, she kept glancing to the right, at the one thing she longed above all else to visit.

Visible in snatched glances over low roofs and between narrow alleys was a small wood. It was a dark smudge in the distance, an enticing place of unknown wonder. Unlike most who might be afraid of a place like that – dark, forbidding, full of hidden dangers – to Isobel it was nothing short of magical. She longed to walk beneath the wild-growing trees, to wander the meandering paths and glimpse the creatures within. Her impressions of what the wood might be like came from the many fantasy books she'd read. Those volumes always seemed to contain a forest or two; ancient, venerable areas with uncounted wonders and teeming with fantastical beings. Whereas for many people she knew, woods and forests were places to be avoided, Isobel had no such trepidation. Deep inside, she sometimes wished she could run away (she knew she never would, though; as with much of her knowledge, she'd read being homeless could be very harsh, especially to a young girl) and hide out in this forest, meeting strange and wonderful entities, having adventures, living a far better life than the one she currently had.

Thoughts of possible future adventures slipped from her mind as she spied the protruding front of the library, a converted Victorian building (she had, of course, read about its history) she found equally as spellbinding as the promise of the woods.

Except, before she reached the grand, old edifice, something else caught her eye.

Stopping in her tracks, Isobel turned slowly to look at the façade that had piqued her interest. It was a shop front. Nothing especially remarkable except for two things: One, it was a shop she'd never noticed before (and she knew it was impossible she could have simply missed it); and two, the display window was full of book piles.

Volumes of every shape, size, and colour were stacked in heaps of varying height. There seemed no discernible pattern or conformity to these towers, yet to Isobel, they also didn't appear to have simply been thrown together without care. Something in their apparent chaotic piling gave an impression of hidden meaning and purpose, if only Isobel could crack the code.

Besides the books – which were more than enough to captivate her – were a number of cardboard display stands. But these didn't have the look of mass-produced, corporate advertisements; instead, they appeared hand-made, painted by a skilled artist to their own imaginative and original specification. Images of characters and places from books old and new, for children and adults alike, adorned these compositions, mingling in ways their creators had no doubt scarcely imagined. And yet, there was something natural about it, a harmonic quality that felt right.

Isobel took a couple of steps back from the window – she'd almost had her nose pressed against the glass, so taken was she with the items on the other side – making sure not to collide with any other pedestrians. She looked up at the sign above the window. It was simple enough. All it said was "BOOKS".

Shrugging, Isobel made up her mind in an instant. The library was a known environment; this was somewhere new and potentially exotic and was therefore a far more enticing a prospect.

Without even a flutter of hesitation she pushed the door open and went inside.

As soon as the door was closed, all sounds from outside – traffic, chattering voices, the soft, mournful wind – were muffled to the point of inaudibility. All that remained were echoes of the old-fashioned bell situated just above the door-frame and even those were soon eaten up in the hush. The silence was heavy with the weight of reverence.

Isobel paused to take in the interior of the shop and let her eyes adjust to the pleasant gloom.

Stretching away in front of her were shelves and shelves of books, stacked floor to ceiling in slightly crooked rows. The corridor created by these bookcases looked far longer than it should have done, disappearing into darkness ahead, though that might have been an illusion created by the lighting; all was washed in warm, honeyed tones of dark-golden light, the source of which Isobel could not readily locate. At irregular intervals were a number of alcoves, suggesting corridors leading off into the depths of the shop. It all had the feel of a labyrinth, a maze, a place of secret nooks and crannies. Of course, Isobel had only ever *read* about labyrinths (and one in particular) not visited them, but they were the kind of thing she loved in fiction, alongside secret rooms and passageways, and doorways to hidden worlds. And again, where other people might feel apprehensive, Isobel felt only joy and excitement.

As if in a trance, she walked forward, one hand trailing over the book spines.

So many books. She'd never seen this many volumes in one place. Isobel didn't think even the library held such a huge amount of books. And the variety. Even a casual glance at the titles suggested these books held stories about every subject possible. Words that implied adventure, intrigue, history, or terror. And, of course, magic and fantasy.

This was a place she could spend hours in; days, even.

She was almost overwhelmed at the choice available. But unfortunately, her time was limited.

The books didn't appear to be shelved in any kind of order; crime rubbed shoulders with science fiction, fantasy with romance. Yet, like the window display, it didn't feel careless or haphazard; on the contrary, she sensed order beneath the seeming chaos. Isobel felt comforted here, as though this place had come from inside her mind, from her very desires. She felt safe.

Isobel moved deeper into the shop, looking for an assistant. She took corridors at random, on a whim. It was only after the fourth or fifth turn that she began to wonder just how big this place was; it seemed far larger than any high street shop had a right to be.

It must be an illusion created by the bookcases and the lighting; the shop couldn't possibly *be bigger on the inside...*

She kept going, not encountering any other customers. And it was a few minutes before she turned one corner and there in a hollow made by outwardly curving bookcases, found a small, wooden desk. Behind that desk sat a woman who must have been the owner.

She was old, her skin wrinkled and worn, yet there was something youthful about her as well. Perhaps it was the light dancing in her eyes, a twinkle that reminded Isobel of childlike wonder. Or it could have been her hair, which though faded, still held all the colours of the rainbow in long, wavy locks.

The woman smiled, not appearing in the least surprised to find a lone eleven-year-old girl wandering through her establishment. It was almost as though she'd been waiting for just such an encounter.

'Well, hello there, young lady. How are you?'

Normally, Isobel was quiet around strangers, unwilling to meet their eyes or engage them in conversation. But this woman had such a warmth about her, a quiet kind of cosy

charm and familiarity – much of which came from her low
and pleasant voice – it made Isobel feel completely relaxed.

'Hi. I'm good. I, um...I like your books.' Isobel winced
inside. *Jeez,* that *sounded lame.*

The woman didn't seem to mind. Her smile grew wider.
'Why, thank you. I've been collecting them for a long time. I
like to think there isn't a collection like it in the world. Quite a
few of them are very rare; unique, in fact.' She winked. 'I'm
Sophie, by the way.' And the woman held out her hand.

Isobel hesitated for a moment, surprised. No one had
ever offered to shake hands with her before. It almost made
her laugh, how grown-up it made her feel. Then she took
Sophie's hand in her own. 'I'm Isobel.'

Sophie's eyes crinkled at the edges. 'That's a perfect
name. It really suits you. I bet you don't let anyone shorten it,
either.'

'How did you know that?'

Sophie shrugged. 'Just a guess. I'm good at guessing.'
Another wink. 'So, let me guess what kind of books you like...'
She held up one hand. 'No, don't tell me. Hmmm.'

One finger pressed against her lips, Sophie glanced up at
the ceiling as if in deep thought. Isobel suspected this was just
for show, but was enjoying the pantomime.

'Okay, let me see...' Sophie quickly looked Isobel up and
down. 'I reckon you like books about...oh, magic and
fantastical lands and such!' Sophie clapped her hands together
and said this last in a rush as if she'd only just thought of it.

Isobel giggled. 'I do, I *do,* I *love* those kinds of books!'

'Excellent. Well, it might be I have a few books like that.
Perhaps, maybe, we can find a few you *haven't* read?' With
that, Sophie got up and walked around the desk to lead Isobel
through the shop.

After a good thirty minutes searching, they were back at

the desk. Sophie was placing the books she'd suggested to Isobel into an old canvas bag, something she'd never seen any other shop do; usually it was thin plastic, or in some cases paper. Not this creased, threadbare yet sturdy looking sack. Isobel loved it. Every volume Sophie suggested had sounded perfect, and promised to introduce her to new authors to love and cherish. But as they'd looked, the time had ticked by, and Isobel had become increasingly aware she needed to start heading home.

Evidently, the snatched glances at her watch had not gone unnoticed. As Sophie put the last of five books into the bag, she said; 'Perhaps you could come back another day. Maybe at the weekend, when you have more time to browse. One or both of your parents could bring you?'

Though the old woman was smiling, it felt to Isobel there was a hint of sadness there, as though she already knew of Isobel's family circumstances. Yet, how could she? Another guess? Perhaps people in similar situations had the same demeanour or aura; maybe Sophie was able to sense this. Regardless, Isobel wasn't about to disclose what her parents were like, no matter how much she liked and trusted Sophie. Though she did feel bad for lying to someone who had been nothing but kind.

'Uh...I'd love that, but we, um... We already have plans the next few weekends, and my parents are real busy most days. I'll be able to come back next Thursday, though, if that's okay...' Well, it wasn't *that* much of a lie (apart from the bit about weekend plans).

Instead of answering, Sophie chewed on the inside of her lip. After a few moments, she reached behind the desk and rummaged around. Eventually – only thirty seconds or so, but an age in which Isobel kept looking at her watch, painfully aware of the seconds racing by, while anxiousness woke and uncoiled within – she resurfaced, clutching a worn, battered brown book in one hand.

She held it out to Isobel. 'I'd like to give you this, Isobel. It's a *special* book, a notebook of sorts. You could use it as a diary, or, do you ever wish you could write your *own* stories?'

Isobel nodded slowly. Another accurate guess from this woman. Isobel did indeed have a vivid imagination. It was something vital, she felt, in picturing the wonderfully alien worlds she read about. And that had translated early on in a secret desire to create stories of her own. Except, the few times she'd tried, she'd been deeply dissatisfied with the results. That didn't stop her from going back again and again, much like a tongue cannot stop probing at a loose tooth.

'Then take this. You might find it helps with the creativity.'

Though Isobel couldn't imagine how, she took the book out of politeness. A quick flick through the pages revealed blank paper yellowed and spotted. Isobel remained sceptical of the book's inspirational qualities, though there did seem to be a slight golden flicker as she riffled through the slim volume. Perhaps a trick of the light.

Placing the book in the bag on top of the other books, Isobel reached into her pocket. 'How much for all this?' It was a query she hadn't allowed to impinge on her enjoyment of the shop, but now, a thin trickle of apprehension scurried through her blood. What if she couldn't afford these volumes?

Except Sophie was waving this aside. 'No, no, you don't owe me anything. Consider them gifts. No payment necessary.'

Isobel couldn't believe it and felt a little ashamed at such kindness. 'I couldn't possibly take them for nothing,' she said, as she continued digging in her pockets.

Sophie leaned over the desk. 'You *can* and you will. Go, enjoy them, and maybe we'll meet again.'

'Well, if you're sure.' A smile and an emphatic nod from Sophie.

It wasn't until they'd said their goodbyes and Isobel was

on her way home that she mulled over something Sophie had said. *"'...maybe we'll meet again.'"*. Not, *'See you next time,'* or *'See you Thursday.'* Strange.

That night, Isobel sat on her bed and read, chewing absent-mindedly on some toast she'd made for her dinner. So excited was she to have new books to read – ones by writers she'd never heard of; though she loved the library, it had a limited stock of books for children, and she'd exhausted most of what she liked – she kept picking one up, reading a few pages, only to switch to another and read some of that. She wanted to consume all the stories at once, live and breathe their worlds.

Eventually, though, the buzz subsided and she settled down into a story where animals talked and fought, lines drawn between species, a tale of heroes and villains. So engrossed was she, Isobel was barely aware when the front door of the flat opened to admit one of her parents. From the muttered complaining and slamming of bags on the kitchen table, she guessed it was her mother.

This was why she preferred to read in her room; though she had the flat to herself most of Thursday evening, the intrusion – and this was how she thought of it – of her parents would no doubt disturb her reading (or homework, or whatever other activity she was occupied with), and she'd have to retreat there anyway. This way, she was left to her own devices while the adults got on with *their* night (usually alcohol related).

Later still, the door opened again as her father finally came home.

Involuntarily, Isobel felt her body tense, her stomach twisting with anxiety. But luckily, it turned out this was one of those rare nights where the dialogue between her parents – and even separated by walls, Isobel could sense it was tense and fractured and full of potential traps – never went above murmured voices. Soon enough, that stopped as they both went to sleep.

Blowing air out through pursed lips, Isobel went back to her book, but found her concentration had fled. Yet it was just a shade too early to go to sleep. She looked about for something to occupy herself with and that was when her eyes landed on the notebook Sophie had given her.

She picked it up. Thumbed quickly through the pages. Again, that golden sheen glimmered, making a battered old blank notebook seem more intriguing than it had any right to be.

Sophie had suggested she might like to try her hand at writing stories of her own.

Why not? Isobel thought.

She picked up a pencil (*the better to rub out inevitable mistakes*, she thought with a wry smile) and opened the journal to the first page. And then sat staring at it, her mind as blank as the paper in front of her.

Where to start?

From her previous few tentative attempts, Isobel knew starting a story was one of the hardest parts. Finding the right scene, the right sentence, the right words. Add to that, she didn't even know what to write about. And the more she concentrated, the more frustrated she became.

Eventually, she put down the pencil and stared up at the ceiling. Maybe the key was to relax. Making a conscious effort to slow her breathing, Isobel stopped trying to force her imagination and let her thoughts simply...drift. Random images popped into her mind and flowed away, various scenes cobbled from memory, dreams, and imagination, none of which had much to do with the others. Eventually, though, her mind turned – as it usually did – to her life, her parents, and her wishes for a better existence. Though this brought with it a tinge of melancholy, it also served to turn her imagination to the woods she longed to visit, and just like that, inspiration struck.

It felt gossamer, vague, so Isobel began writing tentatively, as though her idea was a timid animal she didn't want to scare. But soon the words began to flow and after a few paragraphs, it was as though she could actually smell the earth and trees, feel the breeze caressing her face, and hear the soft chittering and whispering of woodland creatures, both realistic and invented.

She spent hours like this, pushing beyond her bedtime without notice, until eventually she surfaced, blinking her eyes as though rising up from a trance. She yawned and stretched, the journal slipping from her lap onto the bed. A quick glance at the clock; it was late, very late. Time for bed. Tomorrow was the last day of school for that week.

Isobel drifted off, her mind still buzzing from the images she'd been writing about. As she slipped into sleep, she marvelled at how vivid it had all seemed. As if she'd actually been there. She fell asleep with a rare smile on her face.

It was the following Thursday, and yet again Isobel was making her way in the direction of the town centre. Her intended destination was her new-found bookshop. She desperately needed to speak to the Sophie. And far from the excitement and happiness she'd normally be feeling at the prospect of going to a place full of books, she was instead filled with nervousness and worry. It caused her guts to squirm and her hands to tremble. It also made her walk fast, her legs wanting to break into a run.

Without her usual interest in the sights around her, Isobel hurried to the book-shop. Upon arrival, she almost skidded to an abrupt stop.

She stared at the façade in complete bewilderment.

The shop was gone. The building was still there of course – though at this point, Isobel might have believed anything possible – but the shop itself, the books, the displays, even the sign; all were gone.

Her mind whirled. How could this be? Sure, shops closed all the time and it wasn't as if the town was an especially thriving commercial place, but Sophie had given no indication this was coming. And now that Isobel looked closer, it appeared as though the premises had been empty for some time. Dust layered the display ledge, piled at the edges. Spider-webs hung in the corners of the frame, as if they'd been there for years. And that was as much as she could see through the grimy window; the shop itself was in total darkness, and though separated by glass, Isobel had no doubts it would be empty of books.

She took a step back, her thoughts in turmoil. She'd spent the last few days in uneasy anticipation of speaking to Sophie to hopefully find some answers, but now she was at a loss. Maybe if she headed home, she might find something online, but even if she did, how would that put her in touch with the bookstore owner?

Isobel sighed, feeling the urge to cry, mostly in frustration and confusion. It was the journal. Ever since she had begun writing her own attempt at a story in it, her life had changed. The first couple of days were fine, the words flowing, the tale growing, and Isobel taking joy in the act of creation. But soon, her sleep had become affected – *infected*, her mind whispered – thoughts of the forest and the adventures she was writing about seeping into her dreams, making sleep restless. It was as though she were not just writing but *experiencing* the story, the world seeming almost real. On the third night, she'd even found a brown leaf sitting on the bed beside her after a lengthy writing session, but dismissed it as having blown in from outside (furiously avoiding the fact that the window wasn't open and hadn't been since the colder months had come).

It was even beginning to affect school-life, although not

her grades. Not yet. Mr Bleak had actually surfaced from his usual torpor to notice her distraction; perhaps he wasn't as heedless of his students as they liked to think. It had resulted in him sending a letter to her parents, which they'd received the previous day. And for the first time in a long time, her mother had taken an interest in her daughter's academic life.

It hadn't been pleasant. She'd shouted and screamed while clutching the letter in one hand, raining down recrimination and insult on Isobel. The girl was smart enough to know this anger came not from concern but because Isobel had embarrassed the family, embarrassed her mother. She'd sat in a miserable silence until banished to her room, a frankly desirable punishment. All this had taken place before her father had come home. As much as Isobel's mother didn't like her daughter, the woman knew to tread carefully where her husband was concerned; this was exactly the kind of thing that might send him into an incandescent fury.

With nothing else to do, Isobel turned from the strangely abandoned shop and headed home.

As it turned out, she never managed to go online to search for Sophie or what might have happened with the shop.

After making herself some dinner, Isobel turned on the TV as a distraction while she ate, trying to lose herself in one of the many brightly coloured and nonsensical cartoons she rarely watched. But it was no use. The journal, and the unfinished story within, called to her, a siren song that pulled at Isobel's nerve-endings, filled her blood with a near-unbearable fizz.

The more she tried to ignore its pull, the worse it got. And was it really that bad? She'd only stopped writing because she'd been a little frightened by the power of the story.

She still loved that she was able to create something from nothing, that she could invent her own original tale, as amateur and sloppy as the actual words might be. But the intensity of it was a shade overwhelming. She felt some part of her was becoming lost to it. She almost laughed at the notion; as if she really *could* escape into the story, escape her life. Surely that was the one thing she'd been dreaming of for years. Yet now that it felt as though it might actually be a possibility, she was shying away from it. Why? Did she think her mind was cracking, her sanity crumbling? Isobel had read somewhere that only the truly insane didn't question their sanity, but who knew? Perhaps she was simply more comfortable in the life she was familiar with, however miserable, than one that might be better but then again, might not. Better the devil you know, and all that.

Lost in thought, and the cacophony from the TV, Isobel didn't hear the front door open and so wasn't aware her mother had come home until she was standing to one side of the sofa, glaring in cold silence at her daughter.

Isobel leapt to her feet. 'Oh, um...I didn't hear you come in.'

Her mother continued to stare, her eyes hard little stones in their sockets. 'No, of course you didn't. Otherwise you might have had the grace and humility to be in your room, keeping quiet and out of the way. Out of *my* way.'

'I was just watching some cartoons. Relaxing. I didn't...I didn't realise the time.'

Her mother crossed her arms, placing her weight on one leg. '*Relaxing*? Because your life is *so* hard? I've been out all day cleaning, and for a pittance, and you think *you've* got it tough? You don't have a clue, Izzy. You're just a typical, ungrateful brat.'

Isobel felt the familiar bloom of sadness and hopelessness. But beneath that was a hot whirl of anger; anger at the never-ending dismissiveness, at the lack of care and concern, at the crap hand life had dealt her. Most of all, it came from her mother's abuse of her name. As incongruous as it seemed, that was the spark that lit everything else.

Speaking in a low, tight voice, Isobel said, 'Don't call me that.'

'Excuse me?'

'I said... Don't. Call. Me. That!'

Her mother looked at her with wide eyes. 'I'll call you anything I damn well please. I'm your mother.'

It was as if a floodgate burst open. All at once, the kindled embers inside Isobel exploded into a blazing pyre. 'My *mother*? You haven't been a mother to me since I was born! I'm nothing but a...an unwanted burden to you, a responsibility you never wanted. I'm sure you wish I'd never been born, that your life would have been better off without me, that—'

In less than a second, Isobel's mother closed the distance between them, lifted one hand, and swung. The slap didn't have all that much force behind it but the sound of it nevertheless resounded in the subsequent silence.

They stared at each other. Her mother looked just as shocked as Isobel felt, her mouth open in dumb surprise.

Immediately, Isobel felt the sting of tears rise in tandem with a growing burning on her cheek. But she would not cry in front of this woman. Instead, even though her heart was racing, Isobel turned and walked steadily from the living room into her bedroom.

Once there, she allowed the adrenaline to speed up her movements. There was no lock on the door so she grabbed the chair from beneath her small dresser and jammed it under the door-handle, kicking one leg into the carpet to make sure it would hold.

Then she snatched up the journal and her pencil, and sat down on her bed.

All doubts and fears about the book and her writing had

fled. She only worried it was a fantasy her mind had conjured and wasn't the salvation she wished it could be. But still she opened it to where she'd left off and began scribbling furiously, her brow knotted in concentration.

Please work, please, please.

Unlike before, she didn't feel the pull of the story. Maybe she was trying to force it too much. She paused, trying to calm her thoughts, her nerves. That was made especially difficult when her mother first tried the door and then, when she couldn't gain entry, began banging on it, shouting.

'Isobel! Open up, let me in. I...I'm sorry, I didn't mean to do that. You just made me angry. Open this door and we can talk. Please. Let's talk. You can watch anything you want on TV.'

Isobel didn't reply. Instead, she concentrated on slowing her breathing, on centring her mind, recapturing the same feelings she'd had before when writing.

Slowly it came, tentative, tenuous. And threatened to blow away again when her father arrived home and demanded to know what was going on. When her mother explained in breathless tones, glossing over own part in it, he took over at the door.

'Isobel, you open this door right now! Don't make me force my way in there.'

Again she ignored it.

When it was clear Isobel wasn't going to answer or open the door, her father began throwing his shoulder against it. The door shuddered in its frame, the chair creaking under each impact. It wouldn't hold for much longer.

Isobel turned her full attention to the journal. She could sense the thread of the story, now, like a thin, whipping tail. If she closed her eyes, she fancied she could see it. And on the edges of her senses, she was able to smell the forest and hear its sounds – the wind whispering through the leaves, the voices of its denizens.

As the sounds in the flat finally began to fade – the thumping against the door, the shouts of her parents, and the added chorus of neighbours now banging and shouting as well – Isobel closed her eyes, her hand still writing.

Almost there, come on, please...

In her mind, she reached out, trying to grasp hold of the tail.

Nearly...nearly...

It slipped through her hand, once, twice, before she finally wrapped her fingers around it just as – but coming to her as if from a great distance – the bedroom door crashed open, and...

One leg cracking and giving way, the chair wedged under the door-handle collapsed and the door flew open. Isobel's father nearly fell into the room, managing to catch the frame and stop himself.

He stood straight and stepped into the room, looking around first in fury, then in confusion.

There was no sign of his daughter, just a strange scent of dirt and trees that faded even as he noticed it.

He looked about, puzzled. Where could she have gone? The window was closed and didn't look as if it had been opened in months; didn't look as if it *could* be opened. A quick look under the bed showed that was empty and there was nowhere else big enough to hide a person, even one as small as Isobel.

So where was she?

A slight movement drew his attention.

On the bed – the duvet rumpled as though someone had been sitting there and had just got up – was a book. A small, battered brown book, open to the first few blank pages. And as he looked at it, those pages fluttered as if in a breeze, a wind that could not possibly be in this room. As they

fluttered, a sparkling golden sheen wavered across the paper then dimmed.
Then they stopped moving and the book finally lay still.

hat music means to...
Matt Oastler - Guitarist

Sharing a love of music has forged and cemented so many friendships over the course of my lifetime I don't think I could even put a number on it.

From drunkenly singing US punk rock songs with strangers outside venues as a teenager to sharing a road trip with my wife this past weekend singing along to The Beatles; music has been ever present at all the best moments.

I have been lucky enough to play in a band for the best part of 20 years. Playing a show to an audience who visibly get the same kick out of watching us play as I do when enjoying a band is a unique feeling for which I am so grateful to have experienced. It is still a thrill to smash out a tune well in practise, let alone seeing people sing along with us.

Playing music and creating life moments together has created a bond within our band that's as strong as within any family.

Matt play guitar in 3dBs Down, a punkrockska band

from Kent. Formed in 2001 they have released a couple of albums and an EP. The band combine heavy riffs with big choruses, a shit load of harmonies and the odd bit of off-beat ska.

First new album for 14 years is due for release in 2020.

Check out some tuneage here:
https://3dbsdown.bandcamp.com/

And follow the band here for updates:
https://www.facebook.com/3-dBs-DOWN-156058531802/

Matt also plays in melodic punk rock band The Half Strikes:
https://www.facebook.com/thehalfstrikes/

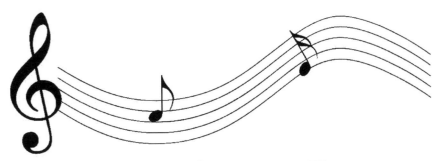

What Music Means To...

Laura Felstead– Music teacher and mean fiddler

"Without music, life would be a mistake" — Friedrich Nietzsche.

Music sounds like emotions feel. Music is a release of energy. Music defines human character. Music is escapism. For me, **music is life...**

Now before you roll your eyes, please be clear that I don't mean that in a sickening, emotional kind of way that makes normal non-airy fairy people want to stick their fingers down their throat but instead in a technical way. Let me explain... Musical activity has defined my course through life for both hobbies and career.

Music is Character Building. Aside from the teaching and learning aspect of music as a child and teenager, it was the discovery of rock, punk and metal music as an adolescent that really defined who I am. Relationships are often built through our similarities in music taste. (I also remember my best friend and I getting thrown out of the primary school recorder club for being cheeky to the teacher but that's more to do with us being little buggers then anything musical). It was also absolutely delightful to be playing pub gigs before I was old enough to buy drinks in pubs!

Music is Team Work. I pursued a music career following studying at college and university. Reading music at university meant that you were already thrown together with other musicians playing in the university symphony orchestra and chamber ensembles. I found this meant my social life was far more advanced from the very first weeks than those studying less practical degrees. I love creating and playing music in ensembles, whether in a punk band, a string quartet or symphony orchestra. You can achieve so much more as group through use of texture and timbre of the instruments ... and it's much more fun!

Music is Confidence. I've been told I come across as being quite calm and together when performing or in public speaking, even when I'm dying inside from nerves. When on stage you can become the person you want to be, the confident being you really want to put across to others but don't have the courage or poise to pull off in everyday life.

Music is Relationships. Relationships have been formed with those I make music with. I can't remember a time when the people I dated weren't musicians(!), and you can't help but feel a certain kind of closeness to your fellow band members having written and learnt songs and tunes collaboratively, sweated it out at band practices and performed them on stage together. You're not just hanging out together as mates, you're actually achieving and progressing at something.

Music is Therapy. I find that a good practise session has the same mental effect on me as exercise, yoga or meditation. It centres oneself concentrating on a physical and mental activity and forgetting all else simultaneously. Music is definitely good for the soul.

Music Makes us Grow. It is widely known that musicians are more likely to excel in other subjects. The left and right cortex of the brain work together when making music in a way that no other activity does. As an instrumental teacher it makes me proud to have contributed to so many childrens' development and to have watched my pupils develop as musicians in all the aforementioned ways.

Laura plays, among many other things, fiddle for Calico Street Riots, you can find out more about them here: https://www.facebook.com/calicostreetriotsofficial/

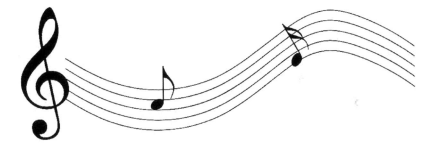

Author Biographies

J.G. Clay

J.G. Clay is a British author, currently residing in the heart of England. Unleashing his unique combination of cosmic horror, dark fiction and science fiction with the first volume of 'The Tales of Blood And Sulphur' in 2015, Clay will be casting his beady eye on Hell, alternative Earths and England's second city in forthcoming works. He promises an endless supply of 'Nightmare Fuel For The Modern Age'.

Away from the printed page, J.G is a bass playing, Birmingham City supporting family man with a fondness for real ale and the Baggie/Britpop era of British Music.

Website: www.jgclayhorror.com
Facebook: https://www.facebook.com/jgclay1973
Twitter: https://twitter.com/JGClay1

Duncan P. Bradshaw

presses pause
holds down record and play
Okay, get ready, don't mess this up like the last thirteen times.
presses pause
Well hello there pop-pickers!
presses stop, rewinds to beginning
For fuck's sake.
presses record and play
Hi, I am Duncan P. Bradshaw, and you can remember my middle initial by thinking of the thing you do when you have had too much lager. I'm like the Enter Shikari of the writing world, impossible to pigeonhole properly. I'm a little bit of horror, a slather of chuckling with a great big dollop of

weird. Can I say dollop? Stuff it, I'm not recording this again. You can keep up-to-date with my writing on my website www.duncanpbradshaw.co.uk or stalk me in real-life, whichever is easiest for you. If you ever feel as if you're the only one in the world who has ever contemplated breeding dining tables, then you are bang out of luck. Thanks for reading. Bye.
presses stop and ejects tape
Bosh. Done.

Christopher Law

Christopher Law's tales of monsters, madness and mayhem have appeared in a number of anthologies, as well as two solo collections - *Chaos Tales* and *Chaos Tales II: Hell TV*. Raised on Heavy Metal and the heyday of late Twentieth Century horror, he doesn't recommend more than one or two for those of a sensitive nature, although there is more to the violence and gore than his teenage desire to write something that 'makes people puke'.

After a far longer break than intended to deal with some personal matters (massive shout-out to anyone caring alone for an ageing parent, or any other loved one with complex care issues) he is planning to return to the fray with two solo releases over the coming months - *Ad Undas*, a poetry collection under the auspices of Burdizzo Bards that is coming very soon, and *Chaos Tales III: Infodump*, which will be a little longer. Hopefully still sometime in 2019, but final edits always overrun.

https://www.facebook.com/evilscribbles/

https://evilscribbles.wordpress.com/

Calum Chalmers

Residing in the sleepy town of Chesham, Calum Chalmers gets to see all the true horrors hidden from the outside World. Old ladies using store bought brownies at bake-sales, geese ram raiding health food shops for quinoa, and God forbid the most horrific of all....school parades.

Oh, and he writes horror too, Google it, there's no direct link because that would be professional.

Lex H Jones

Lex H Jones is a British author, horror fan and rock music enthusiast who lives in Sheffield, North England.

He has written articles for premier horror websites the 'Gingernuts of Horror' and the 'Horrifically Horrifying Horror Blog' on various subjects covering books, films, videogames and music.

Lex's noir crime novel "The Other Side of the Mirror" was published in 2019, with his first published novel "Nick and Abe", a literary fantasy about God and the Devil spending a year on earth as mortal men, published in 2016. Lex also has a growing number of short horror stories published in collections alongside such authors as Graham Masterton, Clive Barker and Adam Neville. He is currently working on both his 'Harkins' book series, the first of which 'The Final Casebook of Mortimer Grimm' is due for release early 2020, and also a trilogy of children's weird fiction books centred around the reimagining of H.P. Lovecraft's mythology.

When not working on his own writing Lex also contributes to the proofing and editing process for other authors.

His official Facebook page is:
www.facebook.com/LexHJones
Amazon author page :
https://www.amazon.co.uk/Lex-H-Jones/e/B008HSH9BA

Twitter: @LexHJones

Em Dehaney

Em Dehaney is a mother of two, a writer of fantasy and a drinker of tea. By night she is The Black Nun, editor and whip-cracker at Burdizzo Books. By day you can always find her at http://www.emdehaney.com/ or lurking about on Facebook posting pictures of witches https://www.facebook.com/emdehaney/

You can also follow Em on Twitter @emdehaney

Her debut short fiction collection Food Of The Gods is available now on Amazon: A perfect corpse floats forever in a watery grave. A gang member takes a terrifying trip to the seaside. A deserted cross-channel ferry that serves only the finest Slovakian wines. Nothing is quite what it seems, but everything is delicious. This is Food Of The Gods.

J.R.Park

J. R. Park is a writer of horror fiction, and was described by DLS Reviews as "a much needed shot in the arm for gritty pulp horror". Often using pulp-horror as his base palate, he likes to experiment with structure and narrative to produce something different. His extreme horror novella Upon Waking saw him try to redress the gender balance in the slasher genre, and saw Scream magazine saying "his mind must be the darkest place in the universe". Other books include The Exchange (Alice In Wonderland meets Reservoir Dogs meets H.P. Lovecraft), Mad Dog (a werewolf in a prison break), Punch (a love letter to the slasher golden age) and Terror Byte (Guy N Smith meets Philip K Dick).

He worked with Matt Shaw to produce Postal, a blood-drenched commentary on society, was Assistant Director on the horror film Monster & runs the Sinister Horror Company.

Find out more at SinisterHorrorCompany.com and JRPark.co.uk

Laura Mauro

Laura Mauro was born and raised in London and now lives in Essex under extreme duress. Her short story 'Looking for Laika' won the British Fantasy award for Best Short Fiction in 2018, and 'Sun Dogs' was shortlisted for the Shirley Jackson award in the Novelette category. Her debut collection, 'Sing Your Sadness Deep' is out now from Undertow Books. She likes Japanese wrestling, Finnish folklore and Russian space dogs. She blogs sporadically at lauramauro.com

Jessica McHugh

Jessica McHugh is a novelist and internationally produced playwright running amok in the fields of horror, sci-fi, young adult, and wherever else her peculiar mind leads. She's had twenty-three books published in eleven years, including her bizarro romp, "The Green Kangaroos," her Post Mortem Press bestseller, "Rabbits in the Garden," and her YA series, "The Darla Decker Diaries."

More information on her published and forthcoming fiction can be found at JessicaMcHughBooks.com.

IG/Twitter: theJessMcHugh
    amazon: amazon.com/author/jessicamchugh
    website: jessicamchughbooks.com

C L Raven

C L Raven are identical twins and mistresses of the macabre. They're horror writers because 'bringers of nightmares' isn't a recognised job title. They write novels, short stories, comics and film scripts. Their work has been published in magazines and anthologies in the UK, USA and Australia. A story of theirs was published in The Mammoth Book of Jack the Ripper, which makes their fascination with him seem less creepy. They've worked on several indie horror films as crew and reluctant actors and have somehow ended up with lead roles in the forthcoming indie horror film School Hall Slaughter. In their spare time, they hunt ghosts, host a horror radio show, look after their animal army, and try to look impressive with polefit. Their attempts at gymnastics should never be spoken about.

Twitter: @clraven

Instagram: clraven666

Facebook: https://www.facebook.com/CL-Raven-Fanclub-117592995008142/

David Court

David Court is a short story author and novelist, whose works have been published in a variety of anthologies including *Visions from the Void, Fear's Accomplice* and *The Voices Within*. He's also had several of his stories narrated on the *Tales to Terrify* and *StarShipSofa* podcasts. Whilst primarily a horror writer, he also writes science fiction, poetry and satire. His last collection of short stories, *Scenes of Mild Peril*, was released by Stitched Smile Publications, and his debut comic writing has just featured in Tpub's *The Theory (Twisted Sci-Fi)*.

As well as writing, David works as a Software Developer and lives in Coventry with his wife, three cats and an ever-growing beard. David's wife once asked him if he'd write about how great she was. David replied that he would, because he specialized in short fiction. Despite that, they are still married.

Website: www.davidjcourt.co.uk

Twitter: @DavidJCourt

CH Baum

By day, CH Baum is a diabolical mortgage professional. By night, he dons his superhero outfit (made up of exactly one pair of torn underwear with weepy elastic) and goes to bed early, ensuring that he gets a full eight hours of sleep. All of this discipline keeps him refreshed and ready to wrestle with your loan application. He lives with his two boys and his stunningly beautiful wife in Las Vegas, Nevada. What happens in Vegas, usually happens without him. He loves to write, ride his bicycle, make furniture, and read. He does all that while avoiding pickles, eggplant, and hummus; because everyone knows those things are just gross.

Other published works by CH Baum:

Gods of Color (Fantasy novel)

The Augment (Fantasy short)

The Conversion of Andrew Currant (Horror Short)

Duplicity at Dugway (Horror Short)

Here Lies Brittney Jean (Horror Short)

And many, many more to come.

Paul M. Feeney

Paul M. Feeney began writing seriously in 2011, and a number of short story acceptances for various anthologies soon followed. To date, he has written two novellas – The Last Bus (2015) through Crowded Quarantine Publications, and Kids (2016) from Dark Minds Press. His work tends towards the dark, pulpy end of the horror spectrum (he has described his work as having a "Twilight Zone" feel), with the odd story or two that's more emotive. In addition to this, he has recently begun writing under the name Paul Michaels, aiming for more nuanced, literary territory; under this name he writes the occasional review for website, This is Horror, with the first Michaels short being published early 2019. He currently lives in the north east of England where he is beavering away on various projects, many of which will be published throughout 2019.

CM Franklyn

CM Franklyn hails from Liverpool but now lives on the Wirral along with her past. Featured in a bunch of anthologies including The Sinister Horror Company's 'The Black Room Manuscripts Vol. 3', and the imminent 'Dystopian States of America' from Haverhill House, you're not likely to find her work anywhere else because she tends not to submit. She should probably change that. She does like to blog, though, and writes poetry in her sleep. As Linda Angel, she's the author of Stranger Companies (Kuboa Press), a collection of experimental (i.e. unedited stream of consciousness) short fiction, which is being polished and preened for re-release in 2020 via Haverhill. As screenwriter Linda Nagle, she was commissioned by First Frame Films to write a web series about human trafficking; tráfico (the lower case 't' really bothers the editor in her) was filmed in New Jersey and NYC. She also has a thing for parentheses (really) and a penchant for italics. You can find her ramblings at www.liberatetutemet.com

Jonathan Butcher

Jonathan Butcher is the author of the novel The Children at the Bottom of the Gardden, the novella What Good Girls Do, and co-author of the novella Demon Thingy with Matthew Cash. He edited the anthology Visions from the Void which features art from his father, and has also had numerous weird, twisted shorter works published. He lives and writes in Birmingham, where he is still working on a political horror novel with the working title Beast of the Earth.

Daryl Lewis Duncan

DLD don't know who the fuck he is,

And nobody knows where to find him,

But leave him alone,

And he will come home,
With a trail of fag ends behind him

Kayleigh Marie Edwards

Kayleigh Marie Edwards is a writer based in South Wales. She mostly dabbles in horror and horror/comedy short stories and plays. She is inspired by Stephen King (of course), Adam Nevill, any and all types of zombie, and Simon from The Inbetweeners. She's the kind of person that says she'll turn up for things but probably won't, but it's only because she doesn't like leaving her house because that's where all her stuff is. And she likes her stuff.

Richard Wall

Born in England in 1962, Richard grew up in a small market town in rural Herefordshire before joining the Royal Navy. After 22 years in the submarine service and having travelled extensively, Richard now lives and writes in rural Worcestershire.

His first short story, "Evel Knievel and The Fat Elvis Diner" (available on Kindle), was soon followed by "Five Pairs of Shorts" a collection of ten short stories, and another short story called 'Hank Williams' Cadillac'.

Richard's stories reflect his life-long fascination with the dark underbelly of American culture; be it tales of the Wild West, the simmering menace of the Deep South, the poetry of Charles Bukowski, the writing of Langston Hughes or Andrew Vachss, or the music of Charley Patton, Son House, Johnny Cash, or Tom Waits.

A self-confessed Mississippi Delta Blues anorak, Richard embarked on a road trip from Memphis to New Orleans, where a bizarre encounter in Clarksdale, Mississippi inspired him to write his début novel, Fat Man Blues.

www.richardwall.org

Matthew Cash

Matthew Cash, or Matty-Bob Cash as he is known to most, was born and raised in Suffolk, which is the setting for his debut novel *Pinprick*. He is compiler and editor of *Death By Chocolate*, a chocoholic horror Anthology and the *12Days: STOCKING FILLERS* Anthology. In 2016 he launched his own publishing house Burdizzo Books and took shit-hot editor and author Em Dehaney on board to keep him in shape and together they brought into existence *SPARKS*: an electrical horror anthology, *The Reverend Burdizzo's Hymn Book*, *Under The Weather** and *Visions From the Void* ** and he has numerous solo releases on Kindle and several collections in paperback.

Originally with Burdizzo Books, the intention was to compile charity anthologies a few times a year but his creation has grown into something so much more powerful *insert mad laughter here*. He is currently working on numerous projects, and his third novel *FUR* was launched in 2018.

*With Back Road Books

** With Jonathan Butcher

He has always written stories since he first learnt to write and most, although not all, tend to slip into the many layered murky depths of the Horror genre.

His influences ranged from when he first started reading to Present day are, to name but a small select few; Roald Dahl, James Herbert, Clive Barker, Stephen King, Stephen Laws, and more recently he enjoys Adam Nevill, F.R Tallis, Michael Bray, Gary Fry, William Meikle and Iain Rob Wright (who featured Matty-Bob in his famous A-Z of Horror title M is For Matty-Bob, plus Matthew wrote his own version of events which was included as a bonus).

He is a father of two, a husband of one and a zoo keeper of numerous fur babies.

You can find him here:
www.facebook.com/pinprickbymatthewcash
https://www.amazon.co.uk/-/e/B010MQTWKK

The Red Aunts
The Red Aunts are an American all-female punk band
that formed in 1991 in Long Beach, California. They have
released five albums; Drag, Bad Motherfucken 40oz (both on
Sympathy For The Record Industry) and #1 Chicken, Saltbox
and Ghetto Blaster for Epitaph Records.

Also From Burdizzo Books

46427384R00197

Printed in Poland
by Amazon Fulfillment
Poland Sp. z o.o., Wrocław